A NECESSARY END

BY HOLLY BROWN

Don't Try to Find Me

A NECESSARY END

Holly Brown

wm
WILLIAM MORROW
An Imprint of HarperCollins*Publishers*

This book is a work of fiction. References to real people, events, establishments, organizations, or locales are intended only to provide a sense of authenticity, and are used fictitiously. All other characters, and all incidents and dialogue, are drawn from the author's imagination and are not to be construed as real.

A hardcover edition of this book was published in 2015 by William Morrow, an imprint of HarperCollins Publishers.

FIRST WILLIAM MORROW PAPERBACK EDITION PUBLISHED 2016.

Designed by Jamie Lynn Kerner

Library of Congress Cataloging-in-Publication Data has been applied for.

ISBN 978-0-06-235638-3

16 17 18 19 20 OV/RRD 10 9 8 7 6 5 4 3 2 1

A NECESSARY END

I'm not sure who said it. I don't know if it was a man or a woman, a small-town sheriff or a big-city cop or a down-and-out drifter or a fortune-teller or a husband or a wife. There's a lot I can't remember, and one thing I do.

"If things keep going like this," he (or maybe she) said, "someone's going to wind up dead."

I probably laughed. Thought how cheesy it was. Melodramatic. But it lodged inside of me and resurfaced the day we met Leah, like a prophecy or a warning. It was easy to ignore, though, with all that was buzzing in my head. It became just another member of the hive.

I know now that there was no other way things could have turned out. Tragedies are inevitable, just like the great love stories, like us.

That's what I tell myself.

CHAPTER 1

Adrienne

More than anything, I want to be a mother.

No, scratch that. It's too desperate. It reeks of years of trying, of thirty-nine, of a dedicated phone line for birth mothers that has only rung twice in the past eleven months, and one of those was a wrong number. "Hello," I said on the latter call, out of breath from running across the house, "hello?!!!" And the voice, a startling baritone: "Is Lisa home?" I'm ashamed to admit this, I never even told Gabe, but I answered, "Are you sure you're not looking for Adrienne? Gabe and Adrienne?" Because the man could very well have been a birth father, a possibility that I hadn't even considered until just that moment. The birth mother could have assigned him to the vetting process, thinking he should make himself useful since he got her into this mess to begin with. One woman's multiplying mess of cells is another woman's greatest desire. "No," the man said, slowly, like I might be cognitively impaired, "I'm looking for *Lisa*." I told him that there was no Lisa here, and it was all I could do not to add, "But if you find Lisa and she happens to be facing an unplanned pregnancy . . ."

The other call was worse. A lot worse. But I've never been someone to dwell on the past. There's so much future to be had.

More than anything, though, I *do* want to be a mother.

Still, humid desperation aside, the sentence should obviously read *More than anything, we want to be parents,* only that's not exactly true. Gabe will come around, though. He's just feeling a little threatened, because once upon a time, I wanted him more than anything, was willing to do anything . . . But that was a long time ago, another life, and now, I'm going to be a mother. Parenthood makes you your best self. You're going to be in the spotlight of that adorable new person's gaze, and you have to be worthy of it.

I will be worthy.

And I *will* be a mother. Because I want it more than those other women on the adoption websites with all their money and loving extended families and better hair (I've been straightening my dark frizzy hair since I was fifteen years old, since before Gabe, since crimping irons reigned supreme). I've got more—what do they call it in the Sissy Spacek movies my grandmother used to watch?—grit. I also come fully equipped with stamina and perseverance and a good body ("big tits and little everything else," a guy in my high school once famously said, and it's still the case). I know that last bit might seem extraneous and I won't say it in the adoption profile, but I made sure to include a full-length photo because appearances matter to a birth mother, especially a teenage one who undoubtedly wants to go back to being hot herself once it's all over. Sure, I'm thirty-nine, but I'm well moisturized and I could run a marathon tomorrow if I cared enough to, if I set my mind to it.

"Can we just get on with this?" Gabe sighs, interrupting my reverie.

"I'm thinking. Are you?"

"Yeah," he mutters, but he isn't. Or rather, he isn't thinking about writing our prospective-parent profile. I can read him like a book. Fortunately for me, he's always been *Choose Your Own Adventure,* sexually speaking, that is.

That won't go in our profile either. But birth mothers will see that he's tall and handsome, with dark hair and dark eyes, like John Stamos when he was on *General Hospital,* that's what I thought when we first met, which shows how long we've been together. How enduring our love is, that's what I should say.

I begin to type. "Our *enduring love*?" he says over my shoulder.

I overlook the tinge of mockery. That's one of the skills you pick up in order to have an enduring love. "Longevity is a selling point. The birth mother wants to know her child will be in a stable home." It's actually our primary selling point. Gabe is a car salesman, which can seem oily, and I teach second grade, which might seem homey but not lucrative or ambitious. They're not aspirational professions, is what I mean. We're not pilots or entrepreneurs or doctors. Our home is a tiny three-bedroom, in a subdivision inside a suburb forty minutes from San Francisco. An expensive suburb—we bought this house for $650,000, probably three times what it would have cost in Dubuque or Tallahassee—but the birth mother isn't going to compare real estate markets. She's going to want bling. Everything she never had, she'll want for that baby.

Best not to think in terms of money or scale, but rather, personality. Yes, the dining room is barely large enough to hold the four-person table where Gabe and I are currently sitting, but it's an awesome table: wrought iron legs, a top made of wavy black and gray onyx. The wrought iron chandelier is shaped like a candelabra, with multicolored gemstones dangling (amethyst, rose quartz, garnet). So there's your bling. And on the wall is a huge canvas—colorful and abstract—and no one has ever guessed that it was the result of Gabe and me, writhing naked and covered in paint. Nothing brings a couple together like a shared secret.

In Realtor speak, our living room is "cozy" (or better yet, "charming"). We had the floors redone in this incredibly rich, dark wood (almost black), and the furniture is all red velvet.

On the wall, sandwiched between windows, is art that we bought at a DIY show at Fort Mason in San Francisco, one of our favorite spots in the city. The piece has rounded double doors made of rough-hewn wood, and inside, a carved quote from Henry David Thoreau: "There is no remedy for love but to love more."

This is the home I built with Gabe, and my default position is to love it. (While overlooking the flat-screen TV positioned above the fireplace, at Gabe's insistence. He says that only invalids watch sports in bed. Does poker qualify as a sport?) Yet as I try to rewrite our adoption profile, all I can see is the inferiority of size.

I never used to feel crappy about where we were in life, about our jobs or our home. I certainly never compared Gabe and myself unfavorably to other couples.

"Do you think the adoption process is turning me into someone else?" I ask Gabe.

He considers for a long minute. He doesn't look happy. "No," he finally says. "You're just you."

Just me? What's that supposed to mean?

No point in going down that road. If we do, we'll never finish this profile today, and we can't afford any detours. Two calls in eleven months is pitiful. Clearly, we need a new marketing strategy.

"If we were a car," I say, "how would you sell us?"

His lips hoist at the corners. "Depends on what they're looking for. You get a read on people and you know whether to push the power of the engine or the safety features. Sometimes the wife is all about safety, and you can tell that the way to make the sale is to talk right to the husband about power, talk like she's not even there. Sometimes people don't have a fucking clue what they're really into."

Gabe can play like he's a tough guy, but really, he's good at selling to people because he likes them. He wants them to feel happy with what they've bought; he doesn't up-sell to people who can't afford it. He's got principles, contrary to what some might assume when they hear his job title.

"Our problem," I say, my thoughts crystallizing as the words leave my mouth—I can practically see them hanging in the air like stalactites—"is that we can't hook everybody. What lures in one person is going to turn another off, on a subconscious level.

"So what we need," I continue, focusing on the laptop screen, "is to stop trying to attract everybody, like I did in the last profile, and write like it's to the one person we want to attract."

"We only need one," he says. I like that he's saying "we," though we both know this is my project more than his. It's like, he plays poker in his free time and I look for our baby. Sometimes I get the feeling he doesn't believe I can really pull this off, and he wouldn't mind if I didn't.

"You don't care if we get the baby," I say, "because you feel like we're enough just as we are." He shifts in his chair, and I can tell that he expects me to be upset, but I'm the opposite. The light's gone on. "That's it!"

"What?" He looks confused but intrigued. For a guy who's so good at reading people, he can't always read me. I've always thought that's another reason for our longevity, and our great sex. The mystery has never leached out of our relationship.

I start typing—it never hurts to make him wait—but fast, screw any mistakes, there's spell-check. My fingers on the keyboard sound like a downpour, like it's raining words that will connect us to the birth mother, a deluge that will deliver our baby. Gabe's leaning forward, more engaged than he's been the whole hour we've been sitting here. I'm writing as Gabe, but I feel like myself again. We're a team, like we've always been.

The profile is a testament to us. It's about the circle of our love that we hope will encompass a baby, but it doesn't have to. We're complete. "We've spent more than twenty years loving each other," it begins, "growing from teenagers to full adults together, and we've never wavered in our commitment. Once we're in, we're all in, and that goes for parenthood, too. We're not waiting for a child to complete us, but we'd love for a child to share in all that we have." I add a line about "finding the right match." We're not looking for just anyone; we're looking, I imply, for *you*.

I sit back, satisfied. All those people on the websites, begging to be picked, and here we are, self-contained, ready and willing but not desperate in the least. This is how we're going to stand out in a crowded marketplace: Play hard to get. Make the birth mothers want to be a part of us; be the club they want to join.

"Is this really how you feel?" Gabe asks as he finishes reading the last sentence. He sounds so moved that I wish it were more than advertising. How much easier life would be if I could only mean it, if I could only feel complete right this instant.

"It's how you feel," I say. I touch his arm. "I'm letting you speak for both of us."

"You even used poker terminology." He smiles, and I hurt a little for him, for his naïveté. But when we get the baby, his heart will be fuller than he ever could have imagined. "See, if it happens, great. If it doesn't, we're still us, right?"

"We're always us." Only it isn't enough anymore. I can't tell him this, but over the past year, I've felt myself loving him just a bit less, like it's leaking out through a very fine sieve. That's not his fault. He can't be any more than my husband, but I need to be more than a wife. I need to be a mother. At a certain point, you have to share what you have, or it diminishes. I don't make the rules. It's biology.

Gabe's the fulfillment of an old dream. The baby is the fulfillment of a new one. How can he compete?

But he doesn't need to. We're going to do this together. We'll love each other even more profoundly through the love we feel for our baby. That's our next incarnation: from sex-crazed teenagers to happily married couple to parents. The shift will be seismic, the increase in feeling exponential. He'll see.

"All-in," I tell him, and he kisses me, in sweetness and hunger.

CHAPTER 2

Gabe

She straddles me, grinding my back into the hard column of the dining room chair; she bucks and howls. I know it's half performance, but so fucking what? She's paying me back for tolerating a Saturday of writing our adoption profile. She's telling me I've been a good boy. I'll take it.

When we're both done, she's sweaty and beaming. She dismounts in a crackle of kinetic energy. I can picture her crossing a line item off the to-do list: Somewhere between "write adoption profile" and "lesson planning" was "hot sex."

I've always loved her energy, the way she can vibrate with it, like her life force is on the outside, right on the surface, when for everyone else, it's hidden. Sometimes she bounces in her seat like a kid when we're about to go out somewhere. And I really have seen "hot sex" written on her to-do list.

As my breathing and heart rate start to slow, I can hear that profile, like a voice-over. Only it's not her voice. It's not mine either. It's some other couple, an act of ventriloquism. Because I'm not jonesing to bring a baby into our circle of love, and she doesn't really think our circle is complete without one, and so even though the love stuff is true, the whole of it feels false.

I want to believe her, that we're enough. Every day I try to show her that we can be, but lately, what comes back . . . I know her too well, is the problem. I know she's capable of deception—of herself, of others. She's sure capable of obsession.

All her clothes are back on, except for her bra. Her breasts swing metronomically under her T-shirt as she moves; it's like hypnosis, watching her. Our house isn't exactly an open floor plan, it's just small, so from the dining room, I look straight into the kitchen, and ninety degrees to the right, I can see her in the living room, fluffing the pillows of the sofa. Sex makes her industrious.

She asked if she's different now. What could I say? It's been more than twenty years. We're both different, like we're supposed to be. People are meant to change. That's why practically no one mates for life anymore. The divorce rate is, what, 50 percent? And that goes for all the second marriages, too. Nobody picks smarter the second time around. They just try to avoid the mistakes they made before, and there are always plenty of mistakes left to make, an infinite number of wrong turns.

I've never asked Adrienne to stay the same, but lately, her different is really different. Unpredictable, and not in the old, good way.

I discovered a high kitchen cabinet overstuffed with baby loot. When I opened it, I was momentarily caught in this monsoon of tiny hats and booties and pacifiers, even a plush blanket with a tiger's head sewn onto it. We're not Jewish, but I definitely get that whole tradition about not filling your home with baby stuff too soon, that it can be a jinx. Didn't she learn anything from the Patty nightmare? Anyone else would have stayed out of the game for years after that one, but not Adrienne.

When she sees a pregnant woman, whatever she's doing, she stops. She goes silent. Everywhere becomes a church. And the look she's giving—it's not normal. It's like she's rapturous and ravenous at once. She asks to touch the woman's belly, and then she rubs like it's Aladdin's lamp, like a genie might come out and grant her wish.

It's been four years since she went off birth control and two years since we got the results of the fertility tests, when we found out that her egg plus my sperm will never equal baby. I've tried to tell her it might not be in the cards for us, and we can be happy anyway. But I don't think she wants to be happy anyway. It's like she can't be a woman if she can't be a mother, which is nuts. She's the most woman I've ever known, and that's the truth.

I can't totally blame her, coming from a mother like hers. She wants to right the wrongs. She wants to be the mother she never had. It's altruistic, almost. But I like to talk about things other than babies, and she doesn't, and that's becoming a problem.

Last week, she did something truly crazy. I was kissing down her body, and I felt this waxiness on my lips. I wiped at my face, and brown smudged my hand. "What the . . . ?" She got this big smile on her face. "Eyebrow pencil," she said. I stared at her. "For my *linea nigra,*" she explained, "the line of dark hair that pregnant women get, right down the center of their stomach." I could only state the obvious: "You're not pregnant." She replied, unfazed, "That's why it's eyebrow pencil."

I had this vision of her carefully filling in the sparse hairs that bisected her stomach, so that it looked like a line of ants marching toward her pubic hair. I was sure she was smiling while she did it. For years she talked about being a mom; somehow it had never occurred to me how badly she'd wanted the experience of being pregnant.

I hugged her and told her it's good that she won't have to get hairy and fat and have her hormones in an uproar, but it was the wrong thing to say. She got up and started cleaning.

She has the mood swings of a pregnant woman. I'll be putting bread in the toaster and she'll whirl around with eyes lit up like a Gorgon's and hiss in a voice full of fury, "*Not that bread!*" Not that bread? What other bread is there? And who gives a shit anyway? It's bread. Adrienne, that's who gives a shit, about all kinds of things she never cared about before.

Meanwhile, she wants us to sit down and write an adoption profile so we can sell ourselves like the perfect couple, the ideal future parents. I know everybody's lying in those things, airbrushing out their flaws, but still. I don't know that it'd be good for her to get her hands on a baby right now.

I'm not baby-proofed either. She asks me what I feel when I imagine being a father. The truth is, I don't imagine, and I feel nothing. I can't see it. If a baby's the sun, like Adrienne thinks, then I'm having my own private solar eclipse. She's got this whole fantasy life—and a kitchen cabinet full of props—and I'm drawing a blank. Adrienne thinks it's sad to feel nothing, but then, she never feels nothing. I tell her nothing's not so bad, she ought to try it sometime. She thinks I'm joking.

I don't tell her that I've been dreaming about Michael, seeing him as a baby. I know those aren't real memories. I was only three years older than him, so there's no way I'm really recalling his crying in his crib. In my dreams, he's been crying for hours. There's no one to pick him up and tell him it's going to be all right. And it wasn't all right, was it?

You know that better than anyone, huh, Adrienne?

I try not to talk about him. Mostly, I keep my guilt to myself, though sometimes when I have too much to drink, it falls out, like loose change from my pocket. Those conversations never go well. Adrienne hears me blaming her.

I don't, though, not exactly. I got caught in her undertow, but that's on me, not her. My problem is, I get acted on, instead of acting. Adrienne's always been the molecule that ignites all the others. You can't complain about people like that; you've just got to admire them, or get out of their way.

There's a list in Adrienne's nightstand of all the things we'll need to buy for the baby. I've got my own list, in my head. It's what we can't do and where we can't go and what we won't be able to afford anymore:

No more raucous sex in dining room chairs—it'll wake the baby.

We'll never tour Italy.

Weekly poker at the Pyramid will become monthly, if that.

We won't sleep for years.

If Adrienne heard my list, she'd think I was being selfish and negative, and she'd be right. But I do think about what a kid needs, too. I really don't know what we'd be like as parents. She's so sure it'll all work out, we'll feel just what we're supposed to, we'll be this great team. "You have a baby, and you *want* to be selfless," she says. "Think what a relief it'll be, to finally have something to think about that's not you."

But what if a baby just destroys what we have and nothing good springs up in its place? Then we'd be unhappy and resentful and faking our way through it, and that baby would be stuck with us, when there are all those great potential parents on the website. We'd have ruined our lives, and an innocent kid's.

Adrienne says don't worry, I'll love the baby as much as I love her.

That's what I'm afraid of.

CHAPTER 3

Adrienne

Hello?" I say breathlessly. It's not the run across the house this time; it's pure anticipation. This could be it.

The birth mother phone is in the nursery. Well, right now, it's the office, a placeholder room, generically furnished from IKEA with nothing on the walls, no love at all, but after this call . . .

"Hello?" I say again. Please, just speak. Please, don't be a wrong number, or worse. Not another Patty.

"Hi." The voice is female and uncertain. No way is it a wrong number. "Is this Adrienne?"

"It is. Hi!" It comes out loud and hearty. I remind myself: Don't come on too strong. Don't scare her away. Remember, we're not desperate. We reworked our profile a week ago, and already, our first caller. We're ahead of the game. "Who's this?"

"My name's Leah. I'm"—she hesitates and then lowers her voice—"pregnant."

I want to scream for joy. Instead, I do a little spin, à la the Jackson Five. Leah's probably too young to even know who they are. "It's really great to meet you," I tell her.

"I'm due in six weeks."

Six weeks! Holy shit, we could have our baby in six weeks. Sooner, even, if the baby's born premature. Leah must be one of those people who crams for the test the night before. "Six weeks is plenty of time to find a good home for your baby," I say. "There are so many loving people who want to raise him. Or her?" My heart is thumping so wildly that I can feel it everywhere, like bass in a tricked-out car. I sit down in the padded desk chair that will soon be replaced by a glider and ottoman. I can see myself rocking that baby to sleep. Six weeks to go; Leah must know the sex, but she hasn't answered yet. "Do you know what you're having?"

"I didn't want to know."

"I can understand that." I'm all for the element of surprise. Green and yellow, that's how we'll set up the nursery. Frogs and ducks. Boy or girl, either one's excellent. "It must be scary, being in your position. Having to make such a big decision."

"You guys seem so happy in your profile. I want my baby to grow up with people who really love each other. It's like, you don't need a baby, you just want one. Some of the other couples—they seem . . ." It's not hard to fill in that blank.

I want to kiss Gabe for giving me the inspiration. I want to kiss myself for writing that profile. We've always been a perfect pair. I find myself rocking slightly, a pantomime of what will be. I can't wait to buy that glider and ottoman. And a gender-neutral mobile for over the crib. Brightly colored fish, maybe, with a matching night-light. "Are you in the Bay Area?"

"No. I'm in Rhode Island." I was so excited, I missed the accent. It's a lot like Boston. She pahked her cah in the yahd.

"Gabe and I grew up in New Jersey."

"I know. It's in your profile."

Right. She knows lots about us, and we know nothing about her. It's a tiny bit unsettling but easily rectified. People love to talk about themselves. "How old are you, Leah?"

"Nineteen."

Hopefully, she didn't drink too much or do too many drugs before she found out she was pregnant. I remember nineteen. Don't be wild, Leah. Don't be like your auntie Adrienne.

"And the father, is he on board with the adoption?" I've heard horror stories about fathers who intercede at the last minute. Well, we're already down to the wire. If Leah's pregnancy were a football game, she'd be getting the two-minute warning.

"He said he'll sign anything. He doesn't care." I hear despair, undergirded by steely anger. "We were supposed to be like you and Gabe. In love for our whole lives. But when I told him I wasn't getting an abortion, he was like, 'Fuck you.'" Another pause. "Sorry. I curse when I'm upset."

"Who doesn't?" I say. Then I think, Shit, I'm auditioning to be her baby's mother. She doesn't want me cursing every time I stub my toe. "I just mean, you can say whatever you want to me."

"When I read your profile, I felt like we had this connection. I look like you, you know." How would I know? I've never seen her. I'm acutely aware of the power imbalance: She's got what I want, and she knows all about me, right down to my appearance. But from where I'm sitting, she's like one of those kids in the yearbook who miss picture day. She's a captioned box that reads, "No photo available."

"I'm a mutt," I say. My parents weren't the type to tell stories about where they came from, let alone where their great-grandparents came from. I assume I'm some European hodgepodge: olive skin, hazel eyes, dark hair. "What about your family? Where are they originally from?"

She laughs. "A mutt. I like that. You have a way with words. In your profile, too."

She's flattering me. That must mean she's a little afraid of rejection herself. Maybe the power dynamic isn't as clear-cut as I first thought. Nineteen years old, six weeks to go—I'd be scared, too, if I were her.

"So I look like you, and Trevor's like Gabe." She turns wistful. "If you and Gabe raise the baby, it's almost like this alternate reality. Like, in another dimension, Trevor and I stayed together and kept loving each other and we became this family."

She wants Gabe and me to be surrogates for her and Trevor? It seems like a creepy little fantasy. But who knows why a birth mother picks a couple, what the attraction is? That could be as good a reason as any. In the big picture, it doesn't matter if she starts out thinking of me as her understudy. I'll be the one playing the role, being the mom, for good.

"You still love him, huh?" I say.

"We were together for more than a year. That's, like, big for me." Her voice turns from rhapsodic to angry as she adds, "But now I pretty much fucking hate him."

And Gabe reminds you of him? I get this weird feeling in my stomach. But that's not her fault. Once bitten, twice shy, and Patty was a scorpion.

This situation is totally different. Leah's young, which means this time, if need be, I'll be the one doing the manipulating. Plus, I don't need to take her every little remark too seriously. Being nineteen is the same as being bipolar. She'll grow up and become someone great. Or she won't. No need to stress about it either way. I've heard that in open adoption, everyone starts out with the best intentions—to include the birth mother in all the holidays and important events, to stay close—and then they inevitably drift. It's a summer camp romance: You promise to write and call and never forget each other, but the story always ends the same.

"You feel betrayed," I say to Leah. "I can understand that. You feel like Trevor should have stood by you, no matter what."

"Like Gabe would have with you."

I think back to the early days of our relationship and I want to believe he would have stood by me if I'd gotten pregnant. If only we'd known it was a medical impossibility. What a waste of good contraceptive devices. "It just goes to show that Trevor wasn't your big love. Your big love is still out there, waiting."

"I'm not going to meet him looking like this. I need to get this baby out already."

I should be glad that she sounds callous, that she just wants the baby out so she can fall in love again; it makes her less likely to change her mind and keep him. But I wonder if a baby can feel, in utero, how little he's wanted, what an imposition his growing existence is. Does she ever talk to him, or sing to him? Or does she go the other way and call him names, scream at him for ruining everything with Trevor?

All I know is, Gabe and I are going to love the hell out of him. Whatever he's been through, we're going to make it up to him.

"I think you're having a boy," I say. "I have this strong intuition. That probably sounds very California, but I was like that in New Jersey, too."

"I can't wait to come to California," she says. "I hate the East Coast. Can you buy me a plane ticket, like, right away? The other birth parents have already offered."

Other birth parents? Is she going on an adoptive-parent tour? "Of course we can buy you a ticket. How soon do you want to come?"

"Like now? You're my first choice, you and Gabe, for obvious reasons. But I need to leave time to meet other people if it doesn't work out. I need to find my baby the best home I can, you know?" She suddenly sounds absolutely perky.

She's just a kid, I remind myself. But I will have to find out her mental health history, and her family's. Maybe she really is bipolar.

No, I don't want to know. If this baby is meant to be ours, we'll deal with whatever comes our way. We're up to the challenge.

It's moving so fast. Normally, that's my preferred speed, so I'll take it as a good sign. And if she wants to interview a number of prospective parents, that means she does care about her baby. It means she doesn't spend her time berating him in utero. She might even sing to him.

Maybe she won't want to give him up, when the time comes. You hear those stories all the time, too. If it's not the father putting the kibosh on the adoption, it's the mother. Read the message boards and you'd think no adoption ever succeeded.

"I'll fly you out today," I tell her.

She lets out a happy little squeal. "See, I knew you were like me. Spontaneous. Don't you need to check with Gabe, though?"

"He'll be thrilled."

It's like one of those infomercials with the digital clock ticking down in the corner: "But wait, if you act now, we'll throw in a *second* baby . . ." Twins—is it possible she's having twins?

This is meant to be. Leah is carrying our baby (babies?). She and Trevor even look like Gabe and me. How amazing is that? What are the odds?

What were the odds of coming across Patty, the devil herself?

"Bring the ultrasound pictures," I say. "Please." Then, "He is healthy, right?"

"I don't know if it's a he, but the baby's healthy, yeah. I've been having regular prenatal checkups and taking my vitamins. Just so you know, I don't drink or smoke or anything anymore."

I ignore the "anymore." We've got a healthy baby boy on the way. Six weeks. Holy shit.

I can't wait to tell Gabe. He's over at the Pyramid. Once I'm done booking Leah's flight, I text him: "Come home NOW. We're having a baby."

CHAPTER 4

Gabe

I hear the text's arrival when I'm in a hand. I raised from middle position with the jack-ten suited (both clubs) and the flop came jack-ten-three, all hearts. So I've got two pair, but no hearts, and the only other guy in the hand is down to his last $150. He pushes the chips to the center of the green felt and says, "All-in." He's not looking at me, not wanting to give anything away. Shit. I was hoping to be the aggressor and put him to the decision, but now I'm in the hot seat.

Still two cards to go. He could already have the flush, if the cards in his hand are both hearts. Or he could have just one high heart, like the ace or king of hearts, and be gambling. Even if I'm ahead now, one of those remaining cards could be a heart. I'd lose a third of my stack. Of course, there could be another jack or a ten, and then I've got a full house. I'd be untouchable. But there are, at most, two jacks and two tens left in the deck. Maybe not even that, if the other guys at the table already folded theirs.

What do I know about my opponent? He sat down not too long ago. Midthirties, Hispanic, quiet, with callused hands, wearing a jacket with threadbare cuffs. He folded the last five hands before the flop. Maybe he just has ace-king, no hearts, and he's figuring that flop missed me. But he didn't reraise me initially, he just called my raise. Wouldn't an ace-king merit a reraise? Ditto for pocket kings, and definitely pocket aces. Maybe he has pocket queens?

Another text. Usually, Adrienne respects my poker time. Maybe it really is important.

I can't think about the hand anymore. I need to check that text. So I call. The bet, that is. It's only a couple hundred dollars. Not that I can afford to be casual with money, when we're staring down adoption costs, but you can't think that way and play poker. You can't play scared. It's a recipe for losing.

He turns his hand over. Ace of hearts, king of diamonds. I hold my breath, waiting for the next card. He's got outs to beat me: A queen gives him a straight, and any heart gives him a flush.

The turn card is the three of diamonds. So there's a pair of threes on the board now. That gives him more outs. If an ace or a king comes on the river, his two pair beat my two pair. I've got a bad feeling.

He's staring at the board. He looks morose, really. So we've both got a bad feeling, and only one of us can be right.

The cuffs on that jacket are practically worn through. He might need the money more than I do. He could have a kid already, or two or three, and he needs to buy formula and diapers. Kids are expensive. But then, should he really be here gambling? First rule: You never put money into a pot you can't afford to lose. Of course, that's my rule; lots of these guys play by their own.

The last card is a two of spades. He missed all his outs, and I get all his money. "Nice hand," he says in a low voice, tapping the felt as he stands up. He's not going to rebuy, which makes me feel rotten.

Three seats separate us. "Good play," I say. "Anything but what I had, I would have folded."

"You had many, many outs," an older Asian man tells the exiting player in his pinched, accented English. I don't know about "many,

many." But we all want to buoy up this particular loser. Part of me wants to give the chips back, like I don't deserve them. It's poker, though. No one's deserving.

I played right. I got my money in as the favorite. That's all you can do.

Ames, next to me, taps the felt in appreciation of my victory. Cards are being dealt, but I don't look at them. I'm staring at my phone. The first text tells me to come home NOW, we're having a baby. The second one reiterates NOW. Apparently, I'm winning all over the place.

Sometimes you'd rather lose, when winning's got so many strings attached.

Ames prods me. "You okay?" he asks. Over the years, sitting next to each other, we've become friends. He's in his late forties, with thinning sandy hair. He's always in faded jeans and a T-shirt advertising something. Today, it's Jim Beam. When we first met, he told me he was in commercial real estate. I've since found out that he owns buildings in questionable parts of town and does all the repairs himself, with no particular urgency. I guess technically, that makes him a slumlord, but he's also a pretty good guy.

"It's Adrienne," I say. "She needs me home."

"Right time of the month?" He grins like he knows the ovulation drill. His kids are ten and twelve.

"No, we . . ." Forget it. "I just have to go."

"In or out, gentlemen?" the dealer asks. The "gentlemen" sounds like an affectation, since he looks like he's barely twenty-one himself. He's in his tuxedo shirt and no bow tie. His collar's askew. It's the first time I've seen him in here. He looks like he was partying all night and didn't have time for a shower before work. He won't last. The Pyramid lacks Vegas-style amenities—hell, it looks like a banquet hall in the Poconos that no one's bothered to renovate since the eighties—but the management runs a tight ship.

Ames slides his cards toward the dealer. I do the same, without having peeked, and stand up. He says, "I'll walk out with you. I should head home, too."

I don't really want company, but what can I say? Ames grabs plastic trays for both of us and we load our chips into them. Red, white, and blue; we're real patriots. We walk up the paisley-carpeted ramp, heading for the booth, where we cash out. I put the crisp hundreds in my wallet.

From the gold railing above, I survey the card room with nostalgia. I feel like something in me is about to die, the part of me that was at home here. The room is large and windowless, ringed with TVs bolted to the ceiling, always showing sports but never poker. I catch a faint whiff of the lousy Chinese food they serve table-side. Some days, you're seated downwind from the lo mein; people touch their greasy food and then their chips and you win a pot and almost wish you hadn't. I don't want to go.

"Come on." Ames claps me on the back and nudges me toward the door. "It can't be that bad." He smiles, revealing one chipped incisor. "Nothing with Adrienne can be that bad."

A few years back, I had him and his wife, Paula, over to our house, testing to see if we could become real friends instead of just poker buddies. Turns out, we couldn't, because of Adrienne. She was a great hostess, like always, and neither Ames nor Paula would have guessed that after she shut the door behind them, she intoned, "Never again." Adrienne makes people like her, no problem, but she's a tough customer herself. Ames and Paula rank among the many couples I've brought in to audition over the years, only to have Adrienne deliver the same pithy verdict. Fortunately, Adrienne's such good company that I barely miss other people.

Now that I'm standing on the precipice of fatherhood, I find myself recalling a conversation Ames and I had that night. He was marveling at our house, how nothing was on the floors but the furniture. "You have your kid, that'll change," he said. "You go out to take a piss in the middle of the night, and it's this toy minefield. Everything plays a different song. One wrong step, and it's a rendition of 'The' fucking 'Wheels on the Bus.' One time, when Natalie was two, I put weight on the wrong floorboard, and this voice comes out of the darkness and says, 'Want to play?' I almost went for my gun, I'm telling you. Had to remember it was the plastic purple octopus. People give you this shit as gifts. Trust me, it's no gift."

"So cleanliness is the first thing to go?" I joked, with a pointed look at his bald spot.

"Well," he said, amending that with a grin, "the third. After your sanity and your hair."

It's all fun and games until your wife texts you to come home NOW, you're having a baby.

Once Ames and I are outside, taking in the view of a parking lot full of lengthy, American-made cars, he shakes a cigarette from his pack and hands it to me. Then he takes one out for himself. I don't really smoke anymore, but it seems like the best idea in the world.

"She says she found us a baby," I say.

"Found? Like in a Dumpster?"

"Like adoption. She must have found a birth mother. She says we're having a baby." I hold up the phone as proof. "We just started looking." Eleven months isn't that long. I was hoping for twice that, at a minimum. It's like I want a long engagement and Adrienne wants to elope.

Ames takes a drag. "Well," he says finally, "congratulations."

I inhale too sharply and start to cough. I would have thought smoking was like riding a bike.

"You're going to love it, fatherhood. It's a pain in the ass, but it's worth it."

"Is it really?"

He squints out at the parked cars, sunlight glinting off their windshields like asteroids. "What's done is done."

I knew it.

"I love my kids, and you'll love yours. Just don't overthink things.

If you spend your time worrying whether you're happy, then you're not. Happiness finds you when you're not looking."

"Unless it doesn't. Adrienne wants this more than anything." I saw that line before she deleted it.

"And you don't."

"I want her to have what she wants."

"Then let her be a mother. Let her do the work."

That's the bargain he's struck. He's got an old-school marriage, where the kids are Paula's domain. There's no way Adrienne would go for a division of labor like Ames's family. She plans to keep working, and she wants me to be a full partner in this, as in everything else; she wants me to want that.

"I've got to go," I say. Another text is coming in. Another NOW. Since when do we talk to each other like that? The kid isn't even here and already I feel like the henpecked husband.

It's always easy to spot my car here, the only hybrid Lexus on the lot. Card players favor gas guzzlers, especially Caddies: old Eldorados and new Escalades. Adrienne's been talking about an SUV. One baby, and we need an SUV. I turn the key in the ignition and remind myself: We don't have one yet. The text said we're *having* a baby. So there's still time to eject from the cockpit.

I think of my buddy Rodney from work, what he said after he learned his wife was pregnant: "You know your life is going to change forever, but at least you've got nine months to kiss it good-bye."

The problem is, I like my life. I love time alone with Adrienne. Last week, we ate kettle corn for dinner with a bottle of wine. Okay, two bottles of wine. I don't want to kiss that good-bye. Adrienne says this'll make us better people, we'll be role models. Jesus. She never used to talk like that either. That kind of stuff made her gag. "Fuck me like a role model," she would whisper in my ear if she overheard someone using a term like that. Maybe I don't want to be a better person; I just want to be happy.

It's not a long drive home, almost all freeway, and I alternate between driving exactly the speed limit and doing ninety. I must look like a schizophrenic. It's the ambivalence made manifest. I need to know what's happening *right now;* I don't want to know, ever.

If I get pulled over by a cop and given a fat ticket, it'll prove I'm not ready to be a dad. Or I can just keep on driving straight to Reno. A poker overnight, the province of the parentless. Show up the next morning and tell Adrienne, "See, I'm not cut out for fatherhood. I'm still a kid myself." Forty-two, and a kid myself. Even I hear how pathetic that sounds.

No cops, no ticket, and I get off at our exit like I'm supposed to, like a good boy. Adrienne yanks the front door open, this massive smile on her face. It's so wide that it's almost creepy, like that clown from *It,* the one that lives in the sewer. The house is redolent with spices. "I'm cooking!" she announces. "Leah gets in tonight at eleven twenty-three."

I follow her into the kitchen. It's small but state-of-the-art, all gleaming steel appliances and expensive granite countertops covered with bowls and implements we never use, like a nylon brush. Who is this woman?

"Leah might not be hungry that late," Adrienne continues, "but the house will smell amazing. First impressions are everything, right? So on a subconscious level, she'll equate us with domestic bliss. And she'll want that for him." Adrienne turns suddenly, her eyes bright and moist. "Do you think we get to name him?"

I am legitimately speechless. Sagging against the refrigerator, I tell myself I don't need to speak. I can just turn on my heel and run. Run away from this possessed woman. Go to Reno, and when I come back in a day or two, Leah will be gone, and reality will have reasserted itself, and Adrienne will be my wife again.

I go into the dining room and sit down. From there, I can look toward the living room, stare longingly at the TV and the night I thought we'd have, or straight into the kitchen, where she's hard at work, kneading dough. Jesus.

"Tell me about Leah," I say.

"She's from Rhode Island. *Really* sweet girl. Her boyfriend, Trevor, wanted her to have an abortion but she wouldn't, and he dumped her, if you can believe it."

"I can believe it."

"She said he'll sign the papers, he's not attached to the baby at all. So that's great news. Oh, and she looks like me, and you look like Trevor. Isn't that amazing?" She doesn't wait for my answer. "The best part is, she's due in six weeks."

"And she's flying out here tonight? Is she supposed to be flying in the last trimester?" If I know that and the mother doesn't—if neither of these mothers do—we're in big trouble.

I see Adrienne's brow furrow. Then she pushes her hair out of her face with her forearm, and it's almost like she's manually smoothed everything over. It's a-okay now. "This is the one," she says quietly. "This baby is meant to be ours. He's even going to look like us."

"It's a boy?" I take a deep breath. If I were going to want a baby, I'd want a boy more.

"Leah doesn't know for sure. But I know." She looks over at me, and her expression is so full of love and hope and wonder that it breaks my heart. I want to be the one to make her look that way; at the very least, I don't want to take it away. But she's talking crazy. Leah's arriving *tonight*? Leah doesn't know the sex, but Adrienne somehow does?

"This is breakneck, Adrienne. This isn't how people do things."

"I know it's fast. But that's because it's fate." Again, she doesn't wait for my response. "Like you said, she can't fly too late in the pregnancy so she needs to do it now."

"It's already too late. What's she been doing her whole pregnancy, smoking crack?"

"She wouldn't do that." Her attention returns to the dough, which she kneads with an almost pathological vigor. "Seriously, I have a good feeling about her. It's overwhelming, being her age and pregnant. Maybe she's been waiting for Trevor to change his mind, to tell her he wants to raise the baby with her." I can tell that Adrienne is convincing herself as she speaks. She nods authoritatively. Yep, she likes that explanation. So it must be true.

"You mean you didn't ask what took her so bloody long?"

"I wasn't going to accuse her. I wanted her to like me. She needs to like us." She looks over at me. "Maybe you could go get your hair cut before she—"

"No."

"Okay, okay. Just a thought." She smiles and raises her sticky hands in the air to indicate her harmlessness. Adrienne is many things, but harmless is not among them.

"She didn't board the plane yet, did she? There's still time to cancel?" Her head whips toward me. "I'm just saying, we can Skype with her first. Get to know each other that way. It's safer for the baby with no air travel. Maybe we can fly out and visit her in Rhode Island, be there for the birth."

Now her eyes are downcast, on the bowl, and I feel the temperature in the room rising. "There isn't time." She pushes it out between clenched teeth.

"What did Hal say?" Hal Grayson III, Mr. "Call me Hal," we're all friends here, especially since he's going to make a mint brokering our baby.

"I can't reach him on a Saturday." Her next glance contains a plea. "She's got other birth parents in the queue."

The queue, like this is Netflix.

"Do you get what that means? She likes us best. She likes how we look and the way we love each other. She wants to meet us *first*. We're her favorites. But if we cancel, she'll go down the list. We'll lose her."

"Then there'll be other birth mothers." It comes out like I want it to—masculine and confident—but she's not buying it. She doesn't want others, she wants this one. It has to be this one.

She's turned into an ice sculpture. Her hands are frozen in the dough, and I can't even see her mouth moving. "This is happening, Gabe. She's flying out tonight. We're picking her up at SFO at eleven twenty-three. You can cut your hair or not. You can drive us to the airport or not." Her eyes flicker in my direction but don't light on me. "This is in motion."

Motion, for Adrienne, is unidirectional. She never reverses.

"Tell me you haven't signed anything," I say. I don't like my tone. Too wheedling. I make it stronger. "If we meet her and we don't like her, we can back out. We put her on a plane back home."

"Do you hear yourself?" Adrienne asks, incredulous. "You want to turn a birth mother away? We don't need to like her. We're not going to raise her."

"But she'll be in our lives forever. Open adoptions—"

"Can be closed," she finishes for me. "If I need to, I'll close it."

She's always been this way, so sure that what she doesn't want open can be closed. Her certainty can sweep you up like a tidal wave, and before you even realize what's happened, you've been carried far far away, so far you can't even see land anymore.

"We'll meet her," I say. "But after that we can still back out. Right? Answer me."

"Yes. But why would we?" She fixes me with a brilliant smile. "She's a teenager, Gabe. You think we can't work this to our advantage? She found *us*. She wants *us*." There are fireworks in her eyes. "*Her baby looks like us.* We've got this in the bag."

"Hello? Hello?"

"Hi."

"This is Adrienne. Are you calling for me?"

"I think so."

"Are you a birth mother?"

"I guess."

"Do you think you'll know soon?" Silence. "Sorry, it was a bad joke. I'm nervous. You're my first caller. I'm just super-happy to hear from you. Can I ask your name?"

"Patty."

"I'm really happy to hear from you. Did I already say that? Sorry, I'm nervous. I already said that, too. I just really want to be a mom. More than anything. And I would try my best to be a great mom to your baby. I really would.

"Patty? You still there?"

"Yes."

"I'm sorry if I'm overwhelming you. I mean, I'm overwhelmed. I just can't believe you called, that this could really happen. I'm not normally like this. I don't normally babble, and I don't normally just start crying with happiness. This is all just . . . it's a lot, you know? This process. The waiting, and the hoping."

"You don't have to be sorry. I'm sorry. I should have waited to call until I felt more together. This just feels really embarrassing. You know, my situation."

"No, no! You totally should have called. Even if you're not sure what you want to do. You get to make calls, right? Weigh out your options. I just want to be an option, that's all. Jeez, I sound like those people who lose at the Oscars, who say it was good to be nominated."

"You sound really nice, actually."

"You do, too. I think we're just both nervous. It's not like either of us have done this before. So maybe we should start over. Okay? Ring, ring. Hello?"

"Hi, my name's Patty. Are you Adrienne?"

"I am."

"I'm pregnant and I don't think I can keep the baby. In fact, I'm pretty much positive I can't keep the baby. And I don't have a good excuse for it either. I'm almost thirty."

"No one needs an excuse."

"I should have known better than to have sex without protection. But I'd just had my period, and I thought he was going to be the real deal. Am I saying too much?"

"No, not at all."

"Thanks. I just . . . like I said, I'm embarrassed. I trusted him, and came to find out he's married with two kids of his own."

"How did you find out?"

"He stopped returning my calls, so I followed him."

"He's the one who should feel embarrassed, tricking you like that."

"It's just such an old story. I can't believe I fell for it."

"Everyone falls sometime."

CHAPTER 5

Adrienne

Gabe puckers his lips a little as he drives, as if he's just eaten a sour candy. You'd think he lost a fight, when really, we're about to get what we've always wanted. I didn't just imagine that, us wanting this together. We used to lie on the grass when we were teenagers (well, I was still a teenager) and talk about what beautiful babies we'd make. Leah's going to be our incubator.

I reach over to touch the hair at the nape of his neck. "I was wrong," I say. He turns to me hopefully. "You look handsome with your hair this length. You don't need a cut." He swivels back to the road.

However he's acting now, he'll put on a good face for company. That's if I know Gabe, which I absolutely do.

The airport is only a few exits away. I start bouncing in my seat. Leah called me when she landed; she should have her luggage by now and be on the curb. Our baby's here.

"One nice thing," I say. "No traffic jams at this time of night."

Gabe's been silent this whole ride, but it's not going to bring me down. Sometimes I have to yank him by the arm to go out, and later he's glad we went. The same goes for this. On a much bigger scale, obviously. This is monumental.

There are only a few days in a life that qualify as truly monumental. This is definitely one of them. We're about to meet the mother of our child. The *birth* mother, I mean; I'm the mother. "Mama." It's going to be his first word. A little person is going to walk this earth and call me Mama. How monumental is that?

I wish Gabe would share this with me. "Dada" will be the second word.

"Time to get excited," I tell him. "There's no do-over. We only meet the birth mother for the first time once."

"And then for the rest of our lives."

Gloomy Gabe. That's what I call him when he gets like this. Usually, I say it right before I do something cute, like go down on him. Then he perks right up, literally. But I don't think he'll find it cute if I say it now, when there's no time for a blow job.

I watch the taillights of the other cars, like it's our own private disco, and decide that if he wants to miss out on this, he'll do it alone. I intend to be joyous.

"Sorry," he says. "I want to be happy."

"Then do it. Please, be happy with me."

"It's all going so fast. We just put up the profile a week ago."

"We *revised* our profile a week ago. Before that, it was eleven months of looking. And before that, years of trying. It's the opposite of fast." I point frantically. "That's our exit! You need to—"

"I know." He cuts me off, just as he cuts off a car in the next lane. A horn blares. He does that sometimes, speaks through his driving. "I want to do a background check on this girl. I mean, haven't we learned anything?"

I stare through the windshield. For Gabe, it's not about this girl; it might not even be about Patty. "We can have this conversation later. After Leah leaves." I can't allow her to hear heated whispers through walls, not when we're supposed to be the perfect couple.

"Terminal One," I say. We drive along slowly through Arrivals. "Stop, stop." I gape out the window. "Holy shit."

I'd thought that Leah might have been overstating our resemblance, but no. It's like my nineteen-year-old self is standing there on the curb—big tits, little everything else, except for a gorgeously compact belly (can she really be six weeks from giving birth?).

I get out of the car and approach her with a feeling of slight disorientation. I think of that old Clairol ad: "You, only better." Leah is me, only better. Same olive skin, hazel eyes, and dark hair, but all the features are sharper and more refined. It's like I'm a sloppy reproduction of a classic painting. Because where I've always been hot, but not actually pretty, Leah is both, even with a stomach like a taut helium balloon. She's in head-to-toe black, wearing scuffed lace-up boots, her dark hair caught up in a ponytail. I wonder if she straightens hers, too.

Gabe is beside me now, also gaping at Leah. He probably assumed she was overselling. Or maybe he thought I was lying, who knows. When he's Gloomy Gabe, he's capable of all sorts of disloyal thoughts that fall away as soon as he's back in his right mind. But he doesn't look gloomy anymore. He's positively lit up, shaking Leah's hand, asking about her flight, telling her no, don't worry about anything, don't lift a finger, I've got your suitcases. Yes, suitcases, plural, three of them, big and red and cheap looking. She brought an entire luggage set.

I hug her—I could swear I feel him kicking through her, reverberating through me, hello, little guy!—and I chatter about how amazing it is that twelve hours ago I didn't even know her, and now she's here, in the flesh. And with so much luggage! (No, I don't say that last part.) She's not saying much, but she's smiling back at me, and smiling at Gabe. Gabe, mostly. Oh, right, he reminds her of Trevor, her lost love. Isn't Trevor the one who did her wrong, though?

Once she's in the backseat of the car, the lap part of the seat belt secured under her belly, and we start to drive, I have this flash, like it's twenty years later, and she's our kid. We're taking her off to college—no, we're picking her up at the airport when she's home for spring break (I subtract the protuberant belly). I almost want to ask her how school's going, but I realize I don't know if Leah's actually in school. I don't know what she does with herself, or what she plans to do someday, after she's given birth and moved on with her life. It's probably too soon for heavy questions.

So what do I ask? Think light. Think whipped cream. Yet I'm stumped. A whole car ride here, and I didn't prepare anything. I like spontaneity, but sometimes it bites me in the ass.

"Your flight was good?" I sound boring. *I'm not boring!* I want to tell her, but you can't tell someone that; you have to prove it. I need to come up with something more exciting, but not too off-puttingly unconventional either. This is an audition for the role of mother.

"It was okay," she answers. "They make you buy your food."

"Airlines are so chintzy now," Gabe interjects. It's a funny word choice, "chintzy," something a New Jersey grandmother would say. Doesn't he realize we're auditioning here?

But Leah laughs. Then she leans forward and curls her fingers around his headrest. It's an oddly intimate gesture. "And they charge you to check bags, too, did you know that? I spent a hundred and fifty bucks on this trip already."

First I think she's flirting with him. Then I think, No, she's telling him she needs money. I bet in her family, if you need money, you go to Daddy.

Gabe doesn't seem to get it. He starts telling her about our flight to Barbados, and then she's all, "Wow, Barbados! I bet the water is really clear and blue. Where is that exactly?" and he's talking about snorkeling and an ill-fated attempt at scuba diving, and she's laughing again. I realize I haven't said anything in whole minutes, so I start describing the hotel and the food. She listens to me politely, like you're supposed to with your elders, but she's still clinging to Gabe's seat and hanging on his words.

"We'll give you the hundred and fifty dollars," I tell her, resigned.

I'm used to people liking me first and then warming up to Gabe more gradually. That's because I start out big, and he starts out small and gets bigger throughout the conversation, but tonight, it's the opposite. I'm not entirely sure what to do. But she likes Gabe, that's obvious, and I should just let her like him.

Wait. Gabe's being who he is at work, when he needs to be on from the first second. I turn to him with a smile, getting it now. Gabe is coming through for me; he's closing this deal for us. I sit back and watch him work.

When we get to the house and open the door, the pulled pork is like smelling salts. Leah is clearly revived. "I'm starving," she says.

"Adrienne was working on this all day," Gabe says. He gives me a proud little smile. I don't know where this Gabe came from, but I'm so glad he's here now. I put my arm around his waist and lean my head against his shoulder. It's authentic, but I still hope Leah notices it.

She's following the smell into the kitchen. I assemble her a plate of pulled pork with roasted vegetables and sourdough bread (I wait for Gabe to tell her I baked it myself, but he falls down on the job a little, which is totally forgivable given what a champ he's been). We all sit at the dining room table, and as Gabe and I watch her tear into the food with abandon, I really do feel like we're her parents, and all we want to do is see her eat, eat, eat, she's so thin, put some meat on those bones, hers and the baby's.

"You're so tiny," I say. "Is the baby tiny, too?" What I mean is, is he underweight, are there problems for which we need to brace ourselves.

"The baby's normal size. They did an extra ultrasound, just to make sure, because I'm carrying so small."

"And your face isn't all distended like some pregnant women's." She looks at me curiously. "Bloated, that's probably a better word." I have to remember she might not be super-educated. She might not love reading, like I always have. One of the great pleasures of my life is going to be reading to that baby, the normal-sized one, who was carried small. I need to get a baby book and write this stuff down so I don't forget any details.

Leah's done eating. We sit smiling awkwardly. It's late, especially for her, with the time difference; she probably needs to get to bed. We can do all the real talking tomorrow. Tonight was all about first impressions, and I think we scored. But one last thing . . .

"Can I see the ultrasound pictures?" I ask.

She licks her fingers slowly, one by one, not looking at me. "I was in a total rush to pack, and I thought I knew where they were, but it turns out they're somewhere else."

"And you didn't have time to find them." My chest has constricted. This cannot happen again. Then it comes to me: "Do you mind if I touch your stomach?"

She shifts toward me so immediately and so casually that I feel myself relax, just a little.

"Sure. The baby really likes your cooking."

"How can you tell?"

"He's kicking like crazy. Here, feel." She grabs my hand and places it on her bump.

And I do, I feel him. The sole of his tiny—excuse me, normal-sized—foot strains against the palm of my hand, like an amplified heartbeat. My God, it's actually him. Where've you been all my life? I laugh in delight and relief, because Leah couldn't fake that. This time, it's all real. "Hi, little guy," I say, leaning in so he can hear me better. "You like pulled pork, huh? And homemade sourdough. I'll bake as many loaves as you want." I turn to Gabe. "You have to feel this. Him."

He waves a you-go-ahead hand. "There's not enough room for both of us. She's carrying small."

"No, really, come here." When he does, I place his hand over mine. The baby is strong enough that we both get a jolt. I look up into Gabe's face, hoping it will mirror mine. But maybe he just doesn't want to give too much away in front of Leah; he's playing hard to get.

This, I tell him with my eyes, is our baby. There's no doubt in my mind.

What are the odds that we would meet a birth mother who's practically my twin (separated by twenty years), and the birth father would look like Gabe? They must be a million to one. Yet here she is, and here he is, inside her.

"You're crying," Gabe says, like it's a miracle, like I'm one of those statues of Mary in the convenience store that suddenly rain down tears.

Self-conscious, I lift my hand, and his falls to his side. Scooting my chair back, I start to clear the table. "I made up the air mattress for you," I tell Leah. It's in the office. I bought it this afternoon, along with all the bedding. We don't really have out-of-town guests, no family to come see us. But I'm not volunteering that information. "You must be tired."

"No, not really." She wipes her mouth with a napkin. "Can we stay up and talk?"

"Sure." Gabe gestures toward the living room.

She and Gabe go ahead while I rinse the plates and put them in the dishwasher and generally tidy up. When I enter the living room, I see that they're together on the red velvet sofa, talking animatedly, so I'm relegated to the love seat, solo. But I can still feel our baby reverberating against my hand, and I'm warmed by it. Once you have a child, you're never really alone again.

I start lighting the thick candles we keep in the fireplace. I hope Leah will notice the pictures and mementos on the mantel above, proof of the enduring love that lured her here.

Instead, she's fixed on Gabe. "I hate winter," she's saying. "You don't really get winter in California, do you?"

"We get rain," Gabe says. "And I complain about it like the pansy ass I've become."

She laughs, of course. "How long have you been out here?"

"We moved seventeen years ago," I interject. "Right after I finished college. We took a trip to San Francisco and we were like, yep, this is it. You can be a teacher anywhere."

"And they've got car dealerships everywhere," Gabe says.

"You must know a lot about cars, then." Leah puts her legs up underneath her, surprisingly agile for a pregnant woman.

He holds up his hand. "I never talk business past midnight."

Again, that laugh. It's starting to grate. "But what if I want to talk business?"

"You play by your own rules," he says.

She looks from him to me and back again. "Yeah," she says, "I do. I feel like you guys do, too, like you won't be all uptight about what I'm about to say."

I get butterflies at that—no, not just butterfly wings flapping but something bigger. It's more like a whole pigeon is taking flight in my stomach. "Let's talk business," I tell her.

She shifts her weight a little and smiles to herself, because she's nervous or because it's funny to do this to people, to make them wait on pins and needles and pigeon wings. I don't know which it is; I don't know her. But I feel like I'm about to know her a whole lot better.

"I brought a lot of stuff, right?" she says. "For a weekend trip. That was what you were thinking." I nod. "I was thinking that if everything's good for the next couple of days, if it seems like we fit together, then I don't go back to Rhode Island. I stay here with you until the baby's born."

Gabe is nodding slowly, not like he agrees but like he's willing to entertain her proposal, which is more than I would have expected a couple of hours ago. I don't exactly mind the idea because if she's here with us, she can't be out interviewing anyone else. Six weeks in our home, six weeks of hospitality and heartfelt talks, and she'll feel indebted. It'll be like a promise she's made. She won't be able to back out, even if she wants to.

I start to smile. But she's not finished.

"Then I stay for another year." She's watching our faces carefully, and I feel like this has to be a test. This is the real audition. I keep my face neutral and nod, *Go on*. But she doesn't.

"So you sign the adoption papers but then you keep living with us for another year?" I ask.

She shakes her head. Good, I misunderstood.

"I sign the papers *afte*r the year."

I don't trust myself to speak.

"You're only leasing us the baby," Gabe says. "Then you're the one with the option."

Her lips curve upward just slightly. "I didn't think of it like that, but yeah, I guess it kind of is."

"So after the baby's born," I say, "for the whole first year, he wouldn't really be ours?"

"Oh, no, go ahead and think of him as yours." I already do. But then, she must know that, after my reaction to touching her stomach. I should have kept a poker face, like Gabe. I've put us in a pretty weak bargaining position, since I can't imagine walking away, not now that I've felt him. "See, you've convinced me! I'm thinking it's a boy, too."

My mind whirs like a helicopter blade. A year with a baby that I want but can't fully have? It's like Chinese water torture. Who is this girl? Satan?

No, the last "birth mother" was Satan. This one's just a kid pressing her luck.

Part of me wants to tell her to get out of my house and find her own way back to Rhode Island. But I know that's our child she's carrying. A-million-to-one odds, and we're the one.

"I don't want a baby," Leah says. "I know that. I'm not staying so I can be around him."

"Then why are you staying?" I'm using the present tense, like this is already, inexorably, in motion. That's what I told Gabe.

"I'm staying because birth mothers get a shit deal. They're treated like they're important right up until they have the baby, and then they're just, like, thrown away, sent back where they came from. I'm giving my baby a new life, and I want one, too."

"In California," I say faintly. That's why she responded to our profile. Not because I look like her or because of enduring love, but because we're geographically desirable, and maybe just crazy enough to agree to her terms.

She's nineteen, and dictating terms. I should open that door and tell her to get out.

But not a single limb so much as twitches. My palm is still tingling where I felt our baby kick. Parents can lift cars off their children, are willing to walk through fire. Surely, I can tolerate Leah for a year. Someday, she'll just be a story we tell: Look what I put up with so I could have you, and it was all worth it.

"I don't want to get thrown back to my old life," Leah says. "I want a soft landing. A year, that's enough time for me to get everything together out here. To find a job, or enroll in school. After a year, I can get my own place. Then I'll be nearby, which will be easier for you guys. No plane trips on holidays, I'm right here. I can babysit if you want to, like, take a long weekend somewhere . . ."

She keeps talking, and I'm thinking, She's got to be delusional. To believe she's capable of living alongside her own child for a year without developing a bond; for her to think she can just babysit him occasionally—it's like she doesn't anticipate having any feelings at all.

"This gives you a whole year to change your mind," I interrupt her. "To fall in love with him, and take him with you, and then you're living right up the street with the baby that was supposed to be ours." I didn't mean to say any of that, but the words flew up through my esophagus, like projectile vomit. I'm scared, I realize. More than scared. Irrational as it is, I already love him. But then, love *is* irrational, at least all the love I've known.

Leah gets up and comes over, kneeling in front of me. "I swear to you, Adrienne, I don't want him. I won't. He's yours. But I need your help. I can't go back home." She's on the verge of tears. "You don't know what it's like for me back there, the way people shit on me because of Trevor, because he told them I'm a stupid whore who tried to trap him. I dropped out of school. I need to start over." It's the craziest thing, looking into her face, like young me pleading with old me. Older me, not old.

How am I supposed to say no to myself?

But if she's really nineteen-year-old me, then this could be an act. At that age, I wanted what I wanted, and screw everyone else. I thought that's how the world worked. I had to grow up to grow a conscience.

She looks genuine, all right, but I can't trust her.

My eyes meet Gabe's. He's buying all of it. They say that the best salesmen are also the best customers, the biggest dupes.

Leah can tell she's got Gabe, even without looking at him. That's why she's kneeling in front of me. I'm the hard sell.

"Two other couples said no. One said yes but then they backed out on me a few weeks ago."

So that's why she's thirty-four weeks pregnant and still looking. She wanted other parents, probably the ones with more money and bigger houses. She had to work her way down to us. She's settling. Slumming.

"But I'm glad it didn't work out with them," she says. "Because I saw your profile, and I just went, 'Yes!' " She's staring into my eyes. It's uncanny and disconcerting. "You've got love to spare, so you can let me in. You don't need to be stingy like those other people." Over her shoulder, to Gabe: "Chintzy."

He smiles at her and then rests his eyes on me. It's like they're both pleading. Doesn't he get that this is extortion?

"We'll think about it," I say, and she actually kisses my hand, the one with the ring on it, like I'm the Pope.

CHAPTER 6

Gabe

Three A.M., and I'm standing in the yard in my bare feet. It's a spring night, a perfect sixty-eight degrees, but I want to be cocooned in my bed. Adrienne hauled me outside. She couldn't sleep, and she couldn't be sleepless alone. She tried, though. She made it until 2:57. A valiant effort, before she prodded me awake.

The grass is in need of a mowing, the blades long and soft between my toes. We're at the far end of our yard, at the fence we share with the Olegsons, yet we're still whispering. I tell Adrienne we don't need to act like cold war spies, I could hear Leah snoring when I walked past the office, but she's insistent.

"I don't want her to know what I think of her," Adrienne whispers fervidly.

"If you hate her so much, then let this one go." I picture it like a game at the fair, the pregnant women bobbing along on little rafts, and if you don't shoot one, you'll get the next. Okay, bad analogy. "There'll be more."

"I wouldn't give her the satisfaction."

I can't help it, I yawn.

"We're going forward," she says.

"Seriously?"

"Oh, yeah. She's not going to win. This is our baby, I feel it. I *felt* it. Didn't you?"

If it's a competition, Leah's already winning. What she wants is a soft landing in California, a year lease, and Adrienne is willing to provide one. The question is, do I go along with it?

I'm as shocked as anyone to find that a big part of me actually wants to. But if Leah could see our profile and jump on it, so could another mother with a few weeks to go and no lease. If that happened, I could be a full-on father with no notice at all. With Leah, there's a loophole: I don't need to be full-on, not for months, because there will be two mothers. If that's not a gradual breaking-in period—a soft landing for me, so to speak—then I don't know what is. Adrienne and I can go out on dates while Leah stays home and babysits. It would be like having an au pair for a year.

Plus, my natural reticence about fatherhood would be warranted: No point in getting too attached to a baby that might not be ours. It's like we'd have a yearlong trial run as parents, a money-back guarantee. If at the end of it, we don't want the baby, well, Leah can't make us take him. (Or her. I refuse to indulge Adrienne's sudden conviction that she can divine the sex of unborn children.) Let's say we do back out—a hundred other couples would step up to claim a healthy infant.

Or maybe it turns out that Adrienne and I are great parents, that we make the transition as seamlessly as she's been predicting. Then, qualm-free, we go through with the adoption. We're a family, just like Adrienne wants, but now, it's what I want, too. Leah's deal gives Adrienne and me time to get back on the same page.

Also, I like Leah. I think she's a good kid. Spunky, like a young Adrienne. This is a chance to do something nice for someone in a hard spot. You don't get many opportunities like that. It could be win-win, and those are rare.

Adrienne is so adrenalized she can hardly stand still. She keeps shifting her weight from foot to foot.

"Why are you so mad?" I ask. "She's just going for what she wants. Making lemonade out of lemons." It's what Adrienne would have done.

"Our baby is not a lemon."

"That's not what I meant."

"Shh," she says, casting a glance back to the house. "Machiavelli's sleeping."

"If that were actually true, do you want Machiavelli to be the mother of your child?"

"Our child," she says, correcting me, "and I believe in nurture over nature."

"We don't need to decide this tonight."

"Time is kinda of the essence, don't you think?" She tips her head, like she's trying to get water out of her ear.

"She didn't give us a deadline."

"There are *other couples in the queue*!" She manages to give the impression of yelling without raising her voice. "If we don't say yes quickly, she'll go down the list."

"Then let her go," I say again, but hollowly. I realize that I don't mean it. I don't want her going anywhere. That's our birth mother in there, the one who'll toss in babysitting.

Adrienne studies me closely. She sees something and she's not sure if she likes it or not. "You don't want her to go. You were totally resistant before she got here, and now you want her to stay an extra year. What's the deal, Gabe?" Her hand flies to her hip, which then juts out, the timeless choreography of the suspicious wife.

"I'm doing what you want. I'm conceding."

She purses her lips, scrutinizing me. "I'm going to make this work. She is not going to bond with that baby. That is our baby."

Adrienne's self-regard is so high that she believes she can make this turn out to her specifications, not Leah's. No, it's not just that.

Her competitive streak has been engaged. As they say in reality TV: It is *on,* and she is not here to make friends.

"You really want to do this?" I ask her.

"Do you?"

"I kind of do."

She breaks out into a smile so bright it's blistering. Then her arms are around my neck and her tongue is in my mouth. "I knew this was the one," she says between kisses. I'm dimly aware of the raging impropriety of this whole thing—this isn't how things are done, how families are born, in a whispered conversation on bare feet at three A.M., with the invocation of Machiavelli—but somehow, comfortingly, it's pure us. This, I tell myself, is how Bonnie and Clyde would decide to adopt.

A couple more minutes and a tent-pole later, Adrienne abruptly stops. "We need to talk details."

"Can't that wait?" I reach for her again. "We'll do that with Leah tomorrow." We haven't had sex outside in too long.

She takes a step back. "No, now. It's about the pool table. It has to go in the garage."

The garage smells like motor oil. It's full of junk. The lighting is lousy, and it's drafty in winter. Most significant, it's a *garage.*

I try to communicate all that to her with my eyes. She appears not to understand. "We agreed to convert the office into the baby's room," I say.

"Right."

"So . . . what's the problem?"

"Leah needs a room, too. We have three bedrooms, one of which is currently taken up by your pool table."

I stare at her, doing the math. "Or Leah and the baby bunk together."

Her eyes widen. Out of this entire conversation, that's the thing that sparks incredulity? "Leah and the baby are not going to share a room."

"Why not? She'll probably be breast-feeding—"

Her eyes bulge. "Leah will not be breast-feeding! Do you know how much bonding happens during breast-feeding? Leah is not going to spend an extra minute with that baby."

Unease washes over me. "You can't really spend the year policing her."

"Watch me." She leans in close, and it's like her next statement is in bold: "I'm the mother, not her!"

My unease ratchets up. "Is this really about Leah, or about someone else?" I don't like to even say Patty's name. Best to forget it ever happened, and over the past months, it seemed like Adrienne had. But for a while, she was consumed. It was like Patty had engulfed my wife in flames.

"This isn't about Leah, or anyone else. It's about our child. So whatever I need to do to keep him safe, to keep him with us, I'll do it."

"Leah's a person, too." I don't like that it bears reminding.

"Don't worry about her. I'm going to kill her with kindness."

"And while you're killing her, what happens to us? We're talking about an entire year."

She sidles up to me. She catches my bottom lip between her teeth, and her hand inside my pants is shockingly cold. But it doesn't stay that way for long.

CHAPTER 7

Adrienne

It's a glorious April day—seventy-two degrees, no humidity, the sun bright but not harsh, as if angled through slats—the kind of day that would make anyone wish they lived in California.

Leah casts her own radiance as we sit outside having brunch. Her long dark hair is in two braids, snaking forward on each shoulder. I never wore my hair like that, not even when I was a little girl. She's friggin' adorable, and I'm pretty sure she knows it.

The back terrace of the restaurant is done up like Tuscany (not that I've ever been there, though Gabe and I plan to go one day). We're in a grape arbor, within a suburban downtown. Sleight of hand, a magic trick. It's a perfect metaphor for what I'm trying to do with Leah. I need her to see what she wants in us. Whatever that might be.

Normally, I'm a quick reader of people, but that girl's book is closed. Behind all her "I love your car" and "I love this restaurant" and "I love the weather," behind all the sweetness and light, lurks her true motivation.

It's disturbing, this supernatural sense that I'm meeting my nineteen-year-old self and she's carrying my baby and running a game on me.

Gabe can't see through it, of course, same as he couldn't see through mine half a lifetime ago. But I had good intentions. I wanted to love him forever. What does Leah want?

"I've got to work later," he's telling Leah, "but tomorrow's my day off. Where do you want to go?"

I snap to attention. I don't have off tomorrow. It's Monday, a school day. Maybe I could call in sick? It would mean doing a bunch of work tonight to get ready for the sub, but it might be worth it. I have to do my prep for the week anyway.

"We need to go to San Francisco," Leah says, "obviously." She smiles.

Gabe and Leah touring San Francisco by themselves? Yeah, I'm calling in sick. "Where in San Francisco?" I try to sound friendly and interested as I keep my eyes down on my plate. In case eyes really are windows to the soul, I better keep my blinds shut.

"I don't know." I'm pretty sure Leah's windows are trained on Gabe. "Any suggestions?"

Gabe goes into this spiel about the merits of exploring different neighborhoods versus going to tourist spots, and I'm staring at my egg-white omelet. I can't help thinking about how young Leah's eggs are, how fresh. I didn't pay enough attention in health class, so it wasn't until Gabe and I were trying (and failing) to conceive that I learned women have all the eggs they're ever going to have at birth. It's downhill from there, a slow degradation until they reach their expiration date.

That's how they made it sound at the fertility clinic. Apparently, there's no upside to aging for an egg. It doesn't get seasoned with life experience, it doesn't marinate in self-improvement. No, if I'd gotten knocked up at Leah's age, as selfish and callow as I was, my eggs would still have been all the better for it. They would have been more viable.

Leah, sitting there chomping on a slice of bacon while I avoid yolks, is more viable than I am.

"You're a teacher, right?" she says. "That's, like, such an important job."

"I love the kids," I respond, which is true.

But she's put me over a barrel. If I call in sick, it could look like I'm not devoted to my job—not devoted to the children—and that's not the impression I want to give, in case Leah really is assessing my maternal instincts.

Also, if I call out of work, it could look like I don't trust my husband to be around Leah, and that's definitely the wrong impression. As far as Leah is concerned, Gabe and I are the Greatest Love of All (not the Whitney Houston version of self-love—why did it never previously occur to me that that song could be a paean to masturbation rivaled only by Billy Idol's "Dancing with Myself"?). The Greatest Love of All is supposed to be Gabe and me, as stand-ins for Leah and Trevor.

Besides, I do trust Gabe. His love for me, his basic honesty, his fidelity—none of that is remotely in question.

I just don't trust Leah. I sense her capacity for manipulation, which, combined with his susceptibility to it, could make for a hairy situation. I don't like imagining what information she could get out of him, what promises she could extract.

But if I call in sick and Leah realizes that I have her number, that could queer the deal, irreparably. Leah might be looking for easy marks, and I'll need to play one, at least for a while longer.

I'm managing to think all this as I tell one of my go-to cute-kid stories (complete with lisping mimicry), and Leah is smiling in all the right places. It occurs to me, too late, that I shouldn't remind Leah how cute kids are.

Because it's possible that Leah is just a normal birth mother, and all my suspicions are coming from my last experience. Unfortunately, a normal birth mother is prone to maternal feelings herself, and to second-guessing.

Let her be Machiavelli, if that's what it takes.

Her cell phone is lying on the table next to a pot of orange marmalade. A text is coming in, and she glances down and smiles, with what seems like private pleasure. Then she broadcasts: "The other prospective parents. They want to know if I'm going down to L.A. to see them."

"They must be nervous," I say. "We've been in their position before." Meaning: We're not there now. Meaning: This is our baby, not theirs.

Leah nods, still with that enigmatic smile. "I don't want to pressure you guys, but I do need to know pretty soon what you want to do. If you want me to stay."

It's funny phrasing—this isn't about Leah staying, it's about her baby staying—and it makes me think that Leah is going to be acutely sensitive to rejection. I remember what she said about birth mothers getting thrown away and how that's not going to happen to her. It's the kind of defiant thing I might have said when I was her age.

It's also funny that I'm not feeling more warmly toward my young doppelgänger. Maybe the mistrust isn't about Leah's resemblance to our last potential birth mother/con artist, but about her resemblance to me.

Gabe and I look at each other. We haven't actually talked about this since our middle-of-the-night tête-à-tête. In the cold light of day, we haven't finalized anything with one another, let alone with Leah.

But the next few seconds are crucial, I know. Leah can't feel rejected.

"We want you," I say. "And the baby, of course." Like the baby is an afterthought, like what we've always wanted in our marriage is not a newborn but a nubile version of me traipsing around our house, burning off her pregnancy weight at the speed of nineteen. "Are you sure you want us? You only got here last night. This is such a big decision, and we want you to feel—"

"I want you guys," Leah says. "I'm the kind of person who goes with my gut."

"What does your gut say about us?" Gabe seems mildly curious, or bemused.

I turn to stare at him. This is no time for questioning. Leah is choosing us. This is all proceeding according to plan, sort of.

Leah turns to him, too. Her expression is decidedly softer than mine. Where he's bemused, she's amused. "My gut says you're awesome." I'm pretty sure she's flirting, though her smile encompasses me, too, like a great big hoop skirt. She's choosing us both. We're her new family.

That's what it is. That's what scares me the most. What if Leah tries to latch on and never let go, like a parasite and her hosts? Family is supposed to be forever.

Good in theory.

I can still hear the slur of my mother's voice. She's overweight, lumbering unsteadily to her feet, like a cow on ice. "Don't ever come back then!" she shouts. "You fucking slut!" She's wrong about the slut part. There weren't many others besides Gabe. In my heart, there was none other.

I was nineteen then, I realize. I lost my mother, what little I ever had of her, at the very age that Leah is going to deliver my own child to me. A boy. Please, let it be a boy. Boys revere their mothers, if the rumors are true.

It's almost too perfect, the symmetry: coming full circle, the circle of love, just like I wrote in the profile.

Leah's right. Gabe and I are awesome. No matter what, we're going to stay that way.

"Can I touch him?" I ask Leah. She leans back obligingly, and I place my hand on her belly. I feel around for him. It's my third time today. I'm like a junkie needing a fix.

I mainline my future child, knowing that whatever happens will be worth it. He's worth everything.

CHAPTER 8

Gabe

Another text from Adrienne: "Soooo . . . ????"

So what? I want to text back. So what are you expecting? I'm showing Leah around the city. We went to Fisherman's Wharf and watched the sea lions and poked around in a few tourist-trap stores; visited Golden Gate Park, where I learned Leah isn't much of a walker, at least not while she's this pregnant; and now we're in the Richmond, my favorite neighborhood. Leah seems to like it, too, even though it's overcast, where the wharf was pure sun.

"Are you going to answer that?" Leah asks. She's smiling in this teasing way, like she knows.

But what can she know? That Adrienne is threatened by her, by the two of us being out together? I don't think Adrienne is willing to admit that to herself.

This morning, Adrienne insisted we have sex, and she wasn't quiet about it either. Maybe it was stress relief; maybe she was marking her territory. To be honest, I wasn't that into it. I'm not a big morning-sex guy, and the potential mother of our kid was within earshot.

"What about Leah?" I whispered.

"She likes that we're hot for each other," Adrienne whispered back. "It's part of why she picked us. She wants us to be what she and Trevor weren't."

I don't know about that. I just know that if I were in the guest room, I wouldn't want to hear the future mother of my kid moaning, especially when it sounded kind of fake. Adrienne often sounds a bit theatrical, but all I could think of while we were doing it was how it would sound to Leah. Like Adrienne was putting on a show.

"It's Adrienne," I tell Leah now. "She wants to know if you're having fun."

"Tell her I'm definitely having fun." Leah's got this twinkle, like she's messing with Adrienne, or with me. I don't mind it, it's friendly, but Adrienne would disagree.

The thing is, Leah does sort of twinkle, all the time. Adrienne is obsessed with how much Leah looks like her, thinks it's a little creepy, but I don't really see it that way. I think Adrienne is gorgeous, don't get me wrong, but she was never just as plain pretty as Leah is. Adrienne tortures her hair straight, while Leah's is long and wavy without any kink to it. Adrienne's skin was never so perfect and clear. Leah's the After in the Proactiv infomercials Adrienne and I sometimes watch (they're heartwarming, with all the pizza-faced ducklings turning into swans).

"Having fun," I text back. On the one hand, I figure Adrienne will be pleased. She wants Leah to have enough fun to stick around, but *only* that much. I'm not sure she wants me having fun at all. She wants this to be a job.

But it is fun, showing someone around this great part of the world in which Adrienne and I chose to live. I never get to do it, since we're not in touch with family and all the old friends have fallen away over the years.

That's all it is, me getting to be proud I inhabit the Bay Area, that

I didn't just stay in my NJ burg for life. I have Adrienne to thank for that. It's like I always say: She's a life force. My life force.

So why is she so threatened by this girl?

Leah and I are browsing a little market, the kind you'd find in Chinatown. That's why I like the Richmond. It's this mix of old Chinese ladies with their steel carts bumping behind them and young hipsters. And normal people, too, though it seems to me it's predominantly Chinese and hipster. Leah's a little bit hipster: all in black once again, with those lace-up boots, like the old Doc Martens people used to wear when I was in high school. They might actually be Doc Martens.

She's peering into a freezer case. "Taro-root ice cream," she says. "Sesame ice cream." She's got big round eyes. Sometimes she really does just look like a kid. Does she look like our kid will?

Now, that's what freaks me out. All this shit Adrienne is dealing with, the petty jealousy—it's nothing compared to the simple, insane reality that soon, we'll be parents, fully responsible for the care and feeding of an actual human being. When my brother and I were kids, he noticed I couldn't even keep Sea-Monkeys and Chia Pets alive. "You've got a black thumb," he once said.

"You okay?" Leah asks. "You look a little—I don't know, something."

My laugh comes out shaky. "I am something."

I'm surprised when she takes my hand in hers. Her eyes are intent on my face, as if she's some kind of healer. The weird part is, I do feel steadier. She smiles. "Better?"

"You got special powers? Are you one of the X-Men?"

She laughs. "I get scared out of the blue, too, sometimes. Comes with the territory."

"What territory is that?"

"I'm about to be a mother, and you're about to be a father."

I take my hand away and go to the produce section, which is full of vegetables I don't recognize. The signs are lettered in a few different Asian languages, plus English. Leah follows me.

"Taro root again," she says. She picks it up and runs her fingers over it. It's like a potato that mated with a coconut, the skin thick and dark and a little hairy. "Do you cook?"

"No, Adrienne does." Though not like she cooked for Leah. I want to tell Leah not to expect that for the next year, unless Adrienne's planning to keep up the act for that long. The truth is, I don't know exactly what she's planning.

There it is, that feeling again. But I keep my back to Leah. It's not right, her comforting me. Adrienne wouldn't like it.

Leah picks up another vegetable. "It says this is bitter melon. Looks more like a really wrinkled cucumber, like a little old man."

I laugh. "Me, in twenty years."

"Don't be so hard on yourself. Twenty-five years."

"Ha ha."

An Asian woman, stooped and foreshortened, elbows me out of the way. I thought she wanted to get at the Japanese eggplants, but no. She points at Leah's belly. "When you due?"

"Six weeks." Leah glances at me. "Well, more like five."

Jesus. Why did she lie to Adrienne about the due date? Or did Adrienne lie to me? One of them was buying time.

"You tiny," the woman says. She touches her own stomach. "Tiny, too. But baby big." She spreads her arms, and Leah and I laugh.

"May I?" another woman asks shyly, indicating Leah's belly. She's white, fifty or so, with close-cropped dark hair. "Is the baby moving much?" I have the distinct impression from the quiet of her delivery, the sense of reverence in it, that she's never had children of her own. The Asian woman begins examining the tubers.

"He's not moving right now," Leah says, but she pins her arms back, assenting to the woman's request. Leah has caught Adrienne's certainty about the sex, or she's decided she might as well co-opt the syntax.

The woman runs her hand gently over Leah's stomach. There's something sensual in the touch, and I find myself averting my eyes. But then the woman looks at me and says, "You must be thrilled."

I'm not sure how to respond. She looks so hopeful for us, for Leah and me. She must think that I'm the real father.

"He's going to be a great dad," Leah interjects. I wonder if she really believes that, and if so, what in me suggests it. It might just be what she needs to think. Or a favor she's doing for this childless woman, who is hanging on the answer.

Leah can be kind, I realize.

"My wife is really excited," I say. It feels like Adrienne should be part of this conversation.

The woman stands up and smiles at Leah, clearly assuming her to be my wife. I would think she'd have some reaction to our age difference, perhaps disapproval, but she's apparently too focused on the fantasy. Two loving parents and a baby on the way. "You're beautiful," she tells Leah. "You glow."

"My husband says the same thing."

What the hell? It's one thing to indulge the woman's fantasy, another to— There's no way I can tell Adrienne about this.

"Congratulations," the woman says, moving away, but reluctantly, like she wants to bathe in our light awhile longer. In Leah's glow.

I stalk out of the store.

"What?" Leah says defensively, once we're both out on the sidewalk. People stream by, mildly interested in our sideshow. What do they take us for? Father and daughter? Husband and wife? Man and mistress?

"You lied, that's what." I probably shouldn't be calling her out. I promised Adrienne I'd be on my best behavior.

Another text. Christ. Adrienne and her impeccable timing.

"Short leash, huh?" Leah ribs me. I guess she's thinking it's a way to lighten the mood, but I glower at her. I'm being too real with her. I'm showing her who I actually am.

But I've got this feeling she likes that. She likes me more than she likes Adrienne, and we all know it, including Adrienne. That's why all the texts.

"Why did you do that?" I ask. "In the store." Maybe I can get Leah to be real, too.

"Don't you ever like to pretend?" She shrugs. "It's not like it hurt anybody."

"But . . ." Why pretend *that*? Why my wife?

"We're friends, right?" she says.

I nod.

"So you need to know something about me. Sometimes I do things and I don't know why. And I'm okay with that."

"It's called being nineteen."

I can tell she doesn't like that answer. I can hardly blame her. No one likes being reduced to their age. I know I don't like when people think the things I do are middle-aged clichés. Like when they assume I'm a married guy sleeping with a young girl. I've gotten a few of those looks today, too.

"Friends," I say. "That's a good idea."

"Didn't you say you were going to take me to Lands End?" She tosses her hair back and smiles. "I love that name."

CHAPTER 9

Adrienne

The kids have spring fever. By this time in the year, they've got the routines down; they know how to work in small groups. But today, they keep chattering loudly, squawking and squabbling. I'm presiding over a barnyard.

I flick the light switch. "Lights off, head down. I'm in no mood for this." I believe in transparency with the kids. They need to know I'm a person, too.

I hear some of the bossier kids repeating after me: "Mrs. T's in no mood."

"I'm not in the mood to be repeated either. I can speak for myself."

In the darkness, I glance over at my desk, where my cell phone lies silent and luminescent, my most recent texts unanswered. Where is he? What's he doing?

The kids simmer down. I stew.

Normally, I'm crazy about my kids. All of them, even the little freaks and terrors and attention whores. I love their rampant humanity, how it can be so concentrated and so exterior. Their whole lives are one big game of show-and-tell. They're still mostly naïve and deeply inquisitive. At the beginning of the year, they need constant direction, and redirection. By April, they're at their best: more mature and independent and opinionated. They broadcast their emotions shamelessly.

Each year presents its own challenges in terms of how to merge all the different learning styles and behavior issues (not to mention managing the expectations of the parents who want to make their job yours). Sometimes you have a tough kid who triggers everyone else; sometimes there are clusters of kids who hijack a room. They're so impressionable that they can easily act on each other, a ceaseless game of marbles. So it's marbles for them but chess for me, as I figure out what to do about it all. Generally, I like that.

But not today.

Why isn't he texting me?

I hadn't realized it would be worse for me once the kids got calm. Their cacophony was drowning out some of the noise in my head.

It's not that I think he's doing anything wrong. She's a kid herself. A pregnant kid. Pregnant with *our* kid, mine and Gabe's. It's that I don't like to be ignored, and Gabe knows that better than anyone.

"I'm going to turn the lights back on," I announce, "and I want you all to remember the way you feel right now. The calm. Hold on to that, okay? We're going back to our small groups and you need to *work*. Five, four, three, two, one."

It's amazing how quickly our eyes adjust to the darkness and how glaring the light can seem. The kids blink and look around. For a second, it's like they've never seen the room before. I recently decorated for spring, with lots of blooming and budding. In the corner is our unit on metamorphosis: the Eric Carle type, not Franz Kafka's. The students have painted pictures of their interpretation of *The Very Hungry Caterpillar.* We have 3-D replicas of the various stages of development from caterpillar to butterfly. There are little plastic cocoons that the kids can hold in their hands and, in more rambunctious moments, chuck at one another. We have a field trip planned to see butterflies.

WTF, Gabe?

My students are now doing what they're supposed to, and I sit back down at my desk. I scan the room, wondering which of these kids will look most like my kid and what his temperament will be. I'm a big believer in temperament. I don't think anyone who works with kids on a regular basis can deny it. I'm hoping for one who's outspoken yet sweet, like Michaela; I hope he looks like Cody, because Cody is a dead ringer for Gabe.

Our baby's almost here. If I close my eyes, I can so easily imagine the weight of him in my arms, my lips grazing his forehead. I'll never get to breast-feed, of course, and that pains me. But Leah won't breast-feed either. Not on my watch.

My fingers itch to text again, but there's no point. I'm sure he saw the last one. Another would only look desperate, and desperation does not increase one's attractiveness. He's just in the middle of something, that's all.

What could he possibly be in the middle of? It's not even noon. They wouldn't have gone to see a movie; they're out sightseeing. Sightseeing should make someone eminently available.

The next half hour passes in a vacillating haze of baby fantasies and agitation over Gabe's failure to respond. The kids are remarkably self-contained. Not a single argument, or a raised hand, or a "Mrs. T . . ." Once you're inessential, you realize how much you want to be needed.

"Lunchtime, Mrs. T." Angie points at the hands of the clock. She sounds proud. It takes her a lot longer than the other kids to pick up skills and once she does, she likes to demonstrate them. With her red hair and off-center pigtails, she's got a certain Pippi Longstocking quality. It's hard not to love Angie.

I smile at her. "You're right, Angie. It is."

That means lunch for me, too, though my stomach says otherwise. After I make sure the kids are safely to the cafeteria, I head for the break room, phone firmly in hand.

The break room is windowless, with each wall painted a different color (green, blue, yellow, red). It's like eating inside a Rubik's Cube.

Mel is already there, at our usual table, eating one of those salads that have so much cheese and dressing it might as well be a Big Mac. We greet each other and she launches into a story about her fifth graders' morning antics.

"Hello?" Mel's voice is as bright as the walls. "Are you in there?"

Mel's my best friend at work—my best female friend period—and she knows about the fertility clinic and the adoption process. But she doesn't know what happened with Patty, and she doesn't know about Leah. I've always thought sharing is overrated. Even as a little girl, I was no good at sleepovers. I was in it for the junk food and the movies and maybe a little Ouija board; screw the rest. I opened up to Patty, and see where that got me.

"Rough morning," I say.

"Dominic?" She smiles sympathetically. The good thing about Mel is that she'll fill in any blank you leave.

Mr. Woodhouse is at the table next to us, reading a book and eating a meatball sub. It's stinking up the joint, and it's not even the worst of his smells. I know we're colleagues, I should call him Larry, but I prefer to maintain formality. Keep a little distance between me and Mr. Woodhouse, a.k.a. the Stink Bomb.

"Not Dominic." He's a loudmouth, but that doesn't rattle me. I'm good at my job because not a lot rattles me.

Now, Leah—she rattles me. But I'm not about to say that to Mel. I haven't even admitted it to Gabe.

Mel envies me in a charmingly transparent, self-deprecating way, and she worships Gabe. I wish she could find one of her own. I've come this close to offering her a makeover or calling in the *What Not to Wear* team. They could film her from the bushes in her shapeless cardigans and calf-length skirts, and we could screen the footage in the cafeteria. Everyone would cheer when the gay man/snarky woman duo offered her an all-expenses-paid trip to New York and a new wardrobe, and she'd say yes, her chins aquiver. She has a pretty face, Mel, but then, that's what you always say about overweight people. Somehow, it always seems to be true. She's not tragically overweight, but the Bay Area singles market is pitiless.

I glance at my phone, in case it failed to audibly alert me to a new text message.

"Did you hear from a birth mother?" Mel asks.

"No," I say. "Why would you think that?" It comes out loud and strange enough to attract Mr. Woodhouse's attention.

Mel scoots her chair closer to me. She always smells clean and comforting, like vanilla and nutmeg, like pumpkin pie. "What's going on, really?"

Leah's only been in our lives a few days, but I already feel like I don't know where to start.

Gabe's too honest. I know that sounds crazy to a lot of people, since he's a car salesman, but he really can be honest to a fault. He could have blown this whole thing by now. Maybe he's not texting because he's doing damage control.

Or he's already backed out without even telling me. He's driving her back to SFO right now.

"Adrienne?"

I look up and it's Principal Jorgenson. Shit. I didn't even hear her come into the room, let alone pad up to our table on her little cat feet. She's not even five feet tall, and her hair is mousy brown and shaped like a mushroom. The last principal loved me, but she retired this past June.

Principal Jorgenson gestures toward my neckline. Cleavage. She warned me about the cleavage.

"They're seven years old," I tell her. "They've seen it all before."

She's not amused.

Well, try to force me out. I'm a good teacher, but most important, I have seniority and my union's stronger than she is.

I readjust my V-neck. "It's always slipping," I say. I give her a faux-friendly smile.

She's not falling for it. I hate people like her, the kind who use the word "appropriate" in every third sentence. I have great tits. Deal with it.

"Melanie," Principal Jorgenson says, "I'll need to speak with you later." Woodhouse is eavesdropping, again.

"Can you tell me what it's regarding?" Mel sounds like she's taking a phone message for her mother. She's easily cowed by authority. It's the other reason I'd love to see her in a pair of thigh-high boots. Clothes are powerful.

"I can meet with you right after school. We'll discuss it then. Are you available?"

Mel nods, and Principal Jorgenson whispers off.

Mel moves so that she's practically in my lap. "I bet Blake's mom called about that recess thing," she says.

I can't recall the recess thing. I don't always listen to every single anecdote of Mel's; there are so many of them. "You'll be fine."

"I've only been here two years." The subtext is that she's not like me, she can't just stand up to the principal with impunity. She could get a pink slip at the end of the year, though more than likely, she'd be rehired over the summer. (It's one of the budget tricks to look like the district is saving money.) "And I don't have a husband to pay my rent."

Speaking of my husband, where is he?

"You'll be fine," I say again, turning up the volume on the conviction and the sympathy. It works. Mel's torso relaxes.

I don't know what compels me, but then it's out of my mouth. "We're getting a baby."

Mel leaps up and hugs me. Her happiness is so instant and genuine that I wish I was a better listener, a better friend. I envy the ease of her joy. I've always had trouble being glad for others. I believe there's a finite amount of good luck in the world, and one person's fortune is always to another's detriment. The universe is about balance, with equal parts joy and suffering, and you always have to be vigilant about which side of the scale you're on.

Mel would never think that way. She doesn't think that my having Gabe means she won't find anyone, or that my getting a baby relegates her to childlessness. I hope she's right, but I fear I am.

She resettles herself next to me. "Tell me all about it. Every detail." Her eyes are round and blue and guileless. They remind me of the Cabbage Patch Kid I had when I was a little girl. Tamara Beth, that was the name on the ersatz birth certificate.

"Well," I say, "it's happening soon. The birth mother is thirty-four weeks along."

"That's amazing! You're practically a mom."

Woodhouse's fingers have stilled on the pages. He's probably debating whether it's ruder to congratulate me, thus admitting his eavesdropping, or to ignore my big news.

"I am," I say. "I'm practically a mom." I let the pleasure rise up from my toes and warm my legs and then my stomach. I let it saturate me.

Finally, the text comes in. "At Lands End," Gabe has written. "Beautiful day."

I exhale. So he hasn't blown it. I never should have doubted him. He's a salesman, a born closer. I'll find out later what was so beautiful about it.

CHAPTER 10

Gabe

I should feel bad that I didn't tell Adrienne. Strangely, though, I'm okay with it. For one thing, it's not my secret to tell. Not my life story. Leah needs to decide when (if) she's ready to share it with Adrienne. So I can call it a principled stance, keeping it from Adrienne.

Underneath that is something else. A desire to have the upper hand for once, maybe, to be the one with the secret. Yeah, I've got resentments. Everyone does in a relationship as long as ours. This is just a small way of evening the score, and it's not like it hurts anybody.

It is a little painful, though, watching the two of them interact. Leah and Adrienne are nicey-niceing each other to death. "No, after you." "No, you." "Yes, please." "Thank you." "Thank *you*!" They're both so much more than nice. I feel like Leah started to show me the rest of her, and I like it. I think Adrienne would, too. And vice versa. If Adrienne acted like herself, I bet she and Leah could turn into sisters.

But Adrienne doesn't want Leah for her sister. Adrienne thinks she's only got room for the baby, like there's a love quota and Leah would send her over. Or she thinks that the baby will only have so much love to give, so she needs to get Leah out of the picture ASAP. Caring for Leah would only complicate Adrienne's mission.

There's plenty of time for Adrienne to change her mind, though. Leah's made sure of that.

"This is meant to be," Adrienne whispered tonight, half-asleep, snuggled against me.

I'm thinking she could be right, maybe it was preordained. We could be the answer to a prayer for Leah, and that baby is the answer to Adrienne's prayer. And me, I don't really pray.

Since when do I have thoughts like that? I guess I'm growing up. I'm becoming a dad.

Jesus.

That's as religious as I get.

Hal—that's Hal Grayson III, Esquire—is eyeballing us each in turn. "I've never seen this done before," he says, "and I've been in the adoption business a long time."

"I thought you were in the legal business," Leah says.

He lifts one side of his mouth in a smile, as if to say he likes a sassy young thing, but that's in his personal life, and this is, indeed, business.

He's your prototypical silver fox. In his late fifties, he wears expensive suits and no tie. He always looks freshly ironed. There's a picture on his desk of a comely woman twenty years his junior, and beyond him, a wall of windows overlooking downtown San Francisco. His furniture is clean and modern, chrome and glass, the chairs artistic and uncomfortable.

And he clearly thinks all three of us are nuts.

"I told you on the phone that this was what we're planning to do," Adrienne says, not hiding her impatience. In this office, time is money, quite literally.

The other side of Hal's mouth joins in. He likes Adrienne's sass, too, and she's more of his target demographic, if that photo is any indication.

It's kind of funny, watching Leah and Adrienne tag-teaming, especially given all their careful conversations and polite distance to this point.

"Just let me make my case," Hal says, "to all of you." He looks at Leah first. "You've never had a baby before."

"And you have?"

"I've worked with plenty of young women in your position. Too much contact immediately after the birth just confuses the situation." Meaning, it might make Leah likely to take the baby back. His bow is pointed at Leah, but that arrow's meant for Adrienne. "You've decided that you want your baby to be raised by Adrienne and Gabe. It's best to let them start as soon as possible, without interference."

"You don't know me," Leah says. "I'm not going to interfere, and I won't get confused."

"Hormones can play tricks. The maternal instinct—"

"Is a myth," Adrienne cuts in sharply. "Every woman doesn't necessarily have it, just by virtue of being female, or because she gave birth. Have you ever watched the Summer Jackson show? Last week, there was a story about a woman who killed her three-year-old and hid her body in the freezer for weeks. Where was her maternal instinct?"

I glance at Leah to see how she'll take that. From her face, she thinks Adrienne is sticking up for her, that they're on the same side.

"We should at least consider what Hal's saying," I tell them. "He's more experienced than any of us." Adrienne and Leah give me eerily identical looks, like I'm a traitor. They really could be sisters. In some ways, Adrienne's still a kid herself. If you tell her not to do something, she redoubles her efforts. She wants to prove Hal wrong, to show that we can be the exception. But we don't yet know the reasons for the rule.

"Thanks, Gabe," Hal says. He's not used to having to fight for the floor. "Listen, I'm just looking out for all concerned. Let me tell you, an arrangement like this is not going to be good for Leah. She'll be in a fragile emotional state after giving birth, and separating immediately seems painful but it's the best way. Just rip the Band-Aid off and she can start grieving right away. Delayed grief is the worst."

"Now he's in the psychology business," Leah says to Adrienne. Then to Hal, "I appreciate your concern." Her tone conveys the opposite. She doesn't think Hal has her best interests in mind, and she's right. Adrienne and I are the ones paying him; we're his clients. We've bought his allegiance.

"Ask any psychologist," he rejoins. "A clean break is better."

"But it's an open adoption. It's not a clean break anyway." Leah's got him there.

"Open adoptions have certain parameters. There are boundaries. Once you move in with the adoptive family, for an entire year, those go out the window. What are you going to do, act like a nanny?" His face is a mask of incredulity. "It's nuts." I never expected him to actually spell it out.

"I'm not nuts," Leah says.

"I'm not saying you're nuts. But the idea's nuts."

Adrienne reaches across me and lightly touches Leah's leg. "We can go to a different lawyer if we need to."

Hal looks at me like I might be the last bastion of sanity. "I'll write up any contract you want. It's not my life. But you're making this more complicated than it needs to be, and believe me, it's already complicated. Two mothers and two fathers—"

"There's only one father," Leah interrupts. "Gabe's the only father."

"Has the biological father signed his rights away?"

"No, but he will."

Hal makes a note on his legal pad. "So we'll have to take care of that, too." He looks up at me, almost imploringly. "Reconsider. This is about to get messy."

"We're all adults," Adrienne says with finality. "We've decided that this is the best arrangement for us. Not for everyone, but for us. We want to help Leah get her life in order, and that's what she'll spend the year doing."

"My life's not out of order," Leah says.

"That came out wrong." Adrienne touches Leah again, on the hand this time. "I just mean, you're young. We're going to help you make a fresh start."

A fresh start? There it is again, that un-Adrienne-like language. The nicey-nice.

"And what about the baby?" Hal asks. "Have you thought about what kind of a start in life this arrangement gives her?"

"Him," Adrienne says. "And I resent your implication. I do nothing but think of him."

"I know you're going to love him." Hal looks at Leah meaningfully. "But Leah will, too. Mark my words. It's going to get messy."

"Adrienne's going to be his mother." But Leah's voice, now drained of snark, is much less audible. "I'm just going to be down the hall."

Adrienne seems satisfied with that answer.

Hal isn't. "This might seem like a delicate subject but I'd be remiss if I didn't bring it up. What about breast-feeding?"

"No breast-feeding," Adrienne says, as Leah shakes her head vigorously.

"Breast-feeding is best for a baby. Breast milk is better than formula on every level. It encourages the immune system, and he'll learn problem-solving."

Leah cocks her head, as in, Seriously? *Problem-solving?*

"So now your business is medicine," Adrienne says, bright with irony. Leah scoffs with her. But I'm finding him persuasive.

Undeterred, he continues. "Read the research. It's the best thing. But it's also the best for bonding. And when a child bonds to a mother, the mother bonds to the child. That's a hard bond to break. The hardest. Do you get what I'm saying?"

"I'm not breast-feeding," Leah says sulkily. "So it's not an issue."

"There are tons of issues. If you're in the home, there will be a never-ending, multiplying, escalating series of issues. You'll want to give your child the best start, won't you? So since you're going to be around anyway, you might want to rethink the breast-feeding."

Leah's eyes flash with anger. "Oh, as long as I'm there, I might as well get *milked* ten times a day? That's what you're saying?"

"As long as you're there"—his tone becomes gentle, paternal even—"you'll want to give that baby the best you have. That's what I'm saying. The maternal instinct is strong, and it's real. You think women lift cars off their babies because they ate their Wheaties that morning?" He scans the three of us. "You're all messing with something you can't begin to understand yet, because it's something you don't yet feel. But you will, and then what?"

"Once the contract is written," I say quietly, "can either party break it?"

Hal laughs. "I don't write contracts that you can easily break. If I did, why would anyone pay me?" He looks at me hard. "We're going to try to prepare for contingencies, but if you sign, you'd better be ready for what comes next. Which could be anything."

Adrienne and Leah are watching me. I see that somehow, miraculously, nothing Hal has said has made a dent in either of their resolves. That means that this actually is the right decision, or wrong as they come.

Patty,

Sweetie! That ultrasound! You sure make a pretty baby! I have to admit, part of me wants to know the sex, but the other part of me is so happy that we're going to wait. Gabe and I can learn it together in the delivery room with you.

I know it seems far away, but have you thought about which delivery room? If you want us to fly out to you for the birth, or you want to stay in our house for a while and have the baby here?

Of course I realize we should meet in person first. That's a given. I can't wait until that asshole boss of yours will let you have time off. I can't wait to meet. I feel like we've become such good friends in such a short time that I'm doubly lucky. Not only do I get to be a mom but I get to have a birth mother that I adore, someone I can invite into our lives with no reservations. Honestly, except for landing Gabe, I've never felt like a very lucky person.

The truth is, I don't normally trust people the way I've come to trust you. I don't normally like people the way I like you. It just feels like you're meant to be in our lives, like I could finally have a best friend, a sister even, and that baby—I just stare at the ultrasound all the time. How do I love thee? Let me count the ways . . . I could write a sonnet. Has there ever been a gender-neutral sonnet before?

I have to admit, I find myself peering at it to see if that's a little pee-pee or just a shadow. But I have to remember: Sometimes it's good not to know everything. Sometimes it's good to be surprised.

Xoxo,
Adrienne

CHAPTER 11

Adrienne

We all go to dinner in the city after the meeting with Hal—at an expensive restaurant along the water at the Embarcadero, ostensibly to celebrate—but Gabe is barely talking. Leah and I carry the load, mocking Hal's pompous talk about maternal instinct and breastfeeding when he's probably on his third wife and there were no pictures of kids anywhere in that office. It's the most bonding Leah and I have done so far, so you'd think Gabe would appreciate that. After all, I can tell he's growing fond of Leah, something I intend to use against him later. Well, not against him, more like for the baby.

Alone, in our bedroom, I go down on him, hoping he'll relax, and he does for just a second. Then all the tension returns. I didn't even know that could happen so quickly.

I cozy up next to him and run my hand up and down his arm. Through the gauzy embossed mint fabric of the canopy bed, I see the sandalwood candles that are scenting the room resting on top of our vintage dresser. I can't imagine a more relaxing, sensual setting. But then, I am the one who designed it. I painted the dresser and armoire green and then distressed them myself; I picked out the fabric and draped it over the bed (it's actually from a sari store on University Avenue, in Berkeley).

Maybe Gabe needs something more masculine. I could look online for a candle that smells like pipe tobacco.

But for now, I just hold on to him. "It's going to be okay," I say into his chest hair.

"I'm not sure it is," he says. His brow is furrowed, and even though I'm touching him, it's like he's across the room. There could be a sign with a skull and crossbones and KEEP OUT, that's how closed off he seems.

"Hal is one of those people who assume that because something's not typically done, it should never be done. Contract law is about playing it safe and covering asses, including his. He doesn't know us. He doesn't know how much we love each other or how determined we are. He doesn't know Leah, and the fact that she one hundred percent does not want her baby and one hundred percent wants us to have him."

"Nothing's one hundred percent. You know that better than anyone." A veiled Patty reference, no doubt, highlighting that he sensed something was off long before I did. I don't need any reminders, not when I worked so hard to exorcise that ghost and he barely did a thing to help me.

I sit up so we're no longer touching. "Leah's different. And I think you'd agree, I'm very different this time around."

He drums his fingers against his upper arms. The percussion puts me on edge, but I can't show it. I need to radiate calm. "What if we fall in love with the baby and she does, too? What if we end up fighting over him? We go to court, and someone wins, and someone loses. Probably the kid. He loses someone right out of the gate. Like Hal said, what kind of a start in life is that?"

"We won't lose. You think she'll have money to hire a good lawyer?"

He stares at me. "So you want to screw her out of her child?"

"She came to us. She chose us. Because we're going to give her baby a good life. Even if she changes her mind, we're still going to give the baby a good life. Because he's meant to be ours."

He looks away. "What if he's not?"

"He is. I can feel it. Last time, I was forcing it. This time, it's organic. Look at her. Look at me. If that's not a sign, what is?"

No answer from Gabe, just a deepening frown.

"He's meant to be ours, and I'll tell you why. It's *because* we're taking the tougher path. Sure, we could tell Leah no, this is too complicated. We could listen to Hal, and we could bail on her. But how I know that we're meant to have this baby—this one, not the next one—is because we're willing to fight for him, if it comes down to it. We're willing to deal with the complications because he's that important. It's trial by fire. We'll have proven ourselves worthy."

I didn't even know I was going to make that argument until it was flying out of my mouth, but it's incontrovertible. Last time, it seemed too easy, too good to be true. I let my guard down, and I got burned. Immolated, really. Now we're in a brave new world.

"And then there's Leah," I say. "You want to help her, don't you?"

"Do you?" He searches my face, as if for hairline cracks in drywall.

"A year with us could do her good. It's like I said. She'll get her life together, with our help, and then when she comes to visit on Thanksgiving or Christmas or whenever, our son will get to see a birth mother he can feel proud of." It's not like I'd mind Leah benefiting; it's just not a priority.

"What if she wants to come by more often? She talks like she'll just be down the street. Can you handle Leah having a real relationship with him?"

I try to picture Leah as a member of our family—"Aunt Leah"—and I just can't do it. I can't imagine sharing him like that, day-to-day. She needs to be distant. In the most likely scenario, she'll lose interest over the years. She'll get wrapped up in her own life; she'll move away; she'll have her own family. But if that's not happening, we'll go to Plan B. I'll put in a call to Hal and make sure the contract has no prohibitions against our moving away.

All problems have solutions. Hal was being histrionic, and he's infected Gabe, who's been less than enthusiastic about the adoption process since the beginning.

"I can handle anything," I say. Patty proved that. "Don't hide behind Hal. If you want to back out, say so."

He glares at me. "I'm not some pussy-whipped teenager, Adrienne. I'll say what I want, and I'll do what I want."

"Shh. Leah will hear you."

He shakes his head angrily. "I'm not going to live this way for a year. With the shushing and the nicey-nice bullshit."

"What are you talking about?"

"You. You're not yourself around her. I don't want this Stepford Adrienne for a year."

I'm about to protest that I don't know what he means, but yeah, I know what he means. "You've said what you don't want. But what do you want? Do you want this baby or not?"

The silence is fraught. It feels like there's a spiderweb stretched between us, and one of us is supposed to try to walk across it. This situation with Leah is the most dangerous trapeze act of our marriage. But that's just another reason to do it. I've always assumed Gabe and I are indestructible. If we're not, I need to know. I'm not getting any younger.

"Yeah," he says finally. "Yeah, I think I want this. I want Leah to be the mom."

"The birth mother. Not the mom."

"You know what I mean. I just hate all that PC adoption talk. Birth mothers and adoptive mothers."

"Well, there has to be some way to distinguish."

I'm glad Gabe said he wants this, but I don't like how he said it. Not "I want us to be parents" or "I want to be a dad." Not even

"I want Leah to be the birth mother." What he said was "I want Leah to be the mom." I wonder—and not for the first time—if something else happened on their day in San Francisco. What he left out, and why.

"I'm going to go watch TV in the living room," I tell him. "I've got Summer Jackson on DVR."

He starts to make one of his derisive jokes about how man-hating commentators like Summer and missing women go together like chocolate and peanut butter, but I'm in no mood to laugh along.

I don't sleep well, and in the morning, I don't much like driving away, knowing Leah's on her own in my house. I find myself wishing I'd thought farther ahead and bought some of those nanny-cam teddy bears to place strategically in all the rooms. It's too late now. If they suddenly appeared, she'd know something was up. She's shrewd.

Oh, sure, we're on the same team for the moment: Leah and me versus Gabe and Hal. The optimists versus the pessimists (Hal would say "realist," but that's what all pessimists say). I just don't know how long that will last, how long it can last. Two mothers, one son—there's always going to be tension.

I'm trying to be a good host, though. I printed out different potential destinations and bus schedules. If she takes the bus to the BART station, she can go into the city. "That's always fun!" I told her, way too happy. Gabe's right, I'm not myself around Leah. What he doesn't seem to realize is that's no accident.

Our house is a mile away from the nearest shopping center, and Leah doesn't seem up for much walking. She doesn't look big, but she says she can feel every step vibrating in her belly. She's complaining, yet I'm envious. I want to know what it feels like, all of it, even the unpleasant parts. Even labor and delivery, especially that—I'd kill to give birth.

That'd be a funny slogan on a T-shirt.

It's only a fifteen-minute drive to school, and every second, I'm thinking about Leah. Where she is, what she's doing, if there's anything for her to find. Our medicine cabinets are innocuous. Sure, there are all my antiaging products, and tons of hair products, and that's slightly embarrassing. But they work. I look good. Leah must have noticed that.

I got rid of all my skeletons years ago. My closets are stripped clean. When we moved to California, we were truly starting over. As far as anyone can tell, we're just a loving couple with palpable chemistry. (I don't mind her snooping in our toy drawer, as long as she doesn't try to use any of it.)

She might find one of my stashes of baby gear. But that wouldn't look weird, now that she's here. It would look thorough. We're prepared.

But are we really? As soon as those papers are signed, we need to make lists. To-do lists, checklists, shopping lists.

Hal said he'll have the papers ready by Friday. That's a lot of time for Gabe to consider, and reconsider. When we went to bed last night, he seemed to have come around. He said he wanted the baby, didn't he? I just don't know what the next days will bring. Gabe does a lot of second-thinking. And third-thinking. And fourth . . .

Leah's signing those papers, no question, no hesitation. Unfortunately, at the moment, I feel surer of her than of my own husband.

When Hal presents the contract, his manner practically screams, "It's your funeral." We could have gotten a new lawyer, but that would have delayed the process. The good thing about Hal's discomfort with our decision is that he clearly wants this over and done with, posthaste. It's like he's trying to make a quick getaway from a crime scene. I've been edgy enough just waiting a few days; my poor students need this contract to be completed.

Gabe and I have continued to play tour guide to Leah. It's exhausting to fake good cheer. I can't wait until she has the baby and she can just lie around in her room, recovering, watching TV.

I can't wait until she has the baby, period. I am so ready to be a mom.

We're in the conference room instead of Hal's office, and there's a young female whose job is to keep all the papers in order. She might also be there to witness his repeated disclaimers: "You know I advised strongly against this . . ."

Blah blah blah.

" . . . I've written this to your specifications as I understood them. If you have any questions or see any errors or inaccuracies, speak up. We can still make changes. Once you sign, it's binding." He clears his throat and then looks sternly at each of us (with the exception of his assistant/witness/mistress). "The contract stipulates that Leah will reside with you for a period of one year, commencing with the birth of the baby. Should Leah miscarry, or if the baby is stillborn, the contract is nullified." I remind myself that he's only protecting my interests, but I'm jarred by the starkness of the language. "Shall I continue?" I nod. Gabe is staring at the table like a boy in detention. Leah seems composed. "During that year, Gabe and Adrienne will provide food and lodging for Leah. They will pay the monthly premium for her and the baby's health insurance. They will also pay for any medical expenses not covered by insurance. They're responsible for all copays and deductibles for her and the baby. They will provide four hundred dollars per month for her discretionary spending—meaning, they have no say over how that money is used."

When Gabe's father died, Gabe got Michael's share of the inheritance. It wasn't all that much, since most of the money went to the stepmonster, but we did come away with enough to pay for a couple rounds of IVF and still have some savings. I have a teensy worry about how we're going to cover all that health insurance, plus the baby's expenses, plus Leah's stipend, but we'll manage. We always do.

Hal fixes his gaze on Gabe and me. "You will be solely and entirely responsible for meeting the baby's practical and emotional needs. That is, Leah will not be required to engage with the child in any way. She doesn't have to change a single diaper or do a single feeding, should she choose not to. But should she desire contact, you must allow up to two hours per day—all at once, or in increments—and she is entitled to privacy inside the home. If she wants to leave the home with the child, she has to get your approval. She has declined to breast-feed, and I have stipulated that she will not be permitted to do so, unless it is with your express approval."

"That seems a little harsh," Gabe says.

It's the first thing he's said since we arrived, and it is not an auspicious beginning.

"The contract isn't saying she can't breast-feed," I say. "She just needs to get our approval."

"But it's her—" Was he going to say "her baby" or "her body"? I can't know because he broke off at the sight of my face. "I just don't want to feel like a dictator, that's all."

"It's not a dictatorship," I say. "We'll all talk about things. This is just a way to start an open dialogue."

"That's not what a contract is," Hal says flatly.

I wave a hand. Whatever.

"What if we disagree?" Gabe asks. "Adrienne and me. If I want to approve something and she doesn't. Or vice versa."

He raises an eyebrow. "Well, you'll just have to work that out amongst yourselves first, before you present your united front to Leah."

"Not a problem," I say. Gabe and I have always been able to come to agreement.

"During that year, either party may terminate the contract. Leah may decide that she prefers to raise the child herself. In that case, she has to vacate the home and all financial obligations will cease. There will be no penalty and no reimbursement." It suddenly occurs to me that Leah could string us along for an entire year and still take the baby away. There's no way to legally protect ourselves from that. We wouldn't be able to prove that she did it knowingly; she could say she didn't decide until the end of the year.

I don't even know how to ask the question, not in front of Leah. If we're going into this, we're supposed to trust her. I can't give away yet that I don't. What I trust is my own ability to outfox her, if it comes down to that. With Patty, I was lulled by my own happiness; I was off my game. When I'm on, no one's going to beat me.

"Adrienne and Gabe, you also have the right to terminate the contract. You could give Leah a month's notice to leave the premises, after which time all financial obligations cease. But then you forfeit any legal claims to the child." He watches me intently. "Do you understand so far?" I nod. "Now, if it's for cause—as in, either party has committed a crime or violated the trust and sanctity of the relationship in one of the ways specified on page seven—then it's a different situation. If the baby is thought to be endangered by either party, Child Protective Services must be called immediately for investigation. CPS will make their own stipulations at that time (for example, whether the child needs to be removed from the home and from both parties, or if the child can remain in the home with both parties, or if one of the parties must leave).

"Leah, if you're found to have abused the child in any way, Adrienne and Gabe would be able to petition the court for your legal rights to be terminated and for the adoption to move forward immediately."

As a teacher, I'm legally required to report suspected child abuse. I've had my dealings with CPS over the years, and I've seen them make mistakes. I've seen them overreact and underreact. So there are no guarantees once CPS gets involved. But the employees are harried and overworked. They could be ripe for manipulation. They could prove to be my loophole, my last resort, if it comes to that.

Leah doesn't need a loophole. All she needs to do is decide she wants to leave, and she takes the baby with her. But if Gabe and I want her out while keeping the baby, we might need a little help from the state.

Not that I'm planning to screw Leah. I intend to honor the contract. But I've learned in life you can never absolutely rule anything out.

"I told you this was going to be messy," Hal says with an undisguised note of pleasure.

I notice Leah is watching me closely. "It's irrelevant," I say. "No one's going to hurt this baby."

Gabe looks like he's eaten bad fish. I just have to hope that he holds it together long enough to initial and sign in a hundred different places.

"Barring any unforeseen circumstances," Hal says, "on the baby's first birthday, we'll all reconvene so that Leah can relinquish her parental rights and we can write up the open adoption agreement. That will be enforceable under California law. However, it's not binding until it's set forth in a written agreement by a judge—essentially, a court order. It'll spell out how much contact there will be between Leah and the child, whether it's pictures or letters or visits. It'll be specific—how long a visit will be, how often—and it'll state that all communication with the child will go through the adoptive parents, through Gabe and Adrienne."

"So we can't complete and file all the paperwork now?" I ask. "Even if it doesn't take effect for a year?" It would seem safer that way, somehow.

"We can't petition the court for an adoption decree until Leah's ready to terminate her parental rights. And she's leaving her options open."

"It's not like that!" Leah exclaims. "It's not that I want to keep my baby. It's that I need him for protection. Otherwise, they can just throw me out whenever they want. I leave a dish lying around, and I have to worry. I can't live like that."

"We wouldn't do that to you," Gabe says, and I believe him. He wouldn't.

"But you could. If I sign him over to you right after he's born . . ." She lowers her head, her hair falling forward in a heavy curtain to block her face. It's the most upset I've seen her.

"I was trying to follow your directive from the other day, but I would recommend a more standard protocol," Hal says. "Meaning, we write up a document where Leah relinquishes her parental rights immediately after birth (the usual time frame is a few days), and we seek the adoption decree. Then, in a separate document, we have a contract where Leah lives with Gabe and Adrienne rent-free and they pay all expenses, same as I already stipulated. That will be legally enforceable. If we file all the adoption paperwork, Gabe and Adrienne would legally be the parents, with all the rights that entails, and Leah would remain in the home with all the same provisions in place."

Hal is brilliant. He wrote up the contract as we requested, knowing that hearing it read aloud would make it clear how divergent our interests really are from Leah's. He couldn't divide and conquer Leah and me the other day, but he's taking his shot now. Honestly, it's working.

I put on my most trustworthy face as I turn to Leah. "What do you think? It's still a lot of protection for everyone involved, but it does seem cleaner." Say yes, say yes, say yes.

Leah doesn't want to look at me.

"Could you say what specific concerns you have so Hal can address them?" I ask her. "I want you to feel completely comfortable before we sign anything."

I notice she's rubbing her belly almost compulsively. It's a new and disturbing gesture. "Can we take a break?" she says. "I'm not feeling well."

Before anyone can answer, she's out the door. "Maybe we should take some more time," Gabe says. "We don't need to get it done today."

In a low voice, I tell him, "We've already thought it through. We both said we wanted this." He doesn't answer. "I'm going to talk to her." I stand up, and Gabe puts his hand on my arm.

"She just needs some time," he says.

"That's not what she said. She said she's not feeling well. I need to check on her, and on the baby." I turn to the assistant. "Where's the restroom?"

I follow her down the hall and into the restroom. I glance at the marble floor under the stalls and see only expensive pumps. No scuffed black lace-up boots. No Leah.

I take off down the hall, past the offices and then the cubicles and then the reception desk. In my haste, I almost trip on the thick cream carpet. What if she disappears? What if we've scared her off?

I'm surprised by my next thought: Maybe it's for the best.

I must be channeling Hal. Or Gabe.

What if she's collapsed somewhere? What if I've stressed her out so much she's having a miscarriage?

I find her by the gold elevator bank. She's sitting on a bench, staring out the windows at the skyline, her hands crossed over her stomach.

The panic has stolen my breath. I sit beside her, exhaling loudly. "Hi." The floor out here is marble, too, but a somber gray, the color of a San Francisco winter.

"Hi." She continues to take in the view.

"Sorry about that meeting. Sorry about Hal."

"He's just doing his job. Protecting you."

"Well, we don't need his protection. We're all on the same side. You, me, and Gabe."

She smiles a little. "Tell that to Hal."

"I'm sick of talking to Hal. Aren't you?"

She looks right at me. It's discomfiting, how her eyes are so like my own. "I called Trevor earlier."

"Yeah?"

"He told me, and I quote, 'I don't give a shit what you do.'" Now her smile is bitter. "Great guy, huh?"

"So he gets you pregnant, and you're trying to find the baby a good home, and he's mad at you?"

"But the good news is, he's happy to sign away his rights. He can't do it soon enough." I see pain in her face. She really loved him, still does.

"Sorry about Trevor, and about my part in stressing you out any more than you already are. I can't even imagine what it's like for you right now."

She looks out the window again.

"Is everything okay, with the baby? You were rubbing your stomach."

"I don't think I was."

I recall Gabe's concern about her flying in her last trimester. If we've done anything to harm my boy, I don't know what I'll do. "We need to get you in to see a new ob-gyn. Just to make sure."

"He's been kicking like crazy. He's fine."

She's obviously getting irritated. If anyone overheard us, they'd definitely think we were mother and daughter. "We don't have to do this today, if you don't feel up to it."

"No, I want to get it done. I just needed a minute to myself. Hal's cologne was making me nauseous."

I laugh. I couldn't really smell him. It must be the pregnancy, sharpening her olfactory sense. "You mean you don't love Eau de Money-Grubbing Lawyer?"

She smiles, like she's humoring me. She doesn't smile that way at Gabe. Then she turns serious as she says, "I'm just trying to have some control. I need that. Don't you understand?"

I definitely do.

It's the most vulnerable I've seen her and it's hard not to feel for her, but I'm well aware it could be an act. If I want this, it's the original contract or nothing. I'm going to have to give Leah control. Well, the illusion of it.

"I understand," I say.

CHAPTER 12

Gabe

I haven't been sleeping for the past week, ever since I signed that contract.

I came pretty close to walking out, leaving Hal's smug face and his contract behind. But then Adrienne and Leah walked in together, and they were actually *holding hands,* and I thought, I've got no choice now. Maybe a small part of me was relieved that the decision was made, which is a feeling I have more than I like to admit, being married to Adrienne. She is a force, remember. Mostly, I love that about her.

Also, I care about what happens to Leah.

I'm learning more about her all the time. We've become insomniac buddies. She said she can't find a good sleep position, since the baby kicks violently at night. She spends her days sleeping. "I'm a big fat vampire," she tells me.

She tells me a lot of things. There's something about sitting in the half dark at two A.M. that inspires confession. We never turn on the overhead, only a dim corner lamp in the living room. By unspoken agreement, we don't want to wake Adrienne.

For one thing, Adrienne doesn't need to know I'm having trouble sleeping. It would prompt all sorts of discussions and persuasions. She'd feel compelled to convince me that what we're doing is right, and I've had enough of that to last me for a while. She would never tell me not to hang out with Leah, but suddenly, Adrienne would have insomnia, too. She'd want to fuck or make hot chocolate, and while there's nothing wrong with either of those things, I kind of like what Leah and I have got going right now. It's peaceful.

We've fallen into a routine. I lie on the couch with my hand under my head, looking up at the ceiling mostly, and Leah sits in the overstuffed chair, her hair up in a bun, her perfect little Buddha belly hanging over her pajama bottoms. We probably look like some warped version of analyst and analysand. Sometimes we talk, sometimes we just drift along together. Not sleeping exactly, not even dozing. It's like some semiconscious state we induce in one another, in between the slats of our conversation.

Tonight, I touched her belly. She said the baby was kicking something fierce and that it was time for me to finally get to know my kid.

She's right, I've been putting it off. I can't say why, exactly. I'm not ready for him to be real, or I'm worried that even after I feel him, he still won't seem real.

It made me laugh, I'll give her (and him) that. It was like the kid's whole foot slammed into my hand, full force. "He's a ninja!" I said, and Leah laughed, too.

But does he feel real now? Not exactly. He's still this abstract concept I can't quite grasp. He's calculus.

I can say that to Leah, and she doesn't get mad or freaked out. She seems to appreciate the honesty. "He doesn't always seem real to me either, and he's pounding me from the inside out all night," she says.

"How come you're not like this with Adrienne?" I ask.

"How come you're not?"

"I'm exactly like this with her."

Leah gives me a doubting look.

"What? I am."

"If that's what you need to think." Then she smiles sweetly, like, It's all good. "I don't know why I'm different around Adrienne. It's just something that happens. I don't plan it. It's like, the things that come out of my mouth are all . . ."

"Nice."

"Yeah, nice." She grimaces. "Who wants to be nice?"

"People in the Midwest, I hear."

"You can't trust nice." She rubs her belly. "Do you think it would be okay if I had a little bit of wine? I read it can calm the baby down."

"Adrienne would flip."

"Adrienne's not here." She gives me an imploring look. "Please?"

There's nothing in the contract to cover this situation. It's her body, after all. But what if the kid comes out with flippers or something, and I'll have to wonder forever if it was my fault?

"Okay, forget it. If Adrienne says no." There's an edge to her voice.

"Hey, that's not it. Maybe you can get clearance from your new doctor, when you meet her?" Adrienne is taking Leah tomorrow.

"Don't you ever find"—her voice is suddenly dreamy—"that you're different people when you're with different people?"

"Huh?"

She laughs. "Like, it's not a decision. It's just, when I'm around you, I'm one way, and when I'm around Adrienne, I'm another, and around doctors or professors, oh and of course around lawyers, I'm someone else. Around Trevor, I was like this fearless version of me."

"You seem pretty fearless. Coming out to California, striking this deal with us, starting over."

"Can I tell you something and you won't judge me?"

I nod, then realize she's probably not looking at me. She's probably staring at some fixed point on the floor. It makes it easier to tell things you don't want to be judged for. "I promise," I say.

"Trevor and I used to break into houses to have sex. We didn't take anything or mess anything up. Well, we'd mess up their sheets, I guess, or their couch. It was this thing he had. It really got him off. And when I found out I was pregnant, I still did it a few more times, even though I couldn't relax. I kept thinking my baby would be born in jail, like I'd be wearing one of those orange jumpsuits, maternity-style."

I don't know exactly what to say, what she's looking for. Absolution? This is the confession hour. "People get off on all kinds of stuff. You didn't hurt anyone."

"Yeah, that's what I thought. He could talk me into anything. It's kind of embarrassing. Like, where was my mind?"

"On him. You loved him." I'm the last person to judge someone for that. She showed me pictures a few nights ago on her phone. He's one of those people who look distinct in each shot. In some, he looked a little like me; in others, we didn't share the faintest resemblance. He could look sweet; he could look cocky.

"When I talked to him about signing away his rights, he told me he still loved me. He said maybe someday, when this is all over, he'd take me back."

"Like it's a favor?"

"It didn't sound that way at the time. But then a minute later, he's all angry. He said he didn't give a shit what I did with the baby, like it's a sack of garbage or something. I mean, it's our DNA. His and mine, all mixed up together."

We drift for a while, and then Leah asks if I believe in God. I don't know, and she says she doesn't know either. "I think about it sometimes," she says. "Like, if there is a God, what would He think about me using my baby like collateral to get a better life for myself? I think, Would He understand? Because if there's a God, I'm one of His children, too, right, just as much as the baby?"

"I'd think so." Though I'm thinking about the idea of collateral. Adrienne would say that we're in a hostage situation. But she signed us up for it, didn't she? I signed, too. And initialed, over and over.

"Everyone uses everyone. God uses us to do His work on earth; He doesn't just go and do it Himself."

Something's twisted in her logic, but I'm too tired to point it out. I decide to change the subject. "I miss playing poker."

She laughs. "I talk about God, you think poker?"

"I must be an atheist."

"I thought you were the other thing, what do you call it, where you don't know."

"Agnostic."

I yawn. I can't think about all this now. But my initial impression is that Leah's right. Everyone uses everyone. We're using Leah to get a baby, she's using the baby and us like a railroad ticket to a new life. If we're all to blame, then no one's to blame. Adrienne would sure endorse that logic; she's always used it when it comes to Michael.

"So let's play poker," Leah says. She sounds suddenly full of energy. I remember surges like that from when I was younger, being struck by lightning.

But I'm yawning again. "Tomorrow night," I say, standing up to return to bed. It's the first time either of us has acknowledged that this nightly communion is a routine, one I suspect she looks forward to as much as I do. I tell myself it's not disloyal to Adrienne, even if it goes unmentioned. There are some things she's better off not knowing, not that she'd ever agree with that. I'm no hypocrite: I let her keep secrets for my own good, too.

Crawling into bed beside Adrienne, I reach for her, always. Sometimes she stirs, sometimes she even talks in her sleep. As far as she knows, I've been here all along.

CHAPTER 13

Adrienne

I flip through a copy of *Maternity Monthly* and then toss it aside. It's been more than a half hour. What are they saying in there? Is anything wrong with the baby?

I'd assumed Leah would let me come into the exam room with her while she met her new doctor. I would have stepped outside or turned away for the actual physical exam: a woman's right to privacy, her body is her own, it's her temple, all that crap. But you'd think I'm entitled to ask questions, seeing as the baby she's carrying is intended for me.

Instead, the receptionist called Leah's name and she leapt up, saying, "I'll be back soon." I was too surprised to protest. In her wake, I realized that Hal hadn't covered this contingency in the contract, so I'm shit out of luck, legally. I'm not her mother, though the receptionist clearly thought I was during check-in.

I shouldn't take it personally. These appointments must stir up a complex brew of emotions for someone in her position. Still, I thought Leah and I had gotten closer after the talk by the elevator bank, after we returned hand-in-hand and I signed away my life for the next year.

I want to witness the ultrasound, to see my baby moving in real time. Then I'd know, with absolute certainty, that all this is real. I mean, I'm almost sure now. I touch Leah's belly a lot, and I don't see how those kicks could be faked. But absolute certainty is pretty tantalizing, and it's right inside that exam room, just out of reach.

If I knocked on the door, would Leah have the heart (or the balls) to deny me?

It might feel good momentarily, but I have to think big-picture here. Leah has a year to renege. I can't afford to have her storing up little resentments.

Yes, it chafes, but I have to let Leah feel like she's in control. That's the only way to wrest it away from her later.

There's a pregnant woman about my age sitting across from me. Speaking of resentments, I can't help but feel a few when I see her. I don't know why she should get to do it herself, while I'm at the mercy of Leah's uterus.

She notices me looking at her and smiles. I smile back, though it feels tight and unnatural across my lips. I lower my eyes to communicate that I'm not up for talking. I've noticed that pregnant women in their late thirties and beyond are eager to share their good fortune. There's this vibe of excited relief, of "I thought it might never happen for me but here I am!" that I don't feel like ingesting.

A few more minutes, and Leah reappears. She gathers up her jacket and walks toward the elevators, not saying anything. She stabs the button. "How did it go?" I ask.

She shrugs.

"What does that mean? Is he healthy? Is everything okay?"

"Yes," she says with an air of condescending über-patience. "I told you he was fine, and he is. He's totally healthy."

Air whooshes out of me. I hadn't even noticed that I'd stopped breathing for a minute there. "Did you like the doctor?"

"She's okay." The elevator arrives. We step in and descend.

Leah obviously doesn't want to talk, but I can't accept that. She left me sitting in the waiting room, she shut me out of the whole wondrous miracle of gestation, and she *shrugged* when I asked how it went instead of leading with his being healthy. Is she toying with me? Is this whole thing one colossal mindfuck? Not again. Never again.

"What did the doctor tell you?" I say challengingly as we walk toward the car.

Leah comes to a dead stop on the pavement. She thrusts a paper out to me that's been clutched in her hand.

I take it and smooth it out. My eyes widen. It's a triptych of him. On thin, shiny paper, there are three pictures of my son. Make no mistake: It is a son. One of the pictures can best be described as full frontal. And there he is, in profile, plus a close-up—a glamour shot—of his beautiful resting face. I can't quite see Gabe or me, but I'll look more carefully later. For now, I need to look at Leah.

"Thank you. He's . . ." Real, that's what I want to say. He's not merely beautiful, he's real, and he's mine.

"So it really is a boy?" she says. I see a hint of pain in her face. She's made a point of never knowing before. Maybe she never even watches the ultrasounds in progress, doesn't want to watch him suspended in amniotic fluid. Gabe's right: Nothing's 100 percent. If Leah is protecting herself, then there can be reasonable doubt.

"You don't look during the ultrasounds, do you?" I ask gently.

She shakes her head. I think she's trying not to cry but when she looks back up at me, her face is hard.

"You didn't want me in there, oohing and aahing, getting all happy, making it real." She doesn't answer, but I know I'm right. I step toward her. "Maybe," I say, my voice soft as down, "you should try it. Make him real." I unfurl the pictures. "You're going to see him soon enough, in the flesh."

Her eyes are a touch frightened, but she does as I've instructed. She tries.

"Beautiful, right?" I say.

"He's okay," she allows, almost smiling.

I'm doing it for me, inoculating her. Any denial on her part is a threat. I don't want her to see him for the first time in the delivery room and be overwhelmed with love. Titration is key.

I'm doing this for him, too. Leah's not ready to be a mother, and she says so herself, all the time. She's not even twenty, she dropped out of college because people were gossiping about her, she seems to have no family or financial support to speak of, and the father gleefully signed his rights away. In her rational mind, she knows the best thing is to give him up. An about-face in the throes of postpartum love and hormones doesn't mean she can provide a good life for him. Gabe and I are the logical choice, the one made in cold consideration rather than hot emotion.

So, men and women of the jury, I rest my case. I direct you to Exhibit A, the ultrasound. Oh, you need to see him. I can't even imagine what I'll feel when I hold him. He will want for nothing, that I can promise. I'll keep him safe.

I'm smiling at him, riding a swell of maternal pride and adoration, when my eyes graze the corner of the paper. I see Leah's name and today's date and the medical group (good, further proof it's real) and then something else: *36w1d*. Thirty-six weeks, one day. Leah's farther along than I thought. Farther than she said.

My baby's practically here.

I like this one better," Leah says. She runs her hand along the edge of the crib. It's a dark wood, which isn't really my taste, but just as significant, it's not in our budget. I feel like telling Leah we can't buy a $1,200 crib because we're going to spend the next year giving her pocket money.

I smile and say yes, that *is* a nice crib, it's among our top three choices, for sure. Then, with my back toward her and my front toward Gabe, I roll my eyes.

He steps up to the crib, fingers the tag, and announces, "This crib is twelve hundred dollars! Hell no!" Instead of being offended, Leah laughs. I'm getting so tired of their language that I can't seem to speak, and of jaunts where we include her like she's already a member of the family.

I move toward a reasonably priced sage-green crib that would be perfect, but on the tag, it says that color needs to be ordered a month in advance.

"White's in stock," I say, masking my disappointment. "They could deliver it this week."

I see Gabe's mouth set in a disagreeable line. He's thinking about his garage-bound pool table.

"You barely play pool anymore," I remind him.

"Well, I won't now." He sounds sulky.

Leah jabs him in the side. "It's *California,*" she says. "How cold will it get in the garage? Wuss."

I should be the one jabbing my husband in the side, joking him out of his snit. Who does she think she is?

The mother of my child, that's who.

I remind myself I'm the one carrying the ultrasound in her purse, I'm the one in love with him already.

"With a white crib, we need to get bedding that pops, you know?" I say to Gabe, ignoring Leah. "We can paint the walls, maybe even hire someone to do a mural."

"How much would a mural cost?"

"I could do it," Leah volunteers.

I look at her in surprise.

"I'm good at art. I've thought before about taking art classes, or something like, I don't know, graphic design, but I'm shit with computers, so I don't know." She crosses her arms across her chest. "Forget it, it's a stupid idea."

"No, it's a great idea," Gabe says. "I mean, unless you're not supposed to be breathing in the paint fumes."

What fumes has Gabe been huffing? It's a terrible idea. Leah painting cows jumping over the moon, or sheep that the baby can grow up to count when he can't sleep—she's just going to get more attached to him. Someday, he'll ask me who painted it, and I'll have to say his birth mom, and she'll be in his thoughts every night. Or worse, she'll have taken him with her and all we'll be left with is her damn mural.

Maybe that's what Gabe wants, deep down. He wants us to try and fail, and then I can get this baby thing out of my system once and for all.

"It could be dark and edgy but beautiful, like your tattoo design," Gabe tells Leah.

Dark and edgy? It's a mural for a baby's room. "What tattoo?" I've never heard her say anything about it. I've definitely never seen it.

"It's the tattoo I'm going to have someday," Leah explains. "I showed Gabe the picture I drew. It's sort of like an enchanted forest."

"Beautiful but a little bit creepy," he adds. He unleashes a huge smile. "Yeah, you should do it!"

"They make nontoxic paint." She says it with a hesitant but growing excitement.

"They do," I say, "but I wouldn't feel comfortable. It's still chemicals, right? Whatever you breathe in, the baby breathes in, too."

"I can do it after I've had the baby," she says, and there's a flash of something in her eyes. Is it defiance? I can't really say no to her, not unless I want to risk offending her about the one thing she says she's good at; until she signs away her parental rights, she holds all the cards. Well, at most, fifty-one of them. The trump card could have "CPS" written on it.

But I'd rather not go there, for everyone's sake. Let's hope she doesn't force my hand.

"It could be, like, a creative outlet or something," she continues. "Like a gift from me to him. You know, a good-bye gift."

"We can talk about it after he's here," I say. "Let's wait and see how you're feeling. Having a baby is a physical trauma, you know?

Not to mention the hormone fluctuations. I don't want you to feel overwhelmed."

"I think I'll be up to it." She's persistent, this one. I really don't know what she'll be like after childbirth, how it'll change her. She could be weaker or more formidable.

"If it's okay, I'd like to see the design. I don't really think 'edgy' and 'newborn' go together." I smile like we're sharing a joke, though Leah and I never share jokes. That's Gabe's department. I look at him, silently asking for backup.

"That's what would be cool about it," he says. "It wouldn't scream 'baby.'" Then he sees my face. "But yeah, we should all agree on the design."

I pretend to study the changing table that matches the boring-ass white crib. I'm trying not to detonate.

Sometimes I get these twinges, painful reminders of how it should be. I should be rotund like Leah, and Gabe and I should have $1,200 to spend on a crib if we want. We shouldn't be buying a crib made of unspecified hardwoods. It should be oak or mahogany, something real and solid. But instead, our money is going to Leah. We finance her new life, and in return, we get her baby. It's a bargain we should never have had to strike. We've been betrayed by physiology.

In contrast to my mood, Leah's suddenly as high as I've ever seen her. She starts spinning this web, describing different images she could do for the mural, and I want to be excited by her excitement, the way Gabe seems to be. Because if she insists on painting a mural, she'll win; I can't risk alienating her.

I once heard a piece of advice: If you want someone on your side, get on theirs first. There's no better way to do that than supporting her aspirations.

This is also a chance for me to hone my maternal instinct. Leah's still a kid. If only I could see her like that, if I could nurture her.

I need to try. I'm going to take her under my wing. We can visit art colleges together. I can help her find herself, give her the courage to follow her dreams, all that clichéd shit. She gets a great life with no regrets; Gabe and I have our family. It's win-win. As Gabe always says, those are rare.

"That sounds great, Leah," I say, offering my most maternal smile.

But she's so deep in her riff with Gabe, she barely seems to notice.

I'm going to be the mother I never had, the one I wanted. That's the pledge I made to myself a long time ago. I can start practicing now, with Leah. If she sees that she's like my daughter, she won't have the heart to steal my son. She's not ready to be a mother, and she'll feel that I am, firsthand.

I have a feeling Leah's parents were as rejecting as my mother. Leah doesn't talk about them at all, and the fact that they clearly froze her out over the pregnancy—that doesn't come out of nowhere. There are myriad small rejections before the big one, death by a thousand cuts.

My mother used to cut me all the time. When I was a little girl, it was paper cuts; later came the slashes. I practically bled out on her furniture and she never even noticed.

I remember being in third grade—third grade, just a little older than my kiddos at school!—and she took me for IQ testing. Ostensibly, it was to see if I qualified for the Mentally Gifted program at my elementary school. But really, I think she wanted to find out my value, the way you'd have an antique ring appraised at the jeweler. Did I sparkle, would I shine, was I someone to be proud of?

My father wasn't home a lot. When he was, he wasn't very interested in either of us. But he was smart (a genius, according to my mother), and she probably thought that a high score on an IQ test would turn his head.

This was before he left, before she let herself eat Marshmallow Fluff and Wonder Bread like it comprised its own food group, before she started drinking herself to sleep every night. She wasn't fat yet, just sturdy. She wanted to be pretty and dressed like a pretty woman in monochromatic clothes with lots of accessories: rings and necklaces and scarves. She flashed and jingled. Her voice was the kind that carried down rows in a theater, along supermarket aisles, to the next restaurant table. She was immune to other people's reactions, except for my father's. He ruled her with his withholding silences, though I'm not sure if that was deliberate. It may have been genuine apathy.

"It'll be fun," she told me the day of the IQ test. "You'll just have to answer a bunch of questions."

Questions to determine how smart I was? It didn't sound fun at all. "I don't want to go," I said.

It wasn't merely that I didn't want to; I was quaking with fear. My insides were in revolt. I spent half the morning in the bathroom with diarrhea. Because I knew, on some level, what my mother was doing. I knew this wasn't just any test, and it wasn't for my own good either.

But a stinking bathroom was no get-out-of-jail-free card, not to a woman with my mother's determination. "What will it take?" she asked. She fingered her oversized gold hoop earrings. "A Barbie maybe? The one you've been wanting with the powder puff on her hand?"

My friend Alexis had that Barbie. You could push a button in her back and she'd powder her nose. I coveted that Barbie like no other. My mom was a hell of a negotiator, and I was buckled into the car within minutes.

"We'll stop at the toy store afterward," she said, parking the car in front of a brick office building. It didn't seem quite fair, but I knew better than to argue. She could be an immovable object.

I can't recall exactly how long I was in there with the examiner. It seemed interminable. The promise of the Barbie receded, and the terror returned, full force. There were puzzles and blocks and, as my mother had said, lots of questions. Everyone said I had a good imagination, but the test didn't seem to be measuring that at all. As it wore on, I felt more and more discouraged and less able to focus. I wasn't smart, after all, and now my parents were going to find out.

When I left the examiner's office, I couldn't look at my mother. I didn't even ask about the Barbie. I felt like I didn't deserve it.

I don't know why my mother didn't stop at the store to buy it for me. She generally made few promises but kept them. I took it as a sign that she knew what a disappointment I was. Maybe she just forgot, or she thought I forgot. If I'd cared, she could have reasoned, I would have reminded her to go to the store.

I hated that Barbie forever after. I wouldn't let Alexis play with her in my presence. And when the IQ test results came in the mail, my mother said, under her breath, "I knew it." She tore the paper up and pushed it way down in the trash can. I'm sure she never said a thing to my father.

All night, instead of sleeping, I thought about fishing the paper out and taping it back together. But then I'd know the truth, and I decided imagining was better. I was good at that.

I could envision all sorts of scenarios: I was a genius, like my dad, but my mother didn't want me to know, she didn't want me to get a swelled head. She didn't want my father and me to have something in common. Or she realized the MG program would only have corrupted me anyway. Maybe I was supersmart in half my brain, and she didn't want me to find out which half. She thought effort was more important than intelligence, and she wanted to make sure I kept working hard.

The last one is actually my own belief. It's what I focus on with my students. I never praise anyone for being globally smart. Instead, I'm specific. I tell them exactly what they're good at, and what they're not, and that few things in life come down to innate ability. It's about effort and perseverance. By the time my second graders leave my class, they can all define "tenacity." Some of them even possess it.

The IQ test became a turning point. I knew I couldn't trust my mother, that she wouldn't deliver on her promises, and that she didn't really see much good in me. I was smart enough to realize that I was on my own in the world. It's always been up to me to make things happen, with creativity and cunning and perseverance.

Help Leah, and I help myself.

Win-win.

CHAPTER 14

Gabe

I've started teaching Leah poker. She's got great instincts. She intuitively knows when to fold, when to bluff, and when to go all-in and put me to a hard decision. Or maybe I'm just easy to read in the middle of the night. Maybe the candelabra above the dining room table turns it into an interrogation room. Whatever it is, when it comes to Leah, I seem to have a tell.

Before I started playing poker, I watched on TV. There were *High Stakes Poker* and *World Series of Poker* and *World Poker Tour* and *Poker After Dark*, not to mention the random televised tournaments I'd frequently stumble across. Six or seven years ago, when I first got hooked, I tried to pull Adrienne along with me. She was tolerant, willing to "watch" while reading a magazine or doing her nails or playing, of all things, computerized Yahtzee, the tiny handheld kind made for airplanes. When I'd say, "You really need to see this hand," she'd dutifully train her eyes on the TV, but it always ended up making me feel more alone than alone did. I could tell she just didn't get the appeal, and I'd turn self-conscious, thinking maybe it was a stupid thing to be excited about, one person outmaneuvering another with some cards and a bunch of chips.

But then I started to play live at the Pyramid, and I loved it so much that I didn't need her approval anymore. Sure, you fold most of your hands preflop, but even when you're not in the hand, there's still so much to pay attention to. The information is just out there, like a pocket begging to be picked. You watch people's faces and see how they match up with their betting patterns. You start to figure out your opponents' tendencies. Then, when you're in a hand, you exploit those tendencies. How often in life do you get the chance to fleece other people right out in the open?

The first night I played with Leah, I handicapped myself (no bluffing, which in heads-up play is a pretty huge handicap). So she won, even though I had tried. By the end of the second night, it was obvious she was a natural, which meant that on the third night, we just went at it. I didn't go to bed until four in the morning, and then I couldn't sleep right away. I was too busy replaying hands in my head, the way I do after a good session at the Pyramid.

"Where were you?" Adrienne murmured, eyes closed.

"Couldn't sleep," I said, and fortunately, that was enough of an answer for her.

Tonight, Leah's eager to play. She spent the day reading my favorite poker tome: Dan Harrington's book on cash games.

"I'm thinking," she says as we divvy up the poker chips, "that we should play for real money."

"Can you afford to do that?"

"Maybe you could spot me a hundred dollars or two hundred dollars. What do people usually sit down with, at the Pyramid?"

"At the low-stakes table? Two hundred dollars."

She smiles. "Then spot me two hundred dollars."

"So if I win, I just get my own money back. If you win, I'm out four hundred dollars?"

"I'll give you back your initial investment."

"So I'd be out two hundred dollars?"

Her face turns serious but her eyes are still on the chips. "Do you really think four hundred dollars is a fair allowance? I'm having your baby."

I feel a certain creeping unease. "It's not 'my' baby. It's our baby. Adrienne's and mine."

The truth is, I still can't quite think of it as our baby, no matter how many times Adrienne presents the ultrasound. The first time, she was looking at me really closely, waiting for my reaction. The good news is, I finally felt something. The bad news is, I felt, strongly, "He's not mine."

I mean, obviously. We're adopting. Intellectually, I've always known there's none of my genetic material in there. I assumed, though, that it wouldn't matter to me. I'm not a caveman; I'm enlightened, mostly. But I look at him, and while he's cute—well, he's not uncute—I just feel it, that oppressive not-mine-ness.

I read somewhere that newborns look more like their fathers. Evolutionary biologists theorize that it works that way so the father knows for sure it's his baby, and then he'll want to invest more of his resources in raising the child. He's ensnared by his own narcissism.

What that means is, I'm not unique. In general, men are more invested in their mirror reflections, the visible carriers of their DNA. If it is a universal male trait, then it could be insurmountable. What if I'm truly incapable of falling in love with this kid? What if I've got an alien in my house for the next eighteen years?

Adrienne fell in love at first sight. First kick, actually. I remind myself that's how she felt about me, and I didn't feel it for her. My love for Adrienne took time. Hell, it took more than just time. But when I felt it, it was seismic, an earthquake that tore down everything in its path. Or that's what Adrienne herself did. Earthquake Adrienne, a 9.5 on the Richter scale.

I guess I feel something else, too, when I look at the ultrasound. I'm not proud to admit it, but I'm jealous. Adrienne's like a cartoon character with big pulsing hearts in her eyes every time she stares at that kid. Sometimes it's like she barely sees me at all anymore. She only sees the future.

"Don't you love him already?" she asks me, her fingers lightly stroking his profile.

I don't answer, because I'd rather not lie.

"You will," she says, her eyes still on the pictures. I hope she's right.

"Four hundred dollars a month for your baby—yours and Adrienne's—it's kind of chintzy, isn't it?" Leah continues.

"It's what we agreed to." I start shuffling the cards. "Should I deal?"

"In Hal's office. I mean, he and Adrienne pretty much trapped me."

"Look around. Look at the size of this house. You think I'm made of money?"

Leah fingers a chip contemplatively. "You've got a whole lot more than I do." Her eyes are suddenly bright on mine. "This is my chance, Gabe. My fresh start. I need to save up for my future. Four hundred dollars a month? That's forty-eight hundred dollars I can save for going back to school and getting my own place to live, if I don't spend a single penny of it. If I have no life at all this year."

Don't cry, Leah. I can't take it.

"I should have negotiated for more but you know Adrienne. She's fucking intimidating. My math skills are so bad that I thought it came to way more. It wasn't until we left the office that I figured it all out. I was shaking the whole time, could you tell?"

"No." I was too busy shaking myself. But I can see what she means. "I want to help you, Leah. You know that. But we practically went broke on IVF. Do you even know what that is?" She nods. "Forty-eight hundred dollars doesn't sound like a lot, but on top of our paying your health insurance and medical expenses and food and—"

"I get it, Gabe." She smiles beneficently. "I know you want to help. I get you. I see how Adrienne intimidates you, too."

"Bullshit."

"Gabe." That unwavering smile. "Seriously. I get it. All I'm saying is, when we play poker, can you put up the two hundred dollars for me? Sometimes I'll win, sometimes I'll lose. You're willing to put that money up for yourself when you go to the Pyramid, right? Every week, you can afford to lose that much."

If there's a flaw in her logic, I'm too tired—or too guilty—to find it. "If you win, I'll give you the cash tomorrow. It's in the bedroom." The unspoken: Adrienne's in the bedroom, and you don't rouse the sleeping giant. So yeah, I hate to admit it, but Adrienne can be intimidating.

"Thanks." Leah doesn't look as appreciative as I would have expected, more like this is her due. "Adrienne's been acting different with me, you know?"

"I haven't noticed."

She runs her fingers over a chip the way Adrienne touches the ultrasound. I realize I've never seen Leah stroke her belly like that. "She wants to take me to look at, like, art schools, and she keeps sending me all these links for scholarships and financial aid. She talks about my potential as an artist, even though she's never even seen anything I draw."

"You should show her."

"She should ask. If she's so interested in my potential, right?"

I'll never understand women. Leah doesn't like that Adrienne thinks she has potential? "That's between you and Adrienne."

"I thought you could at least tell me what's up her ass."

"Look," I say irritably, "nothing's up her ass. She wants to help you build a life for yourself. How about a little appreciation?"

I deal the first hand.

I spent hours disassembling, moving, and reassembling the pool table. Adrienne offered to help, but she's mechanically challenged and impatient and I didn't want any of the pieces broken.

"We" decided that the room that formerly housed the pool table will now be the nursery. So the lucky tyke will have dimmer lights, red walls, and sexy-but-classily-framed movie posters. Every baby should be raised in an upscale lounge setting.

Yeah, right. The posters are in exile with me, here in the garage, and Adrienne is off priming the walls. Once the primer's dry, she plans to have one green wall, one blue wall, one yellow wall, and one white wall (which will be Leah's canvas). I know she's hoping Leah will forget about the mural, but that's not going to happen.

In a few hours, once the nursery furniture is delivered, it'll be official. Our old life is dead.

I once asked Adrienne if the fact that we couldn't conceive was our answer. If we were meant to be parents together, wouldn't we be able to do it? She looked at me like I'd just stabbed her in the chest.

But I still wonder that sometimes. If her eggs are murdering my sperm, is someone trying to tell us something?

The pool table is now set up, surrounded by suitcases, workout equipment, broken fans, and other detritus we've been meaning to take to the dump. I sit on a hard-topped Samsonite—it was my parents', the thing's indestructible—and grimace. My joints are aching. I'm an old man, too old to be a father.

If Michael had lived, I'd probably be an uncle. Adrienne would have been an aunt. That might have been enough for her.

Adrienne, the aunt to Michael's kids. It's a perverse thought.

We weren't close, Michael and me. Maybe we would have become that way as adults. I was the golden boy, and he was the freak. That's to hear him tell it, though he always said it matter-of-factly, like you can't fight gravity. I tried to get closer; I tried to be his protector. Obviously, I failed.

If I couldn't be a decent brother, what chance do I have of being a decent father?

I don't even have a dad I can ask for advice. Adrienne never got to meet my mom, let alone learn from her. My mom would have had a lot to teach. I know she wasn't a saint, no one is, but in my recollections, she wasn't far off. Sure, she died when I was seven, before things got complicated. I like to think that if she'd lived, they'd be simpler. Michael would still be here.

My dad remarried quick, within a year, and I could never forgive him for it. Replacing a woman that pure and good and loving with Jessica? Jessica kept up appearances, but in private, she didn't give a shit about Michael or me. Soon enough, my father saw her point.

After I left New Jersey, we rarely spoke. Six years ago, he died, and I thought about flying back for the funeral, but Adrienne said that would just be me keeping up appearances, pulling a Jessica. Sometimes, though, I wish I'd gone. I might have learned something about the old man, knowledge I could summon now.

"Hey," Adrienne says. She's wearing a concerned expression as she wends her way to the Samsonite.

I want to stand but I feel like my knee's locked up.

Adrienne sits down next to me. She rests her hand on my thigh and her eyes on my face. "You okay?" she asks softly.

"Just feeling my age."

She smiles. Her head tips sideways onto my shoulder, her hair spilling over my arm. I like that she doesn't say anything. I like that she knows me so well.

I kiss the top of her head, and close my eyes, and it's almost like dreaming.

Someone broke in my car.

Oh, Patty. Shit. Seriously?

Yep. Broke the windshield.

Will insurance pay?

Just have liability.

Did they steal anything?

My new iPad. U know I saved up for 2 months.

I know. I am so sorry.

It's my fault. I forgot to bring it inside.

Not your fault. You should be able to forget things and not have them stolen.

I should know better. Other people can, but I can't.

You do have the worst luck.

I know. When will I learn?

You're very optimistic. You hope for the best.

Maybe I don't want to learn.

I love that about you. But you need to change it, like, now.

You think so?

Maybe not. If you changed it, you wouldn't be you.

Patty, still there?

Yeah.

You were parked in front of your apartment?

Yeah.

You need to move.

Can't afford to.

I feel so bad. You're a good person. All this should happen to someone else.

Thx.

I want to buy you a new iPad.

No.

Yes.

You already do too much for me.

So I send you a little money sometimes. I want to.

Does Gabe know?

Why?

Just wondering.

I don't tell him every time I have a facial either.

Do you think he likes me? We only talked once.

He likes you. He knows I like you.

So he trusts you. Your judgment.

He married me.

But it's too much. An iPad costs too much.

You deserve it. Just send me another ultrasound and we're even.

Are you sure? I don't tell you things so you'll help. I tell you because you're my best friend.

I'm sure.

CHAPTER 15

Adrienne

I knock on Principal Jorgenson's door and then readjust my wrap dress. It's form-fitting but with no cleavage. I dressed carefully today.

"Yes?" she says. Not "Come in." Nothing welcoming.

I push open the door and give her my Splenda smile. "Do you have a minute?"

She closes her laptop, with obvious reluctance.

I sit across from her. On the bookshelves behind her desk, she's got her various diplomas and certificates framed and arrayed. There are also a ton of plants, the kind with explosive sprouting leaves, like eighties Tina Turner hair. She has no art or framed photos, nothing to suggest a personality lurking beneath her troll exterior. I notice that even though she's sitting way forward on her wooden desk chair, only her tippy-toes make contact with the floor.

"I need to talk to you," I say, "about my maternity leave."

She casts a pointed look down at my flat belly. "How far along?" Not "Congratulations." Nothing warm.

"Sorry, I should probably have said 'paid family leave.' Six weeks to bond with my new baby, after the adoption." I don't bother to explain the intricacies of my arrangement with Leah. I might need Hal to help me with paperwork that would satisfy the district, since there won't be the usual adoption paperwork for a year. For all intents and purposes, that baby will be mine. Everything else is just semantics. "Once the paid family leave runs out, I'd like to take my FMLA through the end of the school year. I realize that's unpaid."

"Through the end of *this* school year?" Her eyes narrow slightly in calculation as I nod. "When is the mother due?"

"She's thirty-seven weeks now."

"Out of how many?" Principal Jorgenson doesn't have any kids of her own, but I thought everyone knew the answer to this one. Or she's baiting me, because there's some regulation that says I was supposed to ask for my maternity leave four weeks in advance, or six. She'd know all the regulations. She's that type. She's a pointillist, where I'm an impressionist.

"Forty."

How can her quiet be so disquieting? Maybe I shouldn't have sent the e-mail out to notify the parents already. What if the troll actually says no?

Then I'll go anyway. I'm sure the union will have my back, but even if they don't, I'm going. That baby is the most important thing in my life, and this could be my first chance to prove it.

"I'm really sorry to be missing the end of the school year," I finally say when I can't take the silence anymore. "I love the end of the year, how they've gone from these tentative kids to little citizens. You know?" I smile, but either she doesn't know or she won't give me the satisfaction of an assent. I have this tight feeling in my chest, out of nowhere, and it reminds me of being a little girl again, wanting my mom to approve of me, knowing she never will.

"So you're giving me short notice to find a long-term replacement," she says. The corners of her mouth turn down.

"I'm giving you almost as much notice as we had. We just made the connection with our birth mother."

She clearly disapproves of that also, of this slapdash way of acquiring a child. My mother would, too.

It's annoying, how the thought of becoming a mother makes you think of your own. In my case, nothing good can come of that.

"It often happens this way," I find myself saying, wanting to convince the troll, wanting to win her over, hating myself for it. "It takes birth mothers a while to find the right match. One set of adoptive parents falls through, and new arrangements have to be made."

"So you're the second choice?"

Of course she'd seize on that. Her stare reminds me of my mother's: imperious, all-knowing, like she can see through me, can see what no one else can. She can see what I've done, and she thinks it disqualifies me. She thinks I don't deserve this.

"I'm going to be a good mother," I blurt. "I'm going to give this baby everything I have."

The troll breaks eye contact as she nods—not in agreement, but in eagerness to get on with her day. She's ready to vanquish me. Opening her laptop, she says, "I'm sure it's for the best."

Is that what passes for congratulations? "Thank you."

"I mean," she adds, "it's good that you're going to tack the FMLA onto the paid family leave. It's too disruptive for the students if you're gone for six weeks and then you come back to close out the year."

I wish I could say it doesn't hurt, that I can write it off as classic troll behavior. But I've been trying so hard with Leah—trying to be kind, to be motherly—and I'm failing. Leah won't accept it. No reciprocation, just polite distance. Leah doesn't want my attention, that's clear. She wants Gabe's. Whenever he's in the room, her focus is on him; her laughter is for him.

It could be innocent. Leah's looking for the daddy she never had. Well, I don't think she ever had him. She won't tell me anything about her family.

But I know that some girls are into older men, chasing the love they never got. I can't help wondering if Leah could be one of those, and if she is, what the next year holds in store for us.

So all that is in the back of my mind—subtext and context—and then there's the way the principal's gaze can turn me into a little kid again myself, and I know that she's given me what I want, she approved my leave, and I should be grateful and clear out of her office. But sometimes things hurt, things that shouldn't, and you just react.

"Are you this way with everyone?" I ask.

"What do you mean?"

"I mean, the traditional thing to say to someone in my situation is 'Congratulations.' It's not 'Glad you won't come back and teach your kids for the rest of the year.'"

"You must have misunderstood me."

"I'm a good teacher."

"I never said otherwise."

"I'm going to be a good mother."

Her expression is one of mild surprise. "I never said otherwise." She pauses. "Congratulations, Adrienne. Job well done."

I feel my face reddening. I can't tell if she's ameliorating or mocking. I don't even know what I'm looking for, but I've made a fool of myself. Just like I always did when I chased my mother's approval, when I should have known better.

"Thank you," I mumble, turning on my heel. I don't say anything to the front office staff as I rush out.

I sit in my car for a while, fighting to calm down. I text Gabe, but I'm not surprised he doesn't answer. He's at work, in the middle of a sale, hopefully. We need the money. FMLA is unpaid, but we have to keep paying Leah.

I'm light-headed. I can hardly breathe. I tell myself over and over, "You're going to be a mother soon," but somehow that only makes it worse.

I have something important to tell you," I say. The class already looks especially alert, since I've brought them into a circle on the rug. I don't usually do that at this hour, and they're very sensitive to changes in routines. Even Dominic looks attentive. It's that time of year when I can see the fruits of my labor. I'm really going to miss them. Oh, Angie, with those braids. You want to nuzzle her and never let go.

But soon, I'll have one that's truly mine, not just on loan for seven hours a day. No matter what the troll thinks, I'm going to be great.

I take a deep breath and prepare to say good-bye. "In a few weeks, I'm going on maternity leave," I tell them. "Who knows what that is?"

Hands shoot up. Of course I call on Angie.

"It's for after you have a baby," she says. "You stay home and feed him and love him and—"

"It can't be that!" Dominic interrupts. "Because she's not pregnant! Look at her."

Angie looks confused and chastened. But then, other kids seem a little confused, too, as they scan the length of my body. Dominic does appear to have a point.

"Angie's right," I say. "Maternity leave is time for a mother to stay home and be with her baby after he's born. It's time for them to learn to love each other. It's called bonding. So that's what I'll be doing. I'm just not the one giving birth."

Angie stays perplexed; others evince a dawning light.

"Do any of you know what adoption is?" I ask, largely for Angie's benefit.

Hands wave. I know that July is adopted, and that she knows it, too, but her hand remains stationary. Maybe she feels some shame about it. Someday, I hope my son will be proud that he's been chosen, but it reminds me of how unpredictable the whole enterprise is. A baby could become anyone, could feel anything. Temperament is king. What do I know about Leah's temperament anyway? She won't let me know her. Trevor sounds like a dirtbag.

There it is again—the trouble breathing, the light-headedness. I thought I was over it by now.

I call on a kid, any kid, and their definition of "adoption" is close enough. I find I'm ready for this to be over already: all the announcing, with its attendant hope of a validating response. I didn't get it from the troll, and it's pitiful to seek it from a roomful of second graders.

"The baby I'm adopting will be born in a few weeks, and then I'll need to be home"—I smile in Angie's direction—"to feed him and love him."

"It's a boy?" she asks shyly. I nod.

"When are you coming back?" Natasha says.

"Not until next year. So these are our last few weeks together. We can talk about how to make them count. What kinds of things should we do?"

Redirection, a teacher's best friend. Move them from the sadness of loss into the excitement of planning. They're still young enough that the "We're going on a picnic, what should we bring?" trick can work.

When our brainstorming session is done, Angie's brow furrows. "Mrs. T," she says, "how come you're not doing it yourself?"

"What's that?" But I have a sinking feeling I know just what she's asking.

"How come you're not having your own baby? How come someone else is doing it for you?"

Eliza, next to Angie, gives her a poke. "Because she's too *old*!" she hisses in a stage whisper. This is what passes for manners.

"No, it's because her body doesn't work right," Timothy says, full of authority. "That's what my mother says."

July is staring down at her feet, probably thinking that she's being raised by a woman whose body doesn't work right. Timothy's mother needs a solid ass-kicking.

"Sorry, Mrs. T," Angie says. "About you being old, or about your body not working."

"Shut up, Angie!" Eliza says.

"Eliza, it's not okay to say that." I clap my hands together and take a deep breath. "Moving on!"

CHAPTER 16

Gabe

Should we tour the hospital sometime this week?" Adrienne asks. She's at the kitchen counter, carving a turkey.

We're having "Spring Thanksgiving." She said it's the start of a new tradition. Since we have so much to be grateful for, it can't be contained in a single day. I'm a little afraid that she thinks this is what motherhood is: the death of edge, the corresponding initiation of cornball rituals. I couldn't even joke with her about it. Come back, Adrienne. Please, come back.

Leah and I are sitting at the dining room table, lit by taper candles. It's a little awkward, like a blind date, as we wait on Adrienne.

"I don't need to see the hospital first," Leah says. "I'll be there soon enough anyway."

"You'll be more comfortable if you see the maternity floor ahead of time," Adrienne says. "You'll know what to expect."

"I'm comfortable now." Adrienne's blunted her edges; Leah sure hasn't. The harder Adrienne tries to mother Leah, the sharper Leah's going to get. When's Adrienne going to pick up on that? She's usually so perceptive about people.

Leah rolls her eyes at me across the table. I stare into the basket of home-baked dinner rolls. The last thing I want is to act as referee.

"Well, I'll schedule the tour just in case," Adrienne says. "White or dark meat?"

Soon, we've all got our plates filled with turkey, gravy, stuffing, sweet potatoes, and bacony Brussels sprouts. "Do you have any wine?" Leah says. "It would feel festive. My doctor says I can have a half glass a few times a week. It won't hurt anything."

Anything or anyone? I can practically hear Adrienne's thinking.

"We got rid of all the wine," she says. "To be in solidarity with you."

She's lying. She just moved the wine rack into the garage. It's in exile, along with my pool table.

"Could you buy me a bottle?" Leah begins to cut into her turkey. "It'll help settle the baby down at night."

I see Adrienne fighting with herself. Finally, she says, "I'd rather you didn't drink. For one thing, you're underage. For another, it's not safe for the baby."

"I checked with my doctor. Don't you think she knows better than you?"

It's the first true belligerence I've seen out of Leah. "Hey," I intercede. "Do we have to do this now? It's Thanksgiving."

"It's April, Gabe." Leah chews her turkey with an unnecessary degree of force. All this stuff probably scares her, too. In a couple of weeks, she's going to eject a person from her body. His nocturnal hyperactivity probably hasn't been the only thing keeping her up.

"And you need to write a birth plan," Adrienne says, her eyes glittering. Now, that's the woman I married. Relentless (though usually in a good way). "That's another reason we should take a trip to the hospital."

"Another reason I need a trip to the liquor store," Leah says.

Without conscious thought, I find myself drawing my head toward my shoulders, like a turtle retracting into his shell. This could get ugly.

Adrienne chooses to laugh, like Leah was making a joke. "Not on my watch, sweetie."

Uh-oh.

"You do know it's my body, right?" Leah says.

"I don't know what medical journals your ob-gyn has been reading, but no amount of alcohol has been established to be safe for a developing baby. She's gambling with your baby. With *our* baby." Adrienne gestures toward me.

"By now, the baby is almost entirely developed, and I've barely had a drink since I found out I was pregnant."

Oh shit. My head can't get any lower.

"*Barely?*" Adrienne sputters. "I thought you told me that you stopped drinking as soon as you found out you were pregnant."

Leah starts to wilt under Adrienne's gaze. "I did, practically. And I was never, like, an alcoholic."

"The baby's fine," I tell Adrienne. "You've seen the ultrasound pictures. Let's talk about something else, okay? Like how great this food is. Thank you for taking such good care of us." Adrienne is still looking at Leah. "All of us: me, Leah, the little guy." The last remark earns a smile cast in my direction. But her focus quickly shifts back to Leah.

"I have been trying to take good care of you," Adrienne says. "I feel like it's fair to expect a few things in return, like a tour of the hospital, and you not drinking until after the baby is born. Once he's here, your body is totally one hundred percent yours again. I won't buy you alcohol since it's illegal, but I won't try to stop you. Just hold off a little longer, please." Her gaze softens. "Please?"

Leah takes a sulky bite of sweet potatoes and then, finally, nods.

Is this what it'll be like to have a teenager of our own?

Despite a potentially incendiary moment, we've all managed to survive intact. That's when Adrienne says, "What about your parents? Have you thought about whether they're going to fly out for the birth?"

You have to know Leah as well as I've come to know her, or you'd miss it. She's deadpan most of the time, but it's there, in the slight twitch of her mouth, and for a split second it's in her eyes. The hurt. The fury at the person who's summoned the hurt.

"It could bring you guys closer together," Adrienne says, mercilessly. No, she's not without mercy. She just doesn't know what I do. I haven't told her what Leah and I talked about that day at Lands End. She's clueless, and it's my fault.

"No," Leah says, and there's a note of warning in it that I can only hope Adrienne will pick up and heed.

"I sometimes think," Adrienne muses, "that if I'd gotten pregnant, things would be different with my mom. She would have had to come back into my life. She could ignore me, but a baby?"

I didn't know Adrienne had any regrets when it came to her mother. She certainly never mentions the woman.

"Thanks for dinner," Leah says, standing up from the table and walking out of the room before she can say anything she'll truly regret.

Turns out I can muster some gratitude today, after all.

CHAPTER 17

Adrienne

Is she sure it's the real thing?" I'm in the hallway, keeping my voice low. "It's so early. Maybe it's false labor."

"She talked to her doctor and was told to go straight to the hospital." Gabe's freaked, but he's trying to contain himself, like I am.

"The same doctor who told her to kick back with some merlot?" Though it occurs to me that that conversation might never have happened at all. I'd have no way of knowing, not being permitted entry to the exam room. True or not, I'm still mad about how Leah baited me at Spring Thanksgiving, after all I've done for her.

But her willingness to show ingratitude distinguishes her from Patty, so there's a silver lining. Besides, this is no time for being pissed. The baby's on the way. We're on our way.

I break out into an enormous smile. "He's almost here, Gabe! Can you believe it?"

"No, I guess I can't." There's a certain crackle to the phone line. I'm on speaker, with the phone lying on the passenger seat, as Gabe drives home to get Leah.

"I'll leave right now and meet you at the hospital."

"Don't do that. Finish out your day. It'll be your last one with the kids, right? Your maternity leave is starting early."

"She's only thirty-eight weeks, right?" Panic seizes me. "That means the baby's premature." I picture him the size of my hand, entombed in hospital Plexiglas rather than his crib at home. We won't be able to hold and kiss and love him, and even Angie knows that's what maternity leave is for.

"Leah said no, he's full term. Thirty-eight weeks is the cutoff, that's what her doctor told her."

Dr. Merlot again. But on this point, I'll trust her. "I'm leaving right now to meet you."

"What about your class?"

"The troll can babysit for the rest of the day. I need to be there, Gabe. I need to know that he's okay." I'm practically done with writing out the framework for my long-term sub anyway. Maybe I can do it by Leah's bedside, as her contractions intensify.

I hear Gabe hesitating. "She doesn't want you there. Not yet, anyway."

"Let me guess: She wants you there, now."

"We're friends. You and Leah haven't been getting along so great."

"That's not my fault! I've been trying!" My voice rings out through the empty hallway. "She was going to drink wine while she's carrying our baby! I have a right to—"

"I know. But she has a right to decide who she wants in the delivery room with her."

"And she wants you. Alone."

"You can come in later, but there's a lot of waiting involved. She said . . ." He doesn't want to finish the sentence.

"What did she say, Gabe?" Each word comes out clipped, staccato.

"She said you make her tense, and that's not how she wants to feel through hours of contractions. She said you can come in when the baby's almost here. I made her promise.

"Wren? You still there?"

"Still here."

"Don't be mad. Be joyful. You're about to be a mother."

But I didn't think it would happen like this: Gabe on the inside, me on the outs.

"Congratulations, baby." His voice is like warm breath on my neck. "We're so close. Let's just do it her way a little while longer, and then we're home free. We've got our son."

I sag against my closed classroom door. Through it, I can hear the natives becoming restless. "How do I get through the day, knowing I'm missing the whole thing?"

"It'll go on for hours, and school's almost over. You'll be at the hospital soon."

"In the waiting room."

"I've got to go. She's standing outside."

"Does she even have her bag packed? Does she know what to bring? I told her to do the birth plan! We haven't even talked names!" I slam my hand into the door, which discharges some frustration and has the bonus effect of making the kids snap to attention for a second.

Gabe speaks directly into the receiver. "I love you. More than anything." Then he's gone.

My poor kids. They didn't stand a chance at holding my attention. I was glued to my cell phone, awaiting each text: Leah checked into the hospital, no problem; she was in early active labor; the baby was in the correct position (as in, he wasn't breech, the delivery would be vaginal, not cesarean); she'd requested an epidural ASAP (of course she did) and was feeling no pain.

Even as I was offering my students good-byes and apologies that we wouldn't get to do all the fun things we'd planned, my mind was elsewhere. I should have been the one in that delivery room, refusing the epidural, because some things in life are meant to be painful. You feel because you're alive; pain is a sort of currency. Leah and her epidural are cheapening the whole experience.

But it is her experience to cheapen, isn't it? It's her delivery. She'll deliver that baby into my arms, and after that, it becomes my experience.

That's in the back of my mind as I give my final hugs of the school year, and as I inform the office they'll need their long-term substitute sooner than planned, and in the car on the way to the hospital. It helps, but only a little.

I almost stopped by Mel's classroom to see if her perpetual sunniness could perform a type of alchemy. Could she turn my bitterness to gratitude? But I went to the parking lot instead because pain is meant to be felt. It's not just currency; it's information. It can tell me what to do next.

I text Gabe when I arrive at the maternity unit. He meets me at the nurse's station, where one bored-looking woman in scrubs is hunting and pecking on a keyboard. I thought the floor would be more kidded up (clouds painted on the ceilings, circus animals on the walls, maybe), but it's generic hospital. White on white.

Gabe's button-down is untucked and wrinkled and the sleeves are rolled up unevenly. There are bags under his eyes, as if he's been here days rather than hours. "Leah said you can come in," he tells me. The queen will see you now.

"Isn't she afraid I'll make her tense?"

"Adrienne." He sighs.

"Did they do an ultrasound?" I ask. I'd love more pictures of him. A few final candids, before he enters the world. This is you, I could tell him, when you were still in the negative integers, minus-three hours old.

"Kid said no paparazzi."

I smile and step forward, taking his hands in mine. "It's really happening."

He smiles back, appearing dazed. Little cartoon stars could be rotating around his head. "There's no stopping it now."

"I'll be nice," I say.

"Be yourself, okay? Don't try to be her mom. Just be regular."

I was myself for Spring Thanksgiving, and look where that got us. I was initially banned from the delivery room. "What did you say to Leah?" What I mean is, how come she's letting me in? What changed?

"I told her you won't say anything about her parents. I told her we don't even have to talk, if she doesn't want to. There's a DVD player in there. She's watching *Blade Runner*." I laugh: Welcome to the world, little guy! The androids have taken over! "I just grabbed a bunch of DVDs and threw them in her suitcase. That's the one she picked. She called it a 'classic.'"

At that, we both laugh. Then he holds my hand and leads me back to Leah's room.

It's one-stop shopping on the antepartum floor: no more wheeling women through the hall to the delivery room. Instead, Leah will give birth in the same room where she's now watching her generation's *Casablanca*. She's propped up in a bed with steel rails along the sides, in a hospital gown with a blanket over her lower half, her hair pulled back in a tight bun. There are a few stress pimples around her hairline that I never noticed before. But basically, she looks gorgeous and calm. Her eyes are on the TV screen suspended in the air about ten feet away. Harrison Ford and Sean Young are contending with a future that looks positively quaint.

A chair is pulled up to the bedside (Gabe's, I imagine), and another chair resides much farther away, near the door (mine, I presume). There are IV poles and other medical equipment stationed around the room, but Leah doesn't seem to be hooked up to anything.

She glances over, gives me a brief smile and a wave. Then she's back to her movie viewing.

Gabe moves his chair back so he can sit next to me.

"Has she done a birth plan?" I whisper to him. He nods. "What's in it?"

"It was like a multiple-choice test. Does she want the baby placed immediately on her chest, does she want him washed off fully, does she want just a rinse . . . We had fun with it, pictured him being run through a car wash, with those fabric strips slapping at him." He looks tickled at the memory.

Really, Gabe? A newborn getting slapped around in a car wash is funny?

He gives me a hard stare. "After he's born, do you think you're going to get your sense of humor back?"

Before I can respond, Leah turns to us. "Could you guys, like, be a little quieter?"

The nurse comes in. Gabe introduces us, like he and Katrina are old friends. What an unfortunate name, Katrina, to be forever linked to devastation.

Katrina has a long, dark ponytail and a springy way of moving, but I think she's in her forties. She shakes my hand and then purifies hers afterward from a pump bottle attached to the wall. "How's it going?" she asks Leah.

"Kind of weird," Leah says. "I'm mostly numb from the waist down. I'm scared to go pee because I feel like I might not know how to use my legs."

She's scared. It's good to hear an emotion. Our baby isn't being born of an android.

"Let me help you." Katrina assists Leah in her dismount from the hospital bed, and then they walk across the room to the bathroom. The back of Leah's gown gapes open, revealing a high, perfect ass and cellulite-free legs. Gabe pauses the movie but keeps watching the screen; I can feel the effort he's making not to look in Leah's direction. Maybe she can't feel the breeze on her ass; she said she's numb from the waist down. She might not know she's flashing us.

But didn't she say "mostly numb"?

I don't like the feeling I have: jealous that my baby's mama has a better ass than I do, pissed that she wants me (and Gabe) to know it.

I take a deep breath and try to expunge all negativity. I want to fill this space only with love and kindness so that my baby takes it in from his very first external breaths. I need to have compassion for Leah. She's a scared teenager who's about to have a baby and then give him away.

But not really. As Gabe said, she's only leasing him.

What if Leah holds him in her arms (slimy, or washed, or lightly rinsed, whatever box she checked) and she loves him so purely and completely that she rescinds right then and there?

"I'm scared, too," I murmur to Gabe, trying to lean into him though our chairs have plastic armrests that make cuddling somewhat prohibitive.

He kisses the top of my head. "Leah's dilating fine. It's smooth sailing."

There's no time to explain what I'm really afraid of, because Katrina is depositing Leah back in bed. "Dr. Florian will be in soon," she announces. "Leah's dilating quickly, so delivery's not far off."

"I don't feel the contractions. Is that bad?"

"We're going to look at a monitor and tell you when the contractions are happening, so you'll know when to push." Katrina pats Leah's arm. "Nothing to worry about." She smiles over at me. "So you're the aunt?"

I blink at her and then at Gabe. He couldn't have given me a heads-up that we have a cover story? I see that Leah is staring straight ahead with a faint smile. Did she tell Gabe not to tell me? Does she think this is a game?

For a second, I consider not playing along. But this is not the time to antagonize her. "Yes," I say, "I'm the aunt."

Katrina slips out the door, the movie still paused.

"Leah felt like it would be easier to say we're the aunt and uncle," Gabe says. "Less explaining."

Gabe hits "Play," and he and Leah get caught up in the denouement.

I fumble in my purse and remove the ultrasound pictures. I run my fingers across them, over his beautiful profile, like I'm a Catholic and the photos are rosary beads.

Someday I'll tell him, "I loved you before I met you. I would have walked through fire for you." Before this is all over, I just might have to.

Dr. Florian comes in as the credits are rolling. She looks like a sensible middle-aged woman, not someone who would prescribe wine for a rambunctious fetus.

"I'm Aunt Adrienne," I say.

Dr. Florian smiles as she sheaths her hand in latex. "Good to meet you." She tells Leah, "Another cervix check, you know the drill." Leah obediently places her feet in stirrups and lets Dr. Florian do her worst.

"It's time!" Dr. Florian removes the gloves and heads for the door. "I'll get the team together and we'll be in shortly."

Leah looks at Gabe, fear plastered across her face. "It's okay," he says. He moves to her bedside and looks down at her. "I'm right here." It sounds like something a husband would say. I have a feeling he's part of her birth plan, and I'm not.

The team swarms the room, in masks and gloves. There's Dr. Florian, and another doctor who hasn't been introduced, and Katrina, and two people on standby near a Plexiglas platform that I assume will hold the baby. Gabe stays where he is, only now Leah is clutching his hand, her eyes wild. I inch closer to where I can see better but Leah can't really see me, still on the periphery.

The doctors are watching a monitor and every time the line spikes, Leah is told to push. Her gown is hiked up, and I can see the thin landing strip of dark pubic hair. Gabe must be seeing it, too. It's hardly an erotic sight, but it is an intimate one. In fact, it's a level of intimacy he and I will never experience.

It goes on for a while, a half hour at least: the command to push, and then the pushing, and still no baby. I want to ask if this is normal; I can't tell if anyone is concerned behind their masks.

Leah falls back against the pillow, clearly exhausted. Sweaty wisps of hair have escaped her bun.

Gabe strokes the hairs back and whispers something to her. She nods, eyes closed, and then she pops up, sudden as a jack-in-the-box, and says, “Fuck this, I’m just going to push the whole time, until he’s out.”

“Of course,” Katrina says. “You don’t have to wait for the contractions.”

“Why the fuck didn’t anyone tell her that?” I’m surprised by the magnitude of Gabe’s anger. I suspected but never knew for sure how much he cares for Leah. Now it’s on full display.

Leah bares her teeth and lets out animal cries that correspond to each push. She wasn’t kidding, she’s going for it. It’s a bravura performance and I have to admit, even though I slammed her for the epidural, she’s admirably balls-to-the-wall now.

Another five minutes, and the doctors are saying, “He’s almost here, one more good push,” and Leah’s a bug-eyed maniac, and Gabe’s literally shouting encouragement (“You’re doing it!” “Good job!”), and I’m swept up in the excitement, in the romance even, and then *he’s here,* slick with blood and mucus. Red-faced and screaming. My beautiful boy. I feel my knees buckling; I’m weak with love.

Leah’s crying and telling Gabe, “Do it, do it,” and I can’t focus on what she means, I just keep staring at *him,* at my little one. My arms are involuntarily outstretched; I can’t wait much longer. I’m crying, too. Only Gabe is dry-eyed.

“Do it,” Leah says, and then I get it. Dr. Florian hands Gabe a scissors, guides him to the right spot, and he cuts the cord. Yet another intimacy he and I can never share. But the important thing is, Leah and the baby are separate entities for the first time. They’ve been severed.

Then the baby is whisked off for a full wash, the works. “He’s perfect, he’s healthy,” Dr. Florian is reporting. Leah nods, but she looks spent, husklike.

He's swaddled in a blue blanket and placed on Leah's chest. Katrina says, "He's hungry," and Leah gets what she means and begins to frantically waggle her head.

"No, no," she says. "Give him to her." She indicates me, and Katrina takes it in stride, as if mothers are always pawning off their newborns on the aunt.

I thought Leah had forgotten I was here, even I'd forgotten myself for a minute in all of it, but here he is, in my arms. My baby—cone-headed and fuchsia and caterwauling at the shock of his emergence into the world—and I'm spurting like a fountain. Gabe comes and puts his arms around me, around both of us, and says, with great intensity, "This is Michael, he has to be Michael."

We haven't seriously talked names, or even gotten the clearance from Leah to do the naming, but it's all been accelerated. Gabe's never said "Michael" before, and now he seems so certain. "What does Leah think about that?" I ask, though I'm not sure what I think myself. It could be exactly perfect or entirely wrong. Our baby, named after Gabe's brother, who loved me, who took his own life. Our baby named after an angel, just like Gabriel.

"Leah already agreed," he says. "We talked about it before you got here." He couldn't have mentioned that sooner, maybe during the credits of *Blade Runner*?

I glance over, wondering if she knows the whole story of Gabe's brother, the story of the three of us. She's on her side in bed, collapsed. Whatever she knows, she's in no position to tell.

I think, without malice or gratification, that she's feeling it now, the pain. But there's a rightness to that. Epidural or not, you shouldn't relinquish a child and feel nothing. That would make you a monster, a Patty.

No, her name should not be in this delivery room, not even in my head. I never need to think of her again. I'm a mother now.

I turn back to Gabe, and to my baby, and I feel something I've never felt before.

CHAPTER 18

Gabe

We're at the hospital practically round-the-clock for the forty-eight hours until Leah and the baby are discharged; Adrienne won't have it any other way. She's determined to prevent them from bonding.

It doesn't look like she has much to worry about. Michael's rooming with Leah in his elevated glass cube, but she stares past him, over him, at the TV, or out the window. I think she might be depressed.

After the privacy and spaciousness of the delivery room, the postpartum room seems cruelly cramped. It's got light brown walls, speckled Easter-egg floors, striped flame-retardant curtains, and it's shared, demarcated by a blue curtain. We get the window, they get the door. The bathroom is equidistant, but it still requires that Leah exit our small sanctum. Adrienne and I go down the hall to the visitor restrooms.

Adrienne sits in the brown pleather recliner by the window, where she feeds Michael formula from bottles and he sleeps against her chest. I've never seen her so contented.

"You should hold him," she tells me. So I do. I have. I try to look fatherly, though I sure don't feel it, but Adrienne is painfully eager to believe.

He doesn't cry much, except when I hold him. The few times Leah has held him at the urging of the nurses, he's stared up at her soberly, curiously, like he thinks they just might be related. Or he thinks Adrienne's suddenly shed almost twenty years.

I don't know what he thinks. I can't get comfortable with this strange being, with all his untransmittable thoughts.

"He's so tiny!" Adrienne says all the time, breathless with love, sotto voce so she won't disturb him as he nestles in the vicinity of her collarbone (he's asleep 90 percent of the time, it seems like). For Adrienne, tiny equals adorable. By that calculus, we could have bought a box of raisins and been done with it.

I sound heartless. Am I heartless?

Adrienne says that with vaginal births, babies tend to come out a little misshapen and bruised. Think about passing a large melon through a narrow canal; it wouldn't make for the prettiest produce. Hopefully, I'll love him later, when he's grown into a nice honeydew, though that wouldn't say anything very complimentary about my character.

It was a mistake, naming him Michael. It creeps me out every time Adrienne says it. But she's come to think it's the ideal way to honor my brother. Leah thought the same thing, and that's why she agreed. I must have thought it, too, in those couple hours when Leah and I were alone together. A lot of things seemed like good ideas then.

Leah hurts. She walks to the bathroom gingerly, and she comes back looking like she's been crying. I pulled a nurse aside and asked if that's normal, all the pain, and she said definitely, it's a swollen mess down there.

Three different lactation consultants have "stopped by." That's what they say: "Just stopping by in case you have any questions!" They're obviously the ones with the question: "Why won't you even consider breast-feeding, for the greatest start in life you can possibly give your little one?" Leah acts like an obstinate deaf-mute during these encounters, staring into the middle distance and shaking her head convulsively. It's the adult equivalent of putting your hands over your ears and chanting, "I can't hear you, I can't hear you!" So they start proselytizing to Adrienne and me instead. Adrienne nods pleasantly and agrees to take their pamphlets, humoring them as she would a Jehovah's Witness. Me, I keep out of it.

On the other side of the curtain, there's a family that's acting just the way they're supposed to. The mom is always breast-feeding (I know because their lactation consultant keeps showing up with remedies for sore, cracking nipples), and the dad is often singing to the kid (whom he calls "little man"), and their family and friends come by with balloons and flowers to have insipidly normal conversations ("It doesn't get any better than this, does it?" "It sure doesn't!").

Meanwhile, our side of the curtain is often silent, except for Adrienne's occasional off-key lullabies and the low rumble of television. Leah's watching *Blade Runner* again, for the third time. I've offered to go out and buy her any DVD she wants (I'd welcome the errand), but she says she likes the repetition. Despite the fact that it's one of my favorite movies, I suspect I'll never watch it again.

Thankfully, all is well with mother and baby, so we're getting discharged in the next couple of hours. Another day, and I might have died of claustrophobia.

"Leah?" A woman of indeterminate age with lank hair has walked around the curtain. Her eyes are an extreme blue, in marked contrast to her overall nondescript appearance. Colored contacts, probably. "I'm Veronica, one of the hospital's social workers."

"Yeah?" Leah eyes her with wariness and reluctantly pauses the movie.

"This must be Michael." Veronica smiles over at Michael, who's taking a bottle from Adrienne.

"Yes, this is Michael." Adrienne sounds as proud as if she gave birth to him herself. She's proprietary already, and that makes me worry for her. He's not ours yet, though I have to admit, Leah's not showing any signs that she's going to take him back. She doesn't look like she's got anywhere near that much fight in her. With Adrienne, it would be gladiatorial, no doubt.

Veronica transfers her smile to Leah. "How's Mom doing?"

Radio silence. Leah's not making eye contact, and Adrienne looks none too pleased with Veronica's nomenclature.

"How are you, Leah?" Veronica tries again.

"Glad I'll be out of here soon."

"Was there something wrong with your stay?"

Leah shrugs.

"If you don't mind my asking," Adrienne says, smiling sweetly, "what does a hospital social worker do?"

"We do all sorts of things," Veronica answers. "It's standard operating procedure for me to stop by before discharge."

Again with the stopping by. "So you can . . . ?" I say. Her obtuseness is grating on me.

"So I can give Leah resources. There are postpartum groups she can attend, for example. Also, I'm here to assess."

"Assess for what?" Adrienne and I ask at once.

"You're her aunt and uncle, correct?" We both nod. "I see that you're very involved. It's good to have family support." Veronica casts a meaningful look at Michael, resting on Adrienne, having fallen asleep on the bottle. "But Leah's the mother, and I need to make sure that she has all she needs to take care of her baby."

"We'll see that she does," Adrienne says. "She'll be living with us for the next year."

Veronica jots that down. "And the baby's father?" She's looking at Leah, but Adrienne answers.

"He's not in the picture."

"I have to be honest," Veronica says. "There have been some concerns. About the dynamics."

I'd suspected the staff found our triad strange. So they've sent in the woman with the fake eyes to be real with us.

"What about the dynamics?" Adrienne asks, keeping her voice even. She's treading lightly.

"Well, what I'm witnessing right now. Leah's detachment. From the baby, from what's going on in the room."

I look at Leah. She's either incapable of speaking or unwilling. I can't entirely blame the staff. She does seem detached, almost to the point of catatonia.

"Leah. Do you believe you can care for your son?" Veronica says it loudly, overenunciating. Of course it's the moment when the revelry on the other side of the curtain has ceased.

"I can care for him," Leah says. "I just don't want to right now."

Veronica clearly didn't expect that answer. I see her writing it down. "If you're depressed, that's not uncommon. We can get help for you."

"It's not that."

"What do you think it is, then?"

Leah looks at Adrienne and then at me. "I'm just going to tell her. Then she'll go." To Veronica, "They're not my aunt and uncle. They're the adoptive parents."

"It's an unusual arrangement." Adrienne slips into the breach, her tone conciliatory, like we're so very sorry we didn't clue Veronica in to our personal business sooner. "Leah felt embarrassed, and we wanted to respect her wishes. She felt more comfortable calling us her aunt and uncle."

"Adoption is nothing to be ashamed of," Veronica says. "Many beautiful families are formed that way. It's not unusual, either."

"Our arrangement's not the norm, though." Adrienne smiles. She likes the thought of us forming a beautiful, not-unusual family. "Leah is going to live with us for a year, like I said. She wants to build a life for herself in California, and we're going to help her with that." As if it's altruism on our part. I wonder if she's managed to convince herself that it is, if that's the story she wants to tell Michael someday.

Veronica pauses. That, her face says, is unusual. "Won't that be"—she feels around for the word—"confusing for everyone? Including Michael?"

"We're going to have very clear boundaries," Adrienne says. "I'm a second-grade teacher, and I believe in boundaries." It's something of a non sequitur, designed to establish her bona fides as a professional maternal figure.

"We've got this under control," I say. "Leah knows we're going to look after her, and we're going to take great care of Michael. Look at my wife. She's already bonded with him." Adrienne gestures toward the serenely sleeping Michael with her chin. "We've got a lawyer who's handling the contracts. There's nothing for you to worry about."

Veronica doesn't like that answer. She stands up. "I have to run this past my supervisor. She'll help me decide whether social services should be involved."

"Involved how?" Adrienne looks slightly alarmed. "There's no abuse here."

"I didn't say there was abuse. I just . . ." She smooths her black pants. "I know you say the dynamics aren't concerning, but Leah seems depressed—"

"If she's depressed," I say, "we'll see that she gets help. You're not listening. We care about Leah. She's been living with us for a while."

"Oh." Veronica isn't sure if that makes our situation more or less troubling. I can see her making a mental notation—more unusual behavior.

Leah looks straight at Veronica for the first time. "Have you ever had a baby?"

"No. But I've been working here for three years and—"

"So you've seen a lot, but you don't *know* a lot. I've been through, like, bucketloads of shit, and I don't get depressed; I handle it. You don't need to worry about me, or my baby. Gabe and Adrienne are my family now."

It's the most Leah's said for the past forty-eight hours. It's practically a soliloquy. I'm proud of her for standing up for herself, and for us, but I glance at Adrienne and she's feeling something entirely different. I don't know if it's that Leah called us her family or that she said "my baby."

"I'm just going to page my supervisor," Veronica says, "and I'll be back in shortly."

"Is there a chance that Leah won't be discharged today?" I ask.

She must be able to hear my desperation. Fortunately, she seems to mistake it for a passionate desire to have Michael home with us. "No, they'll be discharged. Really, the most that'll happen is that social services will stop by your home periodically."

More stopping by. At least we'll have our own door instead of a curtain.

But I notice Adrienne looks almost pleased at the thought.

I'm so sorry, Adrienne. I really thought I'd be able to come out, especially since you're being so great about paying for the flight and hotel. I'm dying to meet you and Gabe, and I want to see San Francisco, I mean, who doesn't, it's like a wonder of the world, right? At this point, I'll be meeting you guys for the first time in the delivery room. It's friggin' ridiculous.

But I asked my boss if I could use unpaid leave and he actually said no, the fucker. He said they couldn't "spare me," like it's a compliment about how important I am instead of just a way for him to have power over me. They can't get someone else to answer the phones for two days? People can't do their own photocopying and faxing and scanning and whatever else? My job's such a joke, but I'm not really laughing anymore.

I need to get my life together, Adrienne. I need to get out of that place. I wish I could be like you, strong and in control. You would never let someone treat you like I get treated. Maybe it's like you say, I'm too nice. It bites me in the ass. You'd be proud, though: I definitely don't think the best about my boss anymore!

Thanks, by the way, for the check. I hate being short so often but you know how the expenses pile up. Getting mugged set me back, obviously. And all those medical expenses for Yuri. This is why people don't take in strays! You never know what'll go wrong. But you know me, I can't stop myself.

Anyway, I'm totally disappointed that I can't come see you for the next month at least, but I'm going to find a way. If I have to quit my job, I'll do it. We need to meet.

Love, Patty

CHAPTER 19

Adrienne

It could be annoying, the way no one mentioned until the absolute last minute that Michael can't leave the hospital without a car seat. But for the past two days, I've been incapable of true irritation. Michael's like Xanax for me. It was that way even before he was born: when I'd rub Leah's stomach or look at the ultrasound pictures. All along, I knew it. He's going to make me into the person I was always meant to be.

Gabe's out buying and installing the car seat, and he should be back soon. Then we'll be able to take Michael home. I can't wait.

Another thing that could be annoying is the way Gabe chose the name, but he won't say it. He says "the baby" or, worse, "the kid."

Yeah, it's a good thing I'm impervious to aggravation, or Gabe would be working my nerves. Like before he left, we were out in the hall, saying good-bye. I felt antsy. I didn't want to leave Michael alone with Leah any longer than necessary. Gabe asked me, "Do you think something's wrong with her?" He meant Leah, of course. "She says she's fine," I answered, "and I'm going to take her at her word."

Over the past weeks, she's let me know, in no uncertain terms, that she doesn't need to be mothered. She's an adult, and she'll take care of herself. But Gabe seems more preoccupied with Leah than he is with Michael.

She is acting weird, though. The TV is turned off, but she's still staring at it, like she's projecting some movie from her mind.

"I'm going to take a walk with Michael," I say, standing up. He's been drowsing in my arms since his last bottle. I adjust his blue knit cap and temporarily lay him down at the end of Leah's bed for re-swaddling. I'm an excellent swaddler. I've been practicing on a doll, but I never let Gabe know. He would have thought I was getting my hopes up, i.e. setting myself up for a massive fall like last time. But I'm the one who's ready, not him and definitely not Leah.

Leah doesn't answer.

"Do you want to come with us?" I ask. "The doctor said it's good for you to move around a little. We'll go slow. This close to discharge, you can just put your clothes on. Then you won't get a draft up your ass." I smile to let her know I can be her friend just like Gabe can.

"I don't want to wear those clothes."

I hate to break it to her, but she still needs to wear maternity clothes. It'll take some time to tone up. Her stomach looks almost the same as it did when Michael was inside. Granted, she was carrying small, but he's a healthy seven pounds, two ounces. What a little stallion he is. I nuzzle his cone-shaped head.

"I don't want to wear those clothes again, ever in my life."

"You say that now." Wow, I sound like such a mom. Wait, I am a mom! I feel myself flush with pleasure. "I just mean someday you're going to meet someone amazing and you'll want to have your own family. Things are going to work out really well for you, Leah. You'll see."

She looks at me with wide, dead eyes.

"Come on." I smile. "Get up. Get dressed. We'll walk together. It'll be good for you."

Lights are on, but nobody's home. So I walk Michael out into the hall, cradling him so that he has proper head and neck support but is facing slightly outward. His eyes don't really focus yet, and they don't stay open long. Still, I give him the tour.

"This is the hallway," I say. Along the wall, there are a ton of pictures of babies—some newborn, some up to a year old and emblazoned on holiday cards—and I point out the cutest ones to Michael. I'm pretty sure the newborns with the perfectly shaped heads were cesarean. I kiss the top of Michael's and whisper that he doesn't need to be jealous, he'll be beautiful soon enough. He is already, in my eyes, but I'm speaking objectively here. Right now, his head looks like a gourd.

We pass the nurses' station, where I pointedly ignore the one who failed to inform me of the car seat rule until an hour ago. I take Michael's little hand and wave it at the others.

A woman is walking toward us in her gown and slippers, her husband protectively holding her elbow. She manages to smile at Michael and me in an absent sort of way. I think how lucky Michael is to have me, someone who can be fully and immediately present. How difficult it must be to bond with your little one when you're in a kind of physical shock.

I dapple his head with kisses. He blinks up at me for a second, and I think, He knows just who I am. He knows I'm Mama.

We poke our heads into the waiting room. I'm feeling cocky, like I want to show him off. There's an entire family in there: a husband, grandma, grandpa, three kids. I'm about to continue my narration when the gray-haired, bespectacled woman rises with a smile and says, "Your first grandchild?"

Have I aged that much in forty-eight hours? It seems all the more egregious to be misidentified by that woman, who is herself clearly geriatric. "No," I say. "He's my son."

She looks embarrassed, her eyes flicking up and down the length of me. "Oh, I didn't realize . . . you're not in a gown . . ."

"We saw you when you first arrived on the floor," the woman's equally elderly husband says, clarifying. "When your daughter was wheeled by. We thought she was your daughter, she looks a lot like you."

"Such a pretty girl," the woman adds, like that's going to make anything better.

If I go out with Leah and Michael, I bet I'll get that a lot: people commenting on how pretty my daughter is, calling me a proud grandmother. They'll think it's a compliment when they tell me what a beautiful little family I have, three generations together in Safeway.

I smile and wave Michael's little hand at them to show all is forgiven, and we make our getaway. But I'll make sure we don't go out, all three of us, unless it's absolutely necessary.

It won't be a problem for Leah anyway. She's clearly not interested in Michael, she doesn't seem to like me much these days (if she ever did), and once she gets her strength back, she'll want to go off and have a life. We're on the same page, Leah and me.

He only needs one mom. Any more would just confuse matters.

That's why it's okay—advisable, even—for Leah not to bond with Michael. That means no breast-feeding, even if the hospital staff acts like it's a death sentence. "But he won't get the mother's antibodies!" one of them said, nearly aghast. Well, I didn't get my mother's antibodies, and that was likely a good thing. Drinking in my mother might have been toxic, have they ever thought of that?

Besides, formula today is way more advanced than it was almost forty years ago. He'll be awash in probiotics.

The main thing is, Michael is going to feel completely and thoroughly loved.

And really, even though Leah doesn't want me to, I'm looking out for her, too. She's way better off not getting too attached to a baby that isn't hers anymore.

CHAPTER 20

Gabe

I've had some lonely moments in my life. But it's never been as pronounced, as unrelenting, as in the past two weeks, since the kid came home.

I was as prepared as I could be for the haze of sleep deprivation. But this feels like something else, something bigger. I've been horny practically every day for twenty-plus years, and suddenly, my libido's on vacation, or on strike. Adrienne hasn't initiated sex, and neither have I. It makes me realize how naturally it just used to happen. It didn't feel like the will of one person; it was the force of the collective. We were drawn to each other inexorably, like static electricity. But now, all that's between us is actual static.

No, this isn't just sleep deprivation. It's the start of a tsunami that's building offshore. I'm too tired to figure out how to stop it.

Adrienne says I'm hyperbolic when I'm exhausted. She might be right. But she and I have never been this misaligned before. When I cut the umbilical cord, was it really my connection to Adrienne?

I've been feeling Michael's presence. Not the kid, but the real one, my brother. It's like he's waiting and watching. But I don't know if it's to warn me about what's coming or to gloat.

Unless that sound really was just a window slamming shut, and I'm conjuring up ghosts. The sleep-deprived mind can play plenty of tricks.

The kid's in his own room down the hall. Adrienne floated the idea of putting his crib at the end of our bed, but I told her if that's what she wanted, we could have left the pool table where it was. Now I'll be damned if I'm going to take it all apart and put it back.

Not that the pool table is the point. What was my point? I can't even remember.

I thought Adrienne would be all about women's liberation and gender equality and fairness, but no. She's fine with doing all the night feedings—all the feedings, period—and all the diaper changes. It's like he's a country she's trying to colonize. She needs to make sure her smell is in his nostrils as much as possible. She needs him to love her the best.

The funny thing is, she doesn't have much competition. Leah stays away, and the kid gives me the willies. Is it just the name thing? Is it his wizened old face? He looks at me, and I think, He knows, and I can't get away fast enough.

He cries in the night—three, four times. Adrienne goes to the nursery to feed him and always stays awhile. She sings, she talks to him, and her voice, it's just suffused with love. It hurts me to hear it. I want to feel that for him, but it's like I'm broken somehow.

The whole time she's gone, I can't go back to sleep. I miss her, and I miss my late nights with Leah, too. I can imagine that Leah's lying sleepless in bed just like I am, but I can't reach her anymore.

The first week after the birth, Leah barely left her room. She said she wasn't feeling well, but she called her doctor and it was nothing to worry about. She didn't seem to be eating. I thought she'd want to let me in (literally and figuratively) but she spoke through the closed door.

Then today, she flounces out of there, smiling, and says she has a plan. Adrienne's sitting on the living room floor with a blanket spread out and Michael on his stomach. She does that three times a day, says it helps him strengthen his neck muscles and prepares him for crawling. She reads books on infant development every chance she gets; she presents these facts to me like gemstones.

Adrienne looks up at Leah. "What's your plan?" I detect a tinge of anxiety.

"I'm going to pump my breast milk for Michael!" Leah casts the most cursory of glances down at him. "What's he doing?"

"Preparing to crawl," I say.

Adrienne misses my irony. "You want to breast-feed? I thought we went over this."

"No. I want you to feed him my breast milk. I can hook myself up to a machine and pump out the milk, and then you give him the bottles. I just need you to buy the machine." She looks down at her phone and then holds it out so that Adrienne can see the screenshot. "The Medela breast pump is supposed to be the best."

"Where's this coming from?" Adrienne asks. I can tell she's trying to sound open and friendly, but she's failing.

"It's better for him to get my antibodies and, you know, whatever else. My milk is way better than formula, they said so in the hospital."

"They said that a week ago. Can you even produce milk now? I thought your supply dries up if you don't use it."

"I just checked it out in the bathroom. I squeezed and, not to be gross or anything, milk totally spurted out!" Leah chuckles. "Plus, it'll help me get thinner quicker."

Adrienne's expression morphs into one of understanding: So that's what this is all about, Leah wanting to get her body back, ASAP.

As if Adrienne at nineteen wouldn't have wanted exactly the same thing.

I can see Adrienne battling with herself—the stereotypical angel and devil, one on each shoulder—knowing that breast milk is best (it was the nurses' mantra, after all) but not wanting the kid to have regular Leah infusions. After all, he already has half of Leah's DNA and none of hers. What happens, she wonders, if he keeps ingesting more Leah? What I can't tell is whether part of Leah's sudden elation is the knowledge that she's putting Adrienne over a barrel.

They might both be crazy, but someone's got to work around here. "I need to go," I say, standing up.

Adrienne shoots me a look. She wants me to find a way out of her quandary, a loophole, a way she can be a good mother while denying her child Leah's breast milk.

I do get it. She just wants to be the kid's mother, 100 percent. But it ain't going to happen. She can't vaporize Leah—not now, not once the year's over. Leah exists, and she made the kid. If Adrienne would accept that, everyone's lives would be easier, including hers. But sometimes I think she's not interested in easier.

"I'm just so tired of being fat," Leah says.

"You're not fat, you just gave birth," Adrienne counters. I sense her lightly concealed irritation. She would have done anything for the chance to give birth. In her mind, it's an opportunity to prove your mettle, to be a superhero for a day.

"Yeah, well." Leah shrugs. "Can you guys buy me the breast pump?"

Adrienne takes Leah's phone. "You did research? This is definitely the best one?"

Leah nods. "I read that breast milk can help prevent SIDS."

Sudden infant death syndrome is on Adrienne's mind a lot. She's told me numerous times that 2,500 babies die of it every year. One day they're here, and the next—poof—they're gone, the life sucked out of them in the night. It terrifies her, the idea of no known cause, the randomness, the giveth and the taketh away. She puts the kid in something called a wearable blanket that zips up the front, so he can't get tangled and accidentally suffocate, and in his crib, he needs to be on his back *at all times*. She says it just that ominously. I think part of why she likes the night feedings is that it's regular confirmation he's still alive.

"I'll order this for you," Adrienne says. "Overnight shipping."

I want to ask how much overnight shipping is, whether a cheaper model might do the job, if she thinks we're made of money, why she can't just put her ass in the car and go get the pump, but I know the most important answer. She hasn't left Leah alone with the kid yet, and she's too worried about germs to take him out anywhere, except for the fourth-day pediatrician visit. "The well-baby check," Adrienne called it. He was well, though I know Adrienne hated having to take a backseat to Leah, who still has all the legal rights, including medical.

"You've got this under control," I say, "so I'm going. Have a good one."

I'm just grateful for work. No one there knows I even have a kid, and I'm planning to keep it that way. I called out sick for a week, and since then, it's been business as usual. I don't have anyone asking me how it's going with the new baby or waxing rhapsodic about the wee ones. I don't feel any pressure to lie and say he's the best thing that ever happened to me.

The kid sleeps eighteen hours a day, so he's hardly providing entertainment. He spits up every time he eats, so much that it's hard to imagine he's getting any nourishment, and he craps like eight times a day. Adrienne doesn't want me changing the diapers but she wants me to "be a part of the process," meaning I have to hover by the changing table and consult about the size and color of his "poop," as she insists on calling it.

She has a specific way of doing everything, and she utters it with absolute certainty. I guess she feels sure, since she's consulted five different guides to caring for your newborn. She says that we can never ever, even for a second, turn our back on the kid while he's on the changing table. I tell her he can't roll yet, where's he going to go? "That's how accidents happen," she says, "when you think you know what they can't do, and then they surprise you."

Funny, I could say that about wives, too.

She swears she can tell all his different cries: "I'm hungry" versus "My diaper's wet" versus "I'm hot or cold" versus "I have gas" versus "I am in some sort of inexplicable pain that will not be soothed no matter how long you rock me or sing to me." Fortunately, we don't hear that last one too often; we dodged the colic bullet. But when he is upset, even if her ministrations don't seem to be making a damn bit of difference, she'll never put him down.

"I'm going to hold you no matter what," she tells him. Over and over, she says, "I'm here with you."

It seems futile, but the one time I said that, she glared at me. "He needs me."

"What does he need you for right now? He just keeps crying."

"He needs me to know he's not alone."

I say, he needs to know he can pull his shit together, alone. That's what life is, and he might as well start learning it now.

But I don't say that out loud.

Adrienne thinks you can't spoil a baby. You can't make him needy, he's needy by definition; he's utterly dependent. Eerily enough, she seems to think that's one of his best qualities.

CHAPTER 21

Adrienne

Gabe and I haven't had sex in two weeks, not since Michael came home. The amazing thing is, I can't seem to care. No, it's more than that. I find it liberating. Not having sexual urges to be satisfied frees up so much time and energy, all of which I can devote to Michael and to getting things done on his behalf (like his laundry; he is a spit-up king, that one!). It feels like I've spent my whole life in service of Gabe and his needs, and I didn't even realize it until now.

I know I didn't actually give birth to Michael (how could I miss that?), but I feel like I'm still living in an oxytocin haze. I suffer with his every cry; I'd do absolutely anything to keep him safe and happy, just like a real mother would.

I need to stop thinking like that. I am his real mother. I am his mother, period. Write it one hundred times on a blackboard, until it sticks.

But having Leah here sometimes throws that into question, which really bugs me. Generally, she ignores Michael. At first, she was in her room all the time with headphones on so she couldn't hear him. I think she spent a lot of time sleeping. Whether her body was just wrecked or she was depressed, I couldn't tell. She wasn't sharing.

She's since undergone a transformation. She used her allowance to buy workout gear and high-tech sneakers, and she goes for long walks around the neighborhood. She's gone for hours.

And now that Leah's mood is lifting, now that she's trying to cook healthy food she picked up at the Whole Foods on her walks, now that she's filling the refrigerator and freezer with the milk she's pumping out prodigiously on her new industrial-strength machine that cost us $400, now that she's hanging out in the living room and lifting dumbbells while she watches TV alongside Michael and me, now that she's *taking over the house* basically, she's started noticing that—surprise!—there's a baby around.

I wouldn't say she seems truly interested in him, or that she looks at him anything like how I do, but she's definitely begun looking right at him. She hasn't made a move to pick him up, and I'm not sure what I'd do if she did. I can't stop her, since she's contractually allotted two hours a day. But I'd have to figure out something. I don't want him getting confused. I don't want *her* getting confused.

Feedings were, briefly, the joy of my life. They aren't as much fun now that it's her milk. Sure, I still love Michael's closeness, but it's different somehow. The milk is a reminder of what she can provide that I can't; it's a reminder of biology, and I'm helpless in the face of that.

I hate being helpless.

This morning, after his diaper change, he was up on the table and I was cooing at him and he was looking like he wanted to smile at me (he's too little to actually smile yet). Leah stuck her head in the room. "Do you need anything from the store?" she said, like the perfect little houseguest. She was in her workout clothes. Less than a week of exercise, and I can practically see the pounds flying off her in tiny sparks.

"No, thank you." I had my eyes back on Michael. He was belted to the table but you can never be too careful. Accidents can happen in a second.

I thought Leah would just say, "Bye," and continue on her way out the door. But instead, she came and stood next to me, over Michael. She smiled down at him. "Hi, little guy," she said.

Get out! I wanted to yell. *Do not talk to him!*

The urge was so strong that it felt nearly biological. Yes, nearly—I can come close, but no cigar.

Leah playfully pulled on Michael's foot, and I could see the pleasure crossing his face. Can he tell that Leah is somehow special? Then she bopped out the door, like she's oblivious to her own power.

It's time to feed him again. Then he'll nap against me for a while, and later, I'll transfer him to his crib so I can get some things done. It's surprisingly easy to never leave the house.

It feels safer this way, with Michael and me cocooned at home. I ordered a stroller but I haven't tried to use it yet. The thought of driving with him terrifies me. I know the car seat has to meet certain standards, but what if I somehow buckle him in wrong? What if someone sideswipes us and he's sleeted with broken glass?

Better not to chance it. He's so tiny, and all he really wants to do is eat and rest and be loved. No reason to leave the house for that trifecta.

He's drowsing against me when there's a knock at the door. Mel. I almost forgot she was coming over today.

I get to my feet slowly and transport him to his room and into his crib. He doesn't stir. Part of me loves that, how undisturbed he is, and another part thinks, It could be SIDS! I reach down and put my hand in front of his mouth and nose for the comforting heat of his breath. The part of me that thinks about SIDS is the same part that feels like I don't deserve him—not his purity or the happiness he engenders. I shouldn't get to love like this.

Mel knocks again. I stare down at Michael and his sweet bald head (it's already becoming more spherical, he's cuter by the hour it seems like), and I don't want to leave him. I want to sit in the glider beside his bed and watch him. I want to feel my bounty. If I don't answer the door, eventually Mel will get the message and go.

No, that would be mean. He'll still be here, I remind myself. He's not going anywhere.

When I answer the door, Mel hugs me tight and long. "I'm so excited for you!" she says, and I know it's the truth. Mel doesn't measure her excitement in tablespoons; in her worldview, there's plenty to go around.

She looks at me, and I see a touch of surprise. It's my outfit. I'm in yoga pants and one of Gabe's long-sleeved T-shirts. I'm dressed like I can't fit into my usual clothes, like I'm the one who gave birth. It's a pleasing fiction, but in her look I'm reminded that it is a fiction. I'm not postbirth; I'm merely slovenly. Then there's my hair. It takes too long to do a full blow-dry when I need to be at Michael's disposal. So I've gone au naturel: glop in a bunch of product, and let it air-dry wavy and wide.

"Come in!" I tell her. She squats down to pick up a large basket wrapped in plastic and tied with a blue ribbon. "That's really sweet of you. You didn't need to do that."

"I wanted to."

We go into the living room and sit on the couch. I notice some spit-up that needs cleaning, so I throw a burp cloth on top of it. She beams at me, as if she's a proud mama herself.

"How's school?" I ask. "How are my kids?"

"I'm sure they're doing great. At least, I haven't heard about any problems." She makes a face that says, Let's talk about *you*! But I'm at a loss for words. I don't know how to begin to explain the changes in my life, and in me. "You're a *mother*! How amazing is that!"

"It's pretty amazing." It is, yet I find myself forcing a smile. This is all so unbearably awkward. Mel seems to belong to another time and place, or I do.

"So cute," she says, gesturing toward Michael's vibrating chair, with the small stuffed birds that dance above his head. I miss him already, just looking at it. "Open your present." She thrusts the basket toward me.

Mel's a whole shower all on her own: Onesies, bibs, hats, washcloths, towels, a quilted changing pad, a stuffed lamb . . . and nearly all of it is monogrammed. Gabe is going to shit. Or it'll act as shock therapy and he'll finally get used to his baby and his brother having the same name. After all, it was his suggestion.

"This is fantastic," I say to Mel, sincerely. "Thank you so much."

"I figured the good thing about shopping after he's here is that I can personalize it."

I run my finger over the onesie. Michael. An angel's name, just like Gabriel.

"Do you call him Mike, or Mikey?" she asks.

"Never."

"I don't know why people need nicknames anyway, when their names are only two syllables long." Good old Mel, always loyal. "I can't wait until he wakes up so I can meet him."

"It'll be a little while. He went down for his nap right before you got here." I don't know what I'm supposed to do with her for an hour or two. There are no more presents, and I can only fondle cloth for so long. "So who replaced me at school?"

"Yolanda Brewer. Do you know her?" I indicate no. "She seems okay. She's experienced."

"Do my kids like her? Are they happy?"

"I think so."

"I bet Jorgenson's glad I'm gone." A congratulations card came from the school, full of well-wishers, signed by everyone from administration to the custodial staff, and the troll had written her name, nothing else. But she can't hurt me now. Michael's the only one whose approval matters.

"Let's not talk about school," Mel says.

"Is there something you're not telling me?"

"Just that I got my pink slip. Not a big deal. They'll probably rehire me." She refolds a towel. "Let's talk about you. You and Michael. And Gabe. Is he totally thrilled? I bet he was hoping for a boy and got his wish."

I want to talk about Gabe's reaction to Michael about as much as she wants to talk about her pink slip. It's something I try not to think about. He's going to come around. How can he not? Michael's an angel.

But then, I can hear Gabe saying, so was Lucifer, once.

The front door opens, and Leah walks in, a grocery bag in her hand. It seems impossible, but her stomach looks even flatter than when she left. She looks four months pregnant now, and, with her cheeks rosy from exertion, extremely pretty.

Mel seems startled. Leah smiles over. "Hi," she says, "I'm Leah."

"Nice to meet you." Mel's eyes flick over to me questioningly: You've got a nanny who exercises during her workday?

Leah stretches her arms above her head, showcasing her tits. Lactating suits her. "I had a killer run."

"Leah gave birth to Michael," I say when the silence is too fraught.

"Oh." Mel smiles at Leah. "You look great."

"I'm getting there. The breast-feeding helps."

"Breast *pumping*," I say.

"Right." Leah looks just a little bit smirky. Sometimes I get the feeling that she likes making me uneasy. I don't get why. I've been nothing but kind to her. It's not like she can see inside my head.

Mel looks from Leah to me and back again. It's like she's one of those dogs at the airport sniffing for drugs.

"I need a shower," Leah says. "See you."

Once she's gone into the bathroom and shut the door, Mel moves closer to me. "What the fuck?" she whispers. It's maybe the second time I've ever heard Mel swear.

"It's kind of a weird situation."

"Yeah, you can say that." Her tone is full of uncharacteristic irony. "That girl is hot!"

"I'm hot, too." Well, not at the moment, not in Gabe's T-shirt, not with this hair, but typically, I'm hot. Mel makes a good point, though. I'm dressed like a new mom, and Leah—in her form-fitting workout gear—is definitely not.

"What's she doing here?"

"She lives with us."

There's no mistaking Mel's shock. "In your house? I didn't think it worked like that. I thought she has the baby and then goes back to where she's from."

"It can work a lot of ways." I'm trying to sound breezy, but she's making me nervous. Unlike Hal Grayson III, Esquire, I believe that Mel really has my best interests at heart. Also, Leah is almost back to her fighting weight, while I haven't been to the gym in almost three weeks. I might still have some old Tae Bo DVDs around somewhere, and Michael does sleep a lot.

"How long is she staying?"

"Only a year."

Mel's jaw actually drops at that.

"It's going to be fine," I say. "It's already fine. She barely looks at Michael. All she cares about is getting her body back. You heard her, that's the reason she pumps her milk."

"Doesn't that bother you? She's his mother, and she lives in the house with him and barely looks at him?"

"She's not his mother," I say fiercely.

"Sorry. I meant—"

"And no, it doesn't bother me. In her mind, she's already given him up. They just happen to be sharing a house."

Mel is visibly struggling for words.

"Thanks for the gifts," I tell her, "and thanks for being concerned. Maybe you can come back another day when Michael's awake."

"You know me, Adrienne. I'm a total optimist by nature, and I don't like to judge, but something is wrong with this picture."

I'm trying my best not to hear her.

"Adrienne," she starts, but I stop her.

"Another day."

Once she's gone, I feel distinctly unsettled. I turn on the TV and flip through the channels. It's almost the halfway point in Summer

Jackson. Gabe thinks the show makes the world seem ugly, all the women and children kidnapped and murdered. I told him sometimes it turns out the women just walked off and started new lives, like runaway brides.

But that is the minority. Mostly, awful things have happened to them. Very occasionally, a man disappears, but that's an even smaller minority.

"The minute someone goes missing, Summer's sure it's the husband or the father," Gabe complains. Ninety-five percent of the time, though, she turns out to be right.

Summer is a former prosecutor and, she says, a crusader for truth. She wants justice for all women and children (and the occasional man). Since she can't be over thirty, it's hard to imagine she actually has much experience in the legal profession. But she couldn't be expected to languish in a DA's office looking like she does, a gorgeous African-American with the proportions of a Barbie doll.

I know Summer's a venal, ambitious ratings grabber. But I've always found her show compulsively watchable. I love a whodunit. Sure, it's mostly just the husband or the father, but sometimes a suspect comes out of left field. Sometimes you get a big surprise. Even if you don't, there's the satisfaction of watching someone pay for their crimes.

Since Michael, though, I don't enjoy Summer in the same way. I think it's because he makes me so acutely aware, all the time, that bad things can happen to good people. Now I watch her show because I have to keep a step ahead, because I want to know what people are capable of, because—as Summer says—knowledge is power. Since I don't leave the house, Summer has become my friend.

"This is Joy Ellison," Summer says, indicating the screen behind her. I stare at the picture: a woman with chin-length dark hair, head thrown back playfully. The photo was taken by someone she loved, or was at least sleeping with. I always feel a tiny bit disturbed when Summer presents her latest missing woman, but this time, it's way stronger. I have Michael now, and so much more to lose than ever before.

"Joy's thirty-one years old," Summer continues, "and was last seen in Denver, Colorado, five months ago. Yes, that's right, five months ago. No one reported her missing until now." She looks into the camera meaningfully. "Her estranged husband, Brad Ellison"—the screen shot changes to a photo of a man with scraggly facial hair and a baseball cap holding a beer can aloft—"just reported her missing."

Oh, Brad, I think. You're in for it. You're about to get the Summer Jackson treatment.

Summer explains that Joy wasn't working and had no local friends in Denver. Brad was living in another state, doing "seasonal work" (another meaningful look from Summer). "Apparently," she says, "he and Joy were out of touch. None of her family members had heard from her either, not for months.

"Five months, to be precise. The police are estimating that she disappeared in early December. That's when she stopped paying rent, failed to pay any utility bills, and there were no more posts to Facebook, where she'd previously been an active user. According to her landlord, people 'skip town all the time.' So the potential crime scene has been cleaned out and rented to a new tenant." What that means to me: no clues, no forensic evidence. Does Summer even think about what kind of life leads to the situation she's describing—no job or friends or anyone to care about you, no one to even report you missing for months? No, Summer's too busy focusing on her prime suspect, the husband.

I have this crazy thought: Could anything go so wrong in my life with Gabe that he'd try to get rid of me? I know I'd never do it to him—well, never say never, but really, I never would. Gabe knows he couldn't shake me off easily; he couldn't just walk away and leave. So would he ever think the way out is to make me disappear?

I obviously need to get out of the house, if I'm having thoughts like this.

But I don't feel crazy, that's the funny thing. I'm crazy for Michael, and terrified of losing him, and yet, I'm also somehow more clear-eyed than I've ever been.

All these years, somewhere inside me, I've felt a small flicker of fear at the remote possibility of losing Gabe. Strangely, it's absent.

Joy's face is back on the screen, with Summer promising to follow the story closely and keep us updated. I'll be watching.

CHAPTER 22

Gabe

Remember to support his head," Adrienne says, admonishing me, "always!"

You'd think I was swinging the kid around like a caveman with a club instead of trying to hold him. Trying to "bond," as Adrienne calls it. But bonding is damn near impossible with her hovering and screeching.

Of course he starts crying. What else is he going to do when he sees Adrienne all freaked out?

It makes me want to hand him back all the same. He doesn't want to be held, I don't need to hold him. We're in agreement, Michael and me.

I can't get used to that name, and it's stenciled everywhere. I've got a burp cloth over my shoulder, and there's a blob of something on top of the "ha." Ha is right. My life's become a cosmic joke.

"Take him back then," I say. "You know you want to."

"No," she says. "I want you two to bond."

"It doesn't seem that way," I mutter. I thrust him into her arms and walk out of the room (I can't get used to calling it a nursery, either).

I go out to the garage to shoot pool, but when I pick up the stick, I find my hands are shaking. I sit down with my back against a leg of the table and try to calm down. Any minute now, she'll come looking for me. She'll tell me she's sorry for being so preoccupied. Obsessed. She'll tell me I'm the one she loves more than anything.

The first time she said that, I was nineteen, and she was sixteen. She was dating Michael. Months later, he was dead. Sometimes I still feel like I killed him. Adrienne says that's crazy, we're all responsible for our own actions, I wasn't the one who slashed Michael's wrists (vertically—if it had been horizontal he might still be here). She says I couldn't have known. But she's wrong. She couldn't have known; I should have.

When my mother died, he was only four. Sure, she didn't choose to leave, but how can a four-year-old get that? She's here and then she's gone and he's on his own.

I tried to look after him. He was a scrawny, pasty kid who kept to himself, wasn't any good at sports or at socializing. He was destined to get picked on. I was good at all that stuff, and I stood up for him. No one was going to bully my little brother, not while I was around.

The problem was, I couldn't always be around. And Michael didn't necessarily want my help. One time, he mumbled something about how if I didn't talk back to those kids, they'd just leave him alone, like I was making him a target.

Maybe he was right, I don't know. I just know he was a motherless kid with a father who'd checked out and a bitch for a stepmother, and who was going to look after him if I didn't?

I think he resented that things came easy to me. I didn't have to study much to get good grades or practice much to be on varsity teams. I didn't have to try hard to get girls.

Michael didn't seem to try at much, though. If life was a competition, he was going to sit it out on the sidelines. His big interest was watching people and drawing them (sometimes realistically, sometimes in caricature). That's how he first got together with Adrienne. Once she realized he was sketching her, she came over and demanded to see it. It must have been good, because she became his first girlfriend.

I was proud of him, getting a hottie like that. But that was about all I thought of her. She was a junior in high school, and I was working my way up at the Chevy dealership. I thought I'd go to college, just as soon as I figured out what I wanted to study. I was smart enough for it. Life was nothing but possibility.

Adrienne was Michael's girl, and it didn't even occur to me that I'd mess that up for him. I was glad he finally seemed happy.

I can still see them together on the living room couch: Michael in his thermal with a band T-shirt over it and ripped jeans, and Adrienne in her tight tops and tiny skirts. They didn't make sense, on a visual level. They didn't even belong at the same lunch table. But she was so sexual, and he was learning that he could be, too. One day, I caught them fucking on that couch, and I told Michael afterward that it was cool, nothing to be embarrassed about, but why didn't he just use his own room? He said that the couch turned Adrienne on more.

So she was doing everything she could to make sure I'd notice her, and eventually, I did. Adrienne's hard to ignore.

In my defense, I never even flirted with her. Because Michael was my brother, and he was finally happy, and I was not going to ruin that.

But of course, I did ruin it.

Adrienne says I never stole her. She's not property.

But I saw Michael's reaction when she flirted with me, how hurt he was. I'd spent my life trying to protect him, and then when it counted, I let him down. It said something about me. When I had nothing to lose, I could stand up for him. Put a good-looking woman into the mix, and then it's every man for himself.

He wasn't a man, though. He was a sixteen-year-old kid, and I was his brother. Because of me, he's in the past tense.

Adrienne's not coming to the garage. She's probably still sitting in the nursery. If it's because she thinks I'm sulking and wants me to work it out on my own, that's one thing. But I've got a feeling she's barely registered that I'm gone.

Michael, you win. You're finally the one she wants more than anything. I deserve that.

By the time I go back into the house, it's after midnight. Adrienne's asleep in our bed for the moment, though the kid will probably howl in an hour and she'll leap to her feet, eager to be of service. So now's my chance.

I knock on Leah's door. I have no idea what time she's going to bed these days. Sometimes we all eat dinner together, but it's often in silence. I feel like I don't know anyone in this house anymore.

I knock again, a little more insistently, and I hear a faint, "Come in." When I push the door open, Leah's sitting on the air mattress, her back against the wall, with what look like two megaphones attached to her areolae, milk dripping into the attached plastic bottles. A quilt puddles around her lower body.

"Sorry, sorry," I say, my face crimson as I spin around.

I hear her laughing. Did I imagine the "come in"? Or did she say it, not caring what I'd see? Or wanting me to see?

"It's okay," she says. "I'm just about done anyway." I realize the sound I've been hearing is a gentle suction—her breasts being vacuumed out—and now she's turning it off.

"This was a bad idea anyway." What I mean is, I shouldn't be here to vent about Adrienne to Leah, of all people. But Leah, of all people, would get it.

"No, let's talk. I've missed you." She sounds so genuine, and those are just the words I've been aching to hear. Wrong woman, mind you, but sometimes you have to take what you can get. "You can turn around now."

She finishes tying her robe. I try not to look at her tits. They're inescapably real, after what I just witnessed. I'm hard for the first time in a long while.

She pours one bottle of milk into the other and tells me to wait while she puts it in the refrigerator. I notice how at ease she seems, like men are in here every night at the tail end of her pumping session.

"Have a seat," she says, patting me on the shoulder on her way out. The only place to sit is her air mattress, the blankets askew. The generalized feeling of wrongness becomes more specific. I'd be sitting on another woman's bed, with that woman in just her robe. Adrienne definitely wouldn't like that.

Adrienne didn't care that I spent the last hour by myself in the garage. She's not too concerned with my whereabouts these days.

I sit.

Leah returns and gets under the covers. Her robe has loosened to hint at cleavage. Accidental? I can't tell. But there's no way to miss that she's getting her body back in a big way.

She notices my noticing, and smiles.

I should go. She's getting the wrong idea. I'm just here to talk about my wife. But isn't that how things often start?

Not this time. I love my wife.

Isn't that what they all say?

I love my wife, but she doesn't give me enough attention. I love my wife, but does she still love me?

"I feel like a fucking cliché," I tell Leah.

She nods, like she gets it completely. I don't see how she could, but it feels good anyway. I'll take even a pantomime of understanding right now.

"She's in love with that baby," I say. "It's like she can't think of anything else. It's not normal."

"It's probably not normal that I barely think about him. What's normal, anyway?"

"Not this arrangement, that's for sure. Hal knows his shit."

She laughs, though I wasn't joking.

"Is this working out for you? Living here, I mean."

"It's going to." The set of her chin, that determined tone—it's so Adrienne that I actually feel like crying. I miss her that much.

"I don't know who she is anymore." Suddenly, I'm pissed. "She says she wants me to be closer to the kid"—your son, that's actually what she said but I can't bring myself to repeat that—"and then all she does is undermine me. She's got to be the authority on all things Michael. She criticizes the way I hold him, the way I change a diaper."

"You don't change diapers."

"Not anymore, I don't."

I know this is off-the-charts disloyal, and I should feel guilty for venting to Leah, but I'm too angry with Adrienne to care. I've been angry for weeks. But I can't tell her that. What would I say? "I'm pissed that you love our son so much"? "I'm pissed that he doesn't feel like our son, but like my brother reincarnated to screw me"?

"Are you okay?" Leah asks. Her hand ventures out from under the covers and inches toward me, serpentine.

I move my hand away. I'm not that pissed at Adrienne.

"I'm just trying to help. You seem like you're falling apart." She sounds defensive. "You're the one knocking on my door."

"You're right." Now that I'm here, I don't know what I hoped to find. She's offering me compassion, but apparently, that's not what I was in the market for. I got to see her tits, but that wasn't it either.

I can't meet her eyes. I feel ashamed, but of what? Of needing at all, maybe.

"I'm losing her," I say.

"No, you're not." A sage look crosses her face. "Change more diapers. Rock him to sleep. Let her see you trying. That's all she wants."

"Has she been talking to you about this?"

"No. But who wouldn't want that? You're supposed to, like, be a father."

Supposed to be. The words beat on me like a hailstorm. "But what if I can't?"

She's got no answer for that.

"Let's play poker," she says. "Spot me two hundred dollars."

It's the best offer I've had in a while.

Hey, Patty. I felt weird after our last conversation. Maybe I said too much. About Gabe and Michael. I just wanted you to know you're not the only one who makes mistakes. I wanted you to stop putting yourself down and placing me on some pedestal. And maybe I wanted someone else to know the whole story so I wouldn't have to carry it around all by myself anymore.

But I know Gabe wouldn't like my telling someone all that stuff, so when you meet him, please don't mention anything, okay? I know he tries really hard not to think about Michael at all because he feels so guilty. Sometimes I think I could let him off the hook if I just told him the whole story, you know, like if he knew who Michael really was and what Michael was really capable of. In his mind, Michael was some innocent lamb we led to the slaughter. While I know I did some fucked-up things in the name of love, I also know it wasn't like that at all. I mean, which is better—for Gabe to think bad things about himself occasionally, or for him to hate his brother forever? I'm just trying to look out for him. That's what you're supposed to do for the people you love.

I'm babbling. But please, keep it between us, okay?

Xoxo,
Adrienne

CHAPTER 23

Adrienne

Go big or go home, and I'm not going home—not to Leah in her spandex, pumping out her world-class tits and eyeballing my baby. She hasn't picked him up yet, and as far as I know, she only touched him that one time, on the foot. But the escalating nature of her involvement suggests I need to take precautions. She must have an iron will not to go near him, since he's totally adorable.

I can't take any chances. I need to start leaving the house with him, leaving her behind.

I've blown my hair out for the first time in weeks, and I put on a short sundress with a halter, since it's a perfect spring day. The dress feels almost like a costume, a relic from my former life. I don't need to display my womanhood this way anymore, when I've evolved into a fuller form of womanhood. But it's a little treat for Gabe. He got in bed late last night and I could feel him erect as a weather vane, pressing into my spine.

Maybe we'll have sex tonight. Or we won't. It's not that big a deal to me, which I take as another sign of my evolution. It occurs to me that some of my libido over the years has been a quest for reassurance:

I affirm my value for Gabe by fucking him silly; I do penance for whatever role I may have had in what happened to his brother; I keep us on an even keel. Our relationship shouldn't require that kind of maintenance. It should be stronger than that.

I strap Michael into his car seat, reading and rereading the instructions, double-checking the diagrams. He seems secure, but even so, I white-knuckle it all the way to the school. Unfortunately, the car seat is rear-facing so I can't see his face. I make lots of noises, hoping for a call-and-response, but he's silent. Panic nibbles at me until we're in the parking lot, where I see that he's fallen asleep.

He barely stirs as I put him in the BabyBjörn. He's used to that, loves when I wear him around the house strapped to my chest as I do household chores. Unloading the dishwasher is way more fun with his feet dangling over my abdomen and his happy gurgles in my ears.

I smooth my dress down over my ass, just in case I happen to run into Principal Jorgenson. I didn't clear my visit with her, and I'll do my best to avoid her. She'd just try to make me feel bad about myself, same as my own mother would have.

I stop off first at Mel's classroom. I've been feeling a little bad about how abruptly I ended our visit last week. She didn't deserve that, when she was just trying to look out for me. I'm not that good with people looking out for me. Leah and I might have that in common.

I knock, and Mel opens the door, smiling with such genuine delight that I know all is forgiven. "I wanted you to meet Michael," I say.

"Hi, Michael!" she says in a high, singsongy voice. She waves me inside. "Everybody, look! It's Mrs. T and her baby!" She doesn't need to tell them his name, it's written across his onesie and across the matching cap. There are tears in her eyes as she turns back to me. "He's just beautiful, Adrienne."

The kids surround us, and Mel makes them Purell their hands from the industrial-sized bottle on her desk before touching any part of the baby. They ask questions about him but none of them ask where he came from. As far as they're concerned, he's all mine, there is no other mother, and I bask in that. It's an impromptu party, and Michael and I are the guests of honor.

I'm in high spirits as I cruise down the hall to my classroom. The door is opened by a plain-looking woman in her late twenties, her hair in a messy bun at the nape of her neck. "Yes?" she says, unsmiling. She looks at me like the interruption I suppose I am.

"Ms. Brewer?" I say.

"Yes?" she repeats.

"Oh, right." I laugh. "We've never met. This is my classroom."

She looks down at Michael, who's drooling a little. I wipe at his mouth with a burp cloth.

"I'm Adrienne. Mrs. T, if you ask the kids. And this is Michael."

"I see that." Her smile seems forced. She doesn't like monogramming? Or babies? Has she been taking etiquette lessons from Jorgenson? She doesn't move out of the way.

"I'd love to see the kids. I've missed them."

"We're prepping for end-of-year testing. It's really not the best time." She probably didn't like that I called it "my classroom." She might be territorial. I get it. I'm no stranger to that emotion myself.

I toggle up and down, and Michael emits an adorable noise. I give her an ingratiating smile. "I really want the kids to meet him. It'll just take a minute."

She finally steps aside. I poke my head in theatrically. "Anyone looking for a babysitting job?" I call out to the kids, before entering the room more fully.

There are exclamations and excited talk. They start to rush to the front of the room, but Ms. Brewer holds up a hand and they halt immediately. It's an impressive display of classroom management.

"It's okay," I tell Ms. Brewer. "They can come up and check him out. I have Purell in the diaper bag."

I have worlds within worlds in the diaper bag, enough for any contingency I could encounter, so much gear that it's making my shoulder ache. I set it down on the floor.

"You said this would only take a minute," she reminds me. To the class: "Stay in your seats. You can ask a few questions, and then we need to get back to the lesson."

All I get is a quick round of show-and-tell? I can see that the kids are disappointed, too, that they really want to be up close. I forgot how little they are. Not when compared to Michael, but still. Now that they're in front of me, I miss them terribly, and it's like they're behind glass. I can't touch them, and they can't touch me.

I glance around the room. Ms. Brewer's given it a complete remodel, and none of my old displays remain. Now there's nothing but poster boards with addition, subtraction, and phonics. She's managing to take all the fun out of introducing the kids to my baby, so I can only imagine what she does to grammar and math.

"Go ahead," she tells them. "Ask your questions."

Understandably, they're stymied for the moment. What should have been enjoyable is now high pressure, a mini-test.

"This is Michael," I say, smiling around at them. "He's three weeks old."

"Do you love him?" Angie asks, stroking her left braid. Oh, Angie, sweetest girl.

"I do." I smile wider. "I love him very much."

"He's not really yours, right?" Dominic says. Such a predictable little asshole he is. I actually feel a swell of affection.

"He's really mine." I keep smiling. "Someone else gave birth to him, but he's my son." Dominic is scraping against an uncomfortable truth, though, one I try to forget: In an ordinary adoption, Leah would have signed her rights away weeks ago. Technically, legally, Michael is still her son.

He lets out a piercing scream. It's his hunger cry. "Sorry," I say to Ms. Brewer. "I'll just get his bottle." It's actually a bottle of ready-made formula; all I have to do is put the nipple on top. It didn't seem sanitary to bring Leah's milk, unrefrigerated. I prefer formula, anyway.

"We should wrap up," Ms. Brewer says. "We really need to . . ."

I ignore her and rummage in the diaper bag. Michael is increasing in volume. A couple of the kids put their hands over their ears, as if it's an air raid. After a few fumbles, I get the nipple on the bottle, and the bottle into Michael's mouth. It's an odd angle, with him in the Björn, so I unstrap him and let him rest sideways in my arms. It's his usual position, but he starts struggling against me. "Sorry," I mutter, my face beginning to flush. "I don't know what's wrong with him."

"Let's all thank Mrs. T for stopping by!" Ms. Brewer says.

"No, really, he'll be fine." I shift him and sing softly, but he's still resisting the bottle. Oh, shit. That's what it is. He's rejecting the formula; he wants Leah's milk, which he's been drinking exclusively. He doesn't want what I can give him. He wants what only she can provide.

I think of Dominic's comment—"He's not really yours"—and the blood pounds in my head, suffusing my face. I've been exposed as an imposter. I'm not the real mother; I can't even feed my child. They're watching me flounder, and fail.

"At home, he never does this," I say. Ms. Brewer is looking at me with sympathy.

I dimly remember the pride I felt in Mel's classroom. But it seems like another epoch, like it happened to somebody else.

CHAPTER 24

Gabe

It wasn't my best day at work, to put it mildly. I'm off my game. Selling cars is about sensing each customer's pulse points, and when and how to apply pressure. Before the kid arrived, I used to coast on my intuition. Now, to use a sports analogy, I've lost my flow.

On the one hand, work's still an oasis. No one knows about the kid, so no one can ask about him. But he intrudes anyway. I get these images of him with Adrienne—nothing that should be creepy, just generic mother-son stuff—and yet, I'm creeped. Then I realize that I'm actually the creep for thinking like I do. It's pretty hard to focus on anything when you're hating yourself.

Today I come home and there's Adrienne, sans kid, hair silky-straight, looking hot in a short dress, smiling and saying, "I made you dinner." The lights are low and there are candles on the table. I want to ask where the kid is, and where Leah is (are they actually off together? Is Leah babysitting?), but I feel like that might kill something. So I'm going to assume that Adrienne's got it all under control.

"I've been neglecting you," she says, twining her arms around my neck and looking into my eyes. It shoots right to my gonads.

"It hasn't been that bad," I say, because I can afford to be magnanimous.

She gives me a kiss on the lips that lingers, though she doesn't open her mouth. I guess she wants to have dinner first. That's okay, I can wait. All signs point to a sure thing.

We drink wine and eat pasta. I'm trying to hurry because who knows how long we've got before the kid has some need she has to attend to.

"I've been so wrapped up in Michael," she says, skewering penne and popping it in her mouth. I pause as she chews. I want to hear the rest of this. But it seems there's no rest. That's it, just an acknowledgment.

That's enough, though. Obviously, she's doing something about it right now. The kid's in his room, presumably, and I see the baby monitor is on the kitchen counter, not on the dining room table with us. She's letting me know it's going to be different from now on.

I put my hand on top of hers. "I understand," I say. "You're finally a mother. You did it."

She grins at me, but there are tears in her eyes. "We did it."

I wait to see if she's going to talk about the elephant in the room, in every room—she loves the kid, and I don't—but instead, she tells me about their first outing.

She makes it funny, focusing on how she dodged Principal Jorgenson and on the stick-up-her-ass sub, Brewer, and on the perils of trying to feed a baby in a Björn. I laugh because she *is* funny, she always has been, but I feel like something's getting left out. There's some underlying pathos in this story. I can see it in her face.

I finish off the last of the pasta and then the wine. I'm aware that we've been sitting at the table for a half hour, and we're on borrowed time. At any moment, that kid could wake up and cock-block.

It's a dilemma: Do I probe to find out what else happened, or do I stick with Adrienne's version?

She'll tell me when she's ready to tell me.

I grab the back of her neck and pull her toward me. We kiss like we're famished. Then we're heading down the hall. As we pass Leah's room, I think I can hear her voice through the door. So she is home, but who she's talking to and what she's saying, that's not my business or my problem. For the first time in weeks, it's all about Adrienne and me.

In the bedroom, we claw each other's clothes off. I feast on her, traveling from her neck to her nipples to her stomach and beyond. After a few minutes, she pulls my head up and guides me inside her. Missionary sex is fine with me. Better than fine.

I could come in seconds, it feels that good to be accepted into her body again, but I want us to do it together. We need to be aligned again.

But when I look into her eyes, there's a sense of vacancy. She looks—is it possible?—a little sad. She's wet and pulsing around me, and I want to take that as an answer. Maybe she's not totally here with me but that's okay. It's normal. She's supposed to be listening for her baby, it's what mothers do.

I don't want to think of Adrienne as a mother right now. Nothing could turn me on less.

Instead, I stop thinking of her as Adrienne. I let myself get lost in fantasy: She's a hot mom that I just met at the dealership, and her baby is down the hall so we need to be quiet, she needs to listen for him, but a part of her doesn't care because she wants me that bad. She saw me on the lot and said, "Him. That guy. I've got to have him."

Her fingernails grip my back, and I grind into her. She had to have me, above all else. It was all she could think about.

I don't look at her face. I won't look into her faraway eyes.

I'm all she could think about. All, all, all . . .

"Oh, God," I hear her say, over and over, and then I let myself go. It's like pulling the rip cord on a parachute and coming down to earth. The adrenaline, the plummeting, the landing.

I fall against her naked chest and heave. Barely a minute passes, and then, as if on cue, the kid starts to cry. Without a word, Adrienne gets up and yanks on a T-shirt and sweatpants. I watch her go.

I can't remember when, if ever, I've resorted to fantasy. But then, I can't remember seeing that look in her eyes. The elsewhere look. When we make love, all she wants is to be with me. So it wasn't just fantasy, it was memory.

But she is somewhere else, right now. She's in the nursery, feeding and rocking him. Soon, she'll be singing.

I could be there with her. Some of the distance between us is my doing. I've been afraid of the kid, imbuing him with some crazy supernatural power. He's not the ghost of my brother; he's a newborn baby. I need to get my shit together.

It's been a few minutes and he's still crying. Normally, he shuts up the second he sees that bottle.

I tell myself to get out of bed and go to her. She put in effort tonight, and now it's my turn. This might be one of his inexplicable crying bursts, and I should be there with her, with both of them. I can rock my son and sing to him, too. We can be a family, if I let us. Who's stopping me? Adrienne never told me to get lost; she never said she doesn't want me around. Sure, she nitpicks, but that could be a test. If I want my wife, I've got to reclaim her.

I do want Adrienne, badly, yet I can't seem to move. In my head, I hear that old Talking Heads song, the one about it not being my beautiful house or my beautiful wife. The one that goes, "My God, what have I done?"

I start coaching myself. Tough-love stuff like, "What kind of pussy doesn't take care of his own wife and kid? What kind of pussy hides out in his bedroom?" I'm channeling Coach Lake, my high school baseball coach. That guy was so scary, he got you to do things you would never have even tried. Come to think of it, he's got that in common with Adrienne, though their methods are diametrically opposed.

The crying's stopped. It's a good omen.

With Coach Lake's help, I manage to pull on my clothes and go to the nursery. The door is closed, and I think of knocking, but that might wake the kid. Michael, that's his name. I need to stop being afraid of it.

I push the door open as quietly as I can, and Adrienne is where I thought she'd be: in the glider, with the kid—Michael—sleeping against her. The empty bottle is on the floor, illuminated by the night-light. As my eyes adjust, I can make out what she's doing: She's trimming his nails with these tiny clippers. Trimming his fucking nails, like she's got all the time in the world. Like there's nowhere she needs to be, no one she needs to get back to.

I retract, pulling the door shut behind me. She never even noticed I was there.

CHAPTER 25

Adrienne

The whole time Gabe is inside me, I just know Michael is going to start crying. I try to forget, but how can you forget your heart? I can feel that he's almost awake, almost hungry—like a sixth sense, no, a maternal sense. I hang in with Gabe as long as I can, and then I speed things along, forcing my orgasm and, in effect, his.

Not even a minute later, it happens: Michael lets out his biggest, baldest cry. I get up and go to the kitchen for a bottle of milk, only to find that all the milk is frozen. Leah must have screwed up and stuck the day's stock in the freezer instead of the refrigerator. I can't substitute formula; I learned that the hard way. I'm cursing Leah, but more than that, I'm cursing myself. If I'd finished with Gabe sooner, or if I'd never started, I would have been ready for this. Michael wouldn't have to wait.

The thing that kills me about Michael is that he doesn't understand waiting. It all feels like life and death to him; he doesn't know I'll be there in just a minute, that I'd never let anything happen to him. I have to prove myself anew every day, every hour. I have to assert my reliability in the face of what, to him, is a daily fight for survival. He's memoryless. It's like the sequel to that Drew Barrymore movie *50 First Dates*. It's 50 First Bottles.

I hear him screaming and I'm hurrying, on the verge of tears myself, and finally, *finally,* I've got his bottle ready. I throw open the nursery door, and there's Leah, in the glider, with Michael in her arms. She's rocking slowly and stroking his hair. His face is beet red and furious, but she looks calm as can be. I stop dead in my tracks. She just looks so much like his mother.

"Since you were busy," Leah says. A veiled reference to Gabe and me, as if I were neglecting my baby in order to have sex? Or is she referencing the frozen milk? Did she do that on purpose to buy herself this little maternal moment? "I was keeping him company for you."

She doesn't leap up to hand him to me. She continues rocking. Obviously, it would be most expedient to simply hand her the bottle.

Michael is yowling. It's a Mexican standoff. Leah isn't reaching for the bottle, but she's not getting up either. She's going to make me ask for my own baby. It's humiliating.

"I can take it from here," I say.

She stands up and hands him off to me without a word. Then, as he suckles the bottle with greedy desperation, she loiters nearby.

I try to focus only on Michael and the fact that I'm the one sating him. The hand that holds the bottle is the hand that rules the world. It doesn't matter that it's Leah's milk that he craves. It doesn't matter that she's started taking an interest in him. It doesn't matter that she's next to us with a self-satisfied expression on her face, one that says, "See how good my milk tastes?"

Inside, I'm roiling, but I have to play it cool.

"He's starting to look like Gabe," she says. "Don't you think?"

"Not really."

"I heard somewhere that newborns start out looking more like their fathers. It's like some trick to prove who the dad is, because you can always tell who the mom is, but the dad, that's, like, not so obvious." She laughs. "Oh, right, Gabe's the one who told me that!"

I don't know why she's suddenly decided to get chatty. We've barely had a conversation since Michael was born. So I really don't know why she's talking about Michael looking like Gabe, and newborns looking like their dads. And I *really* don't know why Gabe was telling her that little fun fact. Or when.

"Trevor looks like Gabe," she muses, "and Michael looks like Trevor, so Michael looks like Gabe."

I rock Michael faster, trying to discharge the panic that's coming over me. I wonder how long Leah's been coming in here and sitting with him, if she's ever fed him his bottle while I slept on in the next room. Maybe she's even fed him from her breast. I'd have no way of knowing.

"I don't blame you," I say, "for wanting to hold him sometimes. For wanting to be close to him."

I'm lying. I totally blame her. She's the one who told me she 100 percent did not want to be a mother. She's the one who enticed me—letting me touch her stomach, giving me ultrasound pictures. She led me on. And now I love Michael so much that he's all I think about.

"It's not that I want to hold him," Leah finally says.

"What is it then?"

"I come in here sometimes when I can't sleep," she says, just above a whisper. "I like to watch him. It helps me relax." She looks at me quickly. "But I don't bother him. I don't pick him up or anything."

I didn't know Leah had insomnia. That doesn't seem to bode well for me. It suggests she might be having second thoughts. Earlier, I overhead her talking on the phone in her room. I couldn't make out the words, but her voice was low and earnest. Confidential.

"You're allowed to pick him up," I say. "It's in the contract." It comes out colder than I meant it.

Who am I kidding? That's just how I meant it. But I don't want her to know what I mean, not yet, not while she can hurt me.

The truth is, if Leah decided to take Michael away, she wouldn't just hurt me; she would kill me. There's no recovering from a love like this.

"No, that's okay," Leah says. "It's your job." She turns on her heel. "Good night."

In her wake, I'm so anxious that I need to stay with Michael extra-long. But I also need to do something, so while he sleeps, I start cutting his nails. They're so small that it's painstaking work. It requires focus, and that helps, a little. At some point, I look up, thinking I caught a shaft of light or movement or some sudden barely perceptible change, but no, it's still just Michael and me.

Realizing that there's no one else it could be, that Gabe doesn't come to the nursery of his own accord, fills me with loneliness. I thought we'd be doing this together. I thought Michael would be the sun we'd both orbit, astronauts on a shared mission.

I never thought Gabe would turn out to be so selfish. I assumed that after the baby arrived, his heart would grow, inflating chamber by chamber. If the Grinch's could, surely Gabe's would, too.

That's not fair. Gabe just hasn't hit his stride as a parent. Not everyone loves the infant stage. My own father wasn't much interested in me until I was a teenager, so I know that parents can be late bloomers, just like children.

I was in fifth grade when my father moved out. My mother said what she thought was the right thing: "He didn't leave you, he left me." But all that did was underline that I wasn't enough to keep him around. Either he didn't love me much, or he hated her incredibly.

I could understand hating her. I sort of did; with her critical remarks, there was never any pleasing my mother, not if you were me. Suddenly I was stuck with her full-time, full force. My father had muted a lot of her behaviors. She was so desperate to please him that he could tone her down with a withering stare. She'd shrink right before my eyes. I vowed that no one would ever have that kind of power over me.

Once he was gone, my mother's jabs toward me became overt cruelty. She probably resented that I hadn't been enough to retain him. Why she wanted someone whose feelings for her ranged from benign neglect to contempt, I'll never know. I do know that I'd never get her approval again, and after she found Gabe and me in her bed, she was relieved to finally have an excuse to turn her back on me for good. But that came much later.

So I was eleven when my parents divorced, and my mother ate until she became the Michelin Man, and my father took me to his house two weekends a month, where he'd read academic journals and I'd fend for myself. I can still remember how I felt in those years—like there was no place I wanted to be and no one who truly loved me. People like Mel say that my parents probably loved me a lot, they just weren't any good at showing it. Well, what good is love like that? When it comes to love, perception is reality.

I grip Michael a little tighter. When it comes to me, there will be no doubt in his mind.

But what about Gabe?

He'll come around on Michael someday, I know he will. My father did when I was a teenager. It became easier to hold his attention once I was attractive. Not that there was anything untoward in our interactions; he just seemed more curious about me. He liked to hear about my dating life, and I warmed to the attention, embellishing my tales to make him laugh. Meanwhile, my mother seemed angry that boys were interested in me, and though she hadn't raised me with any religion at all, she was newly puritanical. Sex before marriage was a sin, she told me sternly. If she ever caught me . . . She let the sentence go unfinished.

How many times did I have sex with Gabe in her bed before we got caught? Twenty? Fifty?

I was daring her to make good on her threat. I thought she might prove she loved me more than I realized. You win some, you lose some.

My sweet Michael, he's going to be a winner.

CHAPTER 26

Gabe

Raise," I say, tossing the chips into the center. I know I look like a dick, but I don't particularly care. That guy with the goatee has been getting on my nerves for the past hour. He looks young, like he's in college, and probably a good college, like Berkeley. He thinks he's so much smarter than the rest of us. For the most part, it's a working-class crowd at the Pyramid, and Goatee is obviously going to be white-collar. But you don't need a degree to play poker. Sometimes it only slows you down, makes you get in your own head too much, in your own way.

I'm definitely not playing in my head today. I'm full of testosterone, and so far, it's worked out. I've got a mountain of chips in front of me, more than triple my starting stack. I can afford to push Goatee around.

This time, he pushes back. "Reraise." I watch him carefully count out his chips. It's a big reraise, four times my bet.

I've always liked pocket sixes. He might just have ace-king. This is why it's called gambling. "Call."

The dealer starts to lay out the three flop cards. I stare at them, sensing that Goatee's eyes are on me, trying to read my reaction.

Four-four-six. I want to laugh out loud. I just flopped a full house. When you're hot, you're hot. He'll think that there's no way that flop hit me. How could I have called his reraise with a four or a six in my hand? Now I have to hope he has pocket aces or pocket kings. Then I can get his whole stack.

He leads out with a bet that's more than two-thirds of the pot. He wants to take it down right now, without seeing any more cards. Smells like ace-king to me—a hand that sparkles when you first peek at it and then dims fast.

Feigning reluctance, I call. He's got to be putting me on something like pocket tens, and he's wondering if he can run me out of the hand with another bet.

The other guys at the table are paying attention. It's shaped up into a real cockfight, and everyone loves those. They can sense that I don't like Goatee, and he doesn't like me. That's part of the fun. I *like* not liking him. I like this dose of controlled aggression, aimed at someone other than the true target.

I'd hoped the other night was a turning point. Adrienne said she knew she'd been neglecting me, and we finally had sex again, finally spoke in our native tongue. I assumed that her acknowledgment of neglect was a declaration of change, but no, she's gone right back to what she was doing. That feels worst of all. Before the other night, I figured she was too preoccupied with Michael to get what was happening. Fish can't see the water they're swimming in, right? But now I know that she knows, and she doesn't actually care.

There's that old saying: Lucky in cards, unlucky in love. So I guess I'm owed this run of luck, but when put that way, I'm not sure I want it.

The next card is an ace. He's so deliberately expressionless that I'm sure he's got ace-king, and he probably thinks I've got pocket tens, or at most, pocket jacks, and now he's taken the lead.

He makes another big bet. I can play it safe and just call, let him give away his money street by street, or I can go over the top.

I'm feeling over-the-top tonight. "All-in," I say, and begin sliding my rows of chips to the center of the felt.

Goatee looks surprised. It'll take all his chips to call. My play doesn't fit the hands he was putting me on. He glances at his chips almost mournfully, realizing he's probably beat but he's in too deep to back out now. His ego's on the line. After all, I could just have pocket queens. I could be bluffing.

He calls. The last card is a king, but it's not enough. He turns his hand over, and he's got two pair, aces and kings. I'm in no rush to reveal my hand—a real dick move, I know, the slow roll—and the table explodes. No one saw that coming.

"Lucky," Goatee mutters, and he doesn't mean it as a compliment. He means that I had no business calling his reraise in the beginning.

"I knew you'd go all the way with your hand," I say, "so if I hit, I'd take you for everything. Calculated risk."

"That's how you got that big stack, huh? Through calculated risks?" Goatee gives me a twisted smile. He wants me to know he doesn't respect me, no matter how many chips I have in front of me, even if a bunch used to be his. "Fish." He says it half under his breath, but he wants me to hear it.

Without even thinking, I'm on my feet. "What the fuck did you just say?" I've never taken poker personally in my life, but all of a sudden, I want to kill the little asshole.

Goatee doesn't move a muscle. Next to me is a short Latino whose name I've never learned, but we've played together for years. He stands up (he's all of five foot three) and puts a hand on my chest. "It's only poker," he says. "Sit down."

I deflate as quickly as I puffed up. The heat rises to my face. "Sorry," I say, to no one in particular, as I take my seat. I almost got myself kicked out of here because of some jackass kid. I need to get back under control, in every way.

Goatee pulls out a wad of cash for a rebuy. He won't look at me. I've got way more chips than anyone else here, but in his mind, I'm just a fish, an amateur coasting on luck. I want to tell him I've put in years at these tables and I'm not a lucky guy, not by a long shot. I shouldn't care what he thinks, though. He's just some college student blowing his parents' money.

Now, I wouldn't mind that kind of luck—being at the beginning of my life, not tied down, full of ideals that haven't failed me yet. I wouldn't mind a do-over.

As it is, I've got a kid I don't want (there, I said it) and a wife I love too much. Adrienne's like Chinese finger cuffs: The more I struggle to break free, the tighter the vise. It's probably always been that way, only I never knew it before. You don't dream about freedom until you realize you're trapped.

CHAPTER 27

Adrienne

I have a small cooler full of Leah's milk. The diaper bag is well stocked. Michael's looking great in his monogrammed sleep-and-play (what we called "pajamas with feet" when I was growing up). All I need is for Gabe to hurry up and finish shaving. He's moving gingerly, like a man with a hangover, but I know he wasn't drunk last night. He was out playing poker, and he says only a total idiot plays drunk.

While Michael and I wait in the living room, I put him on his stomach and watch him try to hoist his head. It's huge in comparison to the rest of his body but those seem to be typical newborn proportions. Someday, he'll catch up to his head. We all do.

I'm antsy because I didn't tell Leah we were going into the city today. She might want to come along, like a member of the family. That's why we need to get going while she's out for a run.

Gabe's taking so long, it's like he wants her to catch up with us. "Gabe!" I call. "Any decade now!"

Michael is getting bored of tummy time, as the books unfortunately call it. I put him in his vibrating chair while I go back through the diaper bag, making sure I didn't forget anything. I refold and repack, trying not to let my annoyance show. I like to look my best for Michael.

"Did you fall back asleep?" I shout to Gabe. In his vibrating chair, Michael startles. "Sorry, little one," I tell him, my voice soft as Brie. His eyelids begin to droop once again.

Since he's buckled into the chair, I decide I can steal away for a moment. I go into the master bathroom, where Gabe is standing with a towel wrapped around his waist, foam on his face, but no razor in his hand. He's staring down into the sink like he's in a trance.

Something's odd about this picture. "Are you depressed?" He might need to see a doctor and get on some medication to help him adjust to all the changes. He's never been the most adaptable guy.

"No, I'm shaving." He picks up his razor, but when he watches himself in the mirror, it's like he doesn't recognize his own face.

"This isn't a joke. You seem off."

"You want to go to the city, we're going to the city." He sounds weary as he drags the razor down his cheek. "Right?" His eyes meet mine in the mirror.

I put my hand on his shoulder. We're still looking at each other's reflection. There's a physical discord to us, like we don't fit together. One of these things is not like the other, not anymore. "What's wrong?" I say gently.

He seems frozen for a long moment, and then he says, "Nothing. Let me just finish shaving, and we'll get on the road. We're going to have a good day." There's a palpable resignation to him.

"You can talk to me." But even as I'm saying it, I'm thinking how long I've left Michael alone in his vibrating chair. He's not crying, but that's not necessarily a good sign. SIDS is silent.

I'm almost relieved when Gabe shakes his head slightly and rinses off his razor. "I'll be there in a minute."

It's not a minute; it's closer to ten. But I'm so grateful to see Michael alive and well in his vibrating chair that I refuse to quibble.

Most important, we still make it out before Leah gets home, despite all Gabe's lagging, despite his taking the time to write her a note telling her where we're going, when we'll be back, and that we're reachable by cell phone. You'd think she was our kid and we were leaving her alone for the first time with no babysitter.

I bite my tongue. I'm not going to blow this outing. Michael was born exactly one month ago today, and we're going to celebrate.

I sit in the back with Michael during the ride to the city. It only makes sense, since his car seat is rear-facing. He needs me next to him more than Gabe does. This will be his longest car ride by far, so I'm at the ready. I've got burp cloths, rattles, blankets, and pacifiers, not to mention the cooler full of milk.

"Slow down!" I tell Gabe.

"I'm only going eighty."

"With a newborn in the car."

"He's been alive a month. That's not all that new."

We never used to bicker like this. Even when we disagreed, it felt playful, sexy even. It was good to have differences—for me to be a woman and for him to be a man. Now it feels oppositional. Michael's polarized us.

Not that it's Michael's fault. He's a month old. Anything that's wrong is our fault. It's our failure to adapt. Well, Gabe's failure. I've taken to motherhood pretty well, even if I have to say it myself. Neither Gabe nor Leah has ever commented on my nurturing skills.

"Just slow down," I say. "Please."

Gabe swerves out of the fast lane, decelerating by ten miles in an instant. The tires don't exactly squeal, but they protest. I place a restraining hand on Michael's car seat and begin singing to him softly. He looks much more content than I feel. Gabe and I don't speak again for the remainder of the ride, but he doesn't attempt any more *Fast and Furious* maneuvers, either.

Even though Fort Mason's parking lot is crowded, Gabe spies someone going to his car and we get the spot without any trouble. A sign of good fortune to come, I tell myself. I know Michael won't remember, but I want his birthday to be special. I don't want it marred by tension between Gabe and me.

It's a gorgeous Bay Area spring day, though a stiff breeze is coming off the water. I readjust Michael's blue cap and momentarily fret that he'll be too cold in just his sleep-and-play. He doesn't own a jacket yet, but we're going to have to buy one if we keep up these San Francisco jaunts. I was going to put him in the stroller (as yet unused) but I figure I'll Björn him instead, for the body heat. Also, I love having him dangle so close to me, like we're on a tandem skydive.

Gabe has the stroller out of the trunk and is trying to figure out how to unfold it. When he looks up, he says, with faint distaste, "You're going to wear him?"

"He'll be warmer."

Gabe tosses the stroller back into the trunk with a clatter. "You ready then?"

I arrange a blanket inside the Björn. Then I smile at Gabe. "See, it's easier for us to hold hands now." I extend my hand and he takes it. We walk from the parking lot over to the long paved promenade along the water. The Golden Gate Bridge is slightly obscured by fog, but I can make out its long, curving piano strings. "It's Michael's first time seeing the Golden Gate. Most famous bridge in the world!" With my free hand, I grab on to his tiny one and point it in the direction of the bridge.

"London Bridge is probably more famous, but we've got more suicides." Gabe's tone is inscrutable, but it certainly doesn't match my happy tour-guide inflection. Then he chants, "Go, SF!"

I feel like he's mocking me, but I shake it off. It's Michael's birthday, and he's out for his first stroll with his parents.

I tug Gabe's hand and we walk along in silence. I want to tell Michael other tidbits, but I don't want to hear what Gabe would say about Alcatraz.

A couple of Rollerbladers pass us and they start grinning at Michael. I grin back. Most of the people going by can't resist a smile at him. Really, Gabe is the only holdout. On a bench, I notice a woman with a baby a little bigger than Michael. She's got a blanket arranged across her chest, but there's no mistaking her activity. Jealousy surges through me. No matter what I do, Michael and I can never have that.

I wish I could feel like I'm Michael's mother, completely. But until Leah signs those papers in eleven months, there will always be reasonable doubt.

I don't know who let go first, but Gabe and I aren't holding hands anymore. He stays close for a few feet, but then he starts walking closer to the water. I realize how much I want everyone walking by to regard us as a family, probably because I don't yet feel like we are one. As we walk, Gabe doesn't seem quite part of Michael and me. He drifts ahead or behind; he doesn't even seem to register the smiles Michael is attracting.

I feel like crying. On Michael's birthday! On his first family outing! This isn't me. Sometimes it's like I've had an infusion of post-partum hormones; if only I'd gotten to have the partum.

"Hey," I say to Gabe, with a brightness I hope I'll soon feel, "do you want to get some stuff for a picnic? The Safeway is right over there. Then we can spread a blanket on the lawn and eat." Michael can lie in the sun. But I don't say that last part. I feel like Gabe's still uncomfortable with the name. And the person connected to it. Both people, actually, past and present.

"Why don't we eat at that foodie restaurant back there? I could use a drink."

I wonder what about this experience makes him want to get liquored up. Then I picture him from earlier, looking at himself in the bathroom mirror, unseeing. I support Michael's head all the time; I can try to do the same for Gabe.

After a pit stop to get the car seat, we head for the restaurant. We're seated right away (another good sign, I tell myself, at a restaurant that's typically jam-packed). We're in the glass-enclosed back room, which juts out over the water. I feed Michael his bottle as I peruse the menu. Seasonal, locally grown, sustainable, vegetarian, vegan options—we're definitely in San Francisco. Gabe gives the menu a cursory glance and then focuses on the wine list.

The waiter is wearing the requisite hip glasses and wants to know if we have any questions about the menu. "You don't serve any hard alcohol?" Gabe asks. It's the question on every new father's lips.

I smile at the waiter like Gabe's just joking, though it's obvious he isn't.

"No, sir," the waiter answers.

"I'll have this one then." Gabe points at the wine list.

"That's only sold by the bottle."

"A bottle's good. We're celebrating." Gabe smiles. "The kid's one month old today."

The waiter smiles down at Michael, as if he's just noticed him. "Happy birthday!"

Michael's eyes are closed in fierce concentration on his bottle. "Thanks," I say on his behalf. "I'm ready to order. Goat cheese omelet."

"Excellent choice." He pivots toward Gabe.

"I'll have whatever's good."

"Do you like kale? And nettles? Because—"

"Kale's great." Gabe's manner is beyond dismissive. It's embarrassing. I'm sure the waiter is thinking we're some trashy bridge-and-tunnel family, which isn't far from the truth, at the moment. Except we don't even seem like a family.

Something's wrong with us. The patrons glancing over can feel it. The waiter can feel it.

Michael, at least, seems blissfully unaware. He falls asleep on his bottle as if there's nothing out of the ordinary. We are, after all, the only family he's known, the only one he's got. I hold him close for a few minutes, making sure he's really out, and then I ease him down to the floor and into his car seat. All the while, Gabe is looking out the window. Michael and I might as well not even be here.

He's ruining this. I can't even speak through my disappointment and fury. What I'd say, if I did—there might be no going back.

For distraction, I start looking over the wine list. I realize that based on where Gabe pointed, he must have bought a hundred-dollar bottle of wine. "What were you thinking?" I whisper to him angrily. We have to pay Leah every month; we have all Michael's expenses. We didn't need a whole bottle of wine. I won't be having any; I drink when I'm happy.

"It's house money," Gabe says loudly. "I made more than eight hundred dollars last night playing poker—"

I motion for him to lower his voice. We are not sitting among the kind of people who make their money playing poker. We have a sleeping baby at our feet. "Just because you won money," I say in a low, tight voice, "doesn't mean you have to blow it. You know we could use that money."

"It's not your money." His voice isn't as booming as before, but the next table can still hear every word. "It's my bankroll."

I bend down to check on Michael before I answer. "This is not the conversation I want to be having. It's inappropriate."

He scoffs at me. "*Inappropriate?* We used to hate that word. We hated the people who used it, the ones who want to tell everyone how things are supposed to be done." He leans in and finally turns down the volume in order to growl, "Who are you?"

If I didn't know better, I'd think he was already drunk. But there's no way he drove us into the city drunk. Is there?

The waiter returns with our $100 bottle of red. I smile at him with extra force as he uncorks it and pours a small amount into Gabe's glass for approval. Gabe takes it down like a shot and says, "Perfect." Then in a cockney accent, "Please, sir, may I have another?" The waiter is twenty-five, at most. He doesn't get the reference, or Gabe.

He fills both of our glasses and asks if we need anything else. I thank him profusely, as if to make up for the domestic drama he's having to witness.

"See," Gabe says when the waiter's gone. "That's what I mean."

"What are you talking about?" I say through clenched teeth.

"You're not acting like you. Ever since the kid got here. You're worried about what everyone else thinks, how they see us. You've become . . . conventional." The way he says the word, it's like he thinks he's really putting the screws to me.

Since Michael came along, I do find myself wanting to be conventional. I want to be a regular mom, able to breast-feed my son on a bench instead of bottle-feeding him some other woman's milk. I want to be taken for a regular family. But Gabe's making that impossible, and I can only hope I'll be able to forgive him for that.

That night, I'm holding Michael and watching Summer Jackson. I've been recording all the episodes on DVR, not wanting to miss any of the Joy Ellison coverage.

I should feel more, seeing her. But with the life she lived, of course this day would eventually come. I'm following the developing story with a strange mixture of avidity and detachment. Is it because Michael is consuming all my emotion and I can't spare any for Joy?

Summer is interviewing Brad Ellison, who is apparently too stupid to realize that he's the prime suspect. Has he never watched the show before? Sure, she's being nice now, taking it easy on him, but that's just to get him talking. Later on, she'll use clips from the interview to dismantle his story. There's nothing she loves more than using a husband's own words against him.

"So you were in Arizona, doing day labor?" Summer confirms.

"Right." He's in his early thirties, and his hair is shellacked with gel. He's wearing an ill-fitting button-down shirt. You can tell he's used to T-shirts and jeans and baseball hats. He seems thrown to even be sitting across the table from a woman as beautiful as Summer Jackson. She must have flown him in for this, instead of just doing it by video. That means she really plans to nail him later.

"How long had you and Joy been separated?"

"Going on a year."

"But you still love her, I imagine?" Summer uses her most syrupy, sympathetic voice.

"Yeah, I love her. She was a great girl. I mean, she's a great girl." Uh-oh, that slip is going to cost him. "We just weren't getting along, is all. I always wanted to get back together with her someday. I thought that if money wasn't so tight . . ."

"You fought a lot over money?"

"We didn't fight a lot." He shifts in his seat, starting to wonder if Summer is his ally after all. He couldn't have watched a few episodes on YouTube? "But when we fought, yeah, it was about money. Joy got stressed out a lot. It would put her in a bad mood."

"Whose idea was it to separate, Brad?"

"We both thought it was a good idea. My buddy told me that I should come to Arizona, that the work didn't dry up as much in the winter, so I moved there."

"You actually moved there in the summer, though, isn't that right?" He nods. "Did you and Joy talk often in the beginning, and then it petered out? Or did you fight and decide not to talk for a while?"

He obviously realizes she's emphasizing fighting, but there's nothing he can do about it. "We decided not to talk for a while. That's why I didn't know when she went missing."

"Do you think it's possible that she just took off? That she started a new life?"

"Maybe. She had a lot of dreams."

He's clearly lying.

"Or," Summer asks, "do you think someone did this to her? Someone made her disappear?" Long pause.

Now's when he's supposed to get misty. But he can't manage to do it. "I think someone might have hurt her, yeah. That's why I'm here. I want to ask people out there to come forward with information. I know a lot of time's passed, but if you know something, you need to tell the police. You need to help us find her."

Summer leans in toward him. "You know that with so much time passing, the chances of her being alive—they get slimmer."

"But you find people with your show, don't you? I mean, that's what you're doing here, right?" Oh, Brad, that kind of naïveté is going to be your downfall.

Summer affects a modest look. "I do my best, Brad."

I thought we ended this convo last night.

Sex does not = agreement, Wren.

What do you want me to do? Cut her off?

No. Pull back. She's not going to be Aunt Patty. That was just a fantasy.

Don't tell me what's what.

But you get to tell me what a shit father I'm going to be?

I shouldn't have said that. I said sorry.

I don't want to fight again.

Me either.

But this isn't over. You can't trust Patty.

You don't know her like I do.

That's why I can see clearly. She was acting weird.

She's my best friend.

You've never said that before.

Maybe I knew you would just judge her, like you are.

Not fair.

True, though?

She's a disaster. She'll drag you down. She'll drag us down. I don't trust her.

You already said that.

You won't hear me.

It wasn't a good visit, but that doesn't mean you can't trust her.

She barely saw us. When she did, she was acting weird.

You already said that!

It's not just about us. It's about the baby.

It's going to be an open adoption. She's going to be in our lives.

But we can control how. How close she gets. Hal said so.

I'm not going to screw her. She's had enough of that.

Between her boss and her cat and carjackings and

muggings and whatever else.

Don't make fun of her.

I don't think it's funny at all.

This is supposed to be about the baby. Right, Wren? When did it become about Patty? She's a grown woman.

Let's talk about this later.

You're mad.

If you don't trust her, you don't trust me. You don't trust my judgment.

You still there?

You didn't say you trust me.

You didn't say you trust me either.

CHAPTER 28

Gabe

That stuff is amazing," I say as I walk in the room. "I can't even smell it."

Leah pauses, holding her paintbrush high in the air, but she doesn't turn. "The consistency isn't great, but I can work with it."

"Spoken like a true artiste."

I'm still looking at her back, but I can see by the way she stiffens that my comment was not well received. Seems like I can't say anything to a woman today without her bristling. Of course, my behavior at the veghead restaurant was pretty extreme, even before I polished off a $150 bottle of vino. Come to think of it, the wine only improved me, but by then, Adrienne was about done. She was staring fixedly at the view—by which I mean, the kid.

I sit down on the floor near where Leah is working, carefully balancing the glass of bourbon on my knee. "It's going to be beautiful," I tell her. "That's really a special thing you're doing for him."

"Thanks. Can you even tell what it is yet?" She sounds slightly challenging.

I squint at the wall. There are swirls of green and lavender, painted with great care, but no, I can't exactly see it yet. Adrienne and I already approved the sketch, which is a slight variation on the tattoo Leah plans to have someday. It's going to be an enchanted forest. I take a guess: "That's the peacock tree."

She turns, her face as soft and open as I've ever seen it. "Really? You can see it already?" I nod, because when a woman is looking at you like that, what else can you do? It's the most alabaster of lies.

She tilts her head, paintbrush extended, as she studies the wall.

"You look pretty when you work," I say. She makes no response. "I know the paints were expensive. I can reimburse you."

I see her stiffen again. "If I wanted you to pay, I would have asked you for the money. This is a gift."

"Thank you."

"A gift for Michael." The subtext: not for you, or for Adrienne. It stings. I mean, I knew she wasn't going to be handing out presents to Adrienne any time soon, but I thought she and I were friends. She was the one who said it first, that day we went to Lands End. She said a lot of things that day.

I take a long sip of the bourbon. Calm down, I tell myself. Only an asshole would use any of that against her.

"Well," I say, "thank you on behalf of the kid."

"You need to stop that." She's dabbing a bit of darker green around the edge of one of her swirls. "His name is Michael. You suggested it, now get used to it."

In the past, when she's admonished me, it's been flirty. Not this time.

"Or give him a nickname," she continues. "But 'the kid' just sounds . . . I don't know, it sounds shitty. It sounds like he's just an annoyance to you." She spins and regards me. "Is that all he is?"

I find I can't meet her eyes. The truth is, he's a lot more than just an annoyance.

My problem could be solved right now. I tell Leah that this was all a mistake, I thought I could be a dad but I just can't, and she'll have to look for new adoptive parents. It occurs to me, for the first time, that she's still assessing Adrienne and me for fitness as parents, and that she loves Michael. This year isn't only about Leah's getting her feet under her in a new city but about making sure that she picked the right parents for her son. Maybe she loves him more than she expected to. Maybe she's having second thoughts.

But if I confess the truth to Leah, if I tell her the whole story of my brother, and she hightails it out of here with the kid under her arm, Adrienne's going to know. I would have destroyed what she thinks is her greatest chance at happiness, her chance at family. There's no way she'd ever get past that.

"I love him," I tell Leah, knowing I have to make it true. For Adrienne's sake, and for my own. "I'm just having a hard time showing it."

Leah studies me an extra few seconds. "You probably shouldn't have named him after a dead guy."

There's a lump in my throat. "Probably not."

"I bet you can legally change it. There might even be a grace period. Like, I don't know, a ninety-day money-back guarantee, sort of. You should start thinking about different names."

"That's a good idea. I'll talk to Adrienne about it."

Leah smiles, happy she's solved my problem. She likes me, I know she does, and she wants this arrangement to work out. She's laying down roots here, painting this mural. This is supposed to be her baby's home.

I stand and walk up behind her. "You really are talented," I say in a low voice. I watch her stiffen up, but it seems different this time. She's definitely not offended.

Adrienne knows I'm in here with Leah, and I like that. Let Adrienne think it's "inappropriate," her new favorite word. Some jealousy could do her good. She's got Michael cuddled up in our bed right now, and she needs a reminder that I exist.

I'm not proud that I got drunk on our first family outing and that Adrienne had to drive us home. But the old Adrienne would have laughed it off. She would have told me I was a very bad boy; we would have come home and she would have given me a spanking and all would have been fine with the world. But it's like she's changed the terms of the marital contract without consulting me.

She was mad that she had to drive home (she's a feminist, why's it a man's job to do all the driving anyway?), and she was stressed out because we were stuck in traffic leading up to the bridge; she couldn't see how the kid was doing because he was facing out the back window. I offered to ride in back with him, but she told me no, and then she was bitching because she couldn't tell what was happening. I told her if he had a problem, we'd know; he's not exactly subtle, with that bleat of his. She shouted, with zero irony, "SIDS is a silent killer!"

I said, "I'll get in the back with him right now," and she said, "No, you've done enough." I still don't know what that meant. Then she started talking to herself about how the day's ruined and worst of all, we didn't even get any pictures. As if the point of having an experience is to capture and Facebook it, that's how conventional she's become. When I called her conventional, she didn't even deny it. "It's not like I want to remember this anyway," she said. But I know she will.

"Well," I say to Leah, "good night."

"Good night." She doesn't turn but I feel like it's intentional, like she can't. I could just be overestimating my magnetism. I want to think that someone still finds me attractive in this house.

I drain my glass during the walk to the kitchen. Before I get into bed with Adrienne, I'll brush my teeth and use Listerine. Adrienne will probably still smell the booze on me, but at least she'll know I cared enough to try to conceal it. She'll know I was thinking of her.

The lights are low in our room, and Adrienne's sitting up against the headboard. She turns off the TV as I come in. The kid is across her lap, facedown, and she's rubbing his scalp gently. It's her latest obsession with him. He's just developed this dandruff-type condition called "cradle cap." It's probably flurrying down on our sheets right now. Adrienne says it usually clears up on its own, but despite that, she seems to love tending to it. She's been washing his scalp every day and massaging it with her fingertips. It's like it gives her life purpose. My unvoiced suspicion is that's because she doesn't actually have that much to do. I mean, he sleeps upwards of eighteen hours a day, and all she has to do is feed him Leah's milk. With all his spitting up, there is a lot of laundry, but it's not like she has to go out and beat it against a rock. I don't really understand how her days pass. Reading about SIDS, probably.

I climb in bed next to her. "Leah doesn't want us to pay her back for the paints," I say. I think Adrienne will like that, but instead, her eyes narrow.

"Why's that?" She sounds flinty.

"It's a gift."

"We don't need her gifts. It's a business arrangement."

This is not the way I was hoping the conversation would go. We're supposed to be making up. I probably shouldn't have had that extra finger of bourbon.

"Michael's going to sleep in here with us tonight," she says. "I don't really feel comfortable with him going back in the nursery."

"It doesn't even smell. Go in and check."

"I'd rather not." She eyes me sideways. "I thought you were playing pool. What were you doing in the nursery?"

"I wanted to see how the mural's coming along. I think it's going to be really nice. She's working hard on it."

"I'm glad she has a hobby. But as soon as she moves out, we're going to paint over it." She stares at me hard. "Do not tell her that."

"I wouldn't." Though it doesn't seem right to me, painting over the gift his mother left for him, especially when I can see how much it means to Leah. But I'm not going to say that tonight. "Listen, I'm sorry about what happened at Fort Mason. Let's try again next weekend. I've got Saturday off. I'll be on my best behavior."

Adrienne is watching her fingers stroke the kid's head. "He only turns one month old once."

I move in a little closer. "I know. That's why I'm sorry." I wish I could tell her what I just did for her, how I lied to make sure we can keep the kid that I don't actually want. I wish she could begin to understand how much I love her and the lengths to which I'd go. She did it once for me; I'm just returning the favor.

I want to tell her about my conversation with Leah and realizing that the name "Michael" was a mistake. It's keeping me distant from the kid. For one thing, it's making me want to call him "the kid." There must be some way we can legally change the name. Even if it's a pain in the ass, so what, it would be worth it. I need to bond with my son. I need to stop cringing internally every time I think "my son." I just can't be a father to my own brother, especially given the history. Adrienne, of all people, should understand that.

She pushes against my chest, saying with disgust, "You're drunk." Then, icily, "Do you need to go to AA? Is there a problem we need to discuss?"

"No," I say, leaning back against the pillow, closing my eyes, willing sleep to come quickly and mercifully. "We've got no problems."

CHAPTER 29

Adrienne

Yes?" The kid on the doorstep—there's no other word for him, he's gangly, with raggedy clothes and dark hair that needs combing—is looking agog at Michael. You'd think he'd never seen a baby before. "Can I help you?" My intonation is really saying, "Get off my doorstep." I hold Michael a little tighter, even though I could kick this guy's skinny ass, easily.

"That's him, huh?" the kid says.

"Excuse me?" Michael and I have just woken up from our nap, and I'm still a little fuzzy, but my chest starts tingling. I've got a bad feeling.

"Leah's baby. My baby, I guess." His mouth turns down in a gruesome expression, like the word hurts, and then his lips peel back in a huge grin. "Shit, that's so funny!" He actually laughs.

If I weren't so tense, I'd want to laugh, too. There's something about this kid—Trevor—that's infectious. Well, I hope he's not literally infectious. He does look awfully pale. Am I supposed to invite him in? The last thing I need is both of Michael's biological parents darkening my house.

"Leah's not home," I say. I glance down at Michael in my arms. He's looking at Trevor with fascination, maybe because Trevor is looking back with equal fascination. They're an oddly matched set. I guess it's true that newborns resemble their fathers more. But Trevor doesn't much resemble Gabe. Trevor is no John Stamos. Dark hair, dark eyes, dark eyebrows, but he's so skinny he's concave. How did he land a knockout like Leah? He must have one hell of a personality.

"I actually wanted to talk to you first. Adrienne, right?" I nod. "And your husband's . . ." He pauses. "Don't tell me, I can get this. Grant, right?"

"Gabe."

"Shit." He looks genuinely disappointed. "I thought I was getting better with names. Faces, though, I'm good with those. I, like, never forget a face. I definitely won't forget yours! You look like you could be Leah's mom. That's so rad."

Her older sister, I want to say. "You wanted to talk to me?" I bounce Michael up and down in my arms, but he seems perfectly content. He likes Trevor, probably because of how expressive Trevor's face is and all his broad physical gestures. Trevor is what my mother would have called a "character"; I might preface that with the word "cartoon." But he does have a weird kinetic appeal.

"Can I come in?" He holds his arms up, as if to show he's clean, I can search him. There's an army duffel over his shoulder that has all sorts of pictures scrawled on it. He sees me looking. "Leah did those. She's wicked talented. She's doing a mural for this little critter, right?" He leans in slightly toward Michael and goes, "Boo!" Michael lets out a happy gurgle. "That is one lucky critter."

"Why's that?" I say sharply.

"Because Leah's talented, and she made him, so he'll probably be talented, too. And because you obviously love him a lot, and you live here." He eyeballs our cul-de-sac. "I mean, I wouldn't, like, live here, it's just not me, but it looks like a nice place to grow up. All loving and whatnot."

"So you just wanted to see where he's going to grow up? That's why you're here?"

"Can't I come in?" His hands are still in the air, like this whole conversation has been a stick-up. I finally nod.

He follows me in. "Take your shoes off," I say, testing for compliance, and he immediately unlaces his boots—Doc Martens–type, like Leah's—and leaves them by the door. "Germs," I explain.

"I getcha," he says. "I'll wash my hands, okay?" He strips off his jacket and has a black band T-shirt underneath, like the kind Gabe's brother used to wear. His jeans are tighter than in the old days, but there are the same artsy slashes through them. Goth fashion has made few advances.

At the kitchen sink, he lathers with dish detergent up to his elbows. You'd think he was going into surgery. He's funny, this one.

I spread a blanket out on the floor and put Michael down on his stomach for tummy time, facing away from the couch where Trevor will sit. I don't need Michael watching Trevor any more, getting too attached. Michael stretches his arms out and tries to lift his head. It doesn't work, but you can see he's making progress.

"What's dude doing?" Trevor says, sitting at the other end of the red velvet couch.

"It's called tummy time."

Trevor chortles. "Tummy time! That's awesome."

"Does Leah know you're here?"

"Here's the thing. I've been miserable since she's been gone. I can't eat, I can't sleep, I can't play video games. It sucks, man. Woman, I mean." He smiles at me. He sure doesn't look like a depressed person. "So I'm here to surprise her."

"And then what?"

"And then she comes back with me. It'll be, like, a done deal when she hears that I can't live without her. Yeah, she's got this California bug or whatever, but she knows we belong together."

It's almost too good to be true. With Trevor's help, Leah could be out of here way sooner than a year. But I'm waiting for the catch.

"I know you like having her around," he says. "I know she's been, like, giving him milk, and it's not like you can just buy breast milk on eBay. Or maybe you can. You can find action figures from, like, the nineteen sixties on there, who says you can't buy some chick's breast milk?"

"You already signed away your parental rights," I say.

"Yeah, I know. What would I want them for?"

I look down at Michael, not wanting him to overhear his father's disinterest.

"No offense to the little dude," Trevor adds. "He's pretty cute. He looks like a spider monkey or something. But I'm not going to be somebody's dad. That's, like, wackadoodle time."

"How old are you?"

"Twenty. Listen, I just need a place to crash until I can convince her. We won't fuck on your couch or anything." He looks over at Michael. "Sorry. We won't *make love*." Trevor sounds like there are air quotes in every other sentence. "If we've got to do it, we'll go out to my car."

"You drove here from Rhode Island?" I stand up and pull back the curtains from the window. There's a busted-looking Lincoln that's probably older than Trevor, with some sort of graffiti picture on the side. "Let me guess," I say. "Leah tagged your car."

"I asked her to. She's got mad talent."

I stare at him, hard. I've got to figure out if he's for real. "So you broke up with Leah because she got pregnant—"

"No, I told her I couldn't be a dad. She got mad and broke up with me. She said if I couldn't get my shit together, I could fuck off." His eyes flicker to Michael. "Sorry. I got to work on my language. I'm not used to having a kid around."

"But you didn't want to be with her while she was pregnant."

"Because she was mean! She was always trying to convince me we could be parents together, and when I said no, I'm not, like, dad material, she'd get *pissed*. Like, scary pissed. I never knew before what hormones could do. When I see a pregnant woman coming now, I jump out of the way." I have to laugh. "No, seriously."

Michael gurgles, like he's laughing along with us. He's trying to turn his head to see us better. I squat down and spin him around. He should get to be a part of this conversation, especially since it's going so well. Trevor could be the answer to everything.

"So you and Leah have been talking on the phone," I say.

"Yeah. She sent me a selfie. She's looking hot again already."

"Hot enough for you to jump in your car and drive thousands of miles?"

He grins. "Leah's worth it. We were amazing together. Everyone could see it. It's like, we just took a detour for a while and now we need to get back on the road."

"The road to Rhode Island," I say. "Because you can't live in California."

"I've got five brothers and sisters. I'm in school."

"Isn't the semester still going?"

"I turned in all my papers early. I started driving here as soon as I finished my last final. I've got to get her back, Abigail."

"Adrienne."

"Sorry. But I remember Gabe."

I wonder what Gabe will make of Trevor. I wonder what he'll make of what I'm about to say. "You can't stay in her room. You have to sleep on the couch." He nods, suddenly alert, waiting for the rest of my terms. He's perceptive enough to know there's more. "You've got to stay out of everyone's way. Michael wakes up early, so you've got to get up early. You need to clean up after yourself." He continues to nod. "I don't know what Leah's told you, but she doesn't really touch Michael." If you don't count whatever she's doing behind our backs. It occurs to me that Trevor might know. He could be valuable in more ways than one. "I wouldn't think you'd need to touch Michael either, since you're not here for him, right?" Another nod. "So just respect the boundaries, okay? I'm going to help you get Leah back."

He smiles. "Yeah? That's awesome!"

"People in love should be together. That's how I've always felt." I turn on the TV. It's time for Summer Jackson, which means it's also time for Trevor's next test. Can I still go about my business with his being here? Is he capable of shutting his mouth?

Summer catches all the viewers up on Joy Ellison's story—thirty-one-year-old woman disappeared from Denver, estranged husband didn't report her missing for five months, with no mention yet of a secret or untoward past—and then says, "Tonight I'm bringing you an exclusive scoop: Brad Ellison had a girlfriend in Arizona, and we have her, live!"

"Damn," Trevor exclaims. "That news anchor is hot!" Summer is looking particularly fetching in a white suit that offsets her caramel coloring.

"She's not a news anchor," I say. "She's a former prosecutor. She covers missing-persons cases."

"But first," Summer says, "we've learned that in February 2011, when Joy and Brad Ellison had been married only two years, he was arrested on a domestic violence charge. Now, remember, Colorado has mandatory arrest laws. That means that if the police go out on a domestic violence call, an arrest will be made. The victim cannot drop charges; only the state can decide whether to press charges. In this case, they did not press charges. We have tried to obtain a comment from the district attorney's office, but they have not yet responded."

"So this show is, like, educational?" Trevor asks.

"Not exactly," I say. "Shh." He does.

"We have also learned," Summer continues, "that Joy had several hospitalizations during the course of her marriage to Brad Ellison. When my producers contacted Brad about this, he stated that 'Joy could be clumsy.'" Summer raises an eyebrow slightly before going on. "She went to a different ER each time and always gave the same reason: 'accidental slip and fall.'" If she raised her eyebrow any higher, she'd be a circus performer. "We happen to have Granger Hill with us tonight, who is a psychiatrist with a specialty in domestic violence, as well as a longtime victims' rights advocate."

"So the husband did it?" Trevor says. "He killed her?"

"Sure looks that way," I say.

Summer and Granger engage in some speculation as to why the different emergency rooms, whether Joy could have been ashamed or coerced into lying to protect her abuser, and if women can lose the ability to have children after an attack (as Summer had previously reported that Joy was infertile). They manage never to say Brad Ellison's name, which might be how they can avoid defamation charges. I'm always amazed how Summer's show rides that edge, and that I've never heard of any lawsuits against her from wrongly accused boyfriends, husbands, and fathers. But then, she is a lawyer herself.

I never knew about the domestic violence in Joy's past. What else did she keep secret? Summer might find out for me.

After a commercial break, Summer does a split screen with the Arizona girlfriend. She's peroxided and heavily made up, and she's clearly pissed at Brad Ellison. "I didn't even know he was married until he told me he was going on your show," she says. Summer gives a knowing nod. Nothing these men do surprises her. "I threw his ass out, you better believe that."

"Were you together at the time of Joy's disappearance? In November or December?"

"He was practically living at my house, with me and my daughter." The girlfriend shakes her head angrily. "I can't believe I trusted him! He's such a liar."

"During that time, did he work consistently?"

The girlfriend snorts. "Are you kidding?"

"I'll take that as a no."

"He had his own apartment. This crummy little studio. But he kept most of his crap at my place. And he had a gun, did you know that?"

"He has a gun permit on file."

"Honestly, I think he did it." The girlfriend is fuming. Summer is realizing that she's got a somewhat unreliable witness here, and it's time to wrap up the interview.

"Just one last question. Was there any unaccounted-for time in November or December?" The girlfriend looks confused. "Did he leave your home for a few days at a time? Were there periods of time when you couldn't reach him around the holidays?"

"Oh. Yeah. There was a time when he didn't come over for three straight nights. I was like, What's the deal? Are you screwing around on me? He was like, No, I'd never do that. He said he was just working late and he was tired, so he wanted to stay home."

"Have the police asked you about his whereabouts?" Summer loves when she can scoop even the police.

The girlfriend shakes her head. "But I'm going to call and tell them."

Trevor starts laughing. "That guy is in deep shit. I would not want to be him."

With what I know of Joy, no one would.

CHAPTER 30

Gabe

I knew it was coming. I didn't meet last month's quota, and that's one of the deadly sins as far as Ray is concerned. I arrange my face into what I hope is a reasonable facsimile of caring.

" . . . even now," he's saying, "you're barely listening." The whiteboard behind him shows the inventory, with the sales that have been made this week; my name is scarce. "You've always been one of my best. 'No one closes like Gabe,' I used to say. Now you can't close a fucking door."

Ray's a transplant from Long Island. Like me, he's been in the Bay Area for years. When he's chewing someone out, his East Coast cadences return with a vengeance.

He doesn't like this part of the job, chewing people out. That's rare, in my experience. A lot of times guys get into management just for the privilege of gnawing on other guys' asses. Women might, too; I just haven't encountered any women managers. Selling cars is still largely an old-boys' network.

"Are you sick or something?" Ray asks. "You got cancer?"

I shake my head.

"See, cancer I can understand. But just failing to sell, failing to *scramble* at the end of the month—that I don't understand. Everyone else is finding a way, any way, to make a deal, but not you." His eyes bore into mine. "You too good for the business all of a sudden?" He sounds oddly hurt. I'd say it's a new tactic, a manipulation, but Ray's never been that kind of manager either.

"It was one month," I say. "I'll get my sales up."

"So far"—he gestures toward the board—"it's not looking good."

It's a week into the new month. It never looks good. Now's when we post our fewest sales and largest profit margin. I'm tempted to do the old car salesman's lament: The business isn't what it used to be, everyone's got an app telling them what we paid for the car; they come in like we're about to exploit them when really, it's the other way around. The customer is squeezing the life out of us. Our profit margin is lower than practically any other industry you can name, and yet, we're the ones with the bad rep. We're the snakes in the garden.

Sure, it's true, but Ray doesn't want to hear it. He's well aware. My job is to adapt and to work magic. Charm them so they don't see where we're eking out our profit, whether it's the trade-in or the financing; if it's the end of the month, take the hit and sell the cars at a loss, but you gotta post on the board. Only post. I forgot the cardinal rule, and now I've got to look into Ray's disappointed face.

"I'm on it," I say. I don't like disappointing old men, especially Ray.

He doesn't seem satisfied, and I don't blame him.

I just can't seem to give a shit. Obviously, Adrienne and I need my income more than ever. Her six weeks of paid family leave are ending soon, and then she's got nothing coming in for the rest of the summer. We're hemorrhaging money, between Leah and the kid. I might be able to supplement with my poker winnings. I've been running hot lately.

But that's not the way to think about it. You can't count on winning, no matter how well you're playing. There's always a random element. You can make all the right moves and still get unlucky. Some guy has four outs in the deck, and he hits on the river. It happens. I don't have the bankroll to ride out a string of bad luck.

"Something's wrong with you," Ray says. "You want to talk about it?"

"Problems at home. Nothing I can't solve."

"Adrienne's a good woman. She loves you."

Ray hasn't seen her lately. He doesn't know about Michael. All he knows is that the end of the month came and went, and everyone else scrambled to make deals, and I couldn't muster the energy.

I used to like my job. There was adrenaline in the sale and a rewardingly profane camaraderie with the other guys, the kind that can only result from a unique algorithm of competition, testosterone, and empathy. We're all in the trenches together, we get it like no one else can, but we're not entirely on the same side. With the economy as it is, there aren't enough customers to go around, so sometimes, you've got to take some friendly fire.

But since the kid, I've been keeping to myself. I've got a secret and I don't want anyone trying to razz it out of me. If I stop to think, it hurts a little, that they don't seem to miss me more. Maybe Gloomy Gabe just isn't so approachable. Or maybe they don't miss the numbers I used to post. Less for me means more for them. The pie is not infinite.

I don't know if Ray's just being kind or if he's really failed to notice that my numbers have been decreasing incrementally for the past year. The adoption process has been sapping my strength, like Samson getting his hair cut an inch at a time. Now it's been hacked off, shorn by Michael. I'm practically bald.

"You sure you don't want to talk about it?" Ray says.

"Pretty sure."

"You're telling me you're going to get it together? Can I quote you on that?" I nod and head for the door to the showroom. "Don't think I've forgotten about that black RX either." My hand's on the door, and I don't turn around. "That's rookie shit, Gabe. You're better than that."

I open the door and walk into the showroom. I used to be better than that, than selling a car that's already been sold, than having to go back to my buyer and tell them I fucked up, I can get them a silver RX, let me just check the inventory, no, wait, we don't have that one either, just wait, I'll be right back . . . They didn't wait.

The talk with Ray should have energized me. He's putting me on notice, and I'm the breadwinner for a whole family. Adrienne, Leah, a kid . . . how did this happen? I still can't wrap my brain around it. It makes me feel like I'm in the densest San Francisco fog, and I hear voices in the distance, but I just can't follow them home.

I wander the lot. There's a young guy graduating college in a couple of weeks eyeing a car he's got no business owning and no intention of buying today or tomorrow, probably not for years. But I let him take up my time. In fact, I insist on it. At my behest, we take a long, long test drive, and then I get him into the dealership and over to my desk. I run numbers. I take them back and forth to Ray. The kid looks starry-eyed, shell-shocked. I know the feeling.

"I'm going to give you a great deal," I say. "I'm going to take care of you."

But he's not buying, and he doesn't know how to tell me. The thing is, I already know. I've known the whole time. He's the equivalent of shuffling papers on a desk. He's busywork.

"Go home," I finally tell him. "Think it over. Talk to your parents." He looks at me gratefully, a mouse set free from a trap, and goes.

"You couldn't close?" Ray asks when he stops by my desk.

"He's coming back tomorrow with his parents," I say. "They're big money, I think. Dad's a corporate lawyer. It's going to be a graduation present."

"All cash then? No financing?" Ray squints at me. "No trade-in?"

"Don't worry. I got this one, I'll make it good." I smile confidently, and just then, my cell rings. I glance down. "Adrienne." I look at Ray meaningfully. He remembers our conversation, *problems at home,* and backs away.

"Hey, baby," she says. When did her "baby" start to feel like an affectation or a trick?

"Hey, baby." When did my "baby" start to feel like mimicry?

"How's your day going?" It sounds dutiful. She's playing the good wife.

I stare out at the lot, streamers spinning in the breeze like pinwheels, and think what to tell her.

She doesn't wait for my answer. "I'm having a crazy day here. You won't believe who showed up." Then, to the kid, "You sweet wittle . . . ," followed by a whole sequence of gobbledygook. I never thought she'd be one of *those* mothers. But he loves it, eats it up; it's the only thing he can keep down.

"Who showed up?" I finally break in.

"Trevor."

"You've got to be shitting me."

"No."

"You told him to get off our property, right?"

She laughs, though I definitely wasn't joking. "What are we, the Hatfields and the McCoys? Should I have gotten my shotgun?"

"For Trevor, yeah, I'd say a shotgun's what he deserves."

"If it weren't for him, we wouldn't have Michael."

I'm not even touching that one.

"He doesn't seem that bad, actually. You should meet him."

"You have *got* to be shitting me."

"He's out with Leah right now. They're talking. They've been talking, Gabe. She's been calling him."

I rub my temples, feeling a headache coming on. "This is not good."

"No, it's great. He wants to take her back to Rhode Island with him. Not in eleven months. Right now."

"He's not good people, Adrienne."

"He can get her out of our lives sooner rather than later. That's what I care about." Her tone turns harsh. "What is it you care about?"

I see Ray is standing inside his glass box, watching me.

"I can't be on the phone. Ray's on my ass for last month's numbers."

"That doesn't sound like Ray."

"You calling me a liar?" It comes out, unbidden.

She's quiet for a second. "Who are we becoming, Gabe? I don't think I like it."

I didn't know she even thought about it. It's a start, at least. "I don't like it either."

"Then let's get her out of our house, and we can go back to normal. Help me. Help Trevor."

Was her wondering about us just a way to hit me with the sledgehammer? She's trying to subdue me. "What is it you're asking me to do?"

"Let him stay with us, on the couch. I told him all the ground rules. He'll stay out of our way. He agreed to everything."

"Of course he did! That's how any master manipulator would play it." I can't believe I even need to tell her that.

"It won't be more than a few days, a week tops." She lowers her voice, like we're sharing an intimate moment. "Leah and Trevor have been talking three times a day. You should have seen her face when she came home and he was in our living room. She's completely in love with him."

"Then she needs a shrink! She needs some self-esteem! That guy . . ." I see that Connor is staring at me from the showroom floor. Now I lower my voice, but it's not because of the friggin' intimacy. "I don't want that garbage in my house."

"You're not understanding me," she says crisply. "She wants Trevor, and he wants her. And I don't like the way she's been with Michael lately, like she's getting attached. So what we need to do is play Cupid to two young kids in love." Her tone shifts, so that instead of crunchy autumn leaves, it's melting snow. "There are worse jobs, right? It's a win-win."

I'm not trying to be Leah's dad, but I know a lot more about Trevor than Adrienne does, and I care about Leah way more than Adrienne does. Leah's going off with some psychopath and leaving me behind with this woman that I barely know anymore—that's not how I'd define winning.

"If she goes, we become ourselves again," Adrienne says. "That's what I want. Don't you want that, too?"

More than anything.

Just the sight of Trevor's tricked-out emo car makes me want to start throwing punches, especially since I can tell that's Leah's paint job. It seems pretty fucked up to drive around inside her canvas after the way he treated her during the pregnancy.

I have to force myself into my own house. I'm pissed off at all of them, really: at Trevor for being the asshole he is; at Leah for getting sucked back in, despite the asshole he is; at Adrienne for not caring what an asshole he is and exploiting the situation for personal gain. The good news is, I'm neutral on the kid.

Michael. That's his name, don't wear it out.

Suddenly, I can hear all the schoolyard taunts: "First day with the new feet, *Michael*?" "Is that your face or did your neck throw up, *Michael*?" "Retard!" All of that got leveled at pale, silent, perpetually tripping Michael. The real Michael. My Michael. I protected him, until I didn't anymore. Adrienne would say I couldn't, but she's hardly objective.

Adrienne meets me at the door, the kid—Michael, Michael, Michael—resting against her shoulder. He's somnolent and drooling. I can't ascertain the current state of his cradle cap through his monogrammed hat. That increases his attractiveness, for sure, though it doesn't make me want to reach for him. I can hear Leah laughing, full-throated. I've never heard her laugh like that before. In the middle of the night, we had to keep it muted.

"Leah and Trevor are cooking for us," Adrienne says. "Nice, right?" It's her public voice. Then she adds, much lower, "It's all going great. At this rate, they might elope by the weekend."

She steps aside and I enter. The house doesn't feel like mine, doesn't smell like mine. It smells like friggin' canned tuna and oregano. I fight the urge to retch, though I know it's not just the food.

Leah's in the kitchen with Trevor. I'm debating whether to go in, just get it over with, when they come out into the dining room. Leah's got a huge smile on her face and she says to me, "Hey, Gabe! This is Trevor."

Everything about Trevor is skinny: from his thin, lank hair to his long face to his half-inch belt to the tight jeans he's wearing. He's got *bangs,* for shit's sake. If I look like him, may a sniper shoot me dead.

"Hey, man," Trevor says. His grin is so wide, it's practically a leer. "Thanks for letting me crash. Your house is awesome." He gestures at the oversized wall canvas behind him, the one Adrienne and I pressed our naked bodies against. Funny how you can stop seeing things, how the profoundly erotic can become mundane over time.

"No problem." I force a smile. I'm out of sync with this buoyant crew. I'm the recovering alcoholic at Mardi Gras.

Leah cocks her head at me, questioning and cajoling at once. Don't judge him, she's saying. But I know what I know. I can't forget it, just because she wants to play house with the little cretin.

"We made pasta puttanesca," she tells me. "With tuna."

"I can smell." I bark a laugh. They're all watching me quizzically now, wondering if I'm going to blow up their party. Maybe Leah should show me her tits again, and I'll give her some beads.

I hate this guy. Not Trevor. Me.

My anger seems to have calcified into an omnipresent bitterness.

That's not who Adrienne married. But then, she's not who I married either.

I take a deep breath. It's just dinner. One step at a time, isn't that what the alcoholics say?

"I like spice," I say. I'm referencing the puttanesca, but it's just a few beats too late. Everyone's confused.

Adrienne pipes up. "I'm going to put Michael down in his crib. You want to help me, Gabe?"

I never help. Leah knows that. Does Trevor? How much has Leah told him about the inner workings of my house?

My ears are hot as I follow Adrienne to the nursery, where she very carefully places Michael in his crib. He hasn't been swaddled or put in one of those wearable blankets that make him look like a Roman cardinal. Maybe this is discombobulating her, too, more than she's been willing to admit.

It's mostly dark in the nursery, and she turns to me, moving in close. She takes my face in her hands. Her hands, I notice, smell like baby powder. Her uncontrolled hair has a certain Medusa quality. "I know all of this has been hard on you. Just hold it together a little while longer, and then we're home free."

"In my gut," I tell her, "I just don't think it's going to work that way."

She smiles. Her gaze is unwavering and sure. "Who do you trust: your gut, or me?"

She kisses me hard on the lips, no tongue. It feels like the equivalent of Cher slapping Nicolas Cage, telling him to snap out of it.

But it gets me back to the dining room, and bourbon gets me the rest of the way. Somebody—Leah? Adrienne?—has left me a glass with what must be five fingers in it. I down the hand like it's a shot.

A mellow sort of torpor settles over me as I watch the three of them. Trevor's talking about his cross-country drive, about a run-in with some trucker, and he's doing these crazy gesticulations. He's like the next-generation, Rhode Island version of Pauly Shore. That's not exactly a compliment, but Leah and Adrienne are both cracking up. I have a feeling people tend to like Trevor. He's polite and deferential toward Adrienne and me, and he's just weird enough but not offensively so, and yeah, all right, he's kind of funny.

But he's definitely not what I pictured based on what Leah told me. Breaking into houses so they could have sex? Calling Leah a whore and a cunt? How could Leah be head over heels for the Weasel 2.0?

There has to be more to him than quirk. The fact that I can't picture Trevor saying or doing the nasty things Leah reported, that just confirms that he really is bad news. He's sitting here at my dining room table putting on an act, and he's all the more dangerous because the act is so convincing. Trevor is full of shit, and Leah's forgotten that, and Adrienne doesn't care. So it comes down to me. I'm going to have to save Leah.

I get melodramatic when I've had a hand of bourbon.

Through my alcohol haze, I see how happy Adrienne is. Carefree, for once. Trevor doesn't want a baby, and he doesn't want to live in California, but he does want Leah. Adrienne thinks all our problems are about to be solved.

Adrienne's beautiful when she's carefree. She used to look this way a lot. Before the IVF, before our first adoption profile, before Patty, before she got consumed by what Patty had done to us, before before before . . . It's been years of cares, now that I think of it. Adrienne's had it rough for a long time, wanting something so much and having it perpetually out of reach, like the baby's sitting there on a shelf that's just a little too high.

If I could just trust her now, instead of my gut, then I could believe that by playing along, I'll get my real wife back, my real marriage. Everyone at this table is overjoyed; why not just play along?

" . . . I sent this picture back to my little bro," Trevor is saying. He's holding out his phone to all of us, and we crowd in to take a peek. It's Trevor standing on top of the giant shoe of a gargantuan

Paul Bunyan. "What can I say? He loves Babe the Blue Ox." Trevor's full of wistful affection. Then he turns to me. "Have you got brothers or sisters, Gabe?"

For a second, I think: He knows, Leah must have told him. He's actually trying to take me down, the first night, right here in my own house.

His face is friendly as he waits for my answer. He's already mentioned his memory is for shit. He can barely remember anyone's name, let alone fun (and not-so-fun) facts from their lives. But that could be a cover story, a method of plausible deniability for all the pain he causes.

"No brothers or sisters," I say. "It's just me."

Leah's watching me sympathetically. "Here," she says, walking to the counter to retrieve the bottle of Jim Beam, "have another."

CHAPTER 31

Adrienne

First thing this morning, Trevor was up off the couch, with the bedding folded neatly and tucked behind it. He and Leah ate a quick breakfast and were out the door. Neither of them paid Michael a bit of attention. I thought, This is working out *perfectly*.

Soon, Michael started fussing, and next he was full-on wailing. He refused milk. I realized how warm his little hands were and then how warm his head was. I got the rectal thermometer and laid him over my knee. Amid the sound of his screaming, I managed to insert the thermometer with shaking hands. I've never had to take his temperature before. Even though he spits up all the time, he's never been sick.

Now he is. One hundred degrees, even.

Trevor just got here, and Michael is sick for the first time. Coincidence?

I'm still shaking as I go to call the pediatrician. My worst fear is that I've never deserved this beautiful boy. The ultimate punishment for my crimes, I suddenly realize, is not that I never have a baby at all, but that I have him for a brief time and then lose him. On some cellular level, I've been expecting this.

I need to calm down. Michael won't suffer for my crimes; he won't pay with his life. That's not how this will work. It can't.

The receptionist is an idiot. I repeat my name. "You met me," I say. "I came in with Leah for the well-baby checkup." Only he's not a well baby anymore, is he?

"What I'm saying is, you're not the mother. We have no medical authorization on file for you. Did Leah sign one?"

"I'm sure she did." I'm not sure at all. But I assume my most authoritative tone. "Michael has a fever of one hundred. I need to bring him in."

"Unless there's an authorization on file granting you—"

"If your office misplaced the authorization, that's not my problem. My problem is, my baby has a temperature of one hundred." I jog him up and down in my arms. He's still screaming. Tears are in my own eyes; I can't stand to hear him cry. "He's suffering. He needs medical attention."

"I understand. Please hold." After several minutes of Michael's unrelenting cries, she's back. "Dr. Abrams says that one hundred point four degrees is considered true fever in a baby. If he has other symptoms like irritability or poor feeding or listlessness—"

"Listen to him. Doesn't he sound irritable to you? I want to talk to Dr. Abrams."

"Dr. Abrams can't talk to you. We can only give you general information unless we have a release from the mother. Please have the mother—have Leah—call us."

"I'm the mother! I take care of him all the time. Leah had him, sure, but I'm his mother. The adoption is in the works."

She's quiet a long minute. "Ma'am," she says, "as far as our records are concerned, Leah is his mother. So she'll need to call us back and we can go from there."

"What if I bring him in? Would you actually refuse treatment to a sick baby just because—"

"Ma'am"—her voice is steely—"I've just told you what needs to happen. Now, I understand it's upsetting when a little baby is sick, but we've got legal regulations to follow."

I disconnect the call. I'm about to throw the phone, but instead, I call Leah and hear the tinkling ringtone emanating from her room. She left her phone behind. What nineteen-year-old leaves her phone behind? It must be because she's with the only person she cares about talking to. All she cares about is Trevor. Yes, that's what I was banking on, but now it's blowing up in my face. I don't have Trevor's number.

Pull it together. Think. Do I drive Michael to the ER? I don't want to subject him to that if I don't have to. Just imagining the kind of germs running rampant in a hospital terrifies me even more. Do I show up in the pediatrician's office and demand treatment? Do I call my lawyer and have him insist they provide treatment? If he'd done his job properly, he would have prepared for this contingency. He would have gotten me medical rights. Damn that arrogant asshole.

Think. None of this is helping Michael. Oh, God, why won't he stop crying? "Shh, shh, shh," I croon into the top of his head. It's warm but not hot. He's not burning up. One hundred point four is the magic number, and he's not there yet.

Leah has Trevor's number, and her phone is here, in the house.

I go into her room, which is something I never do. I do my best to pretend this room doesn't even exist, as if it's a landmass that has temporarily split off from the rest of the house. I ignore the unmade air mattress bed and the way her makeup and clothes are strewn across the top of the office furniture, same as I've been ignoring the mural that's been encroaching on the nursery. One of the good things about Trevor's being here is that he's halted the progress.

"Shh, shh, shh," I tell Michael, and he actually seems to be listening. The cries are beginning to abate, thankfully. It might only be wishful thinking, but his head seems slightly cooler. I'll take his temperature again soon.

I dial Leah again. It's the quickest way to locate her cell in the mess.

There it is, sandwiched between makeup brushes and a bottle of leave-in conditioner. I swipe it and take it back to the nursery. I rock Michael as I search through the contacts for Trevor. I notice there's no "Mom" or "Dad." Weirdly, there's one that says "The Home." Is that my home or her parents' house?

Michael lets out a renewed sob, and I feel it all through me, as visceral as if it were my own. I'm furious with Leah for her irresponsibility. How dare she fail to sign a medical authorization, how dare she fail to sign Michael over to me, period, and then be unreachable?

She's not unreachable. She's with Trevor.

I call him, and immediately, there he is, in all his loopy charm. "Yo, Trevor here. What am I doing? You wish you knew!" Then he cackles, and the beep sounds.

"Trevor, it's Adrienne. I need to reach Leah *now*. Michael's sick. Have her call me."

Then I call again. And again. And again. The phone's still off, or worse, maybe it's lost somewhere or dead. Most likely, it's just off, because he's with the only person he feels like talking to. Young fucking love. I could kill the both of them.

My rocking takes on a frenetic quality, and Michael's cries intensify. The two might be related, so I force myself to slow. Yes, I'm pissed at Leah, but Michael's my priority. He needs to be comforted.

I walk at a slow bounce toward the front of the house. It occurs to me that Leah and Trevor could be outside, having sex in Trevor's car (since he promised they wouldn't do it in the house, and I'm pretty sure they were out there last night after dinner). I wouldn't have any problem knocking on their steamed-up windows. But when I look outside, the car's gone.

Maybe they're gone for good. If they take off without signing any papers—medical authorization, adoption, anything—what happens to Michael?

I walk him around the living room, slow as I can muster. I call Trevor again, with the same result. I leave another message, more obviously angry this time. Michael's crying has hit another peak and then fallen off, to my great relief. Is it too soon to take his temperature again?

I wish I had someone to ask. My own mother. A friend. A doctor. As soon as I have the legal ability, I'm switching pediatricians. If I'm lucky, it'll be as soon as this weekend, when Trevor and Leah take their reunion show back to Rhode Island.

What makes me crazy is that I can't kick her out. This doesn't violate Hal's contract. She's so selfish—not signing that authorization, not caring what happens to her child. She's no mother; she's the antimother. This just confirms it.

Returning to the nursery, settling back into the glider, I can feel his body relax more fully against mine. I think he's getting better, but what if he's not? What if he's so sick that he doesn't have the energy to cry? Books aside, what do I really know?

All I can do is wait: for Leah to call back, for some time to pass before I take his temperature again. If I bundle him up and put him in the car and then get him into his stroller and march into the pediatrician's office, it could do him more harm than good. I wouldn't want someone doing that to me when I'm sick. He needs to rest; right this second, he's starting to.

I should call Gabe. These kinds of moments are what husbands are for. But not him, not lately. He was knee-deep in bourbon again last night.

I saw Gabe in Leah's contacts. I have the sudden idea to text him, to pretend to be Leah. He might tell Leah what's really going on with him, since he sure as hell isn't telling me. Or maybe I'd learn what's really going on between the two of them. He was just seeing how the mural was coming along the other night? *Seriously?*

I need to pull it together. He's just having trouble adjusting to the situation, which—everyone seems to agree—is not a normal one: a new adopted baby, a birth mom who won't go home, a birth dad showing up out of nowhere. Anyone would be freaked, right?

Michael looks up at me with his wide brown eyes, his lashes skewering tears. "Are you okay, Mama?" he's asking. "Will it all be okay?"

"Oh, baby," I tell him, "it's going to be fine. You and me, we'll always be fine."

The pediatrician's office said it's not the temperature, it's whether he's irritable, whether he's eating. So I take him into the kitchen with me and remove a bottle from the refrigerator. He begins to drink it lustily. "Thank you," I breathe, touching his sweet and cooling head with my lips.

Leah's phone rings from the counter. I see that it's Trevor. Even though it's felt like an eternity, I know that Leah hasn't actually been out of touch for very long. "Hello," I say flatly.

"Adrienne? Is he okay?" There's no mistaking the concern in Leah's voice.

"I don't know for sure." I let it hang out there, torturously.

"What's wrong with him? Did you call the doctor?" I hear her ratcheting up. "Get off me," she says, muffled, to Trevor.

Now, this I don't need. Her getting upset with Trevor, her seeming invested in Michael.

"He's better," I say.

"Wait, which is it? You don't know if he's okay, or he's better?"

"I think his fever is coming down, and he's drinking milk again. For a while, he wouldn't drink, and he was crying a lot." I stare down at him, wishing he was suckling my breast instead of the bottle, wishing I could provide him that added measure of comfort. "The doctor won't talk to me, Leah. You didn't sign an authorization."

"I thought I did." There's something in her delivery that I just don't believe.

"The office Nazi said they couldn't help me, that they couldn't help Michael, because there was no authorization on file. You need to fix that."

"Sorry." But she doesn't sound sorry; she sounds peeved. At me, at the doctor's office?

"You should come home now. Stop at the pediatrician on the way and sign the paper. Because I might still need to take him in today. He feels cooler, but I need to take his temperature to be sure."

"I'm coming home so we can go together."

Michael finishes the bottle in record time and lets out a familiar cry. His hunger cry. There is no sweeter sound: He wants more.

I get another bottle for him as I calibrate my reply. It's a delicate moment. "You know," I say, "if you go to the pediatrician's office and sign the paper, you don't even need to come home. You and Trevor can just get back to whatever you were doing."

"No," she says, "that's okay. We're coming home."

As I sit on the couch with Michael drowsing on his second bottle, I find myself contemplating Leah's phone. I've never seriously considered snooping on her before. But it's almost like this whole episode with Michael was engineered to lead me here. I don't want to move and jostle Michael, he needs his rest, and all I have to entertain me is her phone.

I have a right to know what I'm dealing with. She's living in my house; her possibly reprobate (ex-?)boyfriend is sleeping on this very couch.

Gabe wouldn't like it.

But for all I know, there are text exchanges with him, too.

I just need to ever so slightly violate her privacy. I won't even read back very far, just a week or two. That would be enough to let me know what kind of person she truly is.

I don't know how far away Leah and Trevor are, so if I want to do this, I'd better start.

I want to do this. It's not just for me, it's for Michael, too. And for Gabe. I'm protecting my family.

I begin to scroll through, trying to get an overview. Who am I kidding, I'm looking for a conversation with Gabe. But there aren't any, they're all with Trevor. Nothing with "The Home."

Back to the top, the most recent.

T: Come to the couch.

L: No, you come to my bed.

T: Can't. A says not to.

Good boy. "A" must mean me. Of course, he's not supposed to bone her on my couch either.

T: Car.

That's the end of that exchange. Go back farther.

T: Thinkin bout u.

L: U 2.

T: Miss u. Want to touch u.

L: I'm still fat.

T: Saw the selfie. Def not fat. Hot.

They go on like that for a while. I knew there was phone sex; I didn't know there was text sex. Seems inconvenient, all the typing. I guess I'm getting old.

Next.

T: Is she really that bad?

L: She's just fake.

T: Fake isn't always bad. Like, fake tits. They're pretty good.

Wait, are Leah's tits . . . ?

But more important, is she talking about my being fake?

L: She treats G like shit.

No wonder Trevor couldn't remember Gabe's name, if Leah's just calling him "G."

L: He's like this little puppy. You can tell she kicks him.

T: That can be hot.

L: I'm being serious.

T: Why do u care?

Good question, Trevor.

L: I have to live here. I have to watch.

T: U don't have to live there. U can leave.

Go, Trevor!

L: No. This is my life now.

T: Painting on a wall?

L: It's more than that. U know that.

What does he know?

L: I have plans.

T: U have too many plans. U think too much.

L: U don't think enough.

T: True dat.

L: U know I have plans for them.

My luck runs out: I can hear a car pulling up outside and two loud voices. Leah is clearly angry, and Trevor is expressing seven varieties of "What the fuck?"

I try to scroll quickly to see if I can latch on to any more information. Are Gabe and I "them"? From context, it would seem so, but the conversation appears increasingly disjointed. It's clear that Trevor gets references I don't, and that they've talked about this before. But whatever plans she has, Trevor is here to interrupt them. Isn't he?

I close everything up on Leah's phone and toss it to the other end of the couch. I hold Michael closer.

CHAPTER 32

Gabe

The vibe's definitely off when I get home, and allowing for the peculiarity of the cast of characters in my house, that's really saying something. The TV's on, showing some Lifetime telemovie (stalker lovers, isn't it always?), and I can't imagine which of the three of them would have picked that. None of them are watching it, exactly. They seem like they're all just trying not to look at each other. The kid is lying on his blanket in the center of the room, like a turtle stretching his neck, and Adrienne is idly patting his back. No one's talking.

They all look up at me, Trevor the most expectantly, like he thinks a fellow man might save him. He's got that everyone-likes-me grin, but it's bordered by desperation. I get the feeling Leah's not his biggest fan right now. So it's blowing up already, their little romance. I knew she was too smart to fall for him again.

Adrienne's the hardest to read. She even seems disconnected from the kid. "Hey," I say to the room, but really, I'm talking to her.

Her eyes barely move in my direction. She's inscrutable, and I get this shiver. Anything's possible when she looks like that. "Can I talk to you in the bedroom?" I say. "Work stuff." I look at Leah. "You can watch the—Michael?"

Adrienne shoots daggers at me, but she stands up. "Just for a minute," she says, like a warning. To me, or to Leah and Trevor, I don't know.

We go to our bedroom and I start to push the door closed. "Keep it ajar," she tells me.

"What?"

"The door. Don't shut it all the way. I want to be able to hear if anything, you know, happens."

"What did happen today? It's like a crypt out there."

She shakes her head, like she can't even begin to explain. "He's okay now."

"Was he not okay earlier?"

"He spiked a fever for a little while. He seems better now." She glances at the door uncertainly. She's on call, ready for any sign of change. I'm pretty sure he'll be sleeping in our room tonight, or she'll be in his.

"You took him to the doctor?"

She shakes her head again. "Long story."

I sit on the bed and extend my hands to her. Sit beside me, please. Tell me a long story. Sing me to sleep. I need you, too, Adrienne.

I can't say any of that. What I can say is, "But he's definitely okay now?"

"Should be. I've been checking his temperature every hour. It's normal."

"Good." Her face is impassive. "Listen, I've been thinking about what you said, about us getting back on track. How Trevor might help with that."

She waves her hands to tell me shush, they could hear me.

I lower my voice further. "I've got an idea of what could help me."

"Yeah?" She suddenly looks exhausted. Defeated, maybe, and I've never seen her defeated before. Not through the IVF, not even after the debacle with Patty.

"Yeah." I smile at her. "You okay, Wren? Is there anything I can do for you?"

"Bad day," she says. "Tomorrow will be better."

I can hear her fighting to be herself. I'm ready to fight for us, Wren. "I've got a great idea. Let's rename him."

She blinks like she's seeing me for the first time and doesn't particularly like the view.

"I know, it's unusual," I continue, "but we're nothing if not unusual, right? It's not like it's never done. I was reading online. A lot more people change their kids' names than you think. They get the baby home and they're like, 'Hey, that's not a Eugene! That's a Colin!' It's not even hard to do it, legally, I mean. We don't even need Hal."

Distaste crosses her face. "We definitely don't need Hal. Hal is pretty much useless."

"Not entirely. We've got a contract."

She snorts.

I definitely didn't imagine Hal featuring so prominently in this conversation.

"When Leah and I were in the delivery room, we were talking about Michael. My brother Michael," I say, trying again. "We were there awhile, Wren. And I don't know why, he was on my mind. I guess because it was this big moment, I'm about to become a father, and he never will. He never did. You know?" I think she's softening a little, I think she's hearing me. "So I'm sitting there and I get this flash. I have this thought: I'm about to get a redo, I can make it up to Michael. Crazy, right?"

"Because you don't need to make it up to him."

That's not what I meant, but okay. "So I get this crazy idea that somehow, if I give Michael a namesake with a better outcome, it'll all be better. Things will have realigned in some cosmic way. I tell you, Wren, it's like I was smoking pot, really strong pot, like I was practically hallucinating.

"And Leah, she must have been breathing the fumes, too, because she's like, Yeah, that's it. Yeah, I'll name him Michael, and you'll give him a great life, and peace will reign on earth forever and ever, amen.

It's like we were in some revival tent or something, and we both just needed to *believe*. Do you know what I mean?"

The gears are turning in her head. This could go either way. Finally, she says, "Go on."

"That's pretty much the end of the story. We made the decision and we put on *Blade Runner* and you know the rest."

"You didn't think I should be part of the decision? Part of naming our son?"

"It was spontaneous, that's what I'm telling you. I wouldn't have guessed I'd be in the delivery room thinking about Michael, and about my role in what happened to him—"

"How many times can we go over this, Gabe? You aren't responsible for what happened to your brother. You are not—you were not—your brother's keeper. When are you going to get that?"

"There's a lot that you don't get either," I say. "That's why I'm trying to explain."

"So you feel like it was a mistake to name the baby Michael, it was some shared lapse of consciousness between you and Leah, is that it?"

"It's bigger than that. You say you want me to bond with our baby, but I can't if he's got that name. I just can't. There can only be one Michael for me. I must have been high to think it could have been otherwise."

To her, it's just an excuse. I see it in her face. That tears me up more than anything.

Then she tries to paper over that expression, over what's true, with a look of faux-sympathy and the pretense of understanding. "I see you don't like calling him Michael. You never really do call him that. But to me, he's already Michael. I just can't think of him any other way. I don't see your brother in him at all, and over time, you won't either. But in the meantime, let's come up with a good nickname." She gives me a smile. "Something other than 'the kid.' "

I can't smile back. She's trying to work me over, to create the illusion of appeasement while yielding no ground. She's not willing to hear me, or she hears but she just doesn't get it; she refuses to get it. Has she completely forgotten the way Michael died, the circumstances leading up to it, our shared responsibility in it? How can she be so comfortable calling our baby Michael, divorcing it from our past as a couple? Her powers of compartmentalization are stultifying. They'd be the envy of any sociopath.

"'Mickey,'" she's musing. "But would we always want to add 'Mouse' to it? I don't really like 'Mickey,' but I could live with it, if it would help you. 'Mick,' maybe. 'Micah' is a cute one. How do you feel about 'Micah'?"

"Let me think about it," I say.

"Or 'Cale.' But would people think we're talking about kale then, like our baby's a leafy green?" She wants me to laugh, but I'm feeling the opposite. This was supposed to bring us together, but we're even farther apart. "I won't put him in the monogrammed outfits anymore, okay?" She thinks this is a major concession.

"Thanks for listening," I tell her, and she smiles, not registering the sarcasm.

I realize as I open the bedroom door that I didn't need the kid to have a new name as much as I needed my wife to understand why I can't say "Michael." She, alone, can understand. Micah, Mickey, Mick, Cale, Kale . . . They're all just ways to not think about my brother and what I did to him. I can't feel like a father after failing so completely as a brother. But there's no point in telling Adrienne that. She's let me know quite distinctly that she doesn't intend to hear it.

Adrienne goes back to the living room. I hear her urging Trevor and Leah to take a walk or a drive or see a movie (code for "get the hell out") and once the front door slams, I retreat to the garage to play pool (code for "getting drunk alone"). I've got Jim Beam stashed in there but, I quickly realize, no glass. There's no way I'm going to the kitchen, though, when Adrienne is directly in the flight pattern. Swigging from the bottle like an old wino riding the rails is better than facing her right now.

I don't like what I've become. Not the drinking, even, but the slinking. The not-facing.

Tonight, though, I went right at her, and what did it get me? A son named after a leafy green. That's her final offer.

I could go back out there and fight her on it. It would, undoubtedly, get ugly. I might have to say something like, "It's him or me. Change the name, or I'm walking." She'd give in. Probably.

But that conversation—it's sucked the life out of me. I thought if I approached her right, she'd have to hear me.

So maybe it was my approach. I got it wrong, somehow.

In my heart, I don't think that's it.

This is not my beautiful house. Or my beautiful wife. Or my son. Above all, that is not my son.

I take a long pull from the bottle, and then another. Time passes with me sitting on the granite steps of the garage, lost in reveries I can't begin to recount, more feeling than event, sinking down and down and down . . .

"Oof," I say, jumping up and rubbing my back. I didn't even think about the door opening outward when I sat on the steps; it seemed that improbable for anyone to come looking for me.

"Sorry, dude!"

Trevor. Of all people.

Who's still saying "dude"? It occurs to me that it could be some kind of retro affectation, something Trevor rescued from the archives.

"I thought we could rack 'em," he says. "Play some pool. You'd probably kick my ass, though. Leah says you're out here, like, a lot."

The bottle is still in my hand, uncapped, evidentiary. I stow it to the side of the steps, hoping he won't see but pretty sure he does. "I'm okay," I mumble, "at pool."

Now I'm on defense, when I should be on offense, asking where he gets off coming into my man cave. How he even has the balls to show up at my house trying to woo Leah back after what he did.

He should be off in a cave himself, too ashamed to face daylight. He wasn't man enough to be a father.

I'm one to talk.

Trevor is staring at the pool table, the balls neatly aligned inside the triangle, untouched.

"I just finished a game," I say. "I was about to start another."

"I've always had awesome timing. It's, like, my gift."

"They say timing is everything." My tone is sour, but he doesn't pick up on it. Or if he does, he's not letting on. I have this suspicion that Trevor gets a lot of intel with this "Dude, where's my car" routine. People think he's benign when really, he's a tumor that's metastasized to my house.

He removes the triangle and selects his cue. "Mind if I break?" he asks, suddenly formal.

"Sure." I move to pick up my cue. I'm unsteady on my feet, but I try to camouflage it by leaning slightly against the table. The balls splintering apart nearly makes my brain rattle. Oh, let me guess. Trevor's a born pool player. It's one of his other gifts.

He's stripes, and I watch him circumnavigate the table with grace and confidence. He reels off numbers, one after the other, as balls dance into pockets. I'm subjected to his effortless choreography, when all I wanted was a little peace and quiet.

On top of that, he wants to talk. "Leah," he says, "is not having a good night." As if her name is kryptonite, he proceeds to miss his next shot.

"Yeah?" I say. I'm trying not to sound too friendly. It's not bros before hos around here. I shove off from the table and prepare for my first shot. He hasn't made it easy for me. I squint and concentrate.

"I love her, you know?"

My bank shot is wild, embarrassingly so, given Trevor's virtuoso performance. But he's not even looking. He's leaning on his cue stick, staring off as he muses about his great love for Leah.

" . . . She's worth coming all the way out here for, no question.

I mean, we're killer together. You can tell that, too, right? Adrienne sees it. She wants us to work out. She's into love, you know?"

I stifle a belch. If he thinks I'm going to stand here and validate his relationship with Leah, he must be drunker than I am.

"But Leah's different now. It's like, she's a mother, except that she isn't." He pushes his greasy hair back with my pool cue. I feel like snatching it out of his grimy little hands. "I dunno, it's confusing." He looks directly at me. "She likes you, though."

I don't know what to make of it, the "though."

"Like you're the father she never had, or some shit like that. Maybe you can talk to her?"

"About what?"

"About not being so pissed off at me."

Either I'm not following him, or he's unfollowable. He can't finish a complete thought. The whole generation has attention deficit disorder. He was raised by Wii.

When did I get to be so old? When did I become the father Leah never had?

"If Leah's pissed at you, she probably has her reasons," I say. Like, for example, you calling her names and abandoning her for months.

"It's not my fault she left her phone behind. It's not my fault Michael had a fever." He looks sulky. "I don't get it, why she's suddenly all into him."

Oh, man. Leah's into Michael, more than Trevor? Adrienne better not hear about this.

"He's sorta cute, but he's always, like, projectile vomiting. What's that about?" So Trevor's jealous of Michael, too.

"This is better than it was. You should have seen him when he was first born. It was like Vesuvius erupting every time he had a feeding." I take the next shot, because it doesn't seem like he's going to. The ball sails into the pocket, and I don't know why, but I instantly feel lighter.

Trevor laughs. "I guess I should thank him. Leah never used to have tits like this." He lowers his voice. "I couldn't help it, I had to try it."

"Try what?"

"The milk."

"No shit! Are you serious?"

He grins. "It's, like, sweeter and more watery than real milk. Kind of like—have you ever had almond milk? It was a little like that."

I laugh.

"I like Adrienne," he says. I shoot him a look. I'm not that thrilled about his segue from Leah's tits to my wife. "I'm just saying, she's cool. But Leah . . ."

"Yeah, I know. Leah doesn't think so."

"She can't. I'm surprised your whole house doesn't smell like piss. You know, from the two of them marking their territory."

I don't want to like him. I will not like him. Once I'm sober, it'll be like this never happened.

"I think part of why Leah's upset with me," he says, "is because Adrienne was so upset with her."

"Adrienne was upset with Leah? Today, you mean?"

"She didn't tell you? She was trying not to go off, you could just see it."

It's possible Adrienne told me and now I can't remember. Slim chance, but possible. A long story, she said.

"The problem with Leah," he says, "is that the more you tell her she can't do something, the more she wants to do it. So if Adrienne treats her like she can't be a mom, well . . ."

"Reverse psychology."

He lines up his cue stick. "Maybe you should tell Adrienne that."

I have the feeling all our male bonding was leading up to this particular piece of advice. Unfortunately for Trevor, even if I could recall, I'm not really inclined to pass it along.

You're due in a month.

I know. That's why you need to hurry and buy me a plane ticket! :)

JK.

You're not really kidding.

I want to come see u guys again. Don't u want to see me?

It's not that.

What is it?

That hotel cost a lot. Why don't you stay at our house? You could stay the whole month until the baby's born.

I don't want to be in the way.

You won't be.

I never get to go anywhere. I love hotels. It was so much fun last time.

We didn't see you much last time.

I want to see u a lot this time. Especially Gabe. I barely know him.

Then stay at our house.

I just need a vacation, u know? Room service is the best. I felt special.

You can feel special at our house. It'd be easier to get to know Gabe that way.

Patty?

U don't know what it's like for me. I never get to go anywhere.

You just came to SF. Gabe wouldn't like spending all that money on hotels and room service a second time.

He doesn't like me, does he?

He likes you. We just don't have unlimited funds, that's all.

I don't think he likes me.

He needs to get to know you better. At our house. He'd love to have you.

Patty? You still there?

Why aren't you answering?

Is everything okay?

You're freaking me out. Is anything wrong with the baby?

Baby's fine. But I have a lump in my breast. Need to get biopsied.

Oh, no. What can I do?

Nothing. I need to use a PTO day for the biopsy. So tell Gabe he got lucky. I can't come to SF anyway.

It's not like that. Call me. We'll talk, okay?

What happened with the biopsy?

Did you get the flowers we sent?

I'm worried. Are you all right?

I miss you.

Tell me you're okay.

Just tell me the baby's okay.

CHAPTER 33

Adrienne

It was a fitful night's sleep. I don't even know what time Gabe came to bed, and I'm pretty sure that he was drunk again. He's keeping a bottle of bourbon in the garage now. What gets me is that he thinks I'm too stupid to realize it.

I'm practicing behavior modification, like I do in the classroom. Sometimes you have to ignore a behavior to extinguish it. Even getting mad is a form of reinforcement. Gabe's not going to get my negative attention this time; he needs to grow up.

Enough of his excuses. I refuse to humor him and change our son's name. It's high time that he got over this obsession with his brother.

Sometimes I think I should just come clean. Then Gabe would know who his brother really was: not some hapless victim, but a master manipulator, the kind whose strength lies in playing up his presumed weakness. But once upon a time, I decided it was kinder to keep that from Gabe so he could to hang on to a pristine memory of his brother. That's obviously backfiring now.

I wish I could summon more compassion. All I want to say is:

Man up. Be a father. Be a husband. Be something substantial. Right now, he's the ghost, not his brother. But I must be exercising some compassion, because I haven't said any of that. Last night, I was definitely tempted. Who renames a baby?

I glance at the clock: 8:04 A.M. Gabe's still snoring next to me, and Michael should have started crying by now.

I pull on a robe over my pajamas and head for the nursery. The door's open, and Michael's not in his crib. My heart immediately starts to pound as I dash out into the hall. Then I see them in the living room: Leah and Trevor down on the blanket, encircling Michael. Michael is inside their circle. How did this happen? It was supposed to be a circle with Gabe and me; that's what I said in the adoption profile.

I'm inflamed by the utter wrongness of it. I stride down the hall, not even caring what kind of entrance I make. I'm prepared to let fly. This has to stop.

What freezes me in my tracks is that he's smiling. There's drool on his chin and a bib full of spit-up still around his neck and he's just staring at Trevor and Leah in awed delight. Smiling up at his parents.

I feel like a deflating balloon. None of them have noticed me. Leah is doing "this little piggy" with Michael's toes, and Trevor is "whee-whee-whee"–ing all the way through it.

Without turning, Leah says, "We already fed him."

"Passed him back and forth like a football," Trevor adds. "It was awesome."

Et tu, Trevor? I thought he came out here to take her away from all this. They should be on the road back to Rhode Island. That was the deal.

"Does anyone want breakfast?" I say. "I'm going to make eggs." Before they can answer, I'm in the kitchen, slamming the cast-iron skillet down on top of the stove. I shouldn't do that, it's an electric stove with a black ceramic cooking surface. The last thing I need is a hairline crack to remind me forever of this moment, the moment when I lost my son.

No, I haven't lost him yet. I've been his mommy for almost six weeks now. The fact that he saved his first smile for them—that doesn't mean anything.

I don't understand how things have spiraled this badly, this fast. I don't understand how Michael could do this to me. I'm the one who's been changing every diaper, doing every feeding (well, last one excepted), loving him. Where's the loyalty? Where's the justice?

As I crack eggs into a bowl, I'm thinking that maybe I deserve this. Not because of Gabe's brother, but because of my own hubris. I should have known better than to make any deals with a potential devil, after Patty. Leah chose us, sure, but I chose her right back. Of course, when I first met Patty, I had no way of knowing I was dealing with the actual devil.

Not that Patty's her real name. The irony is, even if I'd been able to figure out her true identity, I wouldn't have been able to touch her. Nothing she did was illegal. It's incredible how the most immoral of acts can be entirely legal.

She was in her late twenties. That's what she said anyway, and that's what she looked like the first time I met her in person. There were tiny cobwebs just starting to form by her eyes and they intensified when she smiled, which was often. I liked her. Maybe I even loved her.

She came into our lives after only four months of searching. She was early in her pregnancy, only four months along. The numerology felt like kismet.

Hers was the first call I ever received on the birth mother line. We were both so nervous (well, I was nervous, she was just playing at it, playing me), and that forged its own kind of bond. Neither of us had done this before (or so I thought). When she confided that she was embarrassed to be pregnant by a married man, I empathized instantly. I believed her totally.

She seemed so sincerely flummoxed by her predicament. We talked for hours about her misfortunes. She was the kind of person who was lied to by dates, abandoned by her family, mugged in the grocery store parking lot. Her last apartment building burned down. "But I won't let it harden me," she said. "If I do, then it's like they all win."

I didn't know who "they" were—the terrorists, maybe? I was charmed by her seemingly misguided resolve. I couldn't imagine being so open to the world, so unprotected, and maybe I even admired that in her. It must have been contagious, because I was open to her in a way I'd never been before with a friend, only with Gabe.

Plus, I wanted to love this woman, the mother of my baby. I wanted to trust her. With her life being so full of calamity, it seemed certain that she would never be one of those mothers I'd read about on the adoption message boards, the kind who changed her mind. She could barely handle her life as it was; there was no way she'd throw a baby into the mix. That's what she said, repeatedly, and there seemed no reason to doubt her.

I swore that Gabe and I would do right by her, and I meant it. We would not be another in a series of catastrophes.

She said she couldn't wait to fly out and meet us in person. "I love you guys already," she told me. "I know you're going to be the best mom."

But among her other troubles, she had an ogre of a boss. She was an administrative assistant at a corporation, and she needed another month in order to accrue a PTO day (she'd used all hers up on things like replacing the car windshield that got randomly smashed). I told her we could fly her out on a Friday night and back on a Sunday, it was a short flight, but she said she wanted us to have more time to get to know each other.

I look back, and obviously, I should have seen through her. But she was so convincing. She was the little engine that could, the hooker with a heart of gold. I realize that part of why she seemed so familiar was because she was like something out of a movie. If there were an Oscar given for swindling prospective adoptive parents, she'd win.

We kept talking on the phone, and she kept postponing the visit.

But she was sending me ultrasound pictures and we were so close that I felt sure that Gabe and I were the only parents she could ever want for her baby. I mean, why wouldn't she want us? I was the best friend she'd ever had; she told me so.

Yes, I sent her money a few times. More than a few times. They weren't large amounts, and she never asked directly. But it was clear she didn't earn much, and she was always incurring additional expenses, none of them her fault. She found her cat in the bushes with a broken pelvis after he'd apparently gotten hit by a car. She posted the pictures on Facebook.

That was part of how she fooled me. Her Facebook seemed to attest to her being an incredibly sweet and deeply unlucky woman. Everything that befell her had photographic evidence. Yet, my bullshit detector must have been going off on some level because I didn't tell Gabe that much about the conversations. I didn't tell him about her cat with the broken pelvis or her car with the busted windshield. I certainly never told him about the money.

I think the genius of her performance was that she seemed so trusting herself. The world was giving her no reason to believe in it, and still, she did. She found a way. It made me want to be like her, at least enough to pay her vet bills and buy her a new winter coat and send a little something extra for her birthday.

I opened up to her more and more, told her everything because I knew she'd never judge me. It seemed like a win-win: I got a best friend, and she was going to have my baby. But as Gabe says, win-wins are rare as comets.

I should have thought of that before I let Trevor into our home. I scramble the eggs in the pan and try to drown out the sounds of him and Leah playing with Michael. I will not hear Michael's happy gurgles. I won't imagine his smiles.

Patty did eventually come out to see us. We put her up at a four-star hotel in San Francisco, not because she asked but because it seemed like the right thing to do. She never got to go anywhere; I wasn't going to stick her in a Motel 6. She said she wasn't comfortable staying with us, that it would feel like far too much of an imposition (not that she seemed to mind imposing on our credit card).

During the long weekend, she didn't end up spending much time with Gabe and me. She had reconnected with some old friends on Facebook, she said, who lived in San Francisco now, how cool was that? Indeed, I could read their ebullient posts. I didn't feel like I had any business trying to take her vacation away from her.

Gabe and I met her for brunch in the city near her hotel. She had a new pixie haircut and was quite rounded, since she was seven months pregnant. But she told me that she couldn't feel the baby kicking, he was too far back in the womb, which meant there was no point in my touching her stomach. "My doctor says there's nothing to worry about, the baby's totally normal." She added gaily, "I just have one of those uteruses!"

In retrospect, it was all pretty suspicious. At the time, though, I was heavily invested in her. In just a few months, she was going to give birth to my child. I had all the ultrasounds in the baby book, and I looked at them every night, the way I'd someday read him (or her) bedtime stories. I was sleeping so well.

Throughout brunch, Patty kept answering texts. She didn't ask us anything, really, just rambled on about her favorite parts of the city. But then, it wasn't your average adoptive parents/birth mother interview. She and I were best friends, while she and Gabe were virtually strangers (they'd had a few brief chats on the phone prior). So I chalked up any awkwardness to that: It's always strange when your significant other meets your friends, when you have to navigate two different levels of intimacy at once. It's bound to create unusual dynamics.

"There's something off about her," Gabe said that night.

I wasn't ready to hear that, and we escalated quickly. I told him he was just afraid to be a father. "You don't want to like her," I said accusatorily. "Then you'd have to grow up."

It was one of the ugliest moments in our marriage—in part, because it's turned out to be true.

We ran through the emotional scales: from rage to sadness to disappointment to forgiveness, crescendoing in some of the best sex we've ever had. Sex has always been our way to restore equilibrium and silence dissension.

Patty went home, where the mishaps continued. Her cat was a money pit. But the poor thing was fourteen, he couldn't last much longer even with dialysis. (His kidneys were damaged in the car accident.)

After the visit, I didn't feel the same way about Patty. I felt like maybe she was a bit of an opportunist, especially given how little time she spent with me—her supposed best friend—during her visit. I was hurt and disappointed, but I was still going to be a mother soon. I just needed to focus on that, which was the point of it all.

A month before her due date, Patty wanted to come to San Francisco again under the pretense of getting to know Gabe better. I insisted she stay in our house and that we see a lawyer to finalize the contract. Unlike our previous dealings, I didn't just roll over and accept her terms.

Patty suddenly had a lump in her breast that needed to be biopsied, so she bailed on the visit. I sent flowers to her work instead of money to her PO box. She never did thank me.

In fact, she never contacted me again. She didn't respond to my calls or texts for the next week. Then she defriended me on Facebook, and her cell phone was no longer in service. Gabe had watched one episode of *Catfish* and had the genius idea to search for her pictures under Google Images. If only he'd gotten proactive sooner. We found that Patty had five alter egos, each with her own Facebook page. We couldn't see what was on them (they were private, of course), but I was pretty sure that each page was patronized by at least one prospective adoptive parent and featured pictures of a cat in traction.

Patty broke my heart clean in half. For the last month we were talking, the month when my faith in her was shaken, I sustained myself by dreaming of soon being a mother. I started buying infant paraphernalia and storing it in a high cupboard in the kitchen. Sometimes I'd idly stroke, say, a newborn wool hat while listening to Patty. It soothed me, a fantasy that was soon to become reality.

I didn't even know how to grieve for this baby that would never be mine. I didn't seem to know how to do anything except be angry: at her, at myself.

My fantasies turned to revenge. I had a PO box address for her, and I talked about staking it out. Gabe tried to convince me not to. "What would you do if you found her anyway?" he asked. "Confront her? She's got no conscience."

He didn't get it. I wasn't interested in making her feel bad. I was interested in making all her bad luck come true. When I couldn't sleep—which was often—I'd let visions of her bloody face dance in my head instead of sugarplums. My dreams were full of beautiful, satisfying, cleansing violence.

What chafed wasn't merely her (temporary) destruction of my dream of motherhood. It's that she slipped right past me, as if I were just any other dupe on the street. I've spent my life cultivating a certain distance from others. Then there's Patty, and I'm listening to her woes and sending her checks. I start sharing my secrets in return, so she can tell me I'm a good person. As if she knows the first thing about goodness.

I burned so bright and so hot that for a while, I wasn't even thinking about the birth mother phone. I wasn't thinking motherhood at all. I was on the avenging angel track. Let her pay, and then I'd don my maternal garb. Then I'd be ready.

"Eggs!" I say to Leah and Trevor, clattering a plate down on the dining room table. "Who wants to eat?"

Trevor leaps up. "You got any Tabasco?"

Leah doesn't look away from Michael. "No, thanks."

After Patty, you would have thought I'd have avoided any potential complications. Obviously, plenty of others have already turned Leah down. But I have to agree with Patty about one thing: If I'd played it safe, if I'd stopped trusting myself, I would have been letting them all win.

I think of that text: "U know I have plans for them."

I've been known to make plans of my own. Just ask Patty.

CHAPTER 34

Gabe

I'm getting that feeling again, like baby Michael is really Michael, like my brother is watching me through infant eyes. Today, he's lying on his blanket and laughing at me. "See," he's saying, "you can't get away from me! She won't even let you change my name!"

"He's started smiling," Adrienne announces, "and I made eggs." There's something maniacal in her movements, like she's barely held together with chicken wire and string. I know the feeling.

Leah and Trevor are so happy they seem stoned. Smart money says they had makeup sex sometime in the night. Or maybe they actually are stoned. They're all over the baby. If you didn't know better, you'd think they were just regular parents, any other young family.

No wonder Adrienne's on the warpath.

I enter the kitchen and move in to kiss her neck. She practically jumps out of her skin. "Relax," I say. "It's just me."

"I made eggs," she repeats, like she's a doll who's only programmed with one line.

"I see." One plate's been scraped clean; the other two are untouched. "Did you eat?"

"No. Trevor did." She bustles around, all useless energy. Without Mick (Cale?), she doesn't know what to do or who to be.

I should suggest something for us to do as a family—as in, Adrienne, Mick, and me—but that new toothless smile of his makes me want to crawl out of my skin. It doesn't help, trying to substitute a name. I still know he's Michael. How could I forget?

"Ray called," I say. "They're shorthanded."

She doesn't look at me. It's like she doesn't want to see me lie to her.

"Is it okay if I go in today?"

"Fine," she says, flat as roadkill.

I briefly consider a shave and a shower but I want out of the house as fast as possible. So instead, I go to the master bathroom to wash my pits and douse myself with deodorant. I stuff my bankroll of hundreds into my wallet and head out the front door, yelling, "Bye," over my shoulder.

I drive fast and aggressively to the Pyramid; I get flipped off twice for cutting people off. I'm spreading the joy around.

The lot for the Pyramid is full, so I spring for the valet. It's not a great neighborhood, and I don't like walking it with hundreds in my pocket. I've got a thousand on me now, and I plan to double it.

Once inside, I check the board. There are three guys already waiting for $2/$4 Hold'em. Three's a bad number. Not enough to start a new table, enough for a long wait. The problem is, you can't make anyone vacate their seat. It's a twenty-four-hour joint, and people can sit there for days if they want. If they suck, they want to keep rebuying, thinking they'll hit a streak. If they're winning, they want to ride the rush. In between are the rocks: the ones who fold and fold, waiting on just the right starting hand. Leaning against the dull gold rail, I can look down and spy the Hold'em action, and I'm in trouble. No one's budging.

I see that Berkeley kid—yeah, it's Berkeley, he's actually wearing the UC shirt today—comfortably settled in at one of the tables.

With rows and rows of neatly stacked chips in front of him, he's not going anywhere. Same stupid goatee as last time, with a self-satisfied expression on his face.

He's focused on a hand and doesn't notice me watching him from the rail. I know he'll remember me, though. You remember the guys who felted you.

Part of me would love to get a seat at his table. He's the big stack, and it would be an exquisite pleasure to take that distinction away from him. The other part of me thinks it'd be better at a table where it's just good fun, no testosterone-surging bullshit. But really, if there's no surge, is it any fun at all?

From this vantage point, I can study all his moves. He's in way too many hands, and his big bets are far too predictable. I know I can take advantage.

That occupies my brain for a while, but once it's been fifteen or twenty minutes, I'm feeling antsy. Worse, my mind starts to travel to all sorts of places I haven't been in a long time, places I try hard never to visit. I'm going back to the beginning.

At first, I really did see Adrienne as Michael's girlfriend, only. I was happy for him, and I had my pick of hot girls. I wasn't an asshole or anything; I was honest with all of them. "I'm not looking for a girlfriend," I'd say, and sure, I knew that for some, that was a red flag in front of a bull, they love a challenge, but I never changed my story. Whatever they did, I still wasn't looking for a girlfriend.

I look back, and I can see that Adrienne systematically set about changing me. She wasn't even the prettiest girl I'd been with, but she was the most determined. She was the funniest, too. Über-confident. It did intrigue me, where she got all that sass, why she was with my brother.

That sounds mean, and it felt mean when I had the thought. But I couldn't help it. She was entirely wrong for him. He couldn't stand up to all that attitude. I think he fell in love with her because she was the first girl he ever had, not because she was Adrienne.

And Adrienne? Did she fall in love with him?

She's always told me no, but she didn't tell him no. I used to hear him saying, "I love you," and her saying it right back. I wish she hadn't done that. Then he would have known the score, he would have been prepared. But she was his first, and he was defenseless.

When she was at our house, she'd laser in on me, using information Michael had told her. She'd talk to me about cars; she'd convey all their power and all their sex; she charged up the room.

Michael thought it was for him; he was that innocent. But I could see how he'd be confused. After she did that, they went up to his room and had noisy sex. I couldn't hear him, but I could sure hear her. I'm sure that's how she wanted it.

So yeah, I wondered about her, but I didn't flirt back. I know that for a fact. She'd talk to me, and I'd occupy myself with something. I'd start making a sandwich, or I'd turn on the TV. I hoped she wouldn't break Michael's heart, not on my account.

One day, after she'd been with Michael three months, after they'd exchanged "I love you"s, she cornered me. I remember exactly where I was: in the kitchen, drinking my dad's beer after a long day at work. I don't know where Michael was.

She stood close, and she smelled amazing (it was a smell I've since come to know well), and she said, "I love you more than anything." Then she scampered off like some woodland creature.

It wasn't the "I love you." I knew plenty of girls said that easily. But "more than anything"—it felt like a promise. I'd offered her nothing, and she made me a promise like that.

Adrienne intrigued me, yes, but girls had done that to me before. What they hadn't done was scare me. I felt the weight of inevitability.

I didn't want to mess up what Michael had going. He would have loved his first girl, any girl, but it happened to be Adrienne. He barely knew his mom; that was heartbreak enough. I didn't want to do it to him.

I thought about telling him some story about Adrienne, a rumor I'd heard about her cheating on him. I thought of confronting her and saying she had to tell Michael the truth, it wasn't right, what she was doing to him. I never considered telling him the truth, though. It just seemed too devastating, since he already thought I was golden and he was shit.

What I actually did was nothing. In a way, I'm more ashamed of that than I am of what came after. I was a coward. I let my brother get used; I let Adrienne feel like we were sharing a secret, which led her on. If I could go back to that fork in the road . . .

It's not that I chose Adrienne, not then. Honestly, I'm not even sure I chose her later. She chose me, and it was a centrifugal force.

I spent the next two weeks avoiding my house. I dated ferociously. I was removing myself from contention, letting Michael have Adrienne. I thought I was being a good brother. He'd find out soon enough what he was dealing with, or Adrienne would move on to someone else. She'd corner some other guy and tell him she loved him more than anything.

In my gut, though, I didn't believe that last bit. I had a feeling that phrase, that feeling, was reserved for me. Why, though? What was so special about me? I didn't know, but on some level, it puffed me up. To have done so little but to have earned so much—it was heady in a way I still can't explain.

But I was a good brother (or so I told myself) and I stayed away. Then Adrienne showed up at the Chevy dealership where I worked. I was in the back, stacking parts, and suddenly she was there in front of me. We just stared at each other, not speaking. I'd never before had a truly electric silence, didn't know they really existed.

She moved in close, still not saying anything, and she ran her hands up my torso, and I found myself saying her name. And that was pretty much it.

I told her afterward that it was just sex; I said that she should leave me alone, and she needed to stop messing with Michael's head. She was sixteen, anyway, and I was nineteen. I could get arrested. I deserved to get arrested for what I was feeling.

It wasn't just sex, though. It was fate. I'd never felt anything like it.

She broke up with Michael, and that was the beginning of the end. The end of Michael, but now, I think, the end of me.

All this time, I've treated Adrienne's manipulation like it's some charming quirk of hers. Adrienne's a force, I've always said. She'll use all she has to get what she wants. But maybe that's not just ambition or drive; it's a sickness.

I was nineteen, and I couldn't hold my own against Adrienne. Leah's nineteen now.

I saw the way Leah was smiling at Michael this morning. So pure, so clean. She's had it rough, and maybe she's starting to think that Michael is her second chance. She could be right.

I need to protect her: from Trevor (who's a classic sociopath, just think how he tried to work an old drunk guy at the pool table last night); from Adrienne. Leah's young, but that doesn't mean she can't be a good mother. That baby is her flesh and blood, not ours. She has claims on him at every level—legal, emotional, you name it. If she decides she wants to be his mother, she has that right. I'm not going to let Adrienne take it away from her.

We're not going to destroy another young life.

CHAPTER 35

Adrienne

Yo, Adrienne!" Trevor says, and then laughs. "Has anyone ever said that to you before?"

"Only my whole life," I answer. I force a smile, like we're all friends here. I'm on the couch feeding Michael, but with Trevor and Leah clustered around, it just doesn't feel the same. I'm on edge. "U know I have plans for them" rings in my head. The *u know* means that Trevor is at least aware of her plans, which seems pretty disloyal given my support for his plan to get Leah back. I want to kick his ass out into the street, with Leah soon to follow, but he's still my best hope. Unless he intervenes, she's got another ten months here. Ten months to bond with my baby.

I need to get Trevor alone and ask for the truth. Somehow, I feel like he might tell me. I can't ask for Leah's plans directly, of course, not without giving away that I saw their texts. But there are other ways.

"My dad loved that movie. He loved all, like, five of them," Trevor says. "Even the one with Mr. T."

Leah laughs. "Your father has the worst taste." I feel like it's a jab at me, like Leah's saying any movie with an Adrienne in it is worthless.

"Leah and me were thinking that we'd take little dude out today. Just to the park or something. Leah says he doesn't, like, get out much." Trevor's tone is casual, but he's not looking at me.

Doesn't get out much. Translation: You, Adrienne, don't take him out. As in, you're a bad parent. As in, Leah is judging my parenting and sharing her brilliant maternal insights with Trevor.

I stare down at Michael in my arms, willing myself to calm down. Only Michael. He's all that matters.

And they want to take him away from me—out to the park or something. What's something?

"Could we just, like, borrow your gear?" Trevor continues. "I know he needs a lot of junk. Car seat and all."

"We just want him to, like, see the sun," Leah says.

He gets out plenty. I put him in the Björn and we traverse the backyard together. I show him things. The trees, the weeds, the grass that Gabe can't seem to get around to mowing. Leah doesn't know how Michael and I spend our time.

Unless she's been observing me and I haven't even realized it.

First Leah takes Michael to the park without me, then what? It seems unlikely she'll want to raise him (especially when she's still into Trevor, who doesn't want to be a dad). But those texts show she's no fan of mine and that she doesn't like how I've been treating Gabe. If I don't start doing some damage control, she could decide that she wants Michael with a different family. There are scads of couples on the prospective-parents website who'd be happy to take my place.

"You're right," I say. "The park sounds great. Maybe I could go with you guys?"

They exchange a surreptitious look. It's not the outing they had in mind.

"I trust you completely," I tell them. "I just think it sounds like fun." I look to Trevor, my supposed ally.

"Yeah, that's cool," he says. Leah doesn't glare at him, so that's a start.

It's not going to be easy, sucking up to Leah. But if I want to neutralize the threat that she poses to my life with Michael, it has to be done. Two can play Machiavelli around here. I need to remember that this is all just a means to an end, and this time, I'm getting my happy ending.

"Let me show you how to pack the diaper bag," I say. It's a gamble, including her more rather than less, but once she realizes how much work Michael really is, she's going to bail. "You'll need to know for when you take him out on your own." I turn to Trevor. "You can watch Michael a minute?"

"Uh, yeah." His smile telegraphs discomfort. Good.

The feeding is over, so I transfer a drowsy Michael into Trevor's arms. In a perfectly timed act of collusion, Michael lets out a fetid fart. "I'll change him," I say, "once we're back."

Trevor nods, his nostrils flaring like a thoroughbred's. Leah stifles a laugh as she follows me to the nursery. Once there, I run through a check of the diaper bag, talking the whole time about how many burp cloths Michael needs, extra pacifiers, making sure there are enough wipes and diapers . . .

I'm being intensely boring on purpose, and Leah's eyes are glazing. That's it, Leah. Get a load of the tedium that is infant care. The only thing that makes it worthwhile, really, is that Michael is the absolute most gorgeously phenomenal baby in the world. But I'm not about to point that out. I'm too busy telling her about all the possible contingencies we need to prepare for, emphasizing his abject helplessness and the heft of caregiver responsibility. If she thinks it's all about watching him smile on a blanket, she's getting schooled.

"The thing is," I say, "he's a lot of work, and I know that can be kind of daunting. It's that way for Gabe."

As expected, she wakes up at the mention of Gabe's name.

"It's not just the work, though, with Gabe, or the way we've had to totally and completely change our lifestyles. It's the trauma. Do you know what I mean?"

"His brother's suicide?"

I nod. "Gabe and I were talking the other night about how the memory of his brother holds him back. He really wants to bond with the baby, but he's so afraid to love someone and lose them." I'm making it up as I go along, but I can see Leah's right with me. "He's trying hard to work through it. He might start seeing a therapist. Also, we're playing around with nicknames, because just saying 'Michael' brings so much back for him. But, you know, marriage is about times like this. Standing by people, understanding them. I mean, love is about times like this. You relate, right?"

"Not exactly."

"You're trying to forgive Trevor. Which I think is great, by the way. I can see how much you love each other."

She starts to smile, as if in reverie. I bet they're in his car every night. Not my business, not my problem. Might even be my solution, if Trevor's pillow talk is about going back to Rhode Island. I'm sure the neighbors never see; they're lights–out–at–nine thirty kind of people.

Leah stops at the smile. She doesn't want to give me too much. She doesn't trust me.

Not yet, anyway. But I'm making headway. I smile and lift the diaper bag onto my shoulder. "So that's it! We're ready."

I have Leah join me for a step-by-step diaper change, taking care to point out all the fundamentals and tips I've learned along the way. Fortunately, it is a full dirty diaper—smelly and sticky. It's a nine-wiper. Leah can't keep the distaste off her face. This is going swimmingly.

Then it's time for a lengthy car seat tutorial. Finally, we're off.

The park is a suburban-planning oasis: a small duck pond, different stations where kids can play stagecoach and ride painted horses or sit in a metal box marked "Post Office," climbing equipment and seesaws, swings for the big kids, swings for the little kids. I suggest we start on the big swings, and take the first shift, resting Michael against my shoulder and supporting his neck as I push myself back and forth, my feet never leaving the ground. There's a woman beside me who has her daughter on her lap, a baby who's much bigger than Michael but has a newly hatched look. There are thin blond tufts of hair electrified around her head, anchored by a flowered headband to denote femininity. "How old?" the woman asks, smiling at Michael. Leah answers before I can.

In the ensuing conversation, Leah is playing mom. So the woman beside us naturally assumes I'm the grandmother. "Are you in from out of town?" she queries.

"No," I say. "They all live with me."

I see the conclusions immediately being drawn: that Leah is my daughter, a teen mom, and now I'm supporting her and her boyfriend so they can afford to raise their mistake. But she arranges her face into a blandly pleasant expression that says, No judgment here. Meanwhile, on the other side of us, a mother who's about my age studiously avoids looking at us. I have a feeling she is most definitely disapproving of our quartet.

I try to ignore both sides of us and focus on Michael. "Wheee!" I tell him softly. I'm rewarded with his new gummy smile, and that is definitely reward enough.

Leah and Trevor are lurking next to us, whispering. I think I hear Trevor say, "Then tell her," and Leah steps over to me.

"Could I take over now?"

It's been maybe three minutes. But then, this was her outing. It's also my chance to reestablish some sort of relationship with her. "Sure!" I smile as graciously as I can, but I feel a stab of pain as I relinquish him. She places him carefully against her shoulder and sits on the swing. I can tell that she feels like I did when I first brought him home from the hospital: both mindful of his fragility, and captivated by it. She's likely never been needed before, and it's a heady feeling. Addictive, even.

I stand beside Trevor. We're both watching Leah, but she's only watching Michael, and he's watching her. I know how compelling that gaze can be. She hasn't moved a limb yet, she's too mesmerized by her baby.

Yes, that's her baby. She feels it now, and so do I. So does Trevor, who appears to be every bit as frightened as I am.

They're such a perfect tableau of mother–child love that even the disapproving mother seems to soften. "These are the moments you'll remember forever," the "no judgment" mom tells Leah. Leah's too absorbed to respond. She doesn't even turn her head. She sees nothing, hears nothing, except for Michael.

I see Trevor make his decision: If you can't beat 'em, join 'em. He moves behind Leah, puts his arms around her and Michael, and speaks softly into her hair. She looks up at him and smiles. Then he talks to Michael, who blinks up and smiles, too. Oh, God, that smile. It is the most gorgeous kick to the gut that I could ever receive.

Trevor could join, but there's no place for me. How do you fight maternal love? It's the strongest substance in the world.

That doesn't mean I can't try.

This is just one moment in time, but it doesn't change the inalienable facts. Which are: Trevor is in school, and obviously has no job or he wouldn't be able to drive cross-country on a moment's notice. He's got a slew of siblings; there's no room in his house for him, Leah, and a baby. More significant, he wants Leah, not an infant. Then there's Leah herself. She's clearly got no parental support, no marketable skills, and no job. But above all, my maternal love has more longevity and durability than hers. I will outlast her. If I need to, I'll break her.

I move closer to them and compliment them on their skills. Trevor's pushing is so delicate! And Leah's a champion head cradler! Smile through the pain, that's it. This is my version of childbirth.

I throw in a few flattering remarks about Gabe, how this will be "his kind of thing." I want Leah to remember that Gabe and I are the real parents. Also, I need to sound sweet on Gabe, since our robust love was the reason Leah chose us (that, and no one else would accept her terms). I've always known Leah likes Gabe, and I saw in her texts that my treatment of Gabe was one of her issues with me.

"Yeah, Gabe should come with us next time," Leah says, but she sounds dreamy and faraway. Intoxicated, that's what it is.

"I bet he'd like that. He's more of an outdoors person." It's an asinine thing to say, as if Gabe's love for his baby depends on how much sunlight he's metabolized, as if Michael is a form of seasonal affective disorder.

A few more minutes go by, and then Leah asks the "no judgment" mom, "Do you know where there's a bathroom?" She sounds full of regret. "I have to go all the time since I had this one!" She gestures toward Michael, and her casual ownership shanks me.

The mother smiles. "I hear you. There are port-a-potties over there, past the baseball diamond." She gestures into the distance.

Leah stands up, hesitating. She doesn't want to give Michael back to me any more than I wanted to give him to her.

I step forward, arms outstretched. "There's Purell in the diaper bag," I tell her, ever helpful.

"I'll be right back," she says, warningly. She looks at me, and then at Trevor. She's telling me not to get too comfortable, that she'll be back for Michael; she's telling Trevor . . . what? That he better not reveal her secrets? Her plans?

I get lucky. The baby chick next to us begins to cry, so her mother says a quick good-bye and they vacate the swings. It escaped my notice when the mother on the other side left, but she's gone, too. Now that Trevor and I have some privacy, I intend to take full advantage.

"Do you want to take a turn?" I say, indicating the swing, and Michael. Trevor shakes his head, passing my test. I sit down and kiss the top of Michael's head, murmuring my love for him. "How's it going, with Operation Rhode Island?"

He shrugs.

"Has anything changed? Are you thinking maybe you like it

out here?" My chest is tight. I feel like my whole life depends on his answer. "That maybe you want to be a father after all?"

"No, it's not that." He looks like he doesn't know if he should say more.

"What is it then?"

"I brought up the idea of moving back and she bit my head off. She said, 'Don't you want to spend time with your son? This is, like, your last chance.'"

His last chance. That means she's still planning on letting Michael go, right? "You seem to like spending time with him." What I mean is, stop giving Leah false hope.

"Yeah, this is cool. But it's not like I want him around all the time. I'm doing this for her." He looks directly at me. "Can I stay longer, if it takes longer? I guess I was, like, kind of cocky. I thought I'd get here and she'd look at me and I'd look at her and she'd be all like, 'Take me home, you bag of awesomeness!'" He smiles, but I can see he's hurt.

"You can stay as long as it takes."

"Thanks, Adrienne. You're the best."

Michael lets out a whimper. Sometimes I think he just wants to remind us that he's here. I kick my legs out slightly and the motion soothes him immediately. "Can I ask you something?"

"Yeah."

"How does Leah feel about me?"

He looks like he wishes he didn't have to answer. "It's not like she feels all one thing, you know? You're the mother of her kid. Our kid, I guess." It seems like it still dazes him to say that. Maybe he's been thinking of Michael as just another one of his younger siblings.

"Does she think I'm a good mother?"

"Oh, yeah." He says it so quickly that I feel a surge of relief. "She thinks you're great with him. That's sort of the problem."

"Why is it a problem?"

"You're, like, larger than life. There's no room for her, and she's the one who pushed him out. You get what I mean?"

"You think I need to make more room for her?" As in, more trips to the park? More time for Leah to clutch Michael and stare into his eyes? That sounds dangerous. Unless the alternative is even more dangerous: We're all hard-wired to want what we can't have.

He glances in the direction of the port-a-potties. "I can't tell you what to do."

"She likes Gabe better than me, though, right?"

A certain darkness crosses his face. I'm not sure how to interpret it.

"I know Gabe's been drinking more lately," I say. "He's had trouble adjusting to everything. You know, he was used to it just being us, him and me, against the world. You get how that is, right?" He shrugs, like he's not quite willing to cut Gabe any slack. "Suddenly, there's Michael, and Leah, and now you. It's just a lot to take in."

"Yeah, he's definitely still taking it in." From Trevor, that's practically scathing. It suddenly occurs to me: Trevor really doesn't like Gabe. Is it possible Trevor's been stalling, same as Leah, because Leah doesn't want to leave Michael with me and Trevor doesn't want to leave him with Gabe?

"You haven't gotten to see the real Gabe yet. The real Gabe is . . . he's the most lovable person I ever met, until Michael." I see that Leah is coming back, so my words accelerate. "Gabe and I have been together more than half our lives. We can get through anything. I'm going to support him, no matter what, and he's going to be an excellent father. He is." It's hard to sound vulnerable when you're talking at breakneck speed, but vulnerability is key, because men (even the young ones like Trevor) are a sucker for a damsel in distress.

Leah rejoins us and asks, "What did I miss?"

"Trevor can fill you in," I say.

I offer to take Michael home for his nap while they go out, and they agree. Then I watch the latest episode of Summer Jackson. My nerves are jangling so bad that I think about having a drink myself, but no, I need to keep my wits about me. I have to figure out my next move.

Today, Summer's guest is a "psychological profiler," oozing professional lingo and faux-insights about Joy Ellison's disappearance. Summer sure can milk a case, despite the fact that no body's been found and there are no new leads. She's wearing hot pink today, and the profiler is in dark blue pinstripes. It looks like Barbie's just joined the navy.

"What do you make of the fact that Joy Ellison had no job, no friends, no one to report her missing as the months ticked by?" Summer asks. "What would you guess about her psychological makeup?"

Oh, this ought to be good.

"What it suggests," Pinstripes explains, "is extreme isolation. That's fairly common in a domestic violence situation, especially one serious enough to involve hospitalizations. Domestic abusers are often quite adept at isolating their victims. The woman is made to feel ashamed of her victimization, to believe that she is, in fact, the cause of it. That's what allows the situation to continue for years. Her worldview is entirely shaped by the abuser."

Pinstripes goes on to speculate about the potential kidnapper/killer. "The psychological profile is of someone who becomes very angry when his hold is threatened. Someone with poor impulse control."

"And people who have affairs, are they more or less likely to become jealous and enraged at their spouses?"

"More likely, actually. The fact that they're having an extramarital relationship makes them more paranoid about what their spouse is doing."

"What about a substance abuse history? Would that increase the likelihood of losing control?" Summer isn't saying Brad Ellison's name, but obviously, she's talking about him. Last night, her "scoop" was about his being charged with cocaine possession; the charges were later dropped, which caused Summer to exclaim, "A lot of dropped charges when it comes to this guy! What's all that about?"

"A substance abuse issue would increase the likelihood of violent behavior," Pinstripes affirms.

In the court of public opinion, Brad Ellison has just been found guilty. I'd feel sorry for the guy, but he should have known better. You are who you marry, right?

CHAPTER 36

Gabe

For the first time in my life, I envy guys with standard desk jobs. If I just had my own office—even my own cubicle—I could take a minute. I could regroup.

But my desk is public, on the showroom floor, and Ray is watching me through his glass wall. The month is ticking by, and my sales numbers are still low. The only people I sell cars to are the ones who are really dying to buy a car. That's not many. Fish don't generally jump out of the water and ask for a hook through the mouth. My reeling skills are for shit right now.

I have started trying again. I approach. I use the old lines. But there's no feeling behind them. What I used to have going for me was that I liked people. Apparently, that's the thing that can't be taught or faked. Unless you're Adrienne.

But Leah likes me, and she doesn't like Adrienne. So nah nah nah.

It's agony, sitting here at my desk, exposed, pretending to make follow-up calls. I'd prefer to make actual calls, because it's harder work to come up with one half of a conversation. "So you've been visiting other Lexus dealerships? . . . Infiniti? You can't trust an Infiniti.

They're good-looking but mechanically, they're a joke . . ." I glance over and see that Ray's now occupied with one of the other salesmen. Since no one's within earshot, I keep the phone to my ear, saying nothing, alert for Ray's potential reappearance.

This is no way to live. That's what I find myself thinking a hundred times a day.

I go outside to wander the lot. I hover near a couple, too close maybe, because the wife gives me a look like she fears a mugging. "I'm Gabe," I say, "let me know if you need anything." They nod and move away. I've become a bona fide creep.

I do something I've never done before. "How's your day going?" I text. "Was thinking about you and the baby."

I lean against a CT hybrid, out of Ray's line of sight. Full minutes pass. Then I hear back: "M's great. Smiling a lot. U should give him a chance."

"He's not hurting for attention," I type.

"He needs his dad."

I don't know why it affects me like it does, hearing it from Leah. M needs his dad, she says, and she means me. I'm it. "You home now?" I wait for her answer, but I feel like I can't wait any longer. "I'm coming home."

My job's mostly commission anyway, and I don't have any sales in me today. Tomorrow. I'll turn it around tomorrow.

I stop by Ray's office, poking my head in through the door. "Gotta go," I say. I look back toward the floor, where some of the guys are clustered, hungry. None of them have been complaining about having to pick up my slack. Yuri—the former number two guy around here—has been having a banner month. The rest of them stay away from me, like what I've got might be catching. They're a superstitious bunch. We were never friends exactly, but we used to be buddies. Now I'm on my own.

I'm tired of the self-pity as much as anything. But I feel like I can't catch a break. I lost money at the Pyramid yesterday, and it's still burning me up. It was only a couple hundred dollars, a slow leak rather than one big hand. But I was at the table with Berkeley Goatee, and I had to watch him rake in pot after pot.

"Not home," Leah writes. "Out with T. Talk later?"

"Come in, shut the fucking door," Ray says. "This ain't a drive-by."

I enter, letting the door fall shut behind me.

"Well, sit down."

Now I really feel like a dog. Come in. Shut the door. Sit. I'd quit if I could think of one other thing in the world I'm qualified to do.

"Where have you gotta go?" Ray asks. I zoom in on the concern on his face.

"Home. I'm not feeling so great."

"You don't look great. But that's nothing new."

I try to smile. "Hey, that's my moneymaker you're talking about."

"That's the thing, Gabe. You haven't been making money. Not for the dealership, not for yourself. Did some rich aunt die and leave you a million? You don't need money anymore?"

"I don't need a pep talk, Ray."

"Pep talk? Who's being peppy?" He shakes his head with a mixture of frustration and sadness. I've been seeing that combination a lot lately. "The thing about you is that you need deadlines. You need—what are they called?—boundaries. Otherwise, it's like I'm just giving you a long rope to hang yourself."

I want to tell him I'm not following him, but actually, I am.

"I'm going to let you name the number. You'd better hit it by the end of the month, or, you know." He might as well have drawn a finger across his throat.

I could tell him he can't do this to me, I've got a kid to think about now. Play the kid card, go on. What do I have to lose? My pride left me weeks ago, months. "I'll have the number for you by tomorrow," I say.

"Feel better," he tells me, before pointedly walking over to the board. I let myself out, trying to decide what to do. Do I actually go home, now that I know Leah's not there? Do I go to the Pyramid and press my luck? Stop at a bar?

I want a drink, but I've got to watch it. I need to stay sharp, for Leah's sake. She's swimming with sharks, and I can't help her if I'm drowning myself.

I drive straight home, bracing myself for whatever Adrienne might have in store. But when I push the front door open, she's just sitting in the living room, watching TV, normal as you please. M must be down for his nap. I'm kind of okay with "M"—beats any of the other nicknames Adrienne's tried to float.

"What are you watching?" I ask her.

"Oh, nothing." She looks around for the remote, seeming eager to shut it off. But it's too late. I've already seen the bitch.

I groan. "What's her name again? Autumn?"

"Summer." Now she's decidedly uncomfortable, and the remote is nowhere in sight. "Summer Jackson."

"Summer. Right. A woman disappears, her husband did it. A kid disappears, the father did it. No woman's ever done wrong."

A photo appears on the screen. She's not pretty or unpretty, but she is familiar. By now, Adrienne is about to turn the set off manually; that's what it's come to. Summer is promising a scoop tomorrow.

"No," I tell her. "Leave it on. Doesn't that woman look familiar?"

"She's been missing for a while. You've probably seen the coverage."

"I don't watch these kinds of shows."

"On the regular news, then."

I stare at the woman, trying to place her. "Let me guess," I say. "The husband did it."

Adrienne laughs way louder than the joke warranted. She's nervous, I realize. Or embarrassed, more likely. She's always given the impression that she's some kind of domestic dynamo who never gets a minute to herself. She probably doesn't like my knowing that she's spending her time with Summer Jackson.

Summer Jackson. That's a made-up name if ever there was one.

"Who is she?" I ask. "The missing woman du jour."

"Joy something."

I don't know anybody named Joy. She must look vaguely familiar because of the homogeneity of the genre: The pictures always seem to be of women with windblown hair, on a balcony or a boat, somewhere balmy. It's a curated irony. We're supposed to believe that for these women, life was a beach. It seems sadder that way, to be snatched away in your vacation-going prime.

Adrienne's found the remote underneath the couch. She snaps off the TV and asks, "What are you doing home anyway?"

"My stomach," I say. I learned long ago that the best fake illness is a stomach something-or-other. It's too distasteful for people to ask any questions, and it tends to disappear as quickly as it came.

Adrienne knows that's my illness of choice, but she says nothing. "It's a good thing you picked up some hours yesterday. Did you sell much? Because your last paycheck—"

"I know how much the last check was for. We're still in a recession. Or did you miss that news because you're spending all your time with your pal Summer Jackson?"

My nastiness surprises us both. As if on cue, M starts to cry.

She brushes past me. I sit down and put my feet up, only to realize that the remote has gone MIA once again.

CHAPTER 37

Adrienne

It's a beautiful spring night, an eat-outside-and-drink-white-wine kind of a night. I marinated chicken, and Gabe's manning the grill. Michael and I are sharing a blanket on the grass. He's alternately looking up at me and at the emerging stars.

It's an idyllic scene. If only I could enjoy it. If only I could make Leah and Trevor disappear. Leah would be great TV: Summer and her audience would eat up a young beauty, a young missing mom, like that. Trevor would be the prime suspect. Well, him or Gabe.

Leah and Trevor sit together at the picnic table like a couple of fireflies, alight in their postcoital bliss. Every so often, Trevor makes a goofy face at Michael, and Leah gazes adoringly at him and Michael in turn. It's like she's fallen in love with their little family, the one that I make possible by footing her bills and doing the actual caregiving. Is she some secret genius, turning me into her au pair? Meanwhile, Trevor keeps indulging her fantasy instead of puncturing it. He and I are definitely going to have another talk soon.

They're not the only reason I'm on edge. I didn't like how intently Gabe was staring at the TV yesterday, at Joy Ellison.

Today's scoop wasn't good for me at all. Summer's finally realized that Joy was no angel. Joy's mother was on the show, crying about how she had to cut Joy out of her life five years ago. Joy had been a troubled teen—promiscuous and manipulative and thieving—and as an adult, she'd begun unrepentantly scamming family members, getting them to invest in phony business schemes. "Was that after she got involved with Brad Ellison?" Summer asked. Once she has a suspect in her sights, she stands by her man.

"I don't know Brad," Joy's mother said, wiping at her eyes. "But it was going on long before him. It seems like Joy was born without a conscience."

Summer didn't linger on what Joy's mother said, but obviously, she's going to have to start looking into Joy's past more closely. Soon, she'll discover Joy's con games and her aliases. Even if that doesn't broaden Summer's suspect pool, it's going to have to broaden the police's.

But maybe not. Because Summer had another scoop. Her next guest was a law enforcement officer who talked about Joy's cell phone records. They'd found a text exchange between Joy and Brad in October where she bragged that soon she'd be coming into some "real money, none of this nickel-and-dime bullshit" and he wasn't going to get any of it. If I'm lucky, the police are as lazy and stubborn as Summer.

"Can we presume," Summer asked the officer, "that Brad Ellison might have taken matters into his own hands in order to get some of this windfall?"

"This is an ongoing investigation," the officer said. "I'm not making any presumptions."

But obviously, he can't police the viewers at home. At least I've still got Summer on my side. That's what I'm telling myself.

I have more than enough on my plate right now. Gabe and I need to demonstrate an approximation of our old selves to Leah. She wants her baby to have a loving family, and we've got to be it. It won't be an act for long, because once she clears out of here, we really will become ourselves again. We've got to fake it until we make it, isn't that the AA saying?

Speaking of AA, Gabe is doing his part tonight. He hasn't had any bourbon, hasn't even poured himself a glass of white wine. Leah isn't drinking either, since she's due to pump soon. So it's Trevor and me clinking glasses, toasting this perfect night. Sure, he's underage, but not by much, and I don't think any narcs will be crashing our little party.

I drain my wine and move Michael over on the blanket so that his fingers are in the long grass. He lets out a happy noise and stares at me with wide eyes before returning his gaze to the grass. I love that each individual element of the world is bright and fascinating for him; I just want to be there when he witnesses all of it, bit by bit, blade by blade.

Gabe brings the platter of chicken to the table. "Looks great," I tell him.

"I'll fix you a plate," he says. I'm touched, watching him carefully assemble the salad, corn, and chicken, and place it on the blanket. I'm even more touched when he makes a second plate and then joins me.

"Thank you," I whisper in his ear.

"Kid's into weeds," he says, his voice carrying to Leah and Trevor. "You think I need to worry?"

Leah laughs. Trevor gives no reaction. Even I think the joke's lame, but I'm glad to see Gabe trying. It reminds me of the night Leah arrived, when Gabe stepped up and charmed her. He saw what I needed from him then, and he sees what I need from him now. Gabe reaches toward Michael, and sure, he's petting Michael like a dog, but it's a start. I take Gabe's other hand. This is our fresh start.

As we all eat, Trevor starts talking about some human sexuality museum he and Leah visited. I honestly can't tell if it was in San Francisco and they were there today, or if it was back on the East Coast. He's describing archaic sex toys in humorous detail. He clearly likes center stage. He's got his shtick, and he's not afraid to use it. Though his recitation is funny, it's also gratingly in-your-face juvenile.

"When Mick's old enough to repeat things," I say, "you'll need to tone that down." The remark has a dual purpose. I'm reminding him that a child will definitely cramp his style, but I'm also baiting him to state his true intentions in front of Leah. He's not planning to be around anywhere near that long.

"What's with the 'Mick' shit?" he counters. "I can still say 'shit' for a while longer, right?"

Leah pokes Trevor and says in a low tone, "Gabe doesn't like hearing 'Michael.' They're finding a nickname."

"It better not be Mick." Trevor makes a face. "That's like some aging cockney fucker." He looks at me. "I can still say 'fucker,' right?"

"Is there a problem?" Gabe says. His tone is mild, but the threat is implied in the question.

Leah says quickly, "Trevor has problems with authority. But he knows when to shut up." Her implied threat is much bigger, and Trevor glowers but he goes back to eating. "I need to pump." She heads inside, and after a few minutes of tense silence, Trevor follows.

"Alone at last," I say, throwing myself across Gabe's lap dramatically. He strokes my hair and I look up at him. Darkness is descending rapidly, and the three-quarter moon has an ethereal quality. Michael seems hypnotized by it all. He's never been out at dusk, I realize. But I need to refocus on Gabe. He's been a very good boy tonight, from fixing my plate to petting his son to defending my honor. "I'm thinking that after I put Mick down, you and I can do things we wouldn't want him to repeat." I run my nails up Gabe's arm and back down again. "What do you think?"

"I think 'Mick' isn't really going to work for me. Trevor's right. I keep picturing him strutting around and singing how he can't get no satisfaction."

"I'm not talking about the baby right now." Isn't that what he's wanted all along? For us to have sex and not talk about the baby? I sit up, shaking my head in frustration. Not one bloody thing can be simple, now that there are five of us. We're a pentagon of complications. A pentagram. "Do you want to fuck or not?"

"It's so enticing when you put it that way." His sarcasm smells like a ruse. Not tonight, I have a headache. Not tonight, I'm too annoyed.

I pick Michael up and whisk him into the house. He's crying at his sudden and unceremonious departure, but he calms the second his lips close around the bottle. That, at least, is simple.

I walk him to our bedroom as he drinks. When he's finished, he's sleepy as usual. We're on the bed, and something comes over me, fast and furtive. I strip off my shirt and bra and clutch him to my bare breast. His lips find my nipple immediately, and he begins to suck. There's no milk to be had, and still he sucks.

I find myself wondering: Does he know to suck because it's instinct or because he's done it before? Because Leah's been breastfeeding my baby?

The sucking hurts, and maybe that's because I'm dry. Or maybe it's because I'm not used to the ferocity with which Michael applies himself to the task. Gabe never did it this way.

I can't believe I actually just compared the technique of my baby and my husband. I'm going nuts. This must be what nuts feels like.

I half-expect Michael to cry out in frustration, but he doesn't know any differently. He doesn't know that I should be yielding milk. Instead, he's drinking my closeness in, and it's enough.

I close my eyes and let myself feel that—what it is to be enough.

That night, I dream of Gabe and me in the old Chevy dealership. We're up against the wall, and there's no condom, and I think, If I'm meant to get pregnant, it's okay, it would be Gabe's.

Little did I know. It was never meant to be.

I always wanted Gabe. As a freshman and a sophomore, I'd

watch him and yearn. But I hadn't grown into my looks or my confidence yet, and our paths never crossed. He graduated, and I still thought of him sometimes, hoped we'd run into each other somewhere. Then, in my junior year, after I'd made up for my lack of experience, I caught this weird kid drawing a picture of me. When I found out his last name, it was like everything clicked into focus.

Of course I was wrong to use Michael. But back then, I thought anything was permissible to help fate along. I didn't know how obsessed he'd become or how far he'd go. I only learned that I was his first sex when Gabe told me, years later. I rationalized that Michael was lucky, because he was getting regular sex, and that was definitely not true of all the guys who looked and acted like him.

The sex was surprisingly good, but that might have been because I was fantasizing about Gabe the whole time. Which was much easier to do since I was actually inside Gabe's house, sometimes even on his couch. When I could, I'd wander through his room and rake my fingers over his belongings, feeling the kinetic link.

I've always liked having one single focal point for all my energy. I'm no multitasker. When I was sixteen, Gabe became that focal point, and it remained that way until I was ready to be a mom, until I was thwarted again and again—through IVF, through Patty, and now, maybe, through Leah.

No, it can't happen again.

What Gabe never seemed to realize, what he doesn't want to accept, is that Michael had deeply mixed feelings about him. On the one hand, Michael liked having a cool older brother. He was one genetic degree of separation from a smart, handsome, socially apt jock—all the things Michael wasn't. So there was all this hero worship, which festered into resentment. Michael told me he used to set fire to Gabe's stuff when he was seven or eight; he liked to see people racing into the room, for him. It was my first clue that Michael was not entirely psychologically sound.

But there were others. Like how quickly he started to idealize me. To hear him tell it, I was flawless. He felt that way about Gabe, too, I came to realize. Gabe was perfect, and that made Michael hate him, on some level.

When Michael told me he loved me, I felt bad about leading him on. But I also thought, He's a guy, he'll get over it, he'll find some other "perfect" girl to sleep with. I didn't have a high opinion of guys in general, and Michael was no exception, but Gabe was.

One of the things I've always loved about Gabe is how principled he is. He didn't flirt with me in front of Michael. It showed his decency and his respect for his brother. Sure, I wasn't respecting Michael much, but I thought Gabe ought to. If Gabe had fallen for me right away, he wouldn't have been worth having; he would have been just another guy.

I tried to engage Gabe in conversation, using the information I'd learned from other people about his interests. He was polite but removed. Then one day, I just couldn't contain myself. We were alone and I was crazy about him. It just came out: "I love you more than anything." Then I actually ran away, terrified.

I told myself that the next move was his. Yet for the next two weeks, Gabe avoided me entirely. At first, I was discouraged. Then I got it: He hadn't told Michael, which would have shut the door for good. That meant it was still ajar.

I went to the Chevy dealership, and they told me I could find him in the back room. He was surrounded by shelves of auto parts. I got close, and I couldn't even speak, I was so overwhelmed by him, and his smell, and the moment. I ran my hands up and down his body, smooth as rails, and then there was no stopping us.

The fantasies I used to have when I was with Michael were nothing compared to the reality. But we never kissed, and when it was over, he adjusted my skirt for me and said, "It's just sex."

He was lying, and we both knew it.

"You need to leave me alone," he said. "You have to stop messing with Michael's head." He sounded firm, but there was a plea in it. If I kept coming after him, he would have to give in.

He was right, though. It was time to stop messing with Michael. While Gabe was still at the dealership, I went to his house. I told Michael the truth: that it wasn't working out, that I didn't feel what I was supposed to.

He cried, he begged, he basically debased himself. "We can get the feelings back," he said. "I'll do anything."

I was hoping he'd get angry. I was hoping he'd hate me. This was way worse. But what could I do? There was no going back, no more pretending. It was better for Michael to start getting over me.

For the next week, he called me all the time, pleading. It was summer so we didn't have school. He started following me. I tried being kind and compassionate; I tried cruel. It didn't matter, he wouldn't go away. Finally, I told him I was in love with someone else.

It seemed like it worked, in that he stopped following me. Gabe and I were able to be together in his car after work. It wasn't the classiest, but it still felt magical to me. Gabe wanted to keep us secret, but until when? Until Michael was over me? Until Michael got another girlfriend? Until he went off to college?

Gabe couldn't give me an answer. He didn't want to hurt his brother but he wanted me like he'd never wanted anyone. It was a terrible quandary. I could see that it really ate away at him. I didn't push too hard because I didn't want him to resolve it by ending things between us, and because I didn't want to hurt Michael any more than I had to.

I don't know when Gabe would have been comfortable going public, how it would have played out, but Michael discovered us. He hadn't actually stopped following me, he'd just gotten better at it.

His reaction wasn't what I would have expected. Oddly, he seemed energized. He was furious with Gabe but not with me. "Gabe's a player," he told me. "You're just another girl to him." It's like he thought he was protecting me.

Michael was all hyped up, fueled by his anger at Gabe. I felt like it wasn't even about getting me back but about beating Gabe. Proving that for once in his life, he was superior to his brother.

His whole being seemed to change. I had never heard of bipolar disorder then, but now I wonder if he had it. When people are manic, they can have lots of energy and delusions of grandeur. He told me he wasn't sleeping but he wasn't tired either. "I can do anything," he said, "even get you back." Apparently, people with bipolar can become psychotic; they can crash.

I've told that to Gabe over the years, but he thinks it's just a way to justify our own behavior. "You think I wouldn't have known my brother was crazy?" he said once. Sometimes I wish I'd told him the rest of the story. Then he'd have to feel differently.

The rest is this: One day, Michael's demeanor changed back again. He seemed sad and lost. He asked if I could come to the house, just to talk. "I need a friend," he said. I believed him.

Alone in his room, he told me how much he loved me. "I'd share you with Gabe, if that's what you need," he said. I felt sorry for him, yes, but I also felt, I don't know, flattered. I felt truly loved.

Gabe hadn't yet told me he loved me; he certainly wasn't making any offers to share me. In fact, it was the opposite. He was initially repentant toward Michael—I have a suspicion he offered to dump me but Michael had too much pride to take him up on it—but Michael just stayed enraged. I had the impression he said all kinds of awful things to Gabe, unrepeatable things, and finally, Gabe became angry himself. They were locked in this war, and I was the spoils.

So I was sitting there on Michael's bed, and I had this flash of nostalgia. The sex with Michael had been good, and part of me wondered what it would be like to do it without thinking of Gabe, without needing that fantasy since I now knew the reality.

It's like Michael could see me wavering, and he pounced. He kissed me, and I kissed him back. But afterward, I told him it was a mistake, just like Gabe had once told me. "You need to leave me alone," I said. "It's not going to work between us."

I was thrown by his response. I would have expected crying or begging. Instead, he was lying back against the headboard in this pose of supreme confidence.

"You can't tell anyone, okay?" I said. I didn't mean anyone, of course; I meant Gabe.

It seemed too easy, and it was. Because for the next week, he hounded me. He alternated between pathetic ("Please, just give me another try") and threatening. He said there was a videotape of the last time we were together, with a date and time stamp, and he'd show it to Gabe. "Or," he said, "you could share. The offer's still good." That's when I realized I'd been set up.

I panicked. I didn't think Gabe would understand or forgive me for sleeping with Michael one last time. He definitely wouldn't be okay with sharing.

Michael—pathetic, puny Michael—was just standing there in front of me, so smug, like he'd finally won. He'd beat Gabe, and he'd beat me. I'd never seen him with so much strength and swagger. I'd never hated him before.

On the surface, I gave him what he wanted: He got to see me all the time, whenever I wasn't with Gabe. Be careful what you wish for.

I suppose it would qualify as psychological warfare, but he was the one who fired the first shot. I'd never wanted to hurt Michael before; he'd been collateral damage. When I saw how hurt he was, I'd been genuinely upset. But giving Gabe up wasn't an option. To do so would mean I'd hurt Michael for no reason at all. Wasn't it better for the pain to have had a purpose, for it to be part of a narrative of everlasting love?

I'd seen Michael at his most grandiose, and I couldn't know how long or hard the fall would be. I didn't know how to spot mental illness or what to do about it. I was sixteen years old. All I could see was that Michael was manipulating me. If he'd been doing it for love, I probably could have forgiven that; I'd have understood it. But I felt like it was really about revenge, directed more toward Gabe than me.

What I did to Michael seemed, at the time, like self-defense. I picked at his inadequacies, pulled at them like loose strings until he began to unravel. I let him feel how unwanted he was, while still doing everything he asked. I behaved like a prisoner so that he would soon have to set me free.

It might sound diabolical, but really, I was just a scared kid myself. I was desperately in love with Gabe, having to play double agent to hang on to him. All I wanted was to be done with Michael for good and to be with Gabe only. I mean, why did Michael think his desires should trump everyone else's? Just because he wants someone, it doesn't matter what they want? He wanted power over me; he was coercing sex. It was a form of rape.

One night, he called me over and over again, crying. "You have to love me," he said. "You just have to." I told him that I'd been trying, but it doesn't work that way. "You have to let me go," I said. He told me, "You need to come over or I'm going to kill myself."

Instead of arousing my compassion, it just made me angry. It felt like another brand of manipulation, of control. Here was my rapist, asking for a favor. "Get some sleep," I said. "You'll feel better in the morning."

The next day, I learned he'd slashed his wrists.

I admitted to Gabe that Michael had called me, begging me to love him. I told the absolute truth except for Michael's last line about killing himself. Gabe might think that I didn't do enough to pull Michael back from the brink, and that could be true. But my intention was never to push him over; I just didn't see how close to the cliff he really was.

Gabe's borne a lot of guilt by continuing to see Michael as an innocent victim. But that makes Gabe and me the villains, and I disagree with that version. None of us were innocent. Would a victim blackmail someone with a videotape that never existed? That sounds like villainy to me. Evil begets evil, isn't that how the saying goes?

CHAPTER 38

Gabe

I busted my ass today at work, and just before closing time, I did it. I made the sale. Now I've only got to make another eight before month's end.

By the time I complete all the paperwork and get home, it's almost ten. Leah's on the couch in her pajamas. I get the feeling she's been waiting up for me.

I fold myself into the chair across from her. "Hey," I say. "Where's Trevor?"

"He went to a movie. Adrienne's already in bed." She tucks her legs up under her, like she's settling in. We're about to have a serious talk. "What's up, Gabe?"

"I made a sale. A big one. GS hybrid. Took me all night, but I did it."

"Congratulations."

"The commission should pay for a few cases of diapers." I knit my hands behind my head, aware of a rank smell filtering up from my armpits. It was tense for a while there; I thought the guy was going to walk. "I've still got some adrenaline to burn. You want to go to the Pyramid with me? Play some poker?"

She smiles, sudden and wide. "Seriously?"

"Yeah. Have you been reading your Harrington?"

She shakes her head. I can sense her nervous anticipation.

"You'll do great. You've got the killer instinct."

I've successfully diverted her from whatever she was about to say. Works for me. I don't need any heavy talks. She gets to her feet. "What do I wear?"

I laugh. I never would have expected that question out of her. For one thing, 90 percent of her wardrobe is black.

"Forget it, I'll figure it out. I just need to pump first. I don't want to start leaking at the table."

"That'd be one way to get a guy to fold his hand."

"Or push all-in."

We laugh together, and then she's gone for about fifteen minutes. I think about going into my bedroom to change, but I might wake Adrienne. Better to leave a note on the refrigerator. She'll see it when she gets milk for the next feeding.

I was looking forward to telling her about the sale, though. In the old days, a GS was cause for major celebration.

I still can't believe I turned Adrienne down last night. That's, what, the second time that's happened in our marriage? The first time I had a 103 degree temperature. I don't know what it was; I just couldn't be close to her.

Leah returns. She's brushed her hair and put it back in a low ponytail, and she's wearing red lipstick. "What?" she says.

"You just look . . ." I meet her eyes. "Perfect. You look perfect. You're going to win a grand, I can feel it."

"How much do I need to put in?"

"It's a maximum buy-in of two hundred dollars at the one-dollar/two-dollar table. I wouldn't do less than a hundred dollars, unless you want to play short stack, which doesn't give you any room to open up your game." At her worried expression, I say, "Don't worry, I'll bankroll you."

"If I lose—"

"Then it was just money. Just poker. It's your first time out. Relax, I sold a GS tonight." I neglect to mention it's all I've sold all week, or that I'm on probation. You can't think like that before you play poker. You worry too much about the money, you play scared; you play scared, you fold too easily, you beat yourself.

On the drive to the Pyramid, I quiz Leah: What are the best starting hands? How do you play early position versus late position? How do you calculate pot odds?

After we're parked in the lot, I pronounce her ready as she'll ever be. She's nervous, yeah, but she's also excited. We walk in together, and I can't help it, I'm proud. Ames is waiting on the rail, and he does a double take. I realize what it is: Leah's Adrienne, but younger.

"This is Leah," I say. "She's the birth mother."

"Oh, sure," he says, like everyone antes up with the mother of their adopted child. "Leah. Good to meet you." When she turns to look around, he mouths to me, "Holy fuck." I start to laugh.

"What's funny?" Leah asks.

"Let's get on the list." I steer her over to the board, and we're in luck. We're seven and eight, so within a couple minutes, they've started a new table. Technically, Leah shouldn't sit right next to me—it's bad form—but she's a newbie, and gorgeous to boot, and the Pyramid's not exactly the Bellagio, so no one's going to say anything. We seize prime real estate, directly across from the dealer. Ames leaves a seat between him and me in a nod to protocol.

It's a mix of ages and styles at the table: a twenty-five-ish nerd who can't stop sneaking glances at Leah, a nondescript fortysomething guy I've never seen before, a couple old Asians who couldn't give a shit less about her or anyone else (they're going to raise with aces and kings and ace-kings and pretty much fold the rest), a younger Asian kid who raises big with any two hole cards, Ames, Leah, and me. There are two empty seats, one on each side of the dealer. Leah smiles when anyone catches her eye; everything about her screams "first time out." But if they underestimate her, they're going to be sorry.

Everyone buys in for $200, except for the nerd, who does $75. I whisper to Leah that she should watch out for him: "Any hand he plays, he's got to be prepared to go all-in, so you need to be prepared for that, too." She nods with great seriousness.

Ames leans over the back of his chair and asks me in a low voice, "Has she played before?"

"I've been teaching her."

He groans. "That's all I need."

I'm debating whether to tell Leah some tips on how to neutralize the young Asian kid's loose-aggressive style when Berkeley Goatee takes the seat to the left of the dealer. I start smiling. Now we've got ourselves a game. I'm going to whup his ass, I can feel it. I sold a GS tonight. My luck is changing, and Leah's here to witness it.

Berkeley Goatee notices me, so I immediately whisper to Leah. It's petty, but I want him to know we're together. "I hate that guy," I say, "the one with the goatee." Her eyes land on him.

"Hi," she says.

"Hi." He seems wary, but that might be because he's not used to a girl who looks like that talking to him.

He buys in for $200, and then we're off.

I fold the first hand, and the second, and the third. Ditto for the fourth and the fifth. I even have to fold my big blind to a raise from the Asian kid. It's frustrating, being card-dead when I want to show Leah how it's done.

Leah, meanwhile, is aggressive immediately. She reraises the Asian kid two out of three hands, and he folds both times, though he spends some time thinking about it and studying her. When she's in a hand, she's cold as ice and just as still. Then when she's collecting her chips, she starts blushing and smiling like a geisha. It's genius. It's like the guys are rooting for her in spite of themselves.

"Next time," the Asian kid says, "you better show."

"Or what?" she answers coquettishly. "You'll fold?"

The guys all laugh, and he has to laugh with them.

"This is fun," she whispers to me. I watch her stack her chips, and

I realize this is how I always imagined Adrienne would be, if she ever cared about poker. I feel proud of Leah, which is funny, since the birth mother of your son is not exactly an extension of you, not like a wife.

So maybe it's more like a coach and a player. I've taught her well, and now she's making good.

Nah, it's not really that either. I've never known precisely what it is with Leah and me.

I fold again and again. I'm a spectator here. Finally, I raise with a 3-4 suited. Hey, it's got potential. Any two cards can make a full house with the right board.

Leah, who's acting after me, actually reraises. Jesus.

Then one of the old Asian guys reraises her. I fold, she folds, and he takes down the pot with his aces or kings or ace-king. We don't even see a flop. It's not too exciting, except that Leah is sending me a message. She's here to play, even against me. Because she obviously wasn't reraising me with a premium hand or she wouldn't have folded to that reraise so quickly.

Berkeley Goatee looks at me with a smirk. He noticed Leah's move, too. I wonder what he thinks my relationship is to her. No one's going to guess birth mother. I can only hope no one's guessing she's my daughter. My wife? I'm wearing a ring, she's not. Mistress? I wouldn't mind.

It reminds me of that day when Leah and I went to the Richmond and she pretended to be my wife. I was uncomfortable because I didn't know her intentions and it felt disloyal to Adrienne. I've gotten over that.

Leah goes on to take a big pot from Goatee; I lose one. But I can't blame myself. He had pocket queens, I had pocket jacks, and if our hands had been reversed, we would have each played it the same. I realize that the previous rancor between Goatee and me has evaporated. Somehow, Leah has brokered a détente. It helps that she's beating him every hand they're playing together, and that feels a little like my beating him.

Occasionally, we talk to each other, but mostly, Leah and I address our chatter to the table. Still, I feel close to her. It's why I used to want to play with Adrienne. Later, I know Leah and I will do a postmortem on the various hands; we'll laugh about the other players, and ourselves. So even as I'm having the experience, I'm taking notes on how I want to share it with her once we're alone. What's more intimate than the anticipation of greater intimacy later?

A couple of companionable hours pass. I'm still largely card-dead. I manage to steal a few blinds and win one legitimate pot with a big pair; I'm breaking even. Leah is continuing to accrue fairly steadily. When she reaches a showdown, she's always got the best hand.

Our table's full. There's a hulking black guy to the right of the dealer with a scar bisecting his eyebrow. He's quiet and never makes eye contact. He's a terrible player, doesn't know how to fold, but he knows how to rebuy. I've seen him lose thousands with no visible reaction. Ames says he's heard that the guy's a fixer. I didn't even know fixers existed, outside of a Scorsese movie. "Does he kill people?" I asked Ames, intrigued. "Break their legs? What?" Ames shrugged and said, "Probably. But the real money is in covering his tracks, and theirs."

I like when the Fixer joins my table. For one, it's easy money. For another, how often do you brush up against a real gangster? Sure, I've sold cars to guys with questionable business dealings before, but the Fixer—he's out there committing real violence. Just having him at the table raises the stakes on a level that has nothing to do with poker.

I scoop up some of the Fixer's chips. Ames, Leah, and Goatee do, too. The Fixer lifts all boats.

Then I finally get a real hand, the realest. A couple of aces. But I'm in early position, so I don't want to do a big raise that scares everyone away. I do a min-raise, twice the big blind. People generally don't know what to make of that.

Leah calls. Generic calls. Then the young Asian kid raises big: five times my initial raise. I'm not worried about him. He's just trying to steal, and he thinks my min-raise meant I had something like pocket sevens. Goatee calls. It's the kind of action I was hoping for.

You don't want to have too many people in the pot who can outflop you when you've got a big starting pair, even the best starting pair there is. So I've got to weigh out whether to push all-in now and drive them out (it's already a pretty good haul, my best of the night) or just call and see the flop. They won't expect me to have aces, if I just call. It is a risk, though; I'd prefer to isolate one of them. The old Asian guys would definitely push all-in. But I've got Leah next to me, and I want her to really see what I can do.

I call. Leah calls, too. That means I've got pocket aces, but I'll have three opponents on the flop. I'm not loving this. Generic folds.

Flop comes king-ten-eight, with two clubs. I've got the ace of clubs, but to get a flush, I'd need runner-runner. Those are not good odds, and one of my three opponents could have two clubs in their hand. What is good, though, is that no one can yet have a straight, only a straight draw. If anyone has pocket tens or pocket eights, I'm in trouble. I'm pretty sure nobody's got pocket kings.

I put in an almost pot-sized bet. There are too many draws out there between straights and flushes. But I do want at least one caller. I'm pretty much pot-committed now. On the next street, I'll be all-in.

Leah thinks a while as she watches me. It's a sexy look, like she knows something. I have always wondered if I've got a tell when it comes to her. Then she says, quietly, "All-in."

I'm either way ahead or way behind. If she's got a set of eights or tens, I haven't got much of a chance; I'd need an ace for a set of my own, or a jack and a queen for a straight, or two flush cards. So I've got outs, but it's slim. Or I'm ahead, and she needs to catch her cards.

Part of me wants to beat her, same as any opponent. But the other part—well, her beating me would be kind of a turn-on. I've always loved a woman who won't back down. Despite everything, I still do.

The other guys fold, and watch intently. Every poker session, there are one or two hands that charge the air molecules. This is the one. But with Leah here, I don't think it's just the air that's charged. I'm not the only one who's hard, I assure you.

I push all my chips into the center and turn my cards over. I'm expecting her to do the same, but her eyes are on the board. She's not going to show until she has to. I'm pretty sure she's on a draw.

Ten of hearts, three of clubs. If she was on a flush draw, she's got me.

She mucks, tossing her cards into the center, unseen. Her mouth is set in disappointment.

She had me covered, so she's left with over $100. "That's more than enough to get back in it," I point out to her. She shakes her head to tell me not to bother, she doesn't need my consolation. She's pissed. I'm dying to know her hole cards, if it was a stone-cold bluff and she really had nothing but the will to push me out of the hand, but with her looking like that, there's no way I'm going to ask.

I didn't see it coming, how much she really, really wanted to beat me.

CHAPTER 39

Adrienne

I haven't been able to sleep tonight, so I'm rewatching today's episode of Summer Jackson on DVR. I'm looking for clues: not to her disappearance, obviously, but to how much Summer and the police really know. Summer conceded that Joy seems to be a con woman, and a con woman makes enemies, but then she moved on to the day's "scoop." If the police have traced any of Joy's victims, Summer either doesn't know about it, or she's not telling. It wouldn't surprise me if Summer and the police have some sort of deal: She only reports what they want getting out.

It might just be for ratings, or because Summer can't admit she's wrong, but she's still plugging Brad Ellison as the guilty party. Her scoop today was a second interview with him.

Lucky for me, Summer isn't going to let a little thing like journalistic integrity or a search for the real killer interfere with her coverage.

Poor Brad. You'd think he'd have figured out by now that he's not going to get a fair shake from Summer Jackson. Either he's an eternal optimist, he's a total idiot, or his self-regard is way too high and he actually thinks he can charm Summer and her viewers.

"I'm ready to come clean," he says. Indeed, he is cleaner than last time. He's even wearing a tie, and his hair is shorter, less gelled. I can't imagine he had the money for a PR team so he must have smartened up a little on his own.

"I appreciate that," Summer says, though her voice is hardly welcoming. Neither is her suit, which is a funereal black. For Joy's funeral, or for Brad's? She waits for him to speak so he can hang himself.

He obliges. "Yes, I was dating, but I'm sure Joy was, too. We were separated."

"The woman you were 'dating' says you were practically living at her house."

"She was mad after it came out about Joy. So she exaggerated. I should have told her I was married." Summer nods sternly. "But the whole thing about how I didn't come over to her house around the time Joy went missing—that's BS. There were a lot of times when I stayed away for a few days. Sometimes I was tired from work, sometimes I just had other stuff to do. So it's not like she made it sound."

It's a lousy performance. I know for a fact that he didn't kill Joy, and I'm *still* having a hard time believing him.

"You came on my show," Summer says, "and talked about how you love Joy and wanted to reconcile with her."

"That's true."

"Was Joy a con woman, Brad?"

He shifts uncomfortably. "Not that I know of."

"Were you conning people together, or was that her solo gig?"

"I was off working for my money!" His face reddens. Doesn't he know anything? You can't afford to sweat, and you can't afford to flush, and above all, you *cannot* raise your voice at Summer Jackson. She fells him with a look, and when he speaks, his voice is much quieter. "It was hard, being away from Joy, and not having steady work. The truth is, sometimes I was gone for a few days because I relapsed. Crack, and cocaine. I go to NA. I have a sponsor. But it's hard."

"Have you ever had a blackout during a relapse?"

He turns crimson. "I didn't kill Joy."

"Who said she was dead, Brad?" It's a clever rejoinder, though it doesn't really mean anything. Everyone's presuming Joy's dead by now.

"To answer your question, no, I don't have blackouts. I definitely don't have blackouts where I drive eight hours and hurt my wife."

"Hurt her how?" Summer is enjoying this. Whether it's because she thinks she's got a guilty man on the ropes or because she hates all men or because she specifically hates this man (who, admittedly, is no prize, between the crack cocaine and the DV charge and his lies), I've got no way of knowing. But it is good television, her cat-and-mouse routine. There's nothing Summer loves as much as a particularly stupid, meaty mouse like Brad.

She starts showing clips from his previous interview and the interviews with his ex-girlfriend, law enforcement, and even the psychological profiler talking about substance abuse and poor impulse control. She's systematically dismantling Brad, and in rewatching it, I'm starting to feel dirty myself. Yes, she's able to do it because he's a lying dirtbag with multiple arrests; because he used to beat his wife; because he lied to his girlfriend. Most likely, he knew about Joy's scams and might even have participated in some of them. This is not some upstanding citizen being railroaded. But he is being railroaded, that much I know.

At one point, he says helplessly, "Do I look like a guy who's had a windfall?" and that clinches it. I do, officially, feel sorry for him. I thought he might be too stupid to have self-awareness, kind of like some lower species, but no, he gets what's happening to him. He's ready to gnaw his own foot off to escape Summer's trap. I might be the only one who can spring him.

The knock on the bedroom door makes my heart race. My first thought is that it's the police. Despite Summer's dog-and-pony show, they're actually doing their own investigating, which has led them to me.

But that's so preposterous that I need a new thought, and here's one that's more realistic: It's Gabe, and we've drifted so far apart that he feels the need to knock on our bedroom door.

Trevor sticks his head in. His hair is standing on end, like he's been running his hand through it repeatedly and it's so greasy that it's maintaining the form. His hygiene habits really leave something to be desired.

"Did you see the note?" he asks, thrusting the offending paper toward me.

"Yes."

"He's taking advantage of her, you know."

"Can we talk about this tomorrow?" I should pump him for information; now's a good opportunity, but I just don't have it in me.

He's clearly amped up and not about to let this go. He begins pacing by the foot of the bed. "Do you think Leah planned it? That's why she told me to go to the movies by myself? Do you think they planned it together?"

"It's not a getaway, Trevor. They went to play poker. They'll be back soon." But I feel the tiniest seed of doubt.

He's still pacing. "He has feelings for her. You get that, right?"

"They're friends."

He stops in front of me. "You seriously think that's all it is?"

"Yes, I seriously do. Gabe's got ethics. He doesn't take advantage of young girls, and he doesn't cheat."

"He's messing with her head. He knows her history."

Now, this is news. Gabe knows her history, but I don't? "Sit down." I lean against the headboard and pat the bed. "No more pacing."

"I just think he's taking advantage of her not having a dad. Acting like he's looking out for her, but really, she has to watch out for him."

"I'm not following you."

"You know the story, right?" I nod. I've learned that the quickest way to learn a story is to pretend you already know it. "All kids want to know their parents. They want to be like, 'I've got her eyes,' or, 'I've got his temper.' You know? She doesn't have that. She doesn't remember shit."

"Because she was so young," I say, taking a stab.

"Yeah. I mean, do you remember stuff from before you were three?"

"Not really."

"I bet she doesn't even want to remember. That it was that bad. I fucking hate addicts."

So Leah's parents were addicts, and she only knew them until she was three. "She got taken away from them," I guess.

"Well, yeah." It has the cadence of "duh." He finally pushes back the sari and sits on the bed.

"And they never tried to come back into her life, right?"

"They might not even be alive, who knows. They might have overdosed. They might be in jail. So she hasn't had anybody, and Gabe knows that, and for some crazy reason, she trusts him—"

"She should trust him. He's a good person."

Trevor cocks his head at me. "He doesn't give a shit about Michael. You get that, right? I'd feel better if it was just you and Michael, to be honest."

"Is that how Leah feels?"

"No! I just told you, she trusts him. More than you, actually. Which is nuts."

"That is nuts." I knew from the texts that she didn't like me, but she doesn't trust me?

"You know about all the foster homes and the group homes and about her having, like, nowhere to go once she aged out of the system last year"—I really didn't know any of that, so go on—"but I don't think you know the most fucked-up part, and why she's so susceptible to what Gabe's trying to do. If I tell you, you can't tell Gabe, though. Deal?"

"Deal." Gabe didn't tell me about the addict parents and the group homes, so it's only fair that he should be in the dark about something, too.

Trevor takes a deep breath. "So when Leah was eight, she was going to get adopted. She'd been in a bunch of different foster homes by then, and she never got along with the parents, or they didn't get along with her, whatever. It's hard going into other people's houses, you know?" Not that she seemed to have any problem with it a few months ago. "It's like, they have all their routines and you're just supposed to fall in line. Like, nothing's planned around you, there are always other kids."

"I can imagine."

"But when she's, like, seven and a half, she starts living with this couple. They didn't have any other foster kids, they were just totally devoted to her. They were in their forties, she said. The guy saw that she liked art and he encouraged her. He made a big deal out of her, like she was really special." He looks at me pointedly. "Sound like anyone you know?"

I've never heard Gabe make a big deal out of her, but I have to admit, he encourages her art. I tried to do the same; I just never got anywhere. She's been all about Gabe since her plane first landed. Trevor might be onto something. "I'm listening."

"Leah wasn't going to make it easy on them, even though she wanted her own family, like, bad. She didn't trust people, especially nice people. She'd met them before and they always turned out to have something wrong with them. Like in one foster family, there was the nice uncle, and you know the deal with those guys."

I stare at him. "Are you saying she got molested?"

"Well, yeah." There it is again, the "duh."

"How old was she?"

"Five or six, maybe."

I shake my head. If she were mine, I'd have killed him. I'd have cut his dick off, no question. But she didn't have someone like me to protect her, or it never would have happened, any of it. All this time,

I've been thinking she had parents somewhere whom she was ignoring. I never imagined. Gabe never told me.

"That's evil," I say.

"You want to hear evil, I'm getting to it."

"What did he do to her, the guy who was going to adopt her?"

"He broke her down, man. All her walls. He got her to love him and believe in him. That couple got Leah thinking she was going to have a family. She let herself want that again, even though it's so scary for a little girl who's been fucked over, you know?" I see he's almost crying for the girl Leah used to be.

"She didn't get adopted, did she?"

"The wife got pregnant. It was a surprise, they said. A miracle. They didn't think that could happen to them or they never would have taken Leah to begin with. They decided they didn't have enough for two kids—not enough money, or attention, or love. So they chose their real kid."

"Shit," I whisper. Leah was eight, just a little older than my kids at school. A little older than Angie with her Pippi Longstocking braids. How would a child that small metabolize a rejection that large? She'd never have the faculties. And she wouldn't even have anyone to help her. She'd be all alone in the world, adrift, floating on to the next foster home, and when she got too old for that, group homes. That was Leah's life.

"You know what made me sick? It was how they tried to still seem like good people. Leah said they were both crying when they told her, and they wanted to visit her in her new foster home. They said they'd give her references—*references,* like it's a job interview!—so that the next people could know how great Leah was, that all she needed was a little love, and bam, she'd open up like a fucking flower."

"But Leah wouldn't give them the satisfaction."

"No way. She didn't want anything from them. She shut down and never saw them again. Never connected with anyone she lived with. They were all just a bed and a meal to her. That's why she liked the group homes better. They weren't pretending to be family." He stares at me hard. "But Gabe—he's pretending like he's her family. Teaching her poker, telling her how much he likes her art."

"He likes poker. He does like her art."

"Somehow, her bullshit detector is turned off when it comes to him."

"Why are you so sure he's bullshitting her? What does he have to gain?"

The vein in Trevor's neck throbs. "I was hoping you could tell me."

"You're wrong about Gabe. What you see is mostly what you get." I wish I could sound more definite, but why didn't Gabe tell me about Leah's past? Did he think I'd use it against her? I'm not some kind of monster. Or does he just like having a secret with her?

"'Mostly' isn't good enough when it comes to Leah."

I smile at him. "She's lucky that she has you. I never knew how protective you were until now."

"I just think you need to understand Leah. She can't be blamed for anything fucked up that she does because the most fucked-up thing of all has already happened to her."

"Wait, what are you saying? Is she going to do something fucked up to me, or to Gabe? Or to Michael?"

"I didn't say that." But suddenly, he doesn't want to make eye contact. "Gabe just needs to watch out. You know how they say a wounded animal is the most dangerous? Well, Leah's like the most wounded animal."

"Is she dangerous to me, too?" I touch his arm. "Hey, I need to know. If she's got plans for me, or Michael, or Gabe, you have to tell me. I'm Michael's mother, and it's my job to make sure nothing bad happens to him. He's not going to have a life like Leah's, I swear to you."

"The thing about Leah is, she's bad at plans. She makes lots of them, but when it comes down to it, she's all impulse."

I think of that text, Leah and her supposed plan for Gabe and me. Is Trevor lying? He certainly seemed sincere when he told me that story, but you can't know anyone, not really. Besides, if he was so interested in protecting Leah, would he have thrown her away when she was pregnant, despite knowing her history?

"You can't tell her I told you," he says. "You definitely can't tell Gabe. But you need to watch them both. That's what I'm going to do."

My brain is like a washer agitating. I don't know what to think about anything. My heart aches for eight-year-old Leah, who finally let herself believe and then had everything ripped away from her. But I'm afraid I might soon know the feeling.

Much as I hate that Leah went through that, I'm not going to let it happen to me. And I'm not going to let a girl that damaged, someone who's never even known a mother, cut her teeth on Michael, if that's what her impulse is currently dictating.

"Trevor," I say, "you have to tell her the truth. I've seen how she looks when it's you and her and Michael. She's living in a fantasy about becoming a family. No wonder, with her past. But if that's not what you want, you need to tell her that. You can't lead her on."

"I know. I will."

"Soon. The longer she nurtures the fantasy, the worse it'll be." Believe me, I know what I'm talking about. "I see it taking hold more each day. It scares me."

I haven't admitted that out loud, not even to Gabe. But then, Gabe's not the one who can do anything about it. Trevor is.

I just wish he looked a little more confident right about now.

CHAPTER 40

Gabe

It's after three A.M., and Leah and I are still sitting in the driveway. We talked nonstop during the admittedly short ride home and then tacked on another hour after that. I loved hearing her assessments of Berkeley Goatee, the Fixer, Ames, and all the other personalities that came and went from our table during our tenure. Her analysis of the hands was spot-on and just different enough from my own to fascinate. Mostly, though, we feel the same: that playing poker is about waves of exhilaration, concentration, and boredom, and that there's no more immediately available and equally satisfying way to battle a bunch of near-strangers. And friends, if that's indeed what Leah and I are.

Why the question? Because it feels like a greater bond than mere friendship. She's the mother of my child; she named him Michael when I thought I needed that; she told me to change the name when I needed *that*. She's seeing me at a time when no one else seems to, especially Adrienne. Adrienne's defection hurts, but it hurts less because Leah is in my life.

"You can't go anywhere," I tell her. The adrenaline after a poker session is like truth serum.

Still laughing, she says, "I'm starting to get tired, Gabe. Honestly, if I don't pump soon . . ." She lets it dangle there, and my eyes move involuntarily to her swollen breasts.

"Were you this beautiful before you had him?" Was she always built like a dream, big tits and little everything else? I can't remember where I heard that descriptor before, but man, does it fit.

She doesn't drop her gaze, doesn't shift away with discomfort or annoyance like she did that time when she was painting the mural. "We can't do anything. You know that."

"We can do *some* things." I lean back in the seat and smile at her. I'm not thinking clearly, except that I feel happier than I have in months. No, not months. Since our late-night talks. I felt happy then, too.

"I'm in love with Trevor. You're in love with Adrienne." Her eyes on mine are intense. "Aren't you?"

If I say no, then what? Would it be a lie, even? "I don't know anymore." I glance toward the house. It's the home I made with Adrienne when we fled New Jersey, went into exile, left the scene of our crime far behind. "There's something between us that's bigger than love."

"I have that with Trevor, too." Her eyes flash with something like defiance. "It's called a baby."

"Hey." I want to reach for her hand, but that might be a point of no return. I know those exist, like Adrienne and me in that stockroom more than twenty years ago. I can't destroy Leah like Adrienne and I destroyed Michael. "I'm trying to be honest here."

"It's such an old, gross story. Like Daddy and the babysitter." Her tone has turned savage.

"You were thinking the same thing I was. I need to tell you why it can't happen."

"I don't think like you do, Gabe. Don't lump me in that category."

What category? I want to ask. But I think the answer would just be an attempt to hurt me, like she's been hurt. Her real parents, and then all those foster families, and the group homes—Leah's got scars I can't begin to know.

"I never want to hurt you," I say. "I don't want Trevor hurting you either."

"What makes you think he's going to hurt me? He's in my pocket."

"I've got a feeling about him."

She laughs. "Well, he's got the same feeling about you. What if you're both right? Then I'm really fucked."

"You're not fucked. You're a star. You've got your whole life ahead of you. You can walk out of here with a clean slate. Do you know what I'd give for that?"

She stares at me incredulously. "You really don't get it at all, do you? I had a baby. That's for life, no matter what I do. I used to believe in clean slates, but I don't anymore. So I need to deal with it."

"Listen, I'm going to tell you a story. Then you'll know what made me who I am, what I had to deal with. You'll get me. I don't know why, but I need that. Will you listen?"

She watches me for a long minute, her face softening incrementally by the second. Then she nods.

All she knew was that Michael killed himself as a teenager. Until tonight, she didn't know my role in his death.

Flushed with shame, I begin to tell her the whole truth: how drawn I was to Adrienne, how much it meant to me that she loved me more than anything. That one little phrase was enough for me to blow up my own brother. Yes, I tried to stay away from her, but I failed. I told her to leave me alone, but she still broke up with Michael. I couldn't tell her no and have it stick.

"He was so upset, he became this ghost haunting our house," I tell Leah. "He couldn't sleep or eat. All he wanted to talk about was Adrienne and how he could get her back. I told him she wasn't worth it, that other girls would come along and they'd love him a lot more than Adrienne had. I said I'd heard things about her being with other guys.

"He looked at me like he hated me. He said Adrienne was perfect, she was pure, who did I think I was to go repeating rumors?"

I don't want to go on, but Leah encourages me with eyes that say she'll understand anything.

"He was determined to get her back," I continue. "I'd never seen that side of him. Never seen him want anything that bad, so bad he was finally willing to try. He told me he needed her. I tried to convince him no one needs anyone, it's a myth, it's a Hallmark card, but I was lying. Because I felt like I needed Adrienne, too. She kept coming to my work and waiting by my car, and finally, I gave in." I can't say any more about that, the shame is too great. Choosing sex over your own brother's life?"

"You were, what, sixteen?" Leah asks, full of sympathy.

"I was nineteen."

"My age."

"Yeah. Adrienne and Michael, they were both sixteen. But I was old enough to know right and wrong. Old enough to know you shouldn't fall in love with your brother's first real girlfriend."

She leans her head sideways into the seat. "You can't control everything."

I thought I wanted her absolution but her willingness to excuse me so readily seems to make everything worse. It's like I need to prove to her just how bad I really was. How bad I am. "Wait. You haven't heard the whole story yet."

I take a deep breath and resume. "I was just hoping that if Adrienne and I kept it secret, if enough time passed, then Michael would have to let go of her. Once he didn't care about her anymore, then we could go public, Adrienne and me. I know some people think sneaking around is sexy, but it wasn't for me. I hated it.

"A couple weeks went by, maybe, and somehow, Michael found out. I knew he'd be pissed at me, but the crazy thing was, he was *only* pissed at me. He said I was the one who was supposed to be loyal. He said I was taking advantage of Adrienne, like she was some stray puppy I led home." My breathing is becoming constricted, just remembering. "He said I was jealous and that he'd figured me out. His whole life, while I was pretending to be on his side, I was really trying to keep him down."

"Was any of it true?" Leah asks quietly.

"No! I mean, I was supposed to be loyal, he was right about that, but I'd always looked after him. With my mom dead, it was like a mission. Then he's standing there, telling me he hates me, he's always hated me, and he knows what a shit I really am, and I don't know, I snapped."

"Everyone snaps sometimes."

"I don't mean I snapped and yelled at him, or hit him, or anything that temporary. No, I turned against him. I thought, If he's going to hate me, I'll hate him right back, that ungrateful little fucker. After all the times I stood up for him, made sure no one would bully him, he's going to tell me I meant to keep him down?" I shake my head, wishing I could shake it all loose, that the memories could flurry down and out of my brain forever.

"So you were mad for a while."

"Yeah. But I think it was bullshit. I think I was just looking for an excuse to stay with Adrienne. If I was mad at Michael, then I didn't have to feel bad about what I was doing. Hell, I could even go public with Adrienne, and he'd just have to deal with it. I was looking for a loophole to let me have what I wanted instead of looking out for my little brother." I feel a sob coming on. "He was my little brother, and I screwed him over. I took away the girl he loved. Then when he hated me for it, instead of being sorry, instead of ending things with her for good, I just . . ." Now I really can't go on.

Leah's arms are around me, and I'm crying into her neck. "It's okay," she says.

"No, it's not. He's dead. How can that be okay?"

She doesn't have an answer for that. But what I started, I'm going to finish. I pull myself upright and force myself to tell the rest.

"Until then, until all that stuff with Michael and Adrienne, I believed I was a good guy. I was honest with girls, and I looked after my brother. I didn't try to hurt anybody. But it's like I was never tested before.

"Because it turned into a self-fulfilling prophecy, what Michael had said to me. I became jealous of him. I didn't like that he kept pursuing Adrienne, and I didn't like that she seemed to feel bad for him. For the first time in our lives, we were truly in competition. Michael had always bailed out before and just let me have everything; he figured I'd win anyway, even if he tried. But he wasn't giving up this time."

"You both loved her that much, huh?" Leah sounds wistful.

"We both thought so. I was sure I had the upper hand, because Adrienne didn't love Michael more than anything, if she loved him at all."

"But part of you started to wonder."

"Yeah, you always have to wonder, a little. It's like, when you cheat and then the other person leaves their husband for you, you're never one hundred percent sure they won't do it again, but to you this time."

"Maybe you're right to wonder," she says. "I mean, Adrienne was the one who made it all happen. She pitted you guys against each other."

"Not exactly."

"Yeah, exactly. Why was she with Michael to begin with? To get to you. You tell her to leave you alone but she won't. She's like quicksand. When you're in too deep, when she knows she has you, she breaks up with him. Then she's like, 'Oh, poor Michael.' It's classic."

"Classic what?"

"Classic teenage-girl manipulation." Leah rolls her eyes. "Seriously, how dumb are you guys?"

I want to smile in spite of myself. "So you think I was pretty stupid?"

"I think you were a *guy*. You probably still are." She smiles to show she's kidding. "She worked you over. She worked Michael over."

"But she couldn't know what was going to happen."

"She probably didn't care."

I've had that disloyal thought myself before. I always quash it. "This isn't about Adrienne. It's about me, and what I did to my brother." At least, that was the point of the story. Leah's got me questioning the narrative a little bit. "You don't even know the kinds of ugly things I thought about him in those weeks before he died. He was a fragile kid, and I didn't see him that way. I saw him as the competition. The enemy. Adrienne didn't do that. I did."

"How sure are you?"

"About what?"

"What you did. What she did." Her eyes glitter in the darkness. "I feel like you want me to tell you how bad you are. Is that what Adrienne does for you? Makes you feel bad so then she can make you feel good?"

"No, it's not like that. She doesn't want me blaming myself."

Leah turns away and stares out the windshield. "I don't know if I can let Michael be raised by someone like Adrienne."

I feel a glacial flood of panic. "Whatever Adrienne did then, she's a different person now. You said it yourself: It was classic teenage-girl manipulation. Adrienne is almost forty. She loves Michael more than anything. You can see that."

"I don't like her way of loving more than anything." She still won't look at me.

"I was older. I was his brother. If anyone had the greater responsibility . . ." I'm babbling now, but it's for nothing. Leah heard what she wanted to hear, and she's stopped listening.

CHAPTER 41

Adrienne

"You all know I've been following the case of Joy Ellison," Summer Jackson intones, "the Colorado woman who is presumed to have disappeared at least five months ago, though her husband only reported it six weeks ago. We've learned she had a number of aliases, with the possibility of criminal activity, though no charges were ever brought against her and no witnesses have come forward. Today, there's been a major development. Her body has been found."

I can barely hear the TV over Michael's wailing. He's been crying for much of the afternoon. It's one of his rare and inexplicable jags, the first in a long time, and I wonder if he somehow knows, intuitively, that his mama could be in big trouble. He senses my connection to Joy. Or maybe it's withdrawal symptoms, he misses Trevor and Leah, who are off having afternoon delight. Or maybe it's just gas.

It is loud, though, and painful for both of us. I hate to hear him suffer; I hate to be incapable of easing his suffering. But I do need to hear this special breaking news. I push the volume button on the remote control and let it blare.

Summer interviews a law enforcement officer who explains that the body is badly decomposed, it's too early to say if they'll be able to recover any forensic evidence, but they have been able to confirm that the remains are Joy Ellison's. I'm lucky, I suppose, that it's been just over six months, which I've learned from my reading is the average time it takes a body to wear down to the bones.

In my case—well, Patty's case—it was supposed to be quicker. The ground near the abandoned mine shaft speeds up decomposition, which is why people choose it as a dumping ground. I learned about it in a few quick Google searches: Scott Powell said it was the best place to get rid of a body only a year before he murdered his wife, Susan. Her body has never been found. That makes him as reliable a source as anyone. It's not like I had people I could call: "Hey, what should I do with Patty's body?"

I still can't really think of her as Joy. That's probably been self-serving: I could follow the coverage on Joy in this very removed way, because she's someone that I never met. She had a different hair color and cut; she had a husband I never knew about who might have been beating her. Joy was an abstraction; Patty was all too real.

Between my talk with Trevor last night and Summer's late-breaking news and Michael's crying, my brain is just too crowded. I need to think, desperately.

I do what I swore I never would: I put Michael in his crib to cry himself to sleep. Please, let it be fast. Let it be merciful for both of us.

When I come back to the living room, Summer Jackson is talking to a forensic geologist. She's cutting him off—apparently, he's getting too science-y for her audience's attention span. "Quick and dirty," she says, "tell us the upshot."

The upshot is, the body was dumped in the wrong place. The killer must have intended for the body to decompose quickly, but in order for that to happen, it would have had to be buried deep inside the mine shaft in western Utah. Instead, Joy Ellison's body was simply found in a hole in the ground in western Utah "where the composition of the soil is—"

"So we can assume," Summer says, "that the killer was either in a hurry, under the influence, or just plain stupid. Or all of the above."

The geologist laughs (of course he does, he wants to be invited back). "Those are all valid assumptions."

When I drove out to Denver, my plan was not to kill Patty. Sure, I'd indulged in violent fantasies for a while, but I never would have killed a pregnant woman. Instead, I was going to scare her straight—for me, for the other adoptive parents.

I've never really been a violent person. I mean, sure, there was that one time in high school with Tatiana, but that surprised me more than anyone. I tended to avoid getting into it with other girls. I could easily walk away from girls calling me a slut, and if they attacked me first, it just devolved into typical hair-pulling, maybe a few scratches, until someone broke it up.

But with Tati, it was different. I'd considered her a friend, someone I'd even confided in about my crush on Gabe. Then one day, she turned on me. She thought I'd spread a rumor when I hadn't, and then she didn't believe my denials. She called me out, said she wanted to kick my ass. I ignored her but she wouldn't stop, so after school, she and I walked up the street to an empty playground. We were accompanied by a bunch of bloodthirsty high school kids who wanted to watch it all go down. Michael was there, and I could see he was excited to be included. He'd never been a spectator to a fight before, and he clearly thought it was one of the perks of dating me. He also seemed kind of turned on by the whole thing.

It started out the usual way: She called me a bitch, I called her a slut, blah blah. So Tati wasn't my friend after all, whatever. I could deal with that.

Then she talked about how she couldn't believe she'd ever been friends with someone as pathetic as me, someone who spent years stalking Gabe, who dated his brother just to get to him, and Gabe had already fucked half the girls here anyway (she gestured around broadly), and what was wrong with me that he didn't want to fuck me? . . .

My head started pulsing in a way it never had before, like my capillaries were about to burst, and I just rushed Tati. I don't know if it was on my behalf, or Michael's, or Gabe's; I'm not sure who I was really defending. Gabe and I hadn't been together yet by that point, and I was starting to think we never would be, but I didn't want Michael hearing any of that. Poor, innocent Michael—that was how I still saw him.

Tati was on the ground, and I just started kicking the side of her head, again and again. People had to pull me back but it wasn't like usual; it wasn't the way they had to extricate one girl's hand from another's hair. No, people were scared: of me, and for Tati. She wasn't moving.

I stood there breathing heavily, looking down at her, and I finally came back to myself. I could see that people were looking at me with a combination of admiration and fear. Tati was out cold, and there was discussion about what to do. Would we actually have to call an adult? It was anathema, involving adults. That's why we walked up to the street instead of remaining on the school grounds. This was teen business.

"Does anyone know CPR?" No one did, no one had paid attention in health class. "Do we call 911? Where's a phone booth?" It was before the days of teenagers having cell phones. "What do we do?"

Weirdly, people seemed to be looking to me for answers. I guess they wanted me to make the decision because I'd be the one responsible, I was the one who could go to jail if anything was seriously wrong with Tati.

I looked for Michael, and he was gone.

Then Tati woke up. Ultimately, she was fine. She had some pretty bad bruises, maybe a concussion, I don't know, but teen business stayed teen business. No police ever got involved.

No one ever talked shit about me again, not that I heard. There was no need for another fight the whole length of high school. Tati never looked in my direction again. And Michael—he never said anything about the fight or about Tati's accusations, not one word.

I'd always thought I could kick someone's ass if it really came down to it. I have a strong self-protective instinct, and it extends to people I love. I never did feel guilty about Tati. Before the fight, I'd never done a thing to her. Afterward, she'd learned her lesson. Maybe I even saved her life. She learned to think twice before she messes with people when she doesn't know what they're capable of. And we really never do know what other people are capable of when their backs are against the wall. If I know anything, it's that people are infinitely surprising.

Patty surprised the hell out of me, and I was determined to repay the favor.

Law enforcement couldn't touch her; I'd already consulted the police. They said that it was "unfortunate" but what I'd done for Patty constituted gifts rather than fraud. She'd never signed any contracts, hadn't violated any laws. It might have been rotten, but it wasn't actionable. The police never even filed a report. (Infuriating at the time, but ultimately, a good thing for me. There was no paper trail, no official connection, between Patty and me.)

When I had to face the fact that Patty had been running a scam on me, Gabe wanted me to let it go and move on. I didn't understand how that was possible. I see now, though, that he never had any investment in Patty or her baby. He was probably relieved that it fell through. All he wanted was for us to get back to normal.

I wanted that, too. But it wasn't going to happen unless she paid for her crime. Even if the law didn't define it that way, I certainly did.

I had off the week of Thanksgiving, and I told Gabe that I needed to get away. I suggested Maui or the Bahamas, knowing full well that his work would never give him the time off so close to the end of the month. His dealership was going to do a huge black Friday promotion, and he was the top salesman. There was no way Ray would approve leave.

Once Gabe's request was turned down, I said that I'd go to a spa alone. I showed him the website for a place in Palm Desert, with a special promotional rate. "It'll be a detox," I said. He thought it was a great idea.

I wasn't entirely lying. I did envision the trip to Denver as a kind of detox, a cleansing ritual. I needed to exorcise Patty once and for all.

I can hear that Michael's sobs are starting to abate. Soon, he'll be asleep. Summer Jackson has moved on to the next story, a new disappearance in Maine.

The whole time Summer's been covering the Joy Ellison case, I've been half-expecting one of the adoptive parents to come forward. I thought someone would want to talk about what Joy had done to them, who she really was. But maybe they had the same fantasies as me, and they were afraid they'd become suspects. Or they were just too ashamed to have been tricked; Joy had turned all of our desperation into gullibility. They probably didn't want to brandish their childlessness for all the world to see. What good would it do for them to come forward, when obviously, the husband did it anyway?

So back in November, the plan was: drive to Denver, stake out the post office branch where Patty's PO box was, follow her home, and scare her. Of course, it wasn't nearly that simple.

For one thing, stakeouts are a lot harder than they sound. I wanted to get a parking space right in front of the post office so I could see the door, but in a busy urban neighborhood, that involved waiting and circling for close to an hour. Meanwhile, I'm also trying to keep an eye peeled for an extremely pregnant woman whom I've only met once in person. Then, when I get the space, I can't figure out how to watch the door without being conspicuous. How do private investigators do it? Are they just not worried about appearing conspicuous? After all, they know they're not guilty of anything.

Once I accepted that I might be conspicuous if anyone cared enough to notice, there was the boredom to contend with. Hours of waiting and watching—it was mind-numbing. A hundred times I wanted to drive away, just go home, put Patty out of my mind, but I told myself I didn't drive twenty hours to reverse course. I'd been obsessing over her for more than a month, and I was going to make something happen if it killed me.

After two hours passed, the meter ran out, and my car had been tagged by parking enforcement. So it was back to circling with a craned neck, and this time, after a half hour, the best I could do was across the street. That meant peering through the traffic, unless I wanted to circle again or get out of the car. I chose the latter, walking into the post office and pretending to peruse the stamps for fifteen minutes. Then I went back to the car, circled again, and finally reparked on the better side of the street with a clear view of the post office.

It occurred to me that Patty might not even make daily trips. Who knew if she was running any current scams? Or she might have five different PO boxes at different offices all over the city. The stakeout might take days. She could be out of town for Thanksgiving, could have connived her way into someone's family celebration. Since the post office would be closed on Thanksgiving itself, that would be a wasted day. If she didn't show up soon, I was screwed. The trip would have been for nothing.

I told myself that maybe that would be a lesson learned. I'm not supposed to get everything I want; better to find forgiveness than vengeance; I have to accept defeat and move on.

Fuck that. I was going to find that bitch, no matter what.

Stakeout Day Two. I'd barely slept, but I was all the more resolved for it. I decided that I'd spend more time in the post office, in case she'd somehow passed right by me. I needed to be able to see her up close and confirm her identity.

It turns out staking out is a skill to be honed. You can get better at loitering; you can improve your surreptitious glances. You get more comfortable pretending to tie your shoes, or holding up different packing materials as if in comparison, with one eye perpetually trained on the door. You lose your inhibitions and realize anew that humans are an incredibly self-absorbed lot. They barely notice anything.

In the early afternoon, a woman approached the row of PO boxes. She was slender, with short dark hair. I was about to turn my attention back to the door, but there was something in her walk, something familiar. As she pivoted toward me, I startled. That was Patty's face all right. But not Patty's belly, as I'd imagined it. Of course it wasn't. Patty was never pregnant.

Somehow, in all the hours I'd spent in violent rumination, I hadn't even considered that possibility. At that moment, it only enhanced her evil. She was tantalizing us with something she herself didn't even possess.

Michael is silent now. I creep down the hall and push his door open as quietly as I can. I need to make sure SIDS hasn't claimed him. No, it's only sleep. I could not love that boy more.

I listen to his breathing and let it work its magic. My thoughts are less frenzied, more focused. Then I tiptoe out. I close the door and lean against it, wanting to stay close to him.

To be clear: When I saw Patty—concave rather than convex—I didn't change my plan per se. I don't remember deciding to kill her. It wasn't premeditated. But things that were beyond the realm of possibility were no longer entirely impermissible.

I don't think Summer Jackson, former prosecutor, would get the distinction.

It was rage, pure and simple. Who plans rage?

I followed Patty outside. She was sorting through her mail and never saw me. See? Self-absorbed. I got in my car, keeping her in sight, and I began to drive slowly beside her. People were honking at me, and I slid down in my seat slightly, not wanting her to recognize me, not yet. I had a hoodie pulled up over my hair anyway, but still. I didn't want to take any chances.

She didn't get in a car, just kept walking. I was forced to tail her for ten blocks in a not-so-nice neighborhood with people swerving to get around me and occasionally yelling obscenities. Somehow, Patty just walked on. For a con woman, she was remarkably oblivious to her surroundings. Her overconfidence was staggering. She obviously thought no one could touch her; nothing bad could happen. This was the woman who'd pretended to be unsinkable in the face of constant calamity. She'd snowed me completely.

I settle outside Michael's room, my back against the door, exhausted. It's always this way when I remember. Fortunately, I'm good at forgetting.

But the body's been found. That was never supposed to happen. Who the hell walks their dog in western Utah near abandoned mine shafts? There weren't supposed to be any remains by now. I suppose it could turn out that I shouldn't have followed the blueprint of Susan Powell's murdering husband, a psychopath who later killed his two children and himself. But her body never was recovered.

It's not my fault. Patty brought it on herself. If she'd had a shred of decency, of remorse, it would have ended differently for her. It might not have had to end at all.

I saw her go into a run-down apartment building, but by the time I found parking and ran in after her, the hallway was empty. It stank of cigarettes and something vaguely medicinal; the carpet was stained and looked like it was made of felt. Patty was destroying people's dreams in order to live like this? Somehow that seemed even more offensive. I read the mailboxes, not recognizing anyone. Now I know which name was hers: Joy Ellison. Then, I was forced into another stakeout.

I sat in my car outside her building for hours. There were few pedestrians, and no one looked at me with even the slightest curiosity. It was the kind of neighborhood where people avoid eye contact.

Finally, she walked outside with a bag of garbage. I leapt from my car and followed her back inside, holding the door open. She didn't look at me or say thanks. Another black mark against her. I hate when people don't thank you for an obvious courtesy. Are we not part of a civil society? Maybe if she'd said thanks, if she'd recognized me, it would have ended there.

Instead, I could see clearly which door she entered: apartment 3.

It was still daylight. I left and drove back to my motel, the one where I'd paid in cash, written in a false license plate number, and signed a false name. If the proprietor had asked for ID, I would have tried somewhere else; he didn't, so the Hi-Tone Motel it was.

Alone in my room, I recalled Gabe's *Catfish* trick: I searched ultrasounds under Google Images. I immediately recognized the third picture that came up. Of course I did, I'd stared at it for enough hours. It was Patty's baby, the one that was supposed to have been mine. She'd passed off someone else's fetus as her own, and she hadn't even been smart enough to cover her tracks. Maybe she figured she didn't need any camouflage, so long as she had the right victim.

I waited until after dark. I realize that might smack of premeditation, but really, I was giving myself a chance to formulate a new plan, or to back out.

That night, I drove back to her building. When I knocked on her door, my mind was racing (kind of like it is now). I had no weapons. I was in no way afraid of Patty, who was shorter and slighter than me and undoubtedly way less adrenalized. I had the element of surprise.

Only she didn't seem surprised to see me. She invited me in, and I had the distinct impression that I wasn't the first angry victim to show up at her door.

The apartment smelled rancid. I wondered what could have been in her garbage that even hours later, the reek persisted. Her decorating was nonexistent. She had the bare minimum of thrift-store living room furniture. In the corner was a rickety desk with a computer on it. Facebook was up.

"Who are you posting as?" I asked. "Which of your alter egos?"

She laughed. She was going to play it as if nothing had gone wrong between us, as if we were old friends who'd fallen out of touch. "Alter egos," she said. "That's funny. Like I'm Superman and Clark Kent."

"More like Lex Luthor."

Again with the laugh. She gestured toward the couch, which I feared might be infectious. "Have a seat. Can I get you anything to drink?"

I hadn't been prepared for hospitality. "No, thanks." I walked around the living room. No pictures, nothing personal displayed.

"Are you sure you don't want to sit down? I know it's not the cleanest, but it's comfortable, I promise." She sat herself, as if to say, Come on in, the water's fine. "I'd love an upgrade, but there's always something going wrong, always new expenses—"

"Where's your cat?"

Without missing a beat: "He died. That's part of why I was out of contact with you. Everything just went to hell. I'd had him for so many years, you know, and he's a member of the family, and there were all these burial expenses."

"You defriended me."

"Really?" Her brow furrowed. "That was a mistake."

"You had my phone number. And my e-mail. If you wanted to stay in touch, you could have."

"I didn't know what to say. I mean, obviously, I lost the baby." She couldn't manage to look sorrowful.

"How does that work medically? When you lose a baby that far along? Was it stillborn?"

She shook her head, like it was too horrible to recount.

"You are the worst actress I've ever seen. Just stop it, okay?"

She stared at me a long minute, and then she started to smile. "Obviously, I wasn't *that* bad of an actress."

"What is wrong with you? Are you just evil? How could you do that to people? I mean, I know I'm not the only one you conned."

Her eyes were hard, and it couldn't have been the first time she was accused of evil.

"How do you live with yourself?"

"You really came all the way here to ask me that?" She smiled. "I didn't think you were that naïve, Adrienne. I thought you were one of those people who get what it takes to survive. I thought we understood each other. I thought we were friends."

"Fortunately, I don't understand you at all."

"What about your brotherly love triangle?" She was smirking at me, like I was the one with a shameful past.

"Fuck you," I said, my teenage self obviously alive and well.

"Well, fuck you, too," she responded, still laughing. "You want to go get a drink?" She stood up.

"Do you think it's a joke, what you did to me? What you're probably still doing to all the other people who want kids?"

"Oh, right. You're here for all of them. This is an intervention. You're here to tell me I need to stop. What a Mother Teresa move." Bitterness settled into the lines of her face. She looked ten years older than when I met her in San Francisco, back when I needed to believe in her. "You and all the rest of them—you like tossing me a few hundred here, a few hundred there. It lets you feel superior. 'We might not be able to have a baby, but at least our lives aren't in the toilet, like Janice's.'"

"Like Patty's. You said your name was Patty."

"Oh, my mistake." She was still scoffing at me, and my anger was tidal and fast-rising.

My age, however, was waning. I'd regressed to elementary school: "Say you're sorry."

"You came for an apology? Then we're done here? Well, okay. I'm sorry."

I had no choice. I hit her. Just punched her right in her mocking little mouth.

I was shocked, staring down at my aching, already bruising knuckles, and so was she, as blood trickled from the corner of her mouth. Then she charged me. After all she'd done to me, she should have just taken her punishment like a woman. If she had, it might have ended there.

But no, *she* charged me. I wrestled with her a little bit and got her on the ground. She was as shitty a fighter as she was an apologist. Once she was on her grimy floor, I started kicking. Boom, boom, boom, in her left temple, Tati all over again.

It might have ended there.

Except she didn't know to give up. She looked up at me and said, "Fuck you." We were a couple of adolescents, and she wouldn't cry uncle, not after everything she'd done. She wouldn't give me any satisfaction at all.

I just kept kicking her, until her eyes closed. Then I kicked a few more times for good measure.

Did I ever think, I'm going to kill her? Or, I might be killing her right now?

No. I just wanted to close her I-won-you-have-no-baby eyes. I didn't even know it was possible for me to kill someone like that. I thought that at most, she was unconscious. She was out cold but she'd wake up—Tati all over again.

Once again, I wasn't about to involve any adults. Because in the police's eyes, she'd committed no crime. At a minimum, I'd just committed assault.

But I wish a jury could have seen her, the remorseless bitch. They would never convict me. They'd know I was the victim.

While I was punting her head, my rage was so complete that I lost contact with the sensory world. No seeing, hearing, smelling, nothing. I was pure energy, I was one with the universe. I coasted on my adrenaline over to her computer and there I found further vindication: She'd been in the middle of writing to someone, talking about her fourteen-year-old cat that needed surgery, posting an eighteen-week ultrasound. My ultrasound.

When she woke up, I planned to tell her that I'd gathered evidence of all her crimes and that she better stop or I would come back. I'd expose her, or I'd do worse. She'd just felt what I was capable of. She was not going to mess with any more adoptive parents, not on my watch.

But minutes passed, and the fury began to drain out of me, like fury will, and I started to feel afraid. Patty hadn't stirred, hadn't made a sound. I had to force myself to go back and squat beside her. What freaked me out the most was that there was not a spot of blood on her—no, just purple flesh, dented purple flesh on the side of her head. It hadn't caved in, not like in the movies, it had just yielded a little, just enough.

I realized that I should probably touch her, touch that vampire, that sack of human waste. I should confirm if she was breathing. If not, I should put my mouth to her nasty little mouth, breathe the life back into her, my life, as if she hadn't stolen enough. No, I'd pound her chest instead. That was more up my alley. Then she'd sit up, startled, with a dramatic intake of oxygen, like in a Quentin Tarantino movie.

My senses were coming back, one by one. First up was smell. It wasn't the rancid smell from earlier, no, it was something animal, like what a skunk releases when he's trying to save himself. Strong and musky and vile, and I didn't know if it was coming from me or from Patty. Was it Patty's last attempt to save herself? But it didn't work, no, it didn't, and I knew because I made myself hold my hand in front of her crummy little mouth to check for breath and then I made myself touch her rotten forehead, not where it was dented on the side but where you'd check for fever, where the first wrinkles had started to form, the last wrinkles she'd ever have, and Patty was not quite cold but she wasn't warm either, she was no longer human temperature, not *living* human temperature. She was transforming from person to meat.

I saw that there was blood now on Patty's forehead, and I jumped. Patty was bleeding after death, like stigmata or some religious shit. Then I understood: It was my blood. I had dug into my own palms with my nails while I was kicking in Patty's head. I'd dug in deep enough that I was still bleeding, even though time had passed—how much fucking time had passed?—and something needed to happen now. I needed to get out. There was a dead body beside me, and I had made it that way.

I knew what I had to do, but I couldn't do it. I sank fully to the floor in paralysis, that dirty fucking floor, with bits of old food and dust balls and—was that cat hair? Yes, it was. White fluffy bundles of cat hair, from who knows when.

So Patty really used to have a cat. Or she still had one right then, crouched somewhere in the apartment, wondering if his mother was dead. Because Patty was that cat's mother. I had killed somebody's mother.

Patty would have been a terrible mother. Incapable of love, incapable of feeling. If there was a cat there, I'd done him a favor. He was probably lurking nearby, waiting, with yellow eyes, waiting until I left so he could eat his lousy mother's face off. He'd been biding his time for years, praying for an opportunity like this one, that bloodless bitch dead on the floor.

I had to clean up my blood.

But I couldn't move. I kept thinking of that cat and his yellow eyes. He was waiting until I opened a closet or the bathroom door, and then it was my face he'd eat. He'd avenge his mother. Because crappy as she'd been, she'd been his.

This was crazy. I couldn't be killed by a friggin' cat.

It wasn't just any cat, though. It was Satan's cat.

The white ball of hair had attached itself to my hand, affixed with my blood. Hard as I shook, I couldn't seem to dislodge it. Tears were running down my face. I wanted to scream, but I couldn't let anyone come and find me here. There was no one to take care of me, no one at all. I could get a disease here. The place had never been cleaned; that cat probably died in the nineties. Those weren't bits of food, they were rat feces. I needed to get out, or die here, like Patty had.

That did it. I stood up. I washed my bloody hands in Patty's stained sink, shunting aside the stinking piles of dishes. From the detritus, I saw that Patty ate Beefaroni, the kind made by Chef Boyardee, and I almost felt sorry for her, but I couldn't afford it. I shook my hands over and over, this time to dry them, because I didn't want to touch my jeans that had touched that filthy floor and I'd surely never touch Patty's filthy dish towel.

Then I found—of all miraculous things—disinfecting wipes on the kitchen counter, the ones that promise to kill 99.9 percent of all household germs. I had to hope that was true of DNA, too, as I wiped down the keyboard and every other surface I'd come in contact with. That included Patty's forehead, now even colder. The whole time, I was on the lookout for a white long-haired cat, bent on revenge.

There was one last garbage bag, and it had the drippy Chef Boyardee can inside (of course Patty wouldn't recycle, further vindication for me). I gathered Patty's body, folding it in on itself, limb by floppy limb. Rigor mortis would have helped but I couldn't wait around for it to set in.

Gritting my teeth, I had to keep touching her, all over, until she was hidden from view, encapsulated in Hefty. Then I disinfected the apartment, again and again, like Lady Macbeth. It stung my palms, because I was the one with the stigmata. I was the one who had been wronged, and no one should ever forget it, and fuck those yellow eyes, I would tell it to her cat if need be, if it came to that.

But he never came out, never showed himself. The animal scent was still high in my nostrils and I wondered if that was him, had been him all along but I'd been too preoccupied at first to recognize it. Then I finally hoisted Patty over my shoulder and closed the door behind me, a disinfecting wipe cloaking my hand.

I never once thought of calling anyone, least of all Gabe. I knew a husband didn't have to testify against his wife, but I wasn't sure he'd see things as I did. Where I saw justifiable homicide (with big emphasis on the "justifiable"), he might have seen premeditation. Then he'd never be able to see anything else when he looked at me.

The building had a back exit, with a small parking lot. No pedestrians, a straight shot to my car. It's like I was meant to get away with it, to rid the world of Patty/Janice. Maybe I was still powered by adrenaline but it felt like Patty weighed nothing at all. I ran the whole way, tossed her in the trunk, and took off. It wasn't until I'd made it to the highway and gone a few exits that I worked out the rest of my plan. In a rest area, I Googled ways to dispose of a body and stumbled upon Scott Powell's sage advice. When I realized that Highway 80 goes right through western Utah, I laughed out loud. Some higher power had used me to take Patty out; it was so obvious.

There were good reasons to think I could get away with it. The street had been empty when I entered the building; my fight with Patty hadn't been at all loud; no one could link me to her, as she wasn't exactly advertising her victims. Now she'd become one. Poetic justice, that.

For the first couple weeks of December, I was convinced I kept finding white cat hairs on my clothes. Now I'm not so sure. It might have been more Lady Macbeth shit. My conscience was mostly clear, but sometimes I'd think, She was a human being. Then I'd say, Nah, not really.

The truth is, if she'd survived, I would have been way more nervous. I would have expected her to retaliate in some way, would have expected the police (or someone scarier) to show up at my door. She did know where I lived, after all. But it was surprisingly easy to just go about my business, especially since by Christmas, her disappearance hadn't even surfaced (that was when I started following Summer Jackson religiously). I assumed that the mine shaft had taken care of the body. I became even more certain that I'd done the right thing *because* I was getting away with it.

But now that the body's been found, I don't think law enforcement is likely to see it my way. And what about Gabe? He could testify that I was smoldering for weeks before I went to Denver. Husbands don't have to testify, but they can.

Even if I'm never charged, Leah would find out I'm being investigated. What woman would leave her child to be raised by a possible murderer?

There are so many ways I could lose Michael.

I'm slumped over with my head to my knees when Leah and Trevor come down the hall. "Hey," she says.

"Hey." I give her a big smile. "What's up? Where'd you go? Did you have fun?"

They both give me strange looks, Trevor's more empathetic, Leah's bordering on frigid. "When Gabe gets home," she says, "we all need to talk."

I look to Trevor for some clue but he's studying the baseboards with great interest. I resume my former position—one of concession, of supplication. At this point, I can't hope for understanding, only for grace.

CHAPTER 42

Gabe

Adrienne texted to say I can't be late, Leah wants to talk to us tonight.

I've texted Leah a number of times, asking what's going on. She was terse: "U'll know tonite." But I'm pretty sure I already know.

She's going to take Michael away from Adrienne because of what I told her last night. I can see now that Adrienne's been right all along, that Leah did have it out for her. Leah was so quick to conclude that Adrienne's some kind of psychopath, and there's no convincing her otherwise. She's been looking for an excuse, and I gave it to her on a silver platter.

Adrienne loves Michael so much. If anything can break her, this is it. I'll have to live knowing it's my fault.

Leah's stopped answering my texts. I continue defending Adrienne anyway, reminding Leah what a great mom she's been. Adrienne's thrown aside every other thing in her entire life in order to mother that kid. "How else can she prove herself to you?" I ask Leah, to no avail. "Whatever you ask, she'll do it."

I'm useless at work. I don't get within one hundred yards of a sale. Ray doesn't even know what to say; he just shakes his head and points at the whiteboard, then at the calendar. I know, Ray, time is definitely running out.

Entering my house is like walking the gangplank. Leah, Trevor, and Adrienne are already gathered around the table, silent and solemn. Adrienne is staring down at her hands in her lap as if she's never seen them before. She looks like an early-stage Alzheimer's patient in a nursing home: still aware enough to know what's coming and what she's about to lose, helpless to change it.

I have to stop Leah. I'll say anything. I'll leverage the relationship Leah and I have built; I'll appeal to her conscience, or her insecurities, whatever it takes.

"Hi, Gabe," Leah says, sounding perfectly composed.

"You're probably wondering why we've called you here," Trevor says in a Godfather voice. Always the jokester. I could murder him, I really could.

"No, they already know." Leah brushes her hair back from her shoulders. "They're smart. They can guess."

"You want to take Michael," I say.

"We don't 'want.' We are taking him. He's going to live with Trevor and me. We're going to be a family." She sounds proud, like she's finally silencing all her detractors, whoever they might be. I was never among them, but there's probably no telling her that now. I've been her champion. Or has she forgotten everything that doesn't fit with her desires? She sure desired me last night, and I shot her down. Is that what this is about?

"Yeah," Trevor adds, "we're making a go of it." He sounds a lot less confident than Leah.

She must feel it, too, because she casts him the quickest of side glances. That's it, there's the chink in the armor, my opening.

"You think this guy is ready to raise a baby?" I cock my thumb at him. "He's father material?"

"You're one to talk," Trevor fires back. "At least I'm not an alcoholic."

"Haven't had a drink in two days."

"Do they have an AA chip for that?" he jeers. To Leah, "I told you he's an asshole masquerading as a . . . a . . ."

"You know the word 'masquerading'?" I say. "Do you get a chip for that?"

I realize we're both performing for Leah like a couple of monkeys. I look at Adrienne, who hasn't moved. It's like she's going into organ failure or something. This really might do her in, even sooner than I thought.

"Look," I tell Leah, "we need to talk more before you make any final decisions."

"We're talking right now, but you're not going to change my mind."

My eyes are on Adrienne again. I'm having a terrible thought: Did I do this to her on purpose, on some subconscious level? Did I think she hadn't suffered enough for Michael's death, that she'd written it off too easily? Or is it that she transferred her love for me onto a baby, and I wanted to punish her for that?

"How are you going to take care of yourselves plus a baby?" I ask Leah. I'm trying to sound strong but I feel anything but. I'm queasy.

"We have a plan," Leah says.

At that, Adrienne snaps to attention, like she's been touched by a cattle prod. "You had plans for us all along." Her voice is faint. "For me."

"No. They're my plans. For me. For my son." It's like Leah's choosing the words to deliver maximum pain to Adrienne. But why? What did Adrienne ever do except love the baby she'd been promised? Leah made a promise and she's reneging without an ounce of compassion, let alone remorse.

"What the fuck is wrong with you?" I say to her. Now she's the one who's jolted. She's never heard anything close to that tone out of me. "We took you in. We've made a home for Michael, and for you, too. How many people would have done that? Show some respect. If you're going to leave, say thank you, and sorry."

"Don't talk to her like you're her father," Trevor says. "After you've been trying to fuck her."

"If I wanted to fuck her"—I stare him down—"I could have done it last night."

Wrong move. Now Leah's eyes are blazing. "You were too busy confessing all your sins to fuck me!"

Adrienne turns toward me, but with all the energy of a rag doll. "What sins?" she asks quietly.

"Oh, wait," Leah says. "He wasn't confessing his sins, he was confessing yours." She addresses Adrienne. "I know what you did to Gabe's brother. I know you killed him."

"I never told you that!"

"Not in so many words." Leah glares at me. "But you were throwing her under the bus, you just didn't want to admit it to yourself. You don't want to be Michael's father, and Trevor does. I want to be his mother, so that's what's going to happen." She stands up. "There's no point in talking anymore."

"Don't," Adrienne says, full of desperation. "Please don't leave, not tonight. If you're going to take him, let me have a little more time with him first. Stay a week, figure out your plans, and then go, no questions asked."

Leah looks from Adrienne back to Trevor. It's like I'm not even in the room.

"Is this really what you want?" Adrienne asks Trevor. Under the force of Leah's gaze, he finally nods. He's like a bug trapped under a windshield wiper.

Adrienne and I both see that he's the weak link; he's our chance. She's playing it more masterfully than I've been. She always does.

It's time for Adrienne and me to team up. We were great together for so many years; we can be again.

"You already signed away your rights," Adrienne reminds him. "Because you weren't ready to be a dad."

"But I didn't," Leah says. "Remember when we talked in the hospital room?" She's still fixed on Adrienne. "Michael was only a couple days old. You said I was going to meet someone great and have a family of my own. You said things were going to turn out really well for me. Well, it happened sooner rather than later." Her eyes sidle over to me. "I am sorry it's turning out this way. I wasn't trying to be a bitch or anything. It's like that annoying lawyer said, the maternal instinct is really strong. With me, it was just, like, delayed."

"Latent" is probably a better term, and it was activated by Trevor's presence. Since Adrienne was the one who invited him into our home, that means she shoulders some blame, too. We really are in this together, finally.

"We can give it a week, though," Leah says, like she's doing us a big favor by accepting another week's free room and board. I guess she is. Adrienne's nearly begging.

We descend into silence that's broken by Michael's cry. Adrienne starts to rise, but Leah waves her off. "I have to get used to this," she says cheerily. "Night feedings and dirty diapers."

Trevor doesn't move. He's only a little less shell-shocked than Adrienne. So all is definitely not lost.

I slap him on the back. "Congratulations, Dad! Hope you're ready for what you've gotten yourself into." I offer a hand to Adrienne and help her up. She really does seem shaky: Alzheimer's with just a dash of Parkinson's. If this is an act, it's a pretty damn good one.

After we're in the bedroom with the door closed, I tell her we need to work together, we need a strategy. "It's all about Trevor," I say. "Put some weight on that hinge, and the door's going to spring open."

Adrienne stares at me blankly. I would have preferred hatred to this nonrecognition, or maybe it's disregard. "You confessed about Michael. To Leah."

"It was a mistake. Obviously, I see that now. But I never blamed you. Leah's lying." I rush toward her and take both her hands in mine. I kneel down before her for the second proposal of our lives. "Work with me. We can save this. Together, we can make sure we keep Michael."

"You never wanted him here. And now you've made it happen."

Only subconsciously. "No. It was a mistake. I didn't know how she'd spin it. She's twisted. You've said that all along. She heard what she wanted to hear. She wanted to convict you for some crime, so she could feel okay about leaving with Michael."

At the word "convict," Adrienne's lips turn up in a bitter smile. I suppose it's better than the blank face, but not by much. Truth be told, she's freaking me out. I want to see her angry. I want to see her fired up. This stricken, resigned woman—that's not my wife.

"She's trying to play us against each other. Don't you get that?" It's not all Leah. Trevor's culpable, too. He's gotten into Leah's head by promising her what she's always wanted. In fact, she wants it so badly that she can't even see that he doesn't. I give them a month, tops. Then what happens to Michael?

"Divide and conquer," Adrienne says finally. "So that was her plan. It worked." She pulls her hands free and walks into the bathroom. The door slams and locks.

CHAPTER 43

Adrienne

I was in the bathtub all night, fully clothed. At first, I was too distraught to move. All I could think of was an empty nursery, the black hole that would become my life. To be without love or purpose—is there any worse fate?

Then I began running scenarios, calculating odds. Gabe might be the poker player, but I'm a better gambler. I won't shove all-in when a smaller wager will do. That said, I'm not afraid to push when I need to.

See? I did learn something sitting next to Gabe for all those televised tournaments. He didn't understand how I could find it so boring. For me, there was nothing really at stake. Money doesn't count.

I can't blame Leah. I could see tonight that she's still that eight-year-old girl who got the family pulled right out from under her. She wants what everyone wants, and she has to create it herself out of whole cloth. She might have concocted this whole plan just to give Trevor an entire year to change his mind, at our expense (literally). If that's true, I have to say touché. It's a plan worthy of a younger me. If she hates me, I can understand that. After all, I am her natural rival.

What's Trevor's excuse? He has loving parents and a house full of siblings. He still doesn't want to be a father, but he's too chickenshit to tell Leah. He should be able to see the situation clearly; he knows that I'm the best person for the job.

But obviously, he doesn't care about what's best for Michael. So I just need to bring his selfishness to the foreground. I have a week to do it.

I can't trust Gabe or his offer to work together. He betrayed me, telling Leah who knows what about Michael's suicide. He's probably thrilled that Leah's going to take Michael off his hands. If he pretends to put up a fight, he thinks I'll forgive him.

That means I'm in this alone, just as I have been ever since our first adoption profile. Otherwise, how could Gabe have been so detached from the Patty fiasco? He should have been incensed, just like I was. We should have been in *that* together.

I need Michael in my life. I'm his mother. I've earned the title, loving and caring for him since the day he was born.

Gabe's right about one thing: Trevor's the fulcrum. Leah doesn't want to be a single mom, she wants a family. So it stands to reason that if I can get Trevor to back out (which is what he wants to do anyway), then Leah will back out, too. Their family was going to break down soon enough anyway; by accelerating the pace, I ensure that Michael doesn't get caught in the crossfire.

I didn't sleep at all, but after formulating my next steps, I'm mildly refreshed. It helps to take a shower and do my makeup and hair. I have the time, after all. Leah and Trevor are on baby duty and have been all night.

In the adjoining bedroom, I see that Gabe is actually asleep. Irritating, but it confirms my assessment. He doesn't really care about any of this.

I make my way through the house. The door to the nursery is ajar, and I see that Leah is also asleep, upright in the glider. Michael is in his crib, and as I push the door open farther, he turns his head toward me. He's only just learned to follow sounds and movements. He smiles and lets out a gurgle. My baby. My love.

I tiptoe past Leah and pick him up. I hear the soft whoosh of gas releasing. That's how comfortable he is with me, with his mama.

I'm not going to lose him. No way.

I carry him out of the room, taking care not to disturb Leah. But I'm not sure where to go. Trevor is snoring away on the couch, Gabe is still in bed, and I'm surely not going to take Michael into Leah's room.

I feed Michael in the dining room, hoping he won't make any sudden loud noises and wake Trevor. I want to go to work on Trevor soon, but I'm still pushing through my anger. A morning to myself—a morning for just Michael and me—is what I need most.

But I'm not going to get it. Trevor wakes up languidly, one limb at a time. For the grand finale, his head pops up and he lights on Michael and me.

"Good morning," I say, hoping it doesn't come out oxymoronic.

"Morning." His voice betrays nothing of last night. Scratching himself furtively, he bypasses us on his way to the kitchen. Then he joins me at the table with a mixing bowl, a box of granola, and a gallon jug of milk. He proceeds to pour himself what must be five servings of granola (granola Gabe and I paid for), dousing it with an oceanic quantity of milk.

I don't want enmity between us—I can't afford it—but he seems so completely at home that resentment can't help but bubble to the surface. We had an arrangement, and he violated it without apology. Hell, without even giving me a heads-up.

"I thought we were friends," I say, aiming to sound hurt rather than reproachful.

He looks at me with surprise. "We are."

What do I say to that? The boy was born without a clue.

He yawns histrionically. "Rough night." Like I'm going to sympathize. Ingrate. "Leah kept bouncing up to take care of Michael every time he cried. I finally moved back to the couch." What happened to our deal about his staying on the couch every night?

"That's called parenting."

"Not complaining, just sayin' is all." He captures a large spoonful of cereal. "Leah and I were talking about looking at some apartments this afternoon."

"Apartments in the Bay Area?"

"Yeah."

"I thought you were going to bring her back to Rhode Island with you."

He shrugs. "Things change."

"Now you like it here?"

Another shrug. "Are you okay with watching Michael? He'd be kind of a distraction if we had to haul him around all day."

"Babies take up a lot of time and energy. You get that, right?" If they think they're going to move up the street and use me for free babysitting . . . well, I might be available. But I'm not shooting for a consolation prize.

It's slightly humiliating. Being asked to watch him, like I'm already just the babysitter instead of the mother, like Leah has already taken over that role. But for today, more time with Michael is all I want. I tell Trevor, "Absolutely. I'd love to watch him. Whatever you need."

He grins through a mouthful of granola. Disgusting.

It's not too soon to enact my plan, not when I've only got a week. "I want Michael to get the best start in life. Of course I prefer it to be with me, but if I can't have that, I'm going to support you. I don't want you taking Michael to some crappy motel or something. So if you need more time to find a place, if it's longer than a week, that's okay, too."

"Rad. You are, like, the most adaptable person ever."

He's seemingly the most gullible. But I know things aren't always what they seem. "The thing is, a baby's helpless. Completely and totally dependent. You've got to be ready to do everything for him, put him first at all times."

He shifts in his chair with what I hope is discomfort but might just be a quest for better positioning. He looks pretty ergonomically unsound. You can get away with that at his age. If I sat like that, I'd wind up in traction.

As he chews, I go on. "I was thinking last night about selflessness. Because that's what a baby needs, you know? Selflessness, for me, is recognizing that as much as I love Michael, I might not be what's best for him. It might be best for him to be raised by the people who are genetically related to him." He stares at me, moon-eyed, as bile circulates in my mouth. I wonder if I've gone too far.

"Damn," he says finally. "That is selfless." He returns to his cereal.

"I was also thinking about that story you told me. About what happened to Leah when she was eight."

"You didn't tell Gabe, did you?"

"No. I'm keeping it between us." He looks relieved. "I was thinking that Leah has suffered so much, and she's going to want to make sure Michael doesn't suffer at all. That'll make her a good mother, because she'll always put him first, above everything in the world."

I'm trying to underscore the level of sacrifice that parenting requires, since I know he's not remotely equal to the task, but perhaps more important, that Leah will give her all to Michael and there won't be anything left for Trevor. I can't tell if I'm getting through. He's nodding with a faraway look. The subtitles could read, "Sure, Mom." But I'm okay with that. This is just my first sally.

I've only got a week, guaranteed, but it could easily become two, or three. Finding an affordable apartment in the Bay Area won't be easy for two unemployed people and a baby.

Leah makes a wary entrance. I manage a no-hard-feelings smile and a "Good morning." Trevor tells her that I'm going to watch Michael that afternoon, and she nods, like it was a given, rendering thanks irrelevant.

"We're going to take him to the park this morning," she says. Then, an afterthought, "If that's okay."

She's not really asking for permission and we both know it. Still, it's a greater courtesy than she extended last night, "He'll like that," I say. "Do you want me to do a run-through of the diaper bag with you?"

"I remember from last time." Trevor's finished eating, so she takes his bowl and refills it with granola, sloshing milk over the top. "It's like a trough," she says, and he starts making pig noises. Michael turns his head to watch them, recognizing humor in progress. He really will like going to the park with them (fortunate for him, unfortunate for me).

It hurts, giving him up even for a few hours. I'm nervous the whole time. What if they run off with him? What if he falls off the swing and hits his head? What if they forgot important things? For example, what happens if they run out of milk?

Leah will have that one covered, at least, being the supplier of milk. I don't think she pumped this morning; I never saw her carrying milk to the refrigerator. So it's possible she's started breast-feeding him already, in preparation for their exit. She's already becoming his mother, fully.

It's an excruciating two hours. I can't imagine it being for good, never seeing Michael again, or perhaps worse, being relegated to occasional babysitting duties. Watching him grow up from down the street, being his almost-adoptive mother, which is the same as being nothing. I'm not equipped to love him part-time, at the discretion of Leah. I couldn't live like that. But could I live without him totally? What would hurt more? Right now, it all seems intolerable.

When they come back, I'm in the living room, the TV on and unwatched. "How was the park?" I ask them. I try to sound upbeat, auntlike. There's no word for that, is there? "Avuncular" is only for men. Gabe can be avuncular. I'll be nothing.

Stop it. This is not over.

"Michael digs swinging," Trevor says. I'm pretty sure he doesn't get the difference between hanging out and parenting. I need to elucidate that for him, bit by bit.

Leah looks happy, too. "He liked the sandbox even better." She's talking more to Trevor than me.

I need to let her think she's won. That I'm waving the white flag, that I'll be her babysitter if that's all I can get, that I believe she could be the best mother for Michael. But it sticks in my teeth, like grit.

"I wouldn't have even thought to put him in the sandbox," I say, like it's brilliant. His every orifice is being buffed as we speak.

"Yeah, little dude was into the sandbox. I put him on his belly, like this." Trevor lies down and flails his arms and legs like a turtle. Leah laughs at the imitation, and I force myself to laugh, too. See? No hard feelings. We're one big happy family.

I'm knotted up until they finally leave to apartment hunt. Then I get to hold Michael close and smell his hair. I'm grateful for every feeding, every diaper change, every smile. I put him on the blanket on the floor and watch him do his flail—Trevor's impression was right on, actually—and I try not to cry. This is not the last time, I tell myself. This is not the end.

It's hard to tear myself away, even though it's time for Summer Jackson and I really need to watch. I need to stay one step ahead.

Summer looks into the camera with utmost seriousness and says, "Those of you who've been following the Joy Ellison story know that I've had my suspicions about her husband, Brad Ellison. You know Joy's remains have been found. Well, today, my instincts were borne out. Brad Ellison has been arrested for the murder of his estranged wife. On the phone, we have Sergeant Loomis, of the Denver police. Welcome, Sergeant."

Summer embarks on a series of questions that are all designed to further validate her instincts. In prosecutorial fashion, she never asks anything unless she already knows the answer. She probes about Brad's non-alibi, his girlfriend, his poor work attendance, his failure to report Joy missing until months had passed, the past DV charge, his stints in rehab, the angry Facebook messages he wrote her—all of it circumstantial, none of it suggesting why he might have actually wanted Joy dead. But I have to admit, put that way, it's persuasive. Apparently, circumstantial and inconclusive is good enough for Sergeant Loomis. There's no mention of any forensic evidence from Joy's remains.

My first reaction is relief: If they've made an arrest, they're not looking into other suspects, and certainly not looking anywhere as far afield as California. Perhaps the particulars of Joy's scams have never come to light, which means that Brad's non-motive is the only motive going.

My second reaction is that an innocent man is being held for a crime I committed.

But since he is innocent, since there's no physical evidence and no motive, can't any halfwit defense attorney get him off? If he's actually convicted, it's a sign he was guilty of something. He physically abused Joy; he put her in the hospital at least three times. This might just be karma. Besides, who marries the devil? A lesser demon, most likely.

He is, however, innocent of murder.

What Leah said last night about me, that I killed Gabe's brother, Michael—it's something I've thought about before. But I've gone on to be a better person. I teach little kids, and that's penance for Michael, my way of doing good in the world. That has to erase my mistakes. That's all it really was, a mistake. I was sixteen. I hadn't grown a conscience yet.

But what's my penance for Patty? Is it losing baby Michael?

It's possible that I can't hang on to him unless I make it right somehow. I can't let an innocent man take his chances with some crappy public defender. I can't just hope he'll go free.

But if I turn myself in, I lose Michael anyway. And unlike Gabe's brother, Patty deserved to die. Summer Jackson might even agree with me, if she knew Patty's past.

If I got that part of the story to Summer, that could make a difference for Brad. It would certainly cast some reasonable doubt. If Summer knew that Patty pretended to be pregnant time and again, then it would follow that she had lots of enemies. She had five Facebook pages that I knew about, but there were probably others that she'd already taken down. Those were just the pregnancy scams. Didn't she say something about a windfall coming? There's motive right there, for someone.

I could call in an anonymous tip. I'd just need to figure out a way to do it that wouldn't lead the police to my door.

That might be enough to tip the scales in my favor and keep Michael in my life.

I look down at the remote control and a cold wind blows through me. Could it really be . . . ? I blink again. There, straddling the number 2, is a white cat hair.

CHAPTER 44

Gabe

So if I can get you three hundred dollars a month for thirty-six months, we've got a deal?" I say.

It's bullshit, of course. Three hundred dollars a month wouldn't even fly for the CT, and we're talking about an ES. But I feel like I can work this guy. Dwight's got an overbite and a receding hairline; there are pit stains on his dress shirt. He's just left his wife and kids for another woman, Lucy, who's not good-looking but she is young, and Lucy wants that red ES. Her hand keeps creeping higher on his thigh.

"I'll take it to my manager right now," I say. "I just need to know if that's what will make you happy. Three hundred dollars for thirty-six months. What do you say?"

"I say, take it to your manager." He leans back in his seat, trying to look like a master of the universe, but really, he's just exhausted.

I'm going to break that asshole. I need this sale, like he can't begin to know.

Sure, there's the monthly quota that I gave Ray, my job in the balance, but that isn't even it. It's about mano a mano, hand-to-hand combat. Me versus Dwight, the man who chose freedom over family, young pussy over old. I'm getting this sale.

I walk into Ray's office and say, "Dwight wants two hundred fifty dollars a month for the red ES." I'm giving myself some wiggle room for the financing, and there's still the trade-in to be negotiated.

"Get outta here," Ray tells me, like I knew he would.

"Hey, I said I'd try."

Ray grins. "Good to see you trying, Gabe."

It goes on this way for another hour: Me going back and forth between Dwight and Ray, with progressively and incrementally higher numbers, and finally, *finally,* Ray gives me the nod. I go back to Dwight, ready to close.

Dwight's on his cell phone, walking in slow concentric circles, and I give him a thumbs-up. He nods distractedly and does one more loop. Then he hangs up and rejoins Lucy and me at the desk.

"Ray hates to let it go for this price—" I begin.

"Good news, then," Dwight says. "He doesn't have to."

I stare at Dwight and his stupid, shiny forehead—so much forehead—and I know I've been had. "You were talking to another dealership."

"Identical car. Also red." He says this last bit for Lucy's benefit, and she smiles in appreciation. "Better price, better financing, better trade-in. All of it."

"How much better?"

"Sorry about this, but it's just better, all around. They're working on the paperwork right now and will have it waiting for us. We need to go." He stands up and holds out a chivalrous arm to Lucy. "It's just business."

I stand up, too. "I understand business. But there's a little something called decency. I've spent how long with you? Then you leverage all my hard work to get a slightly better deal with someone who hasn't done shit." I'm moving closer to him as I speak.

He isn't about to back away, not with Lucy there. That's fine by me. I feel like kicking his ass right here, in the middle of the showroom floor. "It's not about the price," he says. "I don't like you."

"Oh, you don't? Is that because she does?" I gesture toward Lucy with my chin. The truth is, I haven't registered any particular interest on her part, but he doesn't know that. Insecurity is rolling off him in waves, as copious as his sweat.

Lucy gets in between us. "Let's just go, sweetie," she says. "He's not worth it."

Dwight makes a show of backing away slow, like Lucy has to drag him out. The other salesmen and customers are watching.

"I'm not worth it?" I ask Lucy. "Because this whole time, you've looked ready to suck my cock."

Dwight comes at me, and I stand my ground. He's shoving me and calling me names; I'm calling him names right back. I don't plan to actually throw a punch, not until he does. I'm hoping he does. He has it coming, trying to screw me like he did.

Ray's on the floor now and he pulls me back with surprising force for a near-geezer. He barks into my face, "You take a walk. I'll handle this."

He's right, I do need a walk. I head for an empty bay in the service station and take a couple sips of bourbon from my flask. The testosterone is fast draining out of me. Dwight's beside the point, I know that. What is the point anymore?

Time to face the music, and it's going to be a funeral dirge.

Inside Ray's office, he starts giving me a speech about how he's always liked me, how he hates to do this, but I've given him no choice, no choice at all, and I tell him to skip the wind-up and throw the pitch. Is it effective immediately?

"Yeah," he says with a heavy sigh. "You need to get out of here now. I'll mail your final check."

"Just don't contest unemployment. That's all I ask."

"I'll have to run that past the higher-ups, but I'll try. I'll tell them you've been sick. Cancer's been eating your brain. I'll think of something." He looks more upset than I feel.

"Don't worry about it," I say. "You did all you could."

He frowns. "What's wrong with you, Gabe? That's what I don't get."

"I'm a father now."

"You pulling my leg?"

"I wish I were. We adopted a boy two months ago. Well, not exactly adopted. It's complicated." I head for the door.

"Congratulations," he calls after me, both mystified and sorrowful.

"See you around," I say, though I know I'm not welcome on the floor again after what I just pulled. Ray and I have never seen each other anywhere else.

There's no going home. I can't explain this to Adrienne. She doesn't need one more thing, not one more Gabe screw-up.

I autopilot to the Pyramid. I don't think I've ever played at noon on a weekday before. It'll be good for me to hang out with a new crowd. The unemployed, my new brethren.

I go in and lean against the rail, surveying the tables. The mood seems more somber at this time of day. The room's full of people who are taking themselves (and the game) way too seriously. Maybe they're grim because they're down to their last dollars. Or maybe they're trying to make a small-time living; this is a day at the office.

Then I see a familiar face—well, familiar hair. Leah, with that same low ponytail, the way she wore it when we came here together. With a large mound of chips in front of her, she's looking perfectly at home. Content. In my home. Well, my home away from home.

Does she have to take over everything? When she goes, there'll be nothing left of me, or of Adrienne. She's destroying our lives and she doesn't have a care in the world. Was that her goal all along?

If that's it, then mission accomplished. She's damn near ruined my marriage. Adrienne won't speak to me, she won't even glare; she looks through me.

The Fixer is on Leah's left. His head is down, as usual. He's not blinded by Leah's looks; she's just another poker player. He's equal opportunity: He'll lose his money to anyone, same as he'd kill them. What a refreshingly simple worldview.

I envy the guy.

CHAPTER 45

Adrienne

Mel's already at a table, and she starts waving at me with puppy-dog exuberance. I've never been that happy to see anyone in my life except Michael (and Gabe, once upon a time), but I imagine Mel experiences the feeling with some regularity.

This was a mistake. I'm energetically unsuited.

We hug, and I take the seat across from her. She's been trying to pin down a lunch date for weeks, and I happened to cave at just the moment when she could be useful to me. Go figure.

"What's good here?" I ask, scanning the menu. The restaurant is light and airy, white and cobalt blue (Greece's national colors, I presume), with lots of large, open windows, but it's loud, too. The people occupying the slate-topped tables around us seem carefree and buzzed.

"The moussaka's my favorite. Maybe we can start with the dolmas?"

"Sure," I say. I try to catch the eye of a white-shirted waiter. "I could definitely use a glass of wine." I've practically been a teetotaler ever since Michael came along, as if I'm the one breast-feeding. At the thought of breast-feeding—something Leah might be doing right now—my hands involuntarily clench.

When the waiter shows up a minute later, I order a Manhattan instead. "Dolmas for an appetizer," I add, "and I'll have the moussaka."

"Oh, I didn't know we were ordering yet!" Mel laughs, but ever the good sport, she gets a glass of house white and the souvlaki plate. As the waiter recedes, she turns to me with sudden concern. It's like she's been listening to her own radio station—Sunny Lite FM—and just realized I'm occupying another frequency. "Everything okay?"

"Not even close."

She scoots her chair over and lowers her voice. "What is it?"

"Leah says she's going to take Michael. Trevor's been staying with us. Did you know that?" She shakes her head. "He's Michael's birth father. I wouldn't trust him to house-sit, let alone to parent a child. It's insanity." I push my hair back from my face. "But what about you? What's new?"

"That's awful! How are you holding up?"

"I just need to get him alone, that's all. He's in love with her, so he's feeding into her delusion about being the family she never had. Her parents were drug addicts; she's been in the system since she was three. She's got no parenting skills, she had no role models, you know? And he's an underage drinker with no sense of responsibility. This isn't going to happen. There's just no way." I take a deep breath and smile. "So there's no point in talking about it, really." Press me, I urge her silently. Force me to keep talking about it.

"How can . . . I mean . . ." She seems genuinely flustered. "We have to talk about it. You have to do some"—she feels around for the expression—"anticipatory grieving."

Ick. I hate pop psychology, with rumination substituting for action. Why grieve for something that's not going to happen? Something Mel is going to prevent from happening? She just doesn't know it yet.

Our drinks arrive. I take a generous sip of mine, more of a swig. Too much vermouth, but it'll do.

"Do you think, maybe, you're in denial?" she asks delicately. "Isn't that one of the stages of grief? It might even be the first one, I can't remember." Her brow is furrowed. She's clearly trying to remember, sweet girl that she is. She was a psych major in college.

"I'm not in denial."

"But wouldn't one of the signs of denial be denying that you're in it?"

I let out a sigh, like she just might have me there. She hasn't touched her wine yet, I notice.

"Tell me about you," I say. I'm buying some time for her to drink. I'm going to need her inhibitions lowered. "Tell me how the online dating is going. Please? I need you to take my mind off everything."

Still looking troubled, clearly feeling she's supposed to do more to facilitate my anticipatory grief, she starts to tell me about a back-and-forth she just had with a forty-five-year-old dentist. Then she really warms to it, and the anecdotes begin to pour out of her, pooling on the table between us.

Don't think about Michael, don't imagine where he is right now. Don't picture him smiling at his new parents.

This lunch is part of the long game, I remind myself. Wind Mel up and watch her go.

My brain wanders to Brad Ellison. Summer Jackson is still railroading him with a vengeance. Yesterday, her show featured a woman who lived in Joy's apartment building. The interview wasn't via satellite, but in the studio. That meant Summer had flown the woman in just so she could say that she heard arguing around the time Joy was likely killed. My heart sped up at that, but then the neighbor clarified that she'd heard a male voice in Joy's apartment. She couldn't swear it was Brad's, but when Summer played a bit of Brad's interview, the woman couldn't swear it wasn't him.

Joy's apartment building was a half step above a crack house. That neighbor must have been given an all-expenses-paid trip to L.A. and the chance to be on TV. Summer practically seduced her. She's building a case for the prosecution, using her star power and perks.

Summer's got her teeth in Brad, and she's not letting go.

The neighbor might not even know she's lying. Witnesses are notoriously unreliable. I learned that from Summer herself. It's what she says when she wants to discredit a particular witness, and I noticed she didn't say it before (or after) interviewing the neighbor. Summer wants her audience to believe. She wants Brad convicted in the court of public opinion.

I finish my drink in one swallow. "Aren't you going to drink your wine?"

She pushes it toward me. "Go ahead." Her brow furrows anew. "I feel like you're not even really here."

She could never tell during all those lunches in the break room. But I wasn't tossing back Manhattans then.

"Sorry," I say. If she's forgoing wine anyway, then there's no use stalling. "I just keep thinking about Michael, and about the kind of life he'll have with Leah and Trevor, if it comes to that."

"Of course you do!" Her face is suffused with compassion. Good. We're on our way.

"It's not right for Michael to suffer because of their selfishness, you know? Gabe and I are equipped to be his parents. We can give him a stable, loving home." Fortunately, I've never badmouthed Gabe to Mel so she has no reason to doubt what I'm saying. All she's seen is the love I have for Michael.

She must be thinking of that, because her eyes fill with tears. Perfect.

"It's not like they're child abusers, Leah and Trevor. But it's not far off, is it? Taking Michael away from Gabe and me to live in squalor, when they barely know how to change a diaper, when they've hardly done a night feeding. What are they going to do when he's crying uncontrollably and I'm not there to step in? I feel like," I nearly whisper, "there's just real capacity for violence there."

"With Leah? Or with Trevor?"

"Honestly? With both of them."

She stares at the tablecloth, obviously troubled.

"But what can I do? If I call CPS, they won't substantiate the report. They're about what's actually happened, not what could very well happen. They might think I'm making it up for my own gain. It is just a hunch. But, Mel"—I reach out and touch her arm—"it's a strong hunch. You know how sometimes you have kids in your class and you see their parents, just for a minute, and you know? You *know* something's wrong there. It always turns out to be true, doesn't it? I'm not just seeing Leah and Trevor for a minute. I've been watching them for weeks. In her case, months."

"I wish I knew what to tell you," she murmurs. As if I'm here for advice. Oh, sweet, naïve Mel.

"I don't want to wait for something bad to happen to Michael, and then someone calls in a report. Like an upstairs neighbor, once they've already taken him away from me and moved out. Or someone at the park. I wish someone could see them right now and call in." I study her face. Nothing. "They take him to the park alone sometimes now." Still nothing. "If someone trustworthy saw them there, someone who could call in to CPS, I feel like it could change Michael's life, you know?" Finally, the light begins to dawn.

"Call in and lie, you mean?" Her tone is wary. Why couldn't she have taken just one sip of wine?

"See into the future, and then call."

She looks at me with a directness I've never seen in her before. "Is this why you wanted to go to lunch?"

"No! I'm just thinking out loud. I'd never want you to do anything that went against your conscience. I know you're a deeply moral person." Above reproach, really, which is why CPS would trust her as a concerned citizen who happened to witness abuse at the park.

She nods slowly, her eyes back on the tablecloth. I never expected her to say yes instantly. She needs to let it marinate for a day or two, imagine the terrible life Michael has in store for him if she doesn't act, and then let her conscience be her guide. I'll let her call me, and then I could tell her when Leah and Trevor would next be at the park. CPS would never catch on to the connection between Mel and me; they're harried civil servants.

"I'm going to the restroom," she says. She still won't look at me.

But she leaves her purse behind, with her phone in it. That allows me to enact the other part of my plan, the more immediate one. Making sure an innocent man isn't tried for murder—that will improve my karma substantially.

I reach into my own purse. It feels wrong, not having a diaper bag. It's wrong not to have Michael with me. But there's no time to linger on that just now.

I drain her wineglass, and then I yank my phone free. I have all the Facebook pages bookmarked, all of Patty's alter egos, plus the tip line for Summer Jackson. I'd call the police, but I assume they can trace calls. There's no guarantee an anonymous tip will stay anonymous. Summer Jackson wouldn't have that capability.

I grab Mel's phone and block her number, for good measure. I call Summer's tip line and, thankfully, get a recording. "Joy Ellison was a true con woman," I say. "Brad might have killed her, he might not have. But look at her Facebook pages." I reel off the aliases. Fortunately, the Facebook page she used for Patty is gone; she took that one down herself. "There might be more to the story than you realize."

The dolmas arrive, and I pop them in my mouth, one after the other. My heart is racing. What if they can trace that call? What if it leads them to Mel, and then she leads them to me? But she doesn't know anything about Joy, doesn't know I was ever scammed. As far as she's concerned, Leah is my first birth mother. That's the benefit of never really having confidants; they can't rat you out, even if they want to.

The phone's back in her purse by the time she returns to the table. "Hey," she says, "you ate all the dolmas!" She's trying to sound playful and failing. I can tell that she wants to forget our recent conversation ever happened. But hopefully, her conscience won't let her.

"Sorry. I haven't been eating much lately. Grief, you know." I force a brave smile, and I see her melting. Or at least trying to. She likes to believe the best in people. Hey, she has that in common with the Patty I thought I knew. How come I never realized that before? But with Mel, it's all real. "I'll order you more dolmas. Lunch is on me."

"No, that's okay. I can stand to skip an appetizer." She looks down at her midriff self-deprecatingly.

"You look great." I flag down the waiter and place the order.

"A free lunch is kind of appealing right now. Technically, I'm unemployed."

"You haven't been hired back yet? You will be, don't worry."

She smiles, her natural optimism reasserting itself. For a second, I feel it, too, that this is all going to turn out just fine. I'll free an innocent man, Mel will call CPS, and Michael will be mine for good.

I reach for my wine—well, Mel's wine—and startle. I notice something clinging to the condensation. A wet, white cat hair. I want to ask Mel if she sees it, too (I've had a Manhattan and half a glass of wine), but I can't afford to have her doubting me, not now.

Is it true that you only know you've been in a state of denial once you've left it?

CHAPTER 46

Gabe

I stand at the rail and take in the room. For once, I'm not trying to gauge the quality of the play or to size up opponents. I'm not here for the poker. I'm here to find the Fixer.

It's not like I've made any definite decisions. But Adrienne still can't even look at me. If Leah takes Michael away, she'll never forgive me. I won't be able to forgive myself. So that means all options are on the table.

It's such a clichéd scenario: You don't know what you've got until it's (almost) gone. Last night, when I couldn't sleep, I waited by Michael's crib with a bottle of milk at the ready. The second he stirred, I lifted him up and onto my shoulder. We rocked together in the glider, his pervasive warmth spreading through my body. Then he drank from his bottle, his eyes wide on mine. I suddenly saw so clearly that he's not that Michael; he's this one. He's my son, for another few days. Have I squandered my chance to be not just any father, but his father? Am I too late?

After I put him down, I went into the garage. Not to play pool or to drink, but to cry. To sob, actually. I just kept thinking: I've screwed up the life I could have had with Adrienne, and with Michael.

Then I saw something else with incredible clarity. It was an image of the Fixer. There's a guy who can blow a thousand, two thousand at a pop, without batting an eye. If he can afford to suck that bad at poker, he must be pretty good at something. At scaring people straight. At cleaning up messes. And I'm in a hell of a mess right now.

I can't let Leah and Trevor just walk out with Michael. I can't live knowing I did that to Adrienne. Selfishly, I want to take my shot at fatherhood. Adrienne and I are so far away from each other but I know we're still attached; the cord is thin, it's fraying, but it can hold for a few more days. There's a little time left on the clock.

"Hey, man," Ames says. He lifts his baseball cap and runs his hand through his thinning hair. "Are you on the list?"

I shake my head. "I'm just watching."

He gives me a strange look. It's one thing to watch *World Series of Poker* on TV; it's another to watch the $1/$2 table at the Pyramid. "You don't look so good."

"The baby wakes me up a lot."

"I hear you on that." He glances at the whiteboard. His initials are third down. Seeing the whiteboard reminds me for the hundredth time that I've got no job. Soon, I might have no wife. This is as close to abject as I've ever been. "What's the deal with Adrienne Lite?"

"She's the birth mother."

"You said that the other night."

"Well, it's true," I say, feeling defensive, though I'm not sure I'm being attacked. "She's been living with us for the past couple of months. Just till she gets on her feet."

He whistles. "She's right down the hall? A younger version of Adrienne? It's like an episode of that TV show, *What Would You Do?* You know which show I mean?"

"Not really. Listen, I should get going. But I'm looking for someone. If you see him, could you give him my number?"

"Who's that?"

"It's the guy you were calling the Fixer." I'm trying to sound casual. "We were talking the other day and I said I'd text him some information but then we got in a hand and I never put his number in my phone."

"You were talking? The two of you? He doesn't talk to anyone."

I shrug, though he's not buying my casual act.

"What kind of information do you have for the Fixer?"

"It's not a big deal."

"It's a big enough deal that you're here looking for him." He squints at me. "Are you in some trouble?"

"I just had some time to kill. It's been slow at work, so I'm not working as many hours."

"I thought when it's slow, you car guys work the most hours. You need to be there any time a customer might walk in, day or night. My buddy Jim's always complaining about it."

"He doesn't work at my dealership. You know what, give the Fixer my number or don't. Like I said, it's not a big deal. Have a good session." I push off from the railing and head for the door, leaving Ames's worried face in my rearview.

I probably should have stayed and played poker. Because once I'm home, I'm restless and amped up. Three shots of bourbon don't do much for my nerves, but unfortunately, they make it impossible to turn around and drive back to the Pyramid, or anywhere else.

I haven't heard from Ray yet about whether they're going to contest my unemployment claim. I bet he can't talk to anyone until Monday. The muckety-mucks don't have to work the weekends, not like the grunts. I tell myself I'm glad not to be a grunt anymore, though it never used to feel that way, not when I was good at it.

I'm going to need to get another job. But what? I can't seem to sell right now, and I'm not qualified for anything else. I never made it to college. Adrienne's salary, when it kicks in again, won't cover the mortgage.

We've got some savings. I might have to eat into them for the

Fixer. I don't know what his going rate is or if there's room to negotiate. Does he have a sliding scale for the newly unemployed? Pro bono, maybe?

Adrienne's out to lunch with Mel, and Leah and Trevor went somewhere with Michael. I haven't had the house to myself in I don't know how long. I need to take advantage of this moment. I need to do something really lowdown and dirty.

Online porn is the most obvious thing. But Adrienne doesn't really mind that. She used to feel like it just made things hotter between us. It gave me ideas, spurred fantasies. She wasn't threatened by those women, and she didn't need to be.

What does threaten Adrienne? A certain videotape, if she knew it existed. If she knew I had it.

One more shot of bourbon, and I go deep into the garage. First I have to find our old VCR and hook it up. Then I locate the tape, which is actually a lot easier. It's inside the *Stripes* box, the one with a smirking Bill Murray on the cover. (Adrienne's always had what seems to me an irrational dislike of Bill Murray, of smirking comedy in general.)

I lie down in our bed and push "Play" on the dusty remote. This is some deviant shit, I know it is. Somehow, I've never thought seriously about getting rid of the tape. It's the only way I could ever see my brother again, for one thing. Unfortunately, I have to watch him fuck my wife.

I don't have to. I could stop it while they're still just talking. During the time period when he recorded the tape, Michael was turning his vitriol on me like a fire hose, but on screen, with Adrienne, he was cajoling. Pathetically begging, actually. His final offer, when all else failed? "I'll share you with Gabe," he said.

The tape's degraded a lot over the years. I have to turn the volume way up and listen over a whirring sound, the kind you hear in Vietnam movies where a helicopter is doing a rescue; the picture is warping and grainy. When I first found the tape, Michael had been dead less than a week. I could barely stand to see his handwriting along the side: "Adrienne" was all it said. I didn't want to view Adrienne through his lens. I was already sick with guilt.

But three months later, I was still with Adrienne, in deep. I should have given her up, in light of my brother's having killed himself over her, over the two of us being together, but it was the opposite. I couldn't let his death be in vain. Adrienne and I had to be the greatest love there ever was to justify what we'd done to Michael. So for three months, I tried to prove that. Every minute I wasn't at work, I spent with her. If I wasn't with her, my mind went all sorts of terrible places. But when we were together, she was so consuming, so convincing. She believed in us absolutely, and it was contagious. It was a fever.

Then this one night, she was out to dinner with her dad, I didn't know where. If I had known, I bet I would have shown up at the restaurant like some addicted freak. It was before cell phones, so I couldn't reach her. I was going nuts in my house, and I felt like I might rip my own face off if I couldn't see hers. I remembered the videotape (not that I'd ever really forgotten it).

I saw her face, all right. I saw everything. Michael begging, her considering his offer, and then when he kissed her, she responded. It went fast, like they were hungry for each other. It looked like she'd missed him.

It literally made me puke. While they were still pumping away, I was in the bathroom, retching.

I was so angry with Adrienne. How could she do that to me, or worse, to him? She swore that she'd consistently told him no, they'd never get back together, she was in love with me. "I never gave him hope," she said. But what's going to give a guy more hope than what was on the videotape?

I'd been so caught up in seeing Michael as some kind of archenemy in that last month of his life. But that videotape showed me how desperate he'd become. To make an offer like that just to hang on to

Adrienne—it was like we'd turned him into someone else, some sort of degenerate. We really and truly destroyed him.

Then there was the existence of the videotape itself. This wasn't yet the era of sex tapes, and Michael wasn't much of a groundbreaker by nature. So he must have loved her so much that he just wanted to keep seeing her.

From an objective point of view, the sex was standard. Routine missionary, nothing like what Adrienne and I were doing. But there's a point on the tape where Michael slows down and brushes her hair back from her face. He kisses her forehead; he murmurs in her ear. What did he say? I love you, most likely. You can see that he does. Michael is making love. But Adrienne—what's she doing?

Afterward, she gets dressed quickly, ready to flee. She says what a mistake it was. She asks him to leave her alone. She was using my words, the ones I'd said to her after our first time together.

The videotape confirmed that my brother was a victim. But I couldn't let Adrienne be the villain. Even one night without her was unbearable.

If there was a murderer, it was me. I led Adrienne on. I was older, and she was a lovelorn kid who'd worshipped me from afar for years. I was the drug and she was the addict, even if it sometimes felt like the reverse. She'd loved me more than anything before she even really knew me. I was nineteen, and she was sixteen. I should have had the morality and the self-control to say no and mean it. More than that, I should have had the loyalty to walk away. Because Michael wasn't Adrienne's brother; he was mine. So the betrayal that ultimately killed him wasn't hers; it was mine.

After I first watched the videotape, I decided the best thing was to forget about it. Adrienne didn't love Michael, she was in love with me. Nothing on the tape refuted that. She must have felt bad for Michael and caved. She made a mistake, and that's what she told him immediately after. Of course it was the wrong choice, and she was ashamed. That's why she never confessed. After all, confession is really for the wrongdoer. You pass along your burden to another, and in their pain, they have to decide whether you deserve absolution. Adrienne didn't want to put me in that position. That's what I need to believe.

Now I find myself watching the videotape with a detachment that's nearly clinical. There's no sense of discovery, no element of surprise. Uninspired choreography, stilted dialogue, poor production values—all still there. Now I'm looking for something specific, something that would have wrecked me at the time.

But I can't find it. Without a cameraman to zoom in, I still can't see her face as Michael makes love to her.

I just want to know what she felt for him. It's taken me twenty years to realize that something would be preferable to nothing.

CHAPTER 47

Adrienne

It's day four, and I haven't been able to get any alone time with Trevor. Leah seems to have him on the buddy system. It's like that infuriating season of *Survivor* where Boston Rob never let his compadres take a shit in the bush alone, so the other tribe could never pierce their alliance. It was like watching Jim Jones do reality TV.

No word from Mel, not even a text to ask how I'm grieving. I sent her one to say I enjoyed our lunch, hope to do it again soon!, and her response was, "Yeah, me too!" One exclamation point—that's not even lukewarm on the Mel thermometer.

It feels out of character, which scares me. Unless I just can't really judge character at all, which scares me more.

I was so sure that I could get Mel to make that call, if needed. She was supposed to be my insurance policy. Now everything hinges on Trevor, and that might be the scariest prospect of all.

I was hoping he'd be back to sleeping on the couch now that Leah's doing all the night feedings but no, he's moved into her room. He's shed all pretense of propriety and respect for the initial house rules. We're all living under Leah's rules now.

I need to get to him soon. But how, without alerting Leah? The last thing I want is for her to suspect me and clear out of here early with Michael.

I've been kissing her ass so hard that my cheeks ache. I told her she can take all of Michael's things, right down to the diaper bag, to make sure they get off to the best start. She just nodded, like it's all expected. Maybe she was thinking, What's Adrienne going to do with that stuff anyway? It was insulting. She thinks she's the last birth mother on earth?

Unfortunately, she is the last one as far as I'm concerned. Michael's it. He's my son. I know his smell, his touch, his gurgles, his cries. He's imprinted on me, and I'm imprinted on him.

I've got to get Trevor alone, that's all there is to it.

They're out looking at apartments again. That's a good sign. It means they haven't signed a lease yet. It's also good because it's the only way I can be with Michael during the day. Otherwise, they've been taking him with them. They're logging major hours at the park and I don't know where else. I check him for bruising when he comes back but so far, I haven't found any. He doesn't have so much as diaper rash. As far as I can tell, they're actually taking good care of him. But I believe what I told Mel: If they took Michael permanently, it would be a disaster waiting to happen.

One positive thing came out of my lunch with Mel. Summer got the anonymous tip I left, and she took it seriously. Today, she was showing different screenshots from Facebook and reading Joy's fake posts aloud. "The only conclusion we can draw," Summer intoned, "is that Joy Ellison was a bona fide con woman." While Summer wasn't quite ready to admit that this created reasonable doubt for Brad, I feel like the police will have to.

I'm doing my part to right a wrong, and on a cosmic level, that has to count for something. I've earned a few minutes alone with Trevor. Ten minutes, even. I can see how pinched he's looked these past four days, and he's got a fresh spray of acne across his cheeks and chin. The boy is stressed. He's an egg ready to crack, I know it.

I'm going to have to pull an all-nighter. At some point, Trevor's going to leave Leah's room to take a leak. He'll be bleary-eyed, his defenses down. That's when I'll pounce.

While Gabe's sleeping, I position myself in our doorway. From there, I can see down the hall. I try to read and watch videos on my iPad, though what I'm really doing is thinking. About what-ifs. About plans and loopholes.

The first time Leah's door opens, it's because Michael's crying. I have to give her credit; her response time is impressive. She heads to the kitchen and back down the hall with a bottle of milk. Then she disappears into the nursery.

So she hasn't been breast-feeding; she hasn't shared that particular intimacy with Michael. But she is sharing the intimacy that's been mine since he was born: I'm the one who answers his cries; I'm the one who rocks him and gives him sustenance in the night. My chest aches as I watch her close the door, with cruel finality. Michael's sobs quiet.

Maybe she really is becoming a decent mother. If I'm not able to get through to Trevor, if I can't enact the CPS loophole, if she does take him away from me, I have to hope for that.

But I don't have to hope for it yet.

I think of going into Leah's room now and accosting Trevor. But it's too risky. I don't know exactly how long she'll be in with Michael, or if she'll hear us talking. It's better to wait for a more opportune moment.

It comes an hour and a half later. Just as I'm about to doze off, Trevor stumbles down the hall. He slams the bathroom door, and I get to my feet. When he exits a minute later, I grab his arm. "What the—" he exclaims. I slap a hand over his mouth.

"Come with me," I whisper urgently. Then I lead him by the arm through the house and out the front door. He blinks at me, still half-asleep, trying to process whether he's in the midst of an abduction or a dream. "We have to talk."

"Leah wouldn't like it," he mumbles.

"That's why we need to talk." I'm keeping my voice low. The neighborhood is silent, but for the hiss of a neighbor's sprinkler. "She's got you on a short leash, Trevor. That's not why you came across the country, is it?"

"I don't think I should talk to you about this." He turns, as if to go back into the house.

I run around him and put a restraining palm flat against his chest. "You owe me a conversation, at least. I opened my home to you."

"Because you thought it would help you. Because you wanted to get Leah out of here sooner."

"Is that what she told you?"

He doesn't answer, which means yes.

"Maybe that's what she would do, but that's not how I am. I thought it could work out well for everybody. But that's not how it's turning out."

"It's not turning out so good for you." He looks in the direction of the sprinkler. "I know it sucks, Adrienne. I didn't mean to screw you or anything."

"I know you didn't. Let's be real, Trevor. This isn't turning out so good for you either."

He sits down heavily on the front lawn, which is browning from neglect. It's plausible that our neighbors are going to take up a petition against us if we don't get it together soon. Between our lawn and Trevor's car, we're bringing down the property values.

I sit beside him. "You feel trapped into doing this for Leah. You love her. You want to give her the family she never had. But this isn't you, Trevor. Being a dad. You're an awesome older brother, I can see that. But being a father is different."

"It's not so different."

"Yes, it is." I see his jaw set stubbornly. "On a practical level, how are you going to provide for Michael and Leah? How are you going to live?"

"She's got a bunch of money saved. She's going to pay for the apartment when we're starting out."

"The Bay Area is way more expensive than Rhode Island. The economy's still crap. What kind of job are you going to get? Are you going to drop out of college?"

"You sound like my parents," he mutters. He starts plucking blades of grass out of the lawn. They're dry enough to splinter in his hand. He tosses them aside. "They're wrong, and so are you." He looks up at me. "Besides, you don't care about me. You're all about you."

"Is that what Leah thinks?"

"It's what we both think."

"Well, you're both wrong. Because I'm all about Michael. I want him to have the best home possible. If that's you and Leah, then go for it. But you don't want to do this. You're getting pushed into it. Then you have to turn around and defend it to your family. Believe me, I know what that's like. Gabe and I only got closer after my mom kicked me out. I was going to prove to her that he was my life."

"And it worked out okay."

"Has it really?" I suddenly realize I've started telling the truth.

Maybe Trevor can feel that, because his shoulders slump. "Well, if you and Gabe are all fucked up, why should we leave Michael with you?"

"Because I love Michael more than the whole world combined. Because Gabe and I are going to work it out, or we won't, but regardless, I'm going to give Michael everything. *Everything.* Can you say the same?"

He doesn't answer.

"Your whole family's back east, all your brothers and sisters. You love them. Leah doesn't have that, and I'm sorry for her. I'm sorry she missed out. But why should you miss out?" His silence encourages me further. "Leah's manipulating you to get the family she wants. That's not her fault, with the childhood she's had. But still, you don't have to go along."

"I want to go along," he says, but I hear reasonable doubt.

"Do you know if she really has the money she's talking about? She'd need thousands to float you in the Bay Area. Where would she get that?"

"Her poker winnings. She's got a stack of hundreds in the room."

"She won that much the other night?" I want to wring Gabe's neck. He's managed to give Leah a skilled trade.

"She's been going ever since Gabe first taught her." Trevor pretty much sneers Gabe's name. "When they used to stay up all night."

When they used to—*what*?

"If the reason you're doing this," I say, "is that you don't want Gabe raising your son, you don't need to worry. I'll be the only one on the adoption papers. Most likely, we won't last the year."

Trevor glances at me in surprise. "You'd choose Michael over Gabe just like that?"

"I love Michael more than anything. I swear to you." I touch his arm. "I know you love Leah, but you don't have to sacrifice your life for her. You don't owe her that."

His head falls forward heavily, like it can't support the weight of the decision anymore.

I put my arm around him. "You have to think about three lives here: yours, Michael's, and Leah's. She's got it so you're only thinking about hers."

"When I'm around her, I have trouble thinking clearly." His voice is muffled.

"That's love for you."

I knew the conversation had gone well, but I didn't know it had gone *this* well.

The next morning, Trevor's car is gone. Leah left the letter he wrote her in the center of the kitchen table. It said (with egregious penmanship, spelling errors, and sentences that went on for days) that he was sorry he can't be a dad, not now or any time "son." He was especially sorry he was another guy letting Leah down; he never wanted to be that. He wanted to be her shining "night." But he belongs back in Rhode Island, being an older brother and going to college. "I hope I didn't mess you up too bad for that next guy," he wrote, "because they're out there, guys who'll want you, because you're the most lovable girl in the world."

I'm so focused on the letter, awash in self-satisfaction, that a few minutes pass before I realize Leah's taken Michael, and no, she hasn't left me a note. I check my phone. No text. The diaper bag's gone, along with lots of bottles of milk from the fridge. Where could she have gone? She'd be on foot, with a baby. No, wait, the stroller's gone, too. She could have hopped on a bus. What if it was a Greyhound bus?

"Gabe!" I shout, running into the bedroom. "Wake up!"

He sits up in bed, sleep crunched in his eyes.

"Leah took Michael."

"She probably went to the park again with Trevor."

"Trevor left her."

At that, he snaps to attention. A smile begins to spread across his face.

"She took the stroller. She took the diaper bag, and a whole lot of milk. The breast pump is gone. I knew we shouldn't have bought her that fancy portable one, the kind in its own tote bag. Damn it!"

"Calm down. She'll be back."

"How do you know what she'll do? We have no idea what she's capable of!" A woman scorned, alone with my baby.

"She has nowhere to go. She hasn't found an apartment yet, has she?"

"I don't know what she found!" But I definitely didn't find stacks of hundreds in her room. She's off with my son, and thousands in poker winnings, if Trevor was telling the truth (and why would he lie?).

I got what I wanted, Trevor gone, but at what cost? I thought I'd turned my karma around with Mel's anonymous call. What more does the universe want from me?

Pull it together, Adrienne. This is no time for hysteria. Think.

"Maybe this nullifies the contract," I say. "She gets Michael for a certain number of hours but she's not supposed to just take him. She needs permission."

"We can call Hal."

"Can we call CPS? Does this constitute, I don't know, neglect? It's chilly out there. He's not even wearing a jacket, I bet."

"You call CPS," he says, "and we've got ourselves a war."

"It's a war anyway, isn't it? And she's winning. She has my baby!" I slam my hand into the wall.

I hear an incoming text and race over to my phone. It's Trevor. "Thank u, A." Another text: "I saw the future last nite, clear as a crystal ball." And: "If I did this for her now, Id always do what she says. Id be u & Gabe." Then: "Dont hate on Leah. Shes a good girl." A second later: "She was planning to help u & Gabe get on track. Then she was going 2 leave." That was it? That was her plan all along? "But she fell 4 the baby. She fell 4 family."

It's a text soliloquy. "Where is she now?" I type back.

A long pause. "I dont know."

"Does she still want Michael?"

"I didnt think so."

Trevor thought as I did: that with him gone, with the idea of family receding, Leah would give up. But now she's gone rogue, and I've got no inside man.

CHAPTER 48

Gabe

On our way to the car, I get a text from an unknown number: "At the Pyr now. Who r u." So Ames came through. He got my message to the Fixer, and the Fixer's curious.

If you'd asked me yesterday, I would have said that Trevor's leaving would render the Fixer unnecessary. Even with all that's happened, I still have a soft spot for Leah. She's an orphan, you know? There was no one around to teach her right from wrong. No one to even give her a hug, for fuck's sake.

But this stunt she's pulled does piss me off. Michael's my baby, too. If we don't find them soon . . .

I wonder if the Fixer is as proficient at tracking people as he is at—well, whatever else he does to them. I put the phone in my pocket, hoping I'll never need him.

From the passenger seat, Adrienne calls and texts Leah repeatedly, but it keeps going straight to voice mail. "Can I use yours?" she asks, indicating my cell.

"I'm frozen out, too." Leah hasn't uttered a word to me since the night she announced her departure, and I haven't trusted myself to break the silence. I couldn't risk making things any worse.

"We have to try everything." Adrienne's face is agony crossed with determination, a hybrid I've only ever seen on her.

I hand her the phone and steer us toward the park. There's a light rain falling, and as a result, it's pretty much deserted.

"Let's try the other park. The one off Prospect." Her eyes are on my phone. After she sends the text, I notice that she holds on to it. I see her furtively scrolling up.

"What are you expecting to find?" I think quickly about whether there are any texts on there about getting fired. No, Ray hasn't been in touch yet, and I certainly haven't been volunteering the information to anyone else.

"Nothing." She stares at me. "So who are you, Gabe?" She's quoting the Fixer.

"That's from somebody at the Pyramid."

"I know. It says so in the text. Who are you? And who's texting you?"

I peer out through the blurry windshield. "You don't have to know everything, Wren. Sometimes it's better not to know." I'm thinking of her videotape.

She tosses the phone on the floor and puts her head in her hands. She begins to sob. My arm shoots out awkwardly and pats her back. I feel like a stranger on a bus. "It's going to be okay," I tell her.

"What if he's dead? What if she killed Michael and then herself?"

"You've been watching too much Summer Jackson. That's not Leah." The rain is getting heavier. I turn on the wipers.

"How do you know?"

I don't need to keep Leah's secrets anymore. She certainly felt no compunction about keeping mine. "She's got no parents. She grew up in foster homes and then group homes. You don't think she's tougher than this? She's not going to give us the satisfaction of destroying herself."

"What about destroying Michael?"

"I think she really loves him."

"That's what I'm afraid of." But she pops her head up. The squall is passing.

I drive everywhere Adrienne can think of, and the one place I can think of: the Pyramid. I idle the car outside while Adrienne runs inside. She's back a few minutes later. "What a dump," she says. "Leah's not there."

I feel oddly hurt. I don't know why she had to jab at me now, like that. She knows I love the place. Maybe it's about that text. She might have dropped the subject, but she hasn't forgotten it.

"If you want Leah," Adrienne says, her eyes following the wipers, "you can have her."

"Why would you say that?"

"I'm not going to hold you back. I'm not going to fight for you. Not anymore."

"When have you had to fight for me?"

She stares at me. "Seriously? I've been fighting for you our whole lives. Fighting your guilt about Michael. Trying to let you know we're worth it. I'm done."

"You're done with me?"

She faces straight ahead. The light must have turned green, because I hear honking. I don't give a shit, we're going to finish this conversation.

"Do you want me to go with Leah? Do you want me to go, period?"

"She wants you, she can have you. You can play poker all night long. Heads up, isn't that what it's called?" She makes it sound as suggestive as possible. "But I keep Michael."

I didn't realize she even knew about the late-night poker. "You were obsessed with Michael. That's why I was with Leah. Not *with* her, not like that." The honking intensifies. I hear cars hurriedly switching lanes to get around us. I put on my four-way flashers, like we've broken down. It's not untrue.

"You need to drive."

"Drive where?"

"There must be other places to look. They can't just be gone." Her voice rises at the end.

"He's all you're thinking about, huh? Even now. Even when we're talking about our entire future."

"You need to drive the car. I can't think, sitting here." I know what she means. The blare of the horns makes me want to jump out of my skin, too.

But we're going to settle this now. She doesn't get to dictate our whole lives. "No," I tell her. "We're not going anywhere."

Her eyes are wide with surprise. But she's always liked it, at least a little, when I assume command.

"I know things have changed between us," I say. "I know that it's mostly my fault that we're in this position, that Leah is talking about taking Michael." I see her thinking, Mostly? "Yeah, mostly. Because you made the decision to invite Trevor into our home. If you hadn't we wouldn't be here." She can't argue with that. "But I shouldn't have told Leah the story about Michael. I should have realized she had it out for you and she'd twist it. I shouldn't have given her ammunition."

Adrienne's face is inscrutable. The horns blare on and the rain pelts the car, heavier now, but she hasn't interrupted me yet.

"You've done some shit, too, these last two months. It's not only me. But I know that a lot of it's been me. I don't know if I didn't want to be a father, or if I was freaked out with all the memories about my brother, or if it was just that name, that goddamn name . . ." I take both her hands. "Don't give up on me, because I think I'm ready now."

She looks gobsmacked. It's the last thing she expected to hear. So after all these years, I can still surprise her.

I find myself starting to smile, just a little. "You got to admit, it's been a confusing couple of months. But these past few days, I've started thinking differently about everything, including Michael.

See? I can even say his name." She looks down at her hands in mine. I'm reaching her, I can tell.

I think of coming clean with everything, telling her I lost my job but if she'll believe in me again, I could get it together. But that's for later. I'm pressing my luck as hard as I can. Ironic that I can still see the Pyramid's neon sign from here.

She takes her hands away. "I can't think about any of this right now. I just have to think about Michael."

They say you can get used to anything—you get sensitized, acculturated, something. It's true, I can barely hear the horns through the roar in my ears. A pitch like that and she just rejects it out of hand? That's cold.

"You're only thinking about Michael now?" I sneer. "Like you were thinking about him twenty years ago? When he made you an offer you didn't refuse?"

"What are you talking about?"

"The videotape. Michael said he'd share you with me, and then you had sex with him."

She sits back against the seat, visibly stunned for the second time in five minutes. "I didn't think there really was a videotape. Well, I mean, at first I believed there was, but then . . ." She seems unable to continue.

"Why didn't you ever tell me?"

"Why didn't you tell me you knew about it?"

"Knew about it? I've watched it. I own it."

At that, the blood drains from her face.

"What I don't get is how you could have done that to him," I say. "Given him hope like that. I don't get how you could be so heartless."

"If you think I'm heartless, why are you telling me you want us to be a family? That's always been your problem, Gabe. You're wishy-washy."

I know her so well. She's throwing daggers to avoid having to answer questions and take responsibility. "You let me take the blame all these years, but the date on that video—it was pretty close to Michael's suicide. That hope you gave him, and then the disappointment that must have come after . . . I bet it crushed him."

"I never 'let you' take the blame. I don't think either of us is to blame. That's what I've always said." She's silent a long minute. "I tried to protect you. I guess it backfired."

"Protect me how?"

"Michael wasn't some fragile little waif like you believed. He was an angry, manipulative, disturbed person."

I shake my head. "That's not my brother."

"Would the brother you think you knew have recorded that videotape on purpose so he could blackmail me? So he could force me to have sex with him again and again?" I wait for her to go on—needing to hear, not wanting to listen. "He knew I was in love with you and not him. He guilted me into sleeping with him and he taped it. Then he threatened to tell you unless I kept sleeping with him. I hated it, Gabe. I hated him. All I wanted was to be with you, and he knew that. What he wanted was to ruin it for us. He wanted to get back at you so badly for a lifetime of wrongs, things he never even told you about. He hated you, Gabe. I never wanted you to know that."

I slam back into the seat. "You're lying."

"You know I'm not. He was controlling me with that tape, and he enjoyed it. It was like getting raped every night. I went along because I couldn't lose you."

"You should have told me."

She pauses. "Yeah, I should have. If I had . . ." It dangles there, the thought of what could have been, an alternate reality in which Michael had lived. "I thought the only way out was to turn the tables on him. To seem like I was doing what he wanted, but in little ways, letting him know what I really thought of him. That he didn't compare at all to the man you were."

"You were trying to break him."

"I was trying to get away from him. But yes, I was pissed off. Wouldn't you be, if someone blackmailed you? And in the ugliest, dirtiest way, where you had to give yourself to that person night after night. All to hang on to the love you really wanted." She leans in, forcing me to look into her face. "Think about it. What kind of human being would do something like that to another? Is that the work of an innocent victim?"

"I don't know," I say finally. "I just don't know."

"You don't know if you believe me, or you don't know what kind of person would do that?"

Unfortunately (or fortunately, I don't know which), I do believe her.

"Michael wasn't some sweet sensitive artist. Or at least, that wasn't all of him. He was already jealous of you, and the thing with me just sent him over the top. But that's not your fault. You couldn't have known. You tried to be a good brother. I know you did." I turn my head but she grabs my face, forcing me back. "I never wanted you to know how he felt about you and what he was capable of. I never wanted you to see him for what he really was. But maybe if I had, you would have let yourself off the hook. Then you could have loved our baby right from the start."

I squeeze my eyes shut, but a tear finds its way free.

"I'm sorry, Gabe. I really am. Look at me, Gabe."

I finally do, but it hurts. It's agony. I can see that she understands, for the first time.

"I am so sorry. I never should have done what I did. I never should have used your brother to get to you. It's not enough to say I was young and I loved you. If it meant destroying another person, destroying your brother, I shouldn't have done it. There are some means you just don't use, regardless of the ends."

I twist away again, and this time, she doesn't pull me back.

"I get why you don't want to look at me," she says quietly. "But I'm not Patty." Then again, in a true whisper, "I'm not Patty."

I want to believe her epiphany. It's the first time she's ever ceased to defend herself, the first unvarnished remorse she's ever expressed for what happened to Michael instead of a generalized regret. But it's so damn convenient.

"You say it's not worth it to destroy someone in order to get what you want," I say. "Does that hold for Leah, too? You'll let her have Michael?"

"I'm sorry," she says, "but I can't answer that. Not yet."

Then when? I want to ask, but I'm startled by a knock on the window. I roll it down and see an officer in a rain slicker. "Is there a problem with your car, sir?"

"It overheated," Adrienne says, wiping at her eyes. "We needed to give it a few minutes to cool down. We can try to start it up again."

The cop looks back and forth between us. It's obvious something's not quite right, but he's not sure if it's the kind of domestic drama that falls within his purview. "Everything all right here, ma'am?" He's asking Adrienne, as if she's some abused woman who might need help.

I start to laugh. It's high-pitched, hysterical, exhausted. I sound like I've flown over the cuckoo's nest.

The cop gives me a stony stare. "Ma'am?" he repeats.

Adrienne starts to laugh herself. "We're fine, Officer. It's just been a hell of a day."

He considers us both and then decides to extricate himself as quickly as possible. I don't blame him. "Try starting your car, sir."

I oblige.

"Can you get home, or do you need to pull over to the side and call a tow truck?"

"We've had this problem before," Adrienne says, "and we can get home."

He nods brusquely and walks off, without another word. He is thoroughly done with us.

As the light turns green, I take off, making sure to go precisely the speed limit. I notice that the cop follows us for about a mile.

"Can you think of anywhere else to look," I ask, "or should we go home?"

"Let's go home." She looks at her cell phone and then mine, in case we might have missed anything from Leah.

My mind goes to white noise for the remainder of the ride. I can't process what I've heard about Michael or this sudden change in Adrienne. I think I still want a family with her; I'm pretty sure she's still my life, just as she's always been. What would it even take for me to let her go? What would be left of me if I did?

We open the front door to find Leah in the living room. The stroller and several bags are upended and strewn about. There's a sense of disarray that extends to Leah herself, who's obviously been crying. Michael is lying on a blanket on the floor, kicking his legs and moving his arms. It's like he's practicing to be a crab in a school play. He looks content and unharmed.

Adrienne snatches him up and strips him down just to check. He begins to cry, probably at the suddenness. "Shh, shh," Adrienne says as she scans his body. Finding no bruises, she turns to Leah. "How could you just take him like that?" She rubs his back, and his sobs de-escalate.

"I needed to get out for a while," Leah says, her tone defensive. "It felt claustrophobic."

"This can't go on," I tell her. "You don't get to fuck with us like this. You don't get to fuck with our whole lives."

Leah's eyes are on Michael. "I think it's the other way around."

"What do you mean?" Adrienne asks.

"I'm pretty sure you had something to do with Trevor leaving."

"We didn't have anything—" I start.

"Not you. Trevor hates you. Her." Leah thumbs toward Adrienne.

Adrienne doesn't answer, which feels like an admission of guilt. Michael's pupils dart back and forth, following the conversation. "Gabe's right. This can't go on. We need an answer right now. If you want Michael, you take him with you today." Her eyes fill with tears. "Otherwise, you sign the adoption papers. I can't live like this, in a hostage situation."

Adrienne is going all-in. It's a big gamble, but she must be figuring that there's no way Leah can go now. Because Leah is, quite obviously, devastated. She's putting up a front but she doesn't have the kind of bravado that marked her exit conversation five days ago. She doesn't have the illusion of family anymore, no one to have her back. Part of me feels for her, even though she's been putting the screws to Adrienne, me, and our marriage for a while now.

The problem is, I don't think that even a weakened Leah is going to respond to an ultimatum. Adrienne never would.

So maybe Adrienne's got something else up her sleeve.

"It's not so hard, taking care of him," Leah says, like she's figuring it out as she talks. "He's a mellow baby."

"That's because I've done such a good job!" Adrienne flares. "I've made him that way! He doesn't cry because he doesn't need to, because I anticipate his every need, because I have it all at the ready. Are you going to be that mother, Leah?" She tries again, using a calmer tone. "I know I couldn't have been that selfless at nineteen."

"No," Leah says, "you couldn't have."

I notice that Leah hasn't actually said she's going to take Michael. She's stalling.

"How are you going to support yourself and a child?" I ask. "If you leave today. If you don't have us to buy Michael's diapers and whatever else he needs. If we don't give you another dime."

"I've got it covered. Don't worry about me."

"She has her poker winnings," Adrienne says.

"You barely broke even the night we played at the Pyramid," I say. I resist the urge to remind her that I took a lot of her money during our big showdown hand. She doesn't need me kicking her when she's down.

"My bankroll is almost four thousand dollars." She sounds proud, but she has to be lying. There's no way she's made that much in the past week and a half.

"Bullshit," I say.

"It's true," Adrienne says. "Trevor told me she's been playing at the Pyramid since you first gave her lessons. She's been saving up."

I stare at Leah as I roll the footage backward in my mind. She has the decency to drop her eyes, to look ashamed. But that doesn't change what she's done. It doesn't change that she faked me out at the Pyramid the other night by acting like some newbie. She's been snowing me all along, playing me for a fool, tricking me into destroying my own marriage.

It doesn't change that Leah has caused so much misery and disconnection, that she's ruined my life.

Rage builds up in me, quick as a fireball. This is the woman who's ruined my life.

I'm watching her, and then through the haze of my anger, another face superimposes itself on top of Leah's. It's Patty from brunch in San Francisco, and then it's another Patty, a Patty with darker hair, windblown, smiling on a balcony just like all the missing women, all the Summer women, and I feel like I'm on the cusp of knowing something that I just can't afford to know. As if to ward off that knowledge, as if it's an escape, I'm charging Leah.

My hands close around her throat. This has never happened to me before, this feeling, this color. It's true, you really can see red. I'm squeezing the life out of this woman who's ruined mine, but I can't see her face, only crimson, and then I'm seeing nothing at all.

CHAPTER 49

Adrienne

It all goes so fast. The confrontation with Leah, the ultimatum, Michael on his blanket kicking his legs watching his two mommies, the talk about poker, and then out of nowhere, Gabe's just crazy. He looks like he really might kill Leah.

Did I think, just for a split second, that it might be the answer to a prayer? Trevor's already signed away his parental rights, and with Leah out of the picture, Michael would be mine.

But I'd lose Gabe, too, to prison, and I don't want that. Our talk in the car reminded me how far back and how deep our love goes. It's been in hibernation for a while but it's still here, waiting for the thaw.

I need to stop him. I need to bring him back to his senses. Shouting isn't doing it. Even trying to pry his hands off her neck isn't working. Has he always been so strong?

I wish I had a stun gun. That's it, I need to stun him, and I need to do it now. Leah's gasping for air, turning colors.

I spin around the living room, looking for an object. Everything's too light, insubstantial. I can't stun him with a framed photo or a candle, can I? Hurry, I have to hurry.

I run into the kitchen and see a skillet on the stovetop. It'll have to do. I dash back to find that Leah's eyes have closed.

I don't swing the skillet with much force; I'm only trying to stun him. He just needs to come back into himself and realize what he's doing, who he actually is. Gabe's no murderer. Maybe if there'd been someone in Patty's apartment to stun me, someone like Gabe, I wouldn't be a murderer now.

CHAPTER 50

Adrienne

If only the skillet hadn't been cast iron. I think that a thousand times a day.

I can still see it: Gabe falling to the floor, immobile. Leah tumbling down after him, her body limp. Michael, agog, uncomprehending, his arms and legs flailing. Thank God he can't roll yet. Thank God he can't understand.

Gabe's been in a coma for more than a month. No one's talked to me about pulling the plug, and they better not. There have been incrementally positive changes, like the swelling in his brain has reduced, though the doctors never act positive at all. It's like they think that would be some sort of guarantee and they could get sued for false promises. Would it kill them to give me some hope? I just have to find it on my own, that's all.

He's not dead, I won't let him be dead, but sometimes he looks like that. He's so pale and his eyes are closed most of the time. Sometimes they're open but they can't focus.

Patty's head didn't cave in, but Gabe's did. They tried to put his skull back together, surgery after surgery, but it's like Humpty Dumpty. I don't sit on that side of him, his lumpy oatmeal side.

"Michael's getting so big," I tell him. "He's not crawling yet, but he's thinking about it. He'll be here later. You can hold him."

It's sort of like holding. I put Michael on the bed against Gabe's chest and let him poke around. He seems to like it. Michael, that is. I don't know about Gabe, not for sure, but I've got a feeling.

"You were ready to be a dad," I say, smiling. I always smile when I remember that talk in the car, the breakthrough, the one that was going to turn us back into us. We couldn't find Leah—she was already back at the house with Michael—but we found ourselves. "That's what you were telling me that day. We were going to be a family. You were finally ready."

I couldn't answer his question then: Would it be worth it to destroy Leah in order to have what I wanted most, to get Michael that way? By hitting Gabe, by saving Leah, I told him no, it's not worth it. I proved I'm not Patty. I'm not willing to do things by any means necessary, not anymore.

"I think you'd be proud of me," I say. I'm not just talking about saving Leah that day. I'm talking about all that's followed. "But where were we? Chapter four?" I open James Patterson. Once Michael's here, I'll switch to Dr. Seuss. The machines hiss in a way that Michael seems to find soothing. He sleeps well here, against my breast.

I love being official, knowing that no one can take him from me. Leah signed the adoption papers weeks ago, in the flush of gratitude after I saved her life, but the court order only went through yesterday.

"Excuse me," I hear. I look up and see two police officers in the doorway, a man and a woman. He's got a Cro-Magnon jaw; she's softer looking, like she could be your best friend. Instinctively, I distrust her.

They introduce themselves. He's Officer Rigby, and her name goes right by me, whistles past like wind. He says he's sorry to bother me, she says she's sorry for my loss.

I glare at her. "No one's lost around here."

"For all you've been through," she says, trying to amend it, phony as shit. "Could we sit down?"

"I've already been questioned. So has Leah." I was told no charges would be filed, as I was stopping a crime in progress. They can't renege on that, can they?

Officer Rigby gives me a reassuring smile. "This is about another matter. We're here to ask a few questions about Joy Ellison. You knew her as Patty? She pretended to be pregnant?" His lip curls just slightly with a contempt that I can see is reserved for Patty, not for me. I like this guy.

"Have a seat," I say. "I'll tell you all about it."

I know from Summer Jackson that Joy's husband has been released and the Denver police are trying to find other suspects. But I've decided the best course is almost complete and total honesty: Officer Rigby can know everything except my revenge fantasies, everything except my revenge. That's how I'm living these days. Let the sun shine in, that's my new motto.

Also, some days, I find I just need to talk. Some days, I can't stop. Gabe's become a great listener, but for once, it's nice to hear a male voice in return. Officer Rigby's is quite sonorous.

It's quickly clear that the officers are just trying to find out more about Joy's game. They're tracing its contours. I'm happy to oblige. It's been a hell of a year, and I don't mind their knowing it. Officer Rigby is obviously sympathetic.

"I think there are a lot of victims," I say. "She had a lot of profiles on Facebook."

"I think you're right," he says. "I've been at this for years, and I still can't believe what some people are capable of."

They don't ask my whereabouts around the time of the murder. Hell, forensics still can't even determine when the murder took place. There's no physical evidence to link me, and I'm sure there were no witnesses that night. Really, there's no physical evidence at all, with the body as decomposed as it was. I'm surprised they're even bothering. Joy doesn't seem worth all this trouble, and I tell them so.

"You're preaching to the choir," Officer Rigby says.

The female officer says almost nothing. I wonder what the power dynamics are between them. I wonder if they're fucking. I miss fucking. Now that I can't do it, I miss it a lot.

Strange that the police are here, since even Summer Jackson has moved on. She's following a new missing woman, one with a more pristine backstory. Or so it seems.

As the officers are about to leave, I ask how they found me. "An anonymous tip," she says.

Who . . . ? Whatever. I won't sweat the small stuff.

All I have is the here and now. If this past month has taught me anything, it's that. I need to maintain my focus. That's what it'll take to will Gabe back to Michael and me. It's all about family: Gabe and Michael. Oh, and Leah. She's just arriving. She might have even passed the police at the exit.

"Hey," she says. "I brought you your favorites from the vending machine." She shifts Michael in her arms as she tosses some Funyuns into my lap. Until Gabe was admitted to the hospital, I didn't even know Funyuns still existed. Funyuns and Fanta, my retro hospital snack of choice.

She places Michael in my arms and I nuzzle him gratefully. "Hello, sweet boy. I'm so happy to see you." I breathe him in and then tell him, as always, "Say hello to Daddy."

"Did you enjoy your alone time?" Leah asks.

"We had a good talk." Then I level my gaze at her. Could Gabe have told her about Patty/Joy? He didn't even know that Joy was Patty, did he? Could she somehow . . . ?

No, there's no way.

"Did you finish your enrollment?" I ask. "Did you get that art class you wanted?"

She nods. "If all goes well, I'll take graphic design next semester."

"Maybe by then, you'll have actually finished the mural." I smile to let her know I'm only kidding. There's no rush. She smiles back.

I would never have imagined it turning out like this, with me opening my home to Leah when I didn't have to anymore. Technically, our contract terminated when she signed the adoption papers. But after Gabe's accident, something profound changed between us. Then after the papers were signed, she was no longer the competition. I'm the mom, and that's that.

It helps that Hal's contract is practically an old-school closed adoption: Sure, I know who she is, she knows who I am, but she's got no built-in rights, no guaranteed time with Michael, not even a stipulated Christmas card. That was her idea. She said trust is earned. Then she made me an offer I was hard-pressed to refuse. "I could watch Michael while you spend time with Gabe," she said. "I owe you at least that much. You saved my life."

Of course, there was the incidental benefit for her of having a place to stay, an address from which to enroll in community college, but I get free child care (which will come in really handy when I return to work soon) and instead of siphoning money from the household, she's actually contributing through what I now call her poker fund. You could even argue I'm coming out ahead, since my finances are such a mess. (What with Gabe getting fired and unemployment tussling with me over whether to pay me his benefits. Bureaucratic assholes.) Poor Gabe. I should have been more approachable. He must have thought I'd just come down on him, which I probably would have. I'm much more understanding now.

Anyway, Gabe would never turn up his nose at a win-win. Neither will I.

I see myself in Leah, and I've come to think that if penance is still needed—for Patty, for Gabe's brother—then maybe it's in the form of helping Leah.

Do I know for sure that Leah is sincere? No. But I don't have the energy anymore to search for hidden motivations. I'm just going to take Leah for what she is, the way Gabe did. Maybe I'll even come to love her, like he did.

Because he must have loved her, at least a little, in order for him to go so crazy at her betrayal. I think even she understands that, because she doesn't have any anger toward him at all, only sadness that everything played out as it did. She'd change things if she could, but none of us get that chance. Life only goes in one direction: forward.

Michael is looking into my eyes, grabbing for my nose. "Sweetest baby," I murmur, and let myself revel in my good fortune. Then I stand up and head toward Gabe's bed.

I'm tired of thinking of love as some finite commodity. I'm tired of comparisons. More than anything? That's the wrong way to see it. Now it's about having more than enough. There's love enough to go around, there always was, and if I'd opened my heart to Leah sooner, right from the beginning . . . well, no point in dwelling.

Right now, Gabe's trying to teach me a lesson. Once he thinks I've really learned, he'll come back to me. That's what I have to believe, what I do, in fact, believe. I don't believe in God, but I believe in Gabe. I believe in an all-powerful love—more than one, even. Once I embrace Leah, genuinely, once I give her the family she's always needed, Gabe will know, and he'll return. I'm almost there, I really am.

"Look, Michael," I say, waving his little hand at Gabe, "it's Daddy." Then I curl up against Gabe—he's still so warm, no one can tell me he's not really and truly alive—and Michael occupies the space between us. "Look, Gabe," I say softly, "it's your son."

The writing's been on the (living room) wall this whole time. In the words of Thoreau: "There is no remedy for love but to love more."

If I'd just understood that the circle of love could expand infinitely, if I'd only known it from the beginning, if I'd made room, then none of this would have happened. I wouldn't be sitting here, waiting for Gabe's return. He would never have left.

But this is no time for regrets. It's the time for miracles.

Acknowledgments

I'm thrilled to be working with the Harper/Morrow team once again! Many thanks to my insightful editor, Carrie Feron, her lovely assistant, Nicole Fischer, and the social media–savvy Ashley Marudas. Andy Dodds—on top of having a killer response time, you're also smart and sweet and supportive (three of the best "s"'s.) I'm lucky to have you all in my corner.

I'm so grateful for my agent Elisabeth Weed, who was able to sell this book half written, months before the first was released (which did wonders for my peace of mind). Knowing she believed in me that much, enough to pull everyone else along with her, means more than I can say.

Love and thanks to all my family and friends.

And of course, thank you to Darrend and Daisy. You have to get your own line. Because you're you (well, you're each *you*) and I couldn't love either of you more.

Insights,
Interviews
& More . . .

About the author

About the book

Read on

About the author

Meet Holly Brown

Yanina Gotsulsky

Holly Brown lives with her husband and daughter in the San Francisco Bay area, where she's a practicing marriage and family therapist. She is also the author of the page-turning family drama *Don't Try to Find Me* and the upcoming psychological thriller *This Is Not Over.* Her blog, "Bonding Time," is featured on Psychcentral.com.

Reading Group Discussion Questions

1. Adrienne is thirty-nine, and she and her husband, Gabe, are without a child. Now that she's reaching the end(ish) of her childbearing years, she's obsessed with finding a way to adopt. Did you, or do you, feel pressure to have children?

2. If you couldn't have children, would you consider adopting one or some? Why or why not? If you already have borne a child or children, would you consider adopting?

3. Is being an adoptive parent different from giving birth to a child? Should Adrienne and Leah have different rights as mothers?

4. Throughout *A Necessary End*, Gabe feels ambivalent about becoming a father, while for Adrienne, becoming a mother is essential to her future happiness. Do you think men feel differently about parenting than women do? If so, why do you think that is—biology, social conditioning, or a mix of both?

5. Unlike Adrienne, some women consciously choose not to have children. Can you identify with this choice? Why or why not? Is a woman any less of a person if she decides not to have children? Does the standard hold true for men as well?

6. At the beginning of the novel, Adrienne veers toward the extreme when thinking about motherhood. She rubs pregnant women's bellies, hoards baby clothes in kitchen cabinets, and draws hair down her torso with an eyebrow pencil. ▸

Reading Group Discussion Questions *(continued)*

What do you make of her behavior? Is it normal, or do you side with Gabe's hunch that she's become a little too obsessed?

7. Leah proposes a fairly unorthodox plan for the birth of her baby. What were your initial thoughts when she revealed her scheme to live with Gabe and Adrienne while they raised Michael? Did your opinion change over the course of the book? If you were in Adrienne's or Gabe's shoes, would you have agreed to an open adoption? Why or why not?

8. In Chapter 12, Gabe thinks to himself, "Everyone uses everyone." In a sense, this is true of all the characters in the book—even the minor ones. Would you agree with his assessment? Why or why not?

9. Gabe's behavior is questionable throughout *A Necessary End*. He reneges on his fatherly duties. He slacks off at his job. He even comes on to Leah. A lot of men are frightened by the idea of becoming a father. Given these real fears, is his behavior justified? Did you feel any sympathy for Gabe over the course of the book?

10. Along the same lines, it has been said that the bond between mother and child is unbreakable. Given this fact, does it excuse Adrienne's willingness to do whatever it takes to become a mother? Given Leah's own upbringing, do her attempts at creating a family excuse her actions, even if it means nearly destroying Gabe and Adrienne's marriage?

11. None of the characters in *A Necessary End* are particularly likable. Which one do you feel the most sympathy or empathy toward? Who do you think deserves the most blame? Why?

12. The title of the novel is "A Necessary End." Do you think it's fitting? Why or why not?

13. Holly Brown tells the story from two perspectives: Gabe's and Adrienne's. How would the reading experience be different if Brown also devoted a few chapters to Leah's point of view? Or picked one of the characters and wrote the entire book from his or her perspective, in first person?

14. Toward the end of the novel, Brown throws in a few plot twists that take the story down a shocking path. Did you see any of them coming? Do you think the ending works given the trajectory of the

story? Why or why not? If not, what might be a more suitable option?

15. Given Adrienne's track record with Patty, does it seem credible that she'd willingly enter into another open adoption situation? Does gullibility or a willingness to see the best in people have anything to do with her decision, or should she have been more suspicious from the get-go?

16. Each of the characters keeps secrets from loved ones. Are any of them right to do so, or are the secrets part of the problem?

17. If you could pick the best parent for baby Michael, who would it be: Leah, Adrienne, Gabe, Trevor, or someone else entirely?

18. In addition to being a novelist, Holly Brown is a marriage and family therapist. Does this surprise you? How do you think her other career influences her writing?

Q&A with Holly Brown

Your last novel,* Don't Try to Find Me, *was a family drama with suspense elements.* A Necessary End *is more of a psychological thriller. How do you see your progression as a writer?

I see my progression as an organic one. I write what I'm moved to, and when the character of Adrienne came to me, she just made me laugh. It was like channeling this sassy spirit. I enjoyed writing Gabe, too, but Adrienne was in a class by herself for me. She was just so much fun. She's the spitfire driving the action.

Both of your novels are very interested in family dynamics (a mother and daughter in* Don't Try to Find Me, *and a husband and wife in* A Necessary End*). Since you're a family therapist yourself, how does that influence your work?

Therapy is narrative. The stories we tell ourselves, consciously and subconsciously, shape our behavior and relationships. I spend a lot of working hours helping people figure out what drives and motivates them. That inevitably seeps into my writing, which I hope makes it richer and better.

Who were your inspirations for Gabe and Adrienne? Do they resemble people you know or work with in your therapy practice?

I thought of the situation first, and then thought about what kind of couple would find themselves in it. Who would make that sort of devil's bargain to have a baby? Adrienne emerged first, and then Gabe came into focus, and soon after I envisioned their marital dynamics. They don't really resemble people I know except insofar as their longings are universal. I've certainly known—and worked with—people who go too far in the name of love (or what they believe is love).

The novel has a classic "stranger comes to town" setup, though the twist is, there are actually two strangers: Leah, and then baby Michael. Do you think they have different impacts, or one collective impact on Gabe and Adrienne?

They do pack a double whammy. Leah is younger and prettier and fertile, which sets Adrienne spinning right from the start. Leah's attributes don't escape Gabe's notice, either. But while Adrienne is threatened by Leah, Gabe is much more threatened by (and terrified of) baby Michael. So it's like a tag team of sorts, with Leah and Michael bringing out all of Gabe's and Adrienne's insecurities, buried feelings, and, ultimately, secrets. And of course, having a baby can bring couples together but can also expose all the fault lines. Baby Michael is an earthquake.

Can you explain the book's title?

My original working title was "More Than Anything," which I liked because the things we want more than anything are the greatest motivators for wrongdoing (and rationalizing that wrongdoing). But I understood when the publisher told me it wasn't quite menacing enough.

"A Necessary End" shares the same concept with a more deadly flair. Adrienne believes that to get what she wants more than anything, the ends justify the means; ▶

Q&A with Holly Brown ***(continued)***

from her perspective, the end is necessary—inevitable, even. It's what she tells herself (and the reader) in the prologue, a delusion that allows her to go on rather than crumble under the weight of what she's done.

Have You Read?
More from Holly Brown

For more books by Holly Brown, check out *Don't Try to Find Me* and coming this summer, *This Is Not Over.*

DON'T TRY TO FIND ME

Don't try to find me.

Though the message on the kitchen whiteboard is in fourteen-year-old Marley's handwriting, her mother, Rachel, knows there has to be some other explanation. Marley would never run away.

I'll be okay.

Marley's quiet. Innocent. Sheltered. Growing up in Northern California with all the privilege Rachel never had, what does Marley know about taking care of herself? About being okay?

Rachel might not know her daughter at all. But she does know that she needs to find Marley before someone else does. Someone dangerous.

I'll be better.

The police have limited resources devoted to runaways. If Rachel and her husband, Paul, want their daughter back, they'll have to find her themselves. Paul turns to Facebook and Twitter and launches FindMarley.com.

But Marley isn't the only one with something to hide. Paul's social media campaign generates national attention, and the public scrutiny could expose Rachel's darkest secrets. When she blows a television interview, the dirty speculation begins.

I love you.

The blogosphere is convinced Rachel is hiding something. It's not what they think; Rachel would never hurt Marley. ▸

Have You Read? ***(continued)***

Not intentionally, anyway. But when it's discovered that Rachel lied to the police, the devoted mother becomes the prime suspect in Marley's disappearance.

Is Marley out there, somewhere, watching it all happen . . . or is the truth something far worse?

THIS IS NOT OVER

Beware of your "host". . .

People have always told Dawn she's beautiful, like that's a lottery ticket she can cash in. But at thirty, she's just now getting her college degree and living in a cramped apartment with her husband. Her past (and her parents) are unmentionable.

All she wanted was a nice getaway—to stay in a beach house, to live like money's no object, for just one long weekend. But then Miranda had to send that lying, accusing e-mail. Making it sound like Dawn is filthy, like she's trash.

Miranda can't believe that people would come into her home—granted, her second home—and soil it. She's rented it out for years without an issue (though she's got plenty of other issues, like her grown, drug-addicted son and her checked-out doctor husband).

Two very different women are about to embark on a path of mutually assured destruction, and for what?

It's not just about the sheets.

Some things can never be washed away.

Read on for a sneak peek . . .

Coming Soon from Holly Brown . . .

Chapter One

Dawn

Please note: It is April 23, 2014. You'll have your deposit within seven business days, just like it says on Getaway.com. I've put through a refund to your credit card for the full amount, minus $200 to replace the sheets. I couldn't get the stain out despite professional laundering and bleaching, and it was rather large (gray, about the size and shape of a typical housecat, though the house rental didn't allow pets). That's neither here nor there. At any rate, I already told you about this.

Miranda

That's it, the entire e-mail. No *Dear Dawn* or *I'm sorry you had to stalk me to get your deposit* or *Sincerely* or *All the best*. Just *Miranda*. And does she really think I don't know today's date?

I haven't felt anger like this in I don't know how long. No, I know how long. Since before Rob. He's the antidote for all my inadequacies. I'm good enough because I have him in my life. Because I'm the woman he loves. I'm *that* woman now.

Stop reading. Stop rereading.

But I can't.

I'm sitting at my battle-scarred kitchen table, staring at the screen of my five-year-old laptop in my one-bedroom apartment in a rapidly gentrifying neighborhood in Oakland (soon we'll be priced out), and I've been struck dumb. A stain the size and shape of a housecat? Like my husband and I are, collectively, Pigpen from *Peanuts*, and we leave a cloud of ash in our wake? ▸

Coming Soon from Holly Brown . . . ***(continued)***

I'm an honorable (enough) person, and for sure, Rob is. If we'd ruined Miranda's sheets, we would've owned up to it. I would've contacted her myself, apologized profusely, and said, "Take my deposit, please." No, I would have bleached the sheets, and if that hadn't worked, I would have run out to the nearest Target in a state of abject mortification and bought a new set (because those were not $200 sheets, I promise you that). Then one or the other of us, Rob or myself—whoever had left the ejaculate or the powder or whatever state (solid, liquid, or gas)—would have sought medical attention immediately, because WTF?

But that sequence of events never took place, because there's no way the stain is real. This woman, this Miranda, is trying to scam us out of our $200, half the amount of the security deposit. She's stealing from me, from us.

That's neither here nor there.

She's a thief and a liar, and she's trying to make me feel like I'm filthy, literally. Like I'm beneath her. Sure, she owns an ocean-view house in Santa Monica, and I own nothing, but that doesn't give her the right to . . .

Breathe, Dawn. WWRD—What would Rob do?

He'd let it go, because life is too short for grudges. But then, he's never been wronged, not in any way that matters.

I already told you about this.

Another lie.

What gets me is that she's so undeserving of that gorgeous house she doesn't even need to live in. It's an extra, a spare. I wonder about the opulence of her first home, if that's her second. How does a person like her get a setup like that? Where's the justice in this world? I bet she doesn't even appreciate her good fortune. I would, if it were mine.

I should be studying. This semester's been brutal, and I'm closing in on graduation. My good fortune is in being with Rob, someone who supports me in finally finishing my college degree. It's not every man who insists that his wife devote herself exclusively to her studies. I am incredibly, insanely, painfully lucky.

But I'm so pissed—both about Miranda's actions and the snotty, deceitful tone she used to justify them—that I can't concentrate. Miranda stole my husband's hard-earned money, and how can I just let that go? Not to mention she's stealing my time and my energy. She's hijacking my emotions. I'm a slave to my outrage.

It's not only about the $200 (which I could most definitely use); it's the principle. She's trying to shame me, to make me think I did something wrong, something dirty, in order to buy herself what? A dinner? A pair of cashmere socks? That's after we paid her usurious price for a rental that was, admittedly, beautiful but with no add-ons. No sweet surprises. Not like in Monterey, where we discovered a bidet and two free member passes to the aquarium. We went every day just to stare at the jellyfish, getting lost in their hypnotic undulations, imagining what it would be like to go through life with your own attached parachute, knowing you can never crash.

Monterey was my favorite getaway with Rob, because there was something about that house rental that allowed us to inhabit another life completely for those five days. I could envision a future where Rob and I are members of the aquarium ourselves, regular visitors with our kids, a boy and a girl (twins?) who stand agog as thousands of sardines swim in their circles like a silvery carousel.

It might sound shallow, but I'm pretty confident that Rob and I will have attractive children. Rob's handsome, and I've often heard that I'm beautiful, in an old-school, Christie Brinkley way (blue eyes, big toothy smile, no one suspects that I've been dyeing my long blond hair since I was a teenager).

The truth is, I don't feel beautiful, or even pretty, because I'm barely five foot one and at thirty years old, I still have the temperamental skin of a teenager: always at least one pimple, usually more, plus the brown dots that are the slowly healing legacy of pimples past. I'm constantly trying out new skin care products, no, not just products, entire systems. I start with great optimism ("I think I see something! I'm smoother and more supple!"), only to have my skin reassert itself with a vengeance. When people look at me admiringly, I feel like I'm putting one over on them.

Hopefully, our kids will inherit Rob's complexion, among other things.

But back to Miranda, the matter at hand. It's probably unfair to compare her Santa Monica rental to the Monterey house. I'll compare it instead to the one in Mendocino, a pleasant median: with a hot tub perched on a sea bluff; the kitchen sans the Vitamix that was shown in one of the pictures (but not promised in the text so I couldn't officially complain); the mattress that sagged slightly in the center; and the dun-colored days despite being outside the parameters of fog season.

Miranda's house still loses. Six hundred dollars a night and we had to go searching through cabinets to find replacement lightbulbs. Not to mention how loud the dishwasher was, and the hairline crack in the living room ceiling, and the absence of mini-shampoos or body ▶

washes. I felt her stinginess at every turn. A quarter inch of olive oil left in the bottle, grocery store brand. No spice rack, only salt, pepper, and thyme. How did thyme make the cut? How about some basil, or oregano? Red pepper flakes, for shit's sake?

When Rob and I get away, I'm after five-star accommodations, but in a house rather than a hotel so I can marinate in that lifestyle for a little while. It's the adult version of playing dress-up. I dislike when hosts meet us at the house because then I'm reminded it's theirs, and I have a visual to go with that knowledge. But that's only happened once. Normally, rich people do it like Miranda does, with minimal contact: key in a lockbox, call in an emergency.

Burned-out lightbulbs, lack of basic cooking supplies, and cracks in plaster remind me of my real every day, where things need replacing, and fixing, and sometimes you run out. Vacations are for abundance. While Rob and I are away, money is never an object, and that's the biggest break from real life. I even have a different wardrobe for vacation (slinky cocktail dresses for which I scour consignment shops, and stiletto heels instead of wedges), and I start using Crest White Strips a month out so I can wear the red lipstick that's too much for every day.

I'm reborn in those houses. They scrub me clean of all the debris from my past. I'm Dawn 2.0. Because the true American dream is that you don't have to be who you were, you're not where you grew up, and you're not defined by the family you left behind, or the family that left you behind way before that.

Getaway.com has never let me down before. I read through all the reviews thoroughly before I book. I pay special attention to the three-star ones, which seems to be as low as anyone will ever go, and that's probably because a one- or two-star makes you look like a disgruntled ex-lover, bent on vengeance, not to be widely trusted. As I parse each review, I can tell who has a sensibility similar to mine; I can tell who to believe.

Miranda's house had twenty-seven reviews, and nearly all of them were five stars. There was nothing below a four. People loved the ocean views, the proximity to the pier, and the hospitality, oh, the hospitality! You could call Miranda anytime, no need too small. She recommended the most fabulous Thai food; she knew the best car service. When a toilet broke down on Christmas Day, she had a plumber out there within the hour, and she sent flowers afterward, with her apologies.

Who was *that* Miranda? I would have liked to meet her.

Chapter Two

Miranda

Beware of your "host"

Three stars

I wouldn't have left a review at all, if I didn't feel it was my civic duty to warn others. Sure, there were small issues with the house itself (burned-out bulbs, a light switch that didn't work at all, no toiletries provided, a poorly stocked kitchen in terms of cooking oil, condiments, etc., and also from the kitchen, a more obscured ocean view than it appeared in the pictures—things that shouldn't have been going on given the equivalently priced rentals). But I wouldn't be mentioning any of that, if it wasn't for what happened after we left.

I was checking the "pending transactions" on my credit card to see when my security deposit would be returned. I e-mailed the host, Miranda, to inquire about the delay. Miranda didn't respond to my first e-mail, and her reply to my second was a curt "Just keep checking, it'll show up."

I wrote again a few days later to politely nudge her. I got an extremely unfriendly e-mail that accused me of leaving a stain that was "rather large (gray, about the size and shape of a typical housecat, though the house rental didn't allow pets)." Because of that, she said she was deducting half our security deposit. (Getaway.com won't let me say the amount, but you can do the math.)

WHAT????!!!! She's accusing me of smuggling in a bedraggled cat? My husband and I are clean people, and we're not blind. We would have seen a stain on the sheet. We've never left such a stain on sheets in our entire lives. Gray? Really? And impervious to bleaching? It all seemed pretty crazy to me—like she's just finding a way to keep our deposit, maybe as retaliation for me asking about it? I don't know. All I know is that the sheets we slept on were not worth the money she kept. Maybe she's confusing the dollar amount with the thread count.

But the kicker was when she said at the end of her e-mail, "I told you about this already," which she absolutely did not.

This struck me as extremely shady. I know that other people have had different experiences (there are lots of four- and five-star reviews for this property, which is why we booked it to start with). But I thought we should share our experience and you can factor it into your decision of where to book. ▸

• • •

I cannot believe what I'm seeing. I am a certified hospitable person. I open my home to people, and I let them call me with any problems or questions, at any time. And they do. The kind of people who pay $600 a night for a two-bedroom beach house often have "problems." I answer their calls while I'm in the middle of dinner. I answer their calls when I'm in the dressing room at Barneys. I answer as I'm in my bed, about to drift off to sleep. I tell them, "Second drawer on the left," or "No, that's vegetarian. For pure vegan, try Golden Mean, or Viva La Vegan."

I do my best to be a thoughtful, good person. I volunteer. I let cars merge in front of me on the L.A. freeways during rush hour with a friendly hand wave. I treat people decently—family and friends and guests and strangers—unlike some people who shall go nameless in their reviews.

I know who D.T. is, of course. She's darkened my inbox enough over the past week. Dawn Thiebold actually wrote me FIVE times to ask about her security deposit, sometimes leading with, "Don't know if you got my last e-mail . . ." and signing off with a perky "Thanks!" and in between comes the badgering. If she can afford to stay at my rental, then she can afford to wait until the transaction posts to her credit card, within seven business days as promised.

I don't have much tolerance for people who live beyond their means and then act entitled. She had to change a lightbulb? She was denied her constitutional right to condiments? There was a partially obscured view from the kitchen? She fails to mention that it's "obscured" by a gorgeous purple jacaranda tree in full spring bloom. The living room view is completely unobstructed, as noted in every other review, but not in hers. She doesn't highlight a single thing she likes.

I am a little touchy about the rental, I know that. It was my parents' home in their later years, and I can still see the contentment they felt as they surveyed that ocean panorama. Now my father's gone, and my mother's in her assisted living community, requiring more assistance every day as the dementia worsens, and I never feel like I'm doing enough for her, no matter how many flowers I bring or how much tidying up I do or how often I tell her she's a fantastic mom and I love her. More and more often, she barely registers my presence. It's a terrible thing, being invisible to your own mother.

I try not to take it personally. It's the inexorable aging progress; it's a disease, getting old. No love is strong enough to overcome biology. But I can't help but feel that it should be, that it is for some other family, some other mother, with some other daughter.

My brother George says it's the same during his infrequent visits. He lives in Idaho with his family, so he doesn't have to concern himself with her decline. He doesn't have to watch it, day by excruciating day. He doesn't have to see her falter, and disappear.

He also doesn't have to handle any of the arrangements. I'm the power of attorney, it all falls to me. "It's not like you work," he once told me. As if it's not work to deal with all the guests, being hospitable and available, ensuring that no one's broken anything or stolen anything or left, say, cat-sized stains on sheets. My father had left the Santa Monica house to both George and me, but I bought him out, just so I wouldn't have to feel the resentment of doing everything and then giving him his cut. So that it would be all my work, and all my profit. I convinced Larry that it was a good investment, and one that I would manage exclusively. He didn't know there was a hidden catch. He doesn't need to. Marriages work best with a don't ask/don't tell policy, on a bedrock of what you don't know won't hurt you.

Eva's coming tomorrow, but I always pre-clean the Beverly Hills house. Today it's with some extra fervor, courtesy of Dawn and her review. I scrub the granite countertops and every stainless steel appliance until I can practically see my reflection. Or perhaps that's my angry aura.

I've never been very comfortable with anger. It's important to keep it at bay. Cleaning helps. In this case, it's going to take more than just one room. Fortunately, I've got four thousand square feet.

I love this house. Well, I used to, when I could still see it. Now it's just backdrop, the set against which my life with Larry plays out. We've been here for almost twenty-five years, since Thad was three. I remember when the Realtor first showed it to us: a four-bedroom Spanish villa, just blocks from Rodeo Drive. The feeling was so warm—taupe and burnt orange, the variegated walnut wood floors with matching beamed ceilings, the rounded doorways and fireplaces. Thad was tearing through there, letting out excited yelps. He thought he was home. I wanted it, badly, but Larry was barely past residency back then. Maybe I was still reeling a little from what had happened during the residency and thought more penance was due; we didn't yet deserve such a bounty. But Larry disagreed, and his parents were willing to give us the down payment. He was sure that despite everything, the world should (and would) be good to us.

If you saw only this house—high ceilings, ornate mosaic tiling, terra-cotta interior courtyard, Olympic-size pool–you would think that it had been. ▶

Coming Soon from Holly Brown . . . ***(continued)***

I move into the living room, though dusting isn't nearly as satisfying as a vociferous spray and wipe. I should probably do one of the bathrooms. The master bathroom, maybe. I could clean the expanse of the shower, with its four showerheads.

I'd dressed to visit my mother, in the silk blouse she used to like when she still cared about what I wore, and I strip it off. I pull my shoulder-length ash-blond hair into a ponytail, trying not to see myself as I am: middle-aged verging on old, gaining flab in the midsection despite swimming and strengthening my core four times a week, in the plunge bra that Larry likes, when he remembers to look. Fifty-seven isn't so old.

How old is Dawn? Young, I imagine, from the cadence in her e-mails and her review.

That review. I spritz the marble wall and wipe with such ferocity that I begin to fear carpal tunnel.

What if she costs me future bookings? I've got guests for the rest of April and May, but summer is prime time, and now is when people book for summer. If I lose that income . . .

Dawn has no idea what she's doing to me. Or maybe she does. Maybe she's just that rotten.

No, I simply need to make it clear to her that she's wrong, that this was all a misunderstanding, and she'll be reasonable. She'll take the review down. Most people aren't rotten, they're confused. Like Thad.

What galls me about the review is that it makes me look dishonest, when that's the last thing I am. Not that I reveal everything, to everyone. I'm circumspect, even with Larry. But I would never play fast and loose with someone's security deposit.

I might not have been bubbling over in my e-mail responses, I don't use exclamation points or (God forbid) emojis, but I told her what she needed to know: The security deposit would be returned within the specified time frame. They always are.

I left a voicemail to tell her about the sheets. I know that I did. Could I have left it on the wrong phone number? Hard to imagine making a mistake like that, but then, it was a hectic time. I was concerned by what I'd seen on Thad's Twitter feed, not to mention his Instagram, and he didn't return my calls, not for days.

Maybe I wasn't so pleasant in that phone message, because I was peeved to discover the sheets. On the very rare occasions when guests have left damage in the past, they've informed me. They've apologized. We've worked it out together. When people are honest, I generally don't even opt to charge them. But Dawn slips out the back door and then harasses me about her deposit, as if those sheets could escape my notice. It was like someone had come into my late father's home and taken a dump in his bed (though the stain wasn't feces, because human waste can be bleached out; I raised a child, I know this from experience). I still don't know what caused that gray stain. I don't want to know. But Dawn must.

Even if I give her the benefit of the doubt and say she really wasn't aware, she should have been chastened once I called her attention to it. Instead she came out swinging. She's the "shady" one, not me.

Or she could just be young, and in need of some correction. I'll write to her, we'll clear all this up, she'll delete her review, and that will be that. No harm done. I can forgive most anything, I know that from experience, too.